SPOKEN BONES

A DI FENELLA SALLOW CRIME THRILLER

N.C. LEWIS

Chapter One

*N*OVEMBER 6

It was 7:00 a.m. and still dark in Port Saint Giles. Audrey Robin hurried along the beach. She clutched a black sack, her mind focused on the plan.

In front of her, the dunes sloped down to the blackened sand of the bonfire. Guy Fawkes Night had brought out the locals. It came too late in the year for tourists, and besides, the faded seaside town wasn't on any Cumbria sightseeing map. A bonfire smouldered after the night-time party. The chill sea air tasted of salt and ash.

A skein of barnacle geese honked. Audrey wiped her glasses and watched as they made their way south through the cloud-spotted dawn. Their flight announced the turn of the seasons. November brought cold and dark. She lowered her hood, inviting in the chill, and tightened her knitted red scarf.

Three years had passed since she left Bristol wearing only her summer dress.

It felt like a lifetime.

And in North West England, it was damn cold.

The weather forecast predicted more rain, wind, and chill. But only a light mist hung over the sand. Still, Audrey was glad of her coat, boots, and scarf, all given to her by Maureen Brian.

"A friendship gift," Maureen had said, "to keep you warm through the winter dark."

As Audrey rounded the base of a dune, the breeze eased. She stopped to take in the view. Flat sands stretched off in all directions, but she turned her gaze to the pier. At the end, shrouded in mist, stood the abandoned lighthouse.

"It's been there for two hundred years," Maureen had said. "A relic we need to preserve."

Audrey wasn't sure. She didn't like old buildings. They gave her the creeps. But she was sure about Maureen Brian. Meeting the wee retired artist with unnaturally red hair had been a stroke of luck. And when good luck struck, Audrey grasped it with both hands and milked it for all it was worth.

She let Maureen cluck over her like a Bantam hen its chick. Audrey enjoyed the fuss. Now she owned a two-bedroom cottage, bought at a huge discount thanks to Maureen. The deposit came from the divorce. In truth, she could scarcely afford the mortgage. And, oh God, the repairs! The run-down cottage sucked money into an endless pit.

That's where Maureen came in.

Maureen Brian knew everyone. Painters, plumbers, handymen. All eager to work for rock-bottom prices. With Maureen's help, it worked out. But Audrey knew one thing about luck: it always ran out.

She pulled her coat tighter around her shoulders and fiddled with the scarf. Daylight crept across the beach. Three gulls landed, poked around, and screamed at each other. A fourth gull circled and screeched above her head.

Audrey worried. About the mortgage. About her job. But she worried most of all about how long her luck would last. She worried about the voices in her head. They would grumble soon. Tell her what to do. She didn't want that. They stayed silent when she cleaned up a mess.

Any mess.

Audrey scanned the beach for empty beer cans or crisp packets. Not much to pick up. A paper bag or burnt-out firework. The crowd had listened and taken home their trash.

A win for nature.

That made her uneasy.

The voices would know about the beach. Know her sack was empty. And that would bring them back.

She paused to take in the warmth of the rising sun and watch the green-tinted waves of the Solway Firth. The water shimmered and lapped against the shore. A soft *slush-slush*. The constant beat jangled her nerves until a scurrying began in the back of her head.

With a sense of dread, Audrey turned to look at the town. Was she being watched?

Leafless trees lined the cobbled lanes. Whitewashed houses clustered as if for warmth. A barren landscape in the grey morning light. *Slush-slush*. She clenched her jaw. It didn't stop the scurrying noises. They grew until she thought she could make out vowels.

No. She wouldn't listen. She wouldn't do what they commanded ever again.

A biting wind raced across the beach. Audrey raised her hood, dipped her head, and spun away from the blast.

Pressure.

That's what Audrey felt. The constant *drip, drip* of money from her meagre purse. Repairs, heating bills, even the cost of food.

Drip, drip, drip.

Now she thought of Maureen Brian, retired with a pension and all the time in the world. An artist too, with photos that hung in real art galleries. No cash worries for Maureen. No cash worries for Audrey either, if she stuck to the plan.

It had worked before. Hadn't she run away from Bristol with her husband's cash? Enough for a deposit on the cottage. Planning had worked in the past. It would again. If she were careful.

Audrey clambered up a dune, puffing so hard, twin jets of condensed air swirled from her nostrils. Even at this early hour, there were a few people about. A woman in a bright-pink jacket power-walked next to a man with a dog. At the water's edge, a mother played with a toddler. A person in a mud-brown trench coat hurried away from the blackened debris of the bonfire. From this distance, they were like stick figures in a Lowry oil painting.

Audrey watched and played her secret game—*know thy neighbour*. She tried to put names to their blurry faces. First, the man and the woman with the dog. Next, the toddler and its mother. The piercing shriek of a gull broke her focus. It didn't matter. She'd know their names once she walked closer. Another plus of small seaside-town life. None of the isolation of married life in Bristol's Harbourside.

Marriage... Audrey wondered whether she'd missed the boat. At thirty-seven, there were no children to mother. Everyone in town knew Patrick filed for divorce, and she didn't have the strength to fight it. Although she had grown up in Bristol and married in the same town, she had never got rid of the feeling of being an outsider. The tatters of her marriage gave one more reason to stay away from her home town.

Audrey took a paper tissue from her pocket and wiped her eyes. No, she wouldn't cry. She clambered down the slope to a broken fragment of driftwood. Maybe it would count with the voices? She scooped it up with the keenness of a miner panning for gold. As she glanced towards the blackened bonfire, the scurrying began again. It hovered in her ears like a brooding sea mist.

A gull screamed.

Audrey took a deep breath, set the timer on her mobile phone for three minutes, and performed her daily ritual. With eyes closed, she swayed to the rhythmic slap of the waves and said her secret mantra. The voices dimmed. She felt the warmth of the winter sun on her cheeks. Turning her face into the breeze, she sniffed the scent of seaweed and brine and smoke from the bonfire. She loved life in Port

Saint Giles. This little seaside town was home, the first place she really loved since running away at fifteen. Her drunken mother's council flat was a place to sleep and eat, that was all. Her body swayed, her mouth opening and closing—each word a promise to do what it took to keep things this way.

Her eyes opened. A shaft of sunlight broke through the shield of clouds, casting dimpled patterns across the sand. Audrey repeated her mantra, then gave a prayer of thanks for Maureen Brian.

Now it was time.

With her mind clear and focused, Audrey hurried with quick steps in a direct path to the bonfire. Her focus was intense. The breeze against her face damped out sound. The welcome waves of the man with the dog and the woman in the pink jacket almost went unmet.

"Nice day for it," said the woman.

"Care to join us?" added the man with the dog. "A bracing stroll to the lighthouse and back."

Audrey put names to the faces. The woman was her friend, Elizabeth Collins. And the man was the American pastor, Noel O'Sullivan, with Barkie, his Irish Setter.

Audrey knelt in the sand to pet Barkie, then pointed at the bonfire. "Going the other way. Maybe tomorrow." The dog looked at her with sad eyes, as though to warn her things were going to go wrong. As it opened its mouth to pant, a voice spoke in her mind, but she couldn't make out the words. She shivered, but not from the cold, and told herself to stick to the plan. Everything would be fine if she stuck to the plan. She said, "Meet you tomorrow, then, seven at the pier by the cannons?"

They both nodded and shuffled by. That was another thing Audrey liked about Port Saint Giles. Everyone lived their life to a firm routine. Tomorrow, before daylight, Elizabeth Collins and Noel O'Sullivan would be at the pier. As would she.

Today, though, there remained more to do.

Audrey circled the edge of the bonfire with slow, precise steps. She stooped to pick up a bottle, two plastic cups, and a squished packet of cigarettes. Then she saw the smiling face and red and white strips on a fried-chicken box. Under her annoyed gaze it seemed to grow, dwarfing her earlier hoard.

Vile!

Didn't they realise what litter did to the natural world?

Wrinkling her nose in distaste, Audrey leaned forward and scooped it into her sack. Only then did she see the body. Smallish and curled with a blue headscarf wrapped tight around the head. She couldn't see the face. It pressed against the ash-laden ground as if tasting the sand. But she recognised the strands of unnaturally red hair.

Suddenly she screamed with such force, the vibrations tore at the back of her throat. But not enough to tear the image of Miss Maureen Brian's blackened corpse from her mind.

Chapter Two

F ENELLA SALLOW RELAXED IN the well-worn couch. She refused to think about the job. Today was her day off. Family time. Precious. The kitchen fire crackled and radiated a pleasant glow. Its warmth mixed with the smell of fried breakfast. The rambling farmhouse on Cleaton Bluff offered sweeping views of Solway Firth.

Her husband had bought the house when farm cottages were passé. It came with two acres. One of dozens of derelict stone cottages scattered across Cumbria like forgotten pagan relics. They'd lived there for nineteen of their twenty-six years of married life.

Fenella loved the hardwood floors and oddly shaped door frames. Not so much the windows that wouldn't shut right. They'd kept the ancient landline with a grey British Telecom rotary-dial telephone. And the faux pinewood cassette-tape answering machine. Throwbacks to a simpler age.

They'd added inside toilets. Rewired the electric, and built a drafting studio with floor to ceiling windows for Eduardo. An upgrade to the fitful central heating was next on the list, when his latest comic strip sold. All five children were grown and gone. Well, almost. Katherine, their youngest, always left Winston, now nine, for Guy Fawkes Night. A tradition Fenella cherished.

"I've forgotten something, I know I have."

Nan stood by the stove with a raised spoon, scanning the pots. Fenella's mother had moved in three years earlier when her fourth husband died of a heart attack. The grandkids called her Nan because she couldn't abide the words *Great-Grandma.*

"Ham, eggs, bacon, beans, black and white pudding. Fried tomatoes and mushrooms in garlic butter. Now, what have I forgotten?"

"And pancakes, don't forget the pancakes, Nan," added Winston. "We always have pancakes with lemon and honey the day after Bonfire Night, don't we, Grandma?"

Fenella nodded. She'd let her hair go white years before but couldn't get used to being a granny. But it sounded so sweet when it came from her grandson, and fifty wasn't that old in the grand scheme of things. Her mother remarried for the fourth time at seventy. The husband croaked during an intimate moment on New Year's Eve. And Fenella wasn't convinced there wouldn't be a fifth. Rocking chairs and knitting were not in her mother's future. Fenella hoped they weren't in her future either and said, "Better put on an extra batch of black pudding for me, Mum."

"In the pan, luv." Nan looked over the pots and pans and flipped the bacon. "Now, what have I missed?"

"Nothing Nan," Winston said, looking at the stove. "And lots of pancakes for me; I'm going to eat them all."

The kitchen door opened. A rush of frigid air blew in from the hall. Eduardo leaned on the door frame, smiling at Fenella as their eyes met.

"Good morning, Mrs Sallow; you look yummy."

"Why thank you, kind sir," Fenella replied. "But it's Detective Inspector Sallow to you." She loved her husband. Too tender to be a police officer though. She loved that too.

"What about me!" barked Nan. "I'm the one slaving over the pot. Don't I get a kind word from the man of the house?"

"I see you every morning," Eduardo said. He hovered in the open doorway. "One perk of working from home."

Nan scowled. "Women of a certain age need to hear a compliment now and then. Even if it is only from a fat sod who draws cartoons for a living."

"Aargh!" Eduardo scrunched his face. "Well, at least my detective inspector wife has the day off. And today, oh glory, I get to see her in the morning light rather than under the glow of the full moon."

"What are you trying to say?" Fenella asked.

"Something about werewolves or vampires, I guess," Nan added. "Eduardo, isn't that so?"

Eduardo's lips curved into a banana. "No comment. But you, my dear wife, have been working rather a lot in the graveyard shift lately. And with those damn blood sausages you adore. Makes one wonder."

Fenella raised her mobile phone and wagged it at her husband. "Day off. Mobile off. If you weren't so handsome, I'd tell you to bugger off."

Eduardo rocked from side to side in the doorway. He raised his arms like a mashup between Frankenstein and Count Dracula.

"Shut the door, you soft prat," Nan yelled. "You're letting in a draft."

Eduardo closed the door and eased into the couch. He put an arm around Fenella and kissed her before turning to Winston. "Nan's a slow coach today. Come on Great-Grandma, my stomach's growling."

"Cheeky bugger," grumbled Nan.

After they had seconds of black pudding, Nan drained the last of the pancake batter onto the griddle.

"Can't eat no more," Winston said.

"Don't worry, I'll help." Eduardo patted his stomach. "Can't say no to Nan's pancakes, can I?"

"Oh dear, I knew I forgot something," Nan said. "The telephone in the hall rang earlier. They left a message on the answering machine."

"Wonder who'd call our landline?" Eduardo eyed the batter as it bubbled in the pan. "Must be one of your lover men, Nan."

"Don't be daft." Nan grinned and began to clear the plates from the table. "Sounded like Veronica Jeffery, so I didn't pick up."

Fenella gritted her teeth. *Not important,* a little voice whispered, *and it is your day off.* But the landline rarely rang, and Superintendent Jeffery never called the cottage.

Nan placed the plates in the sink. "Winston, you can dry? Come on, snap to it."

"Aargh, but my tummy's going to burst. I can't move."

Nan thumped her hand on the draining board. Winston jumped from his chair and scurried to help. No one messed with Nan. The children and grandchildren learnt that lesson fast.

"Did she leave a message?" Fenella asked.

"Aye, but I didn't hear what she said." Nan began to fill the sink and squirted soap. "You know how fast she speaks, and even if she slowed down, I can't grasp that police lingo."

Fenella stole a glance at Eduardo. After decades of married life, he'd accepted her calling to the Cumbria Police as she accepted his art. And they'd both accepted the wild swings in hours and income that came with both.

"Take the call," said Eduardo. He flipped the last pancake onto his plate. "We've eaten and we can go for a stroll along the beach at sunset."

"It'll be cold," complained Winston. "And there won't be any fireworks or bonfire or nothing."

"We'll take your torch. You might spot a barn owl," chimed in Nan.

"Can we, Gran?" Winston asked.

"Sure," replied Fenella, reaching for the *on* button on her mobile phone. It pinged, almost dancing out of her hand. For a moment she scanned the list of calls, a cautious trick she'd picked up between sergeant and inspector.

Twelve.

All from Superintendent Jeffery's office.

Fenella left the kitchen and eased into the chair behind the desk in Eduardo's studio. The shuttered blinds blocked out the morning light. But she couldn't settle. She didn't like surprises. With the superintendent, they came aplenty. You never knew what the dragon might throw at you.

With slow steps, she walked to the studio windows, raised the blinds and took in the view. Cumbria countryside. Fields of greens and browns all the way to the blackened slopes of the cliffs. The land bare and beautiful in the sparse November morning light. In the distance, she heard the crash of waves against the shore.

But she didn't dial Superintendent Jeffery.

It had been a restful morning with Nan, Eduardo, and Winston. A big breakfast the day after Bonfire Night was a tradition. One Fenella cherished as if it were a newborn child. She wanted to go back to the kitchen to chat.

Except, of course, the voicemails from Superintendent Jeffery.

Fenella screwed her eyes shut and imagined their farmstead in summer. Meadows in full bloom and lush greens under a dappled blue sky. A day off work might still happen. Yet she knew this to be only a dream.

She'd have to reply.

Better call Dexter.

Detective Sergeant Robert Dexter was her senior in age by three years. He had been her second in command for over a decade. An officer who kept his ears close to the ground. So close, Fenella wondered whether he'd bugged the superintendent's office. There was no better police officer in Cumbria, with his gut instinct and nose for the truth. If he kept off the bottle. It all went to hell when he hung out with Mr Booze.

Dexter answered on the seventh ring.

"What's up Guvnor?" His voice rasped like pebbles dashed against rusted tin.

"It's Jeffery. She's been ringing my phone like it's the Salvation Army Christmas bell. What's going on?"

The line went silent for a long moment. When Dexter spoke, his voice dropped half an octave.

"Nothing that I know of, Guv."

Fenella eased the phone from her ear and glanced at the wall clock —eight forty.

"You at the station?"

"Thought I'd lie in today. Take the morning off."

A tightness crept along her neck. She tilted her head from side to side to ease the tension. Detective Sergeant Dexter, twice divorced and with no friends outside the job, never took time off. Unless...

"You back on the bottle?" But Fenella had already heard a faint slur in his speech. "Come on, Dexter, you know better than that."

"Give me a break, Guv."

Fenella turned from the windows and bowed her head for a few seconds. Static crackled across the line. It burst and faded like surf crashing against rock. She spoke in a whisper.

"You are at your A A meeting this morning, right? Get yourself sobered up." She snorted. Not a pleasant sound, but it fitted her mood. "If Jeffery finds out, she'll have your—"

"The Dragon's got it in for me, you know that."

"Come off it!" But Fenella knew there was truth in his words. "If you show up reeking of booze, she'll have good reason. Don't hand it to her on a plate."

Dexter coughed as though his next words were stuck in his throat. "Jeffery's only concern is her spreadsheets. Or playing up to the chief constable. What about her officers?" Dexter spoke fast. "Guv, it'll be another bleedin' crime initiative. That's my bet. Why can't she leave us to—"

"Don't throw it all away," Fenella replied, cutting into his rant. When he sobered, they'd have a hard chat. And this time she'd have a word with Croll. Detective Inspector Jack Croll, retired. Dexter had worked with Croll for even longer than he'd been her second. If she couldn't get through, Croll would. She slowed her speech, so each word landed with impact.

"Clean up your act. Stay off the booze, and show up tomorrow morning at the station by seven-thirty."

Fenella hung up. She waited thirty seconds and sucked in three long breaths. Then dialled the superintendent. Jeffery picked up on the first ring.

"My office as soon as you can, Sallow. There's been a suspicious death on the beach in Port Saint Giles. I'm assigning you as the senior investigating officer. I'll send a car. You live in the old farmhouse on Cleaton Bluff, don't you?"

Chapter Three

I T WAS JUST AFTER 9:00 a.m. in Detective Constable Hugh Earp's cramped two-bedroom house. Hoar frost covered the neat backyard and the bare branches of his Egremont Russet apple tree shivered. Sue cleared away the plates in the warm kitchen. Six-year-old Nick helped his mum at the sink. Tomas, their cat, curled up on the counter. The radio crackled in the background with the weather forecast.

The weatherman spoke in a rapid voice. Less them thirty seconds until the news, and there was still tomorrow's forecast to squeeze in. A storm had brewed on Bonfire Night. It hovered far out over the Solway Firth and spun in tight circles. As if it waited, the weatherman said, for the festivities to end. Then it rushed towards land as gusts of naked raw chill. It whistled through the cobbled lanes of Port Saint Giles and shook Hugh Earp's apple tree with frigid force.

In the kitchen, however, it was warm. The coffee percolator bubbled with a fresh brew. Sue laughed as Nick aimed squirts of washing-up liquid into the sink. For some time now, Hugh Earp had been gazing at the naked branches of the apple tree.

"Coffee, darling?" Sue asked. "Fresh-ground from the Grain Bowl Café."

"That tree," Earp said, without glancing up. "About time it produced an apple or two. This summer, do you think?"

"Maybe," Sue replied with a touch of uncertainty. She filled a mug with coffee, added two spoons of sugar, and a splash of cream. "Nicky, take this to your dad, darling. Then go read in your room until the school bus comes, okay?"

Nick expertly balanced the mug on his lap, holding it steady with one hand, using the other to apply pressure to a lever on his motorised wheelchair.

"Here you go, Daddy."

Earp looked away from the window. His eyes settled warmly on his boy. The son who came after thirteen years of marriage. The child whose birth he'd celebrated with an Egremont Russet sapling. And the son, who one day, would climb into its branches. Once they'd saved enough money to pay for the trip to America. He knew deep down in his gut that the miraculous surgery would give his son legs to run and play. But it was not yet available on the National Health Service, being so new.

"Untested," his doctor had said with a curt wave of his pen. But he'd referred them to a specialist in Carlisle. The surgeon researched the American procedure with enthusiasm and said, "Not feasible at the moment. Not with the cutbacks in government spending. But certainly worth a try, oh yes. Let me know how you get along with our friends across the Atlantic. I'll write a letter of introduction, if you like."

So, the Earps saved every penny. And one day they'd fly to America. Later, back in England, Hugh Earp would watch young Nick climb high in the branches of his Egremont Russet apple tree. He dreamed of the day his son kicked a ball. That's when he'd race him to the front door and out into the yard to plant another apple tree. That's what kept him going. That's all he wanted in life.

"Thank you, son," Earp said, placing the mug on the table. "Now go do your reading."

"Do I have to, Dad?"

"You heard what your mum said."

"But I have a late start today, don't I, Mum?"

"Eleven," Sue added," on account of Bonfire Night. Can't expect kids to be awake in class when they were up half the night watching fireworks."

"I don't feel sleepy," Nick said. "And, Dad, what about school today?"

"Eh?" Earp said.

"You are giving a talk in Mrs Ledwidge's class about being a police officer," Sue said from the sink. "Haven't forgotten, have you?"

"Told everyone my daddy is a detective," Nick added. "They better be nice to me today, else you'll throw them in prison, won't you, Dad?"

Earp rubbed a hand over his chin. "Today, son?"

"Two o'clock." Sue stared at her husband for a moment. He saw a familiar flicker cross her eyes—disappointment. "If it is too difficult," continued Sue, "I'm sure Mrs Ledwidge will understand."

"Aargh... Dad," Nick said. "Pleeease."

"I'll be there, son."

"Promise, Daddy?"

"Promise."

"Cross your heart and hope to die."

Earp crossed his heart. Not that he had much faith in the divine; being a police officer drained it out of you. Still, Sue insisted on taking Nick to church on Sundays and he made the effort to attend at Easter and Christmas. "And if you listen to Mummy, you can come to work with me sometime, be a policeman for the day. Now go read before I change my mind!"

"Tom, come here," Nick called. The cat turned to look, hesitated as if uninterested, then ambled across the kitchen and jumped into his lap. "Daddy's coming to school today. Don't get jealous. You'll get your turn when we have the blessing of the animals with Vicar Beasley."

With a jerk, the wheelchair came to life. It spun around almost on the spot and whizzed with an electrical click out of the kitchen, along the hall to the bedroom.

Sue sat down, blew on her coffee, then leaned over to whisper in her husband's ear. "A fresh start today, Hugh." She sniffed in the curls of steam as if it were a fine wine. "Hope you like the coffee."

Earp glanced at his cup but did not drink. "Expensive?"

"Aye." Sue knew they couldn't really afford it. "Just a small packet, to celebrate."

"Suppose you might call it that."

"It's a chance to rebuild, Hugh."

"They've shafted me. The whole bloody lot of them."

Sue took a sip and stared out the window at the shivering apple tree.

"Do you hear me?" It would have come out as a shout but Earp didn't what his boy to hear. "Shafted by the Cumbria Constabulary after seventeen years putting my neck on the line for the uniform!"

"Please don't," Sue said as she leaned to take her husband's hand. "A fresh start, Hugh."

He shook his head, swallowed hard, barely able to speak the words. "If it weren't for you and Nick, I'd—"

Sue raised her other hand, palm out. "Please. Don't."

Earp clenched his jaw. "Oh bugger off, Sue." The words seeped through his teeth like the scalding hiss of a kettle on the boil. He didn't want her to leave, realised how lonely he'd be without her, but said it again, anyway. "Just bugger off and leave me alone, will you?"

Sue didn't move, except to lower her hand and release her grip of his with the other. Then she placed both hands palms down on the table. "I don't ask for much, but our son is depending on you. Don't let him down, Hugh. I couldn't bear it if you did that again. Better to tell him you can't—"

"I'll be at the damn school."

"That's what you always say."

"And we'll go out to dinner tonight, the three of us as a family. Nick loves Chinese, or do you fancy a good curry?"

"Don't, Hugh. Please don't give me your word."

"Whatever you want, we'll do it. I'm all in. So we'll go for an Indian feed?"

Sue said, "We don't need fast food, Hugh. We need you."

"I'm here, aren't I?"

"And Nick needs you to accept him for what he is, not what you want him to be."

"My boy will walk. That's what I'm working for, what we are saving for. Not long now until we have the money to go to America. It's what we want, isn't it?"

Sue gazed away from her husband and through the window at the Egremont Russet apple tree. "Dinner together as a family at home is enough. I'll make something special. How about lamb? I've cutlets in the freezer."

"And I'll get a bottle or two of wine, red?" Earp said. "Let's look at some holiday locations for Christmas break. You've always fancied Devon. Nice surprise for Nick."

"No, Hugh. No." Sue sat silent for a while, toying with her hands, and Earp's trained eye couldn't ignore the slight tremble in his wife's fingers or the purple sheen growing slowly along her neck. When she eventually spoke, her voice remained so low it appeared to come from a great distance. "Long ago you promised me the world and have delivered so little. No more dreams, Hugh."

"It's not my fault!"

"It never is."

"It's the job. I'm a police officer, not a nine-to-five office clerk."

"You even made that excuse to your fellow police officers, didn't you?" Sue shook her head, and a single tear rolled down her cheek. "Only they are not a silly woman who loves you."

Earp curled his fists into tight balls and brought them down one after the other. The mugs toppled, sloshing their contents over the table top.

"Go on, trash the place!" Tears streamed down her face. "We need you."

"My God, Sue, I'd just like to smash their bleedin' faces to a—"

All at once his mobile phone rang.

"Earp," he barked. Sue retreated to the kitchen, returning moments later with a dishcloth to wipe the table. He was about to tell whoever it was to go away in unfriendly terms, when he glanced at the incoming number and his voice became instantly alert. "Superintendent Jeffery?"

"Earp," began the superintendent. "I hope you had an enjoyable breakfast. Nice quiet start to the day for you, eh, Detective Constable?"

He hesitated a moment, biting back his annoyance at the way she'd drawn out the last two words. But he swallowed hard and said, "Yes, ma'am."

"Good."

Only one word, but to Earp's ear it sounded like the buzz of an irritated wasp. And he knew whatever came next, it wouldn't be good.

"I'm assigning you to Detective Inspector Sallow," continued Jeffery. "A suspicious death in Port Saint Giles, the beach. You are to work with her, take instruction from her, do as she requests, and no slouching off during the day. Do I make myself understood, Detective Constable?"

Earp closed his eyes and cursed under his breath.

"Yes, ma'am."

"And Earp?"

"Yes, ma'am."

"I've read your file."

He kept silent, already sensing what would come next.

"If you hadn't been so impulsive, you'd still be a detective inspector in the Carlisle Divisional Headquarters, and may I add, with excellent potential of rising even higher through the leadership ranks."

Earp swore.

"What was that?"

"A crackle on the line, ma'am."

"Are you sure?"

"Yes, ma'am. Something to do with a storm blowing in from the Solway Firth. Messes with the signals. It was on the radio news this morning."

The line went quiet for so long, Earp felt the thud of his heart in his throat. Had he stepped over the line, again?

When Superintendent Jeffery spoke, her voice was almost a hiss. "That's what I'd have thought if I didn't know better. But I do know better. You only have yourself to blame; you do understand that, don't you?"

He didn't answer.

"I asked you a question. And when I ask a question, I expect an answer." There was a long pause and Earp felt his heart shrivel. Then came the hiss of the superintendent. "Do you accept responsibility for your actions, Detective Constable Earp?"

"Yes, ma'am."

"And the consequences?"

Earp didn't hesitate this time. He knew the drill. "Yes, ma'am."

"I see there was a push from the powers-that-be to demote you from detective inspector to uniform." Superintendent Jeffery's voice resonated with a high-pitched drone. "Consider yourself fortunate you are still a detective. You have booked an appointment with Dr Joy Hall?"

He gritted his teeth, trying to stop the irritation from showing in his voice. "Yes, ma'am."

"I want a weekly report on your progress. Dr Hall is one of the best, an old college friend. And if I hear so much as a squeak from her, your sorry arse will be back on the beat. Understood?"

Earp stared at the Egremont Russet apple tree, then closed his eyes and swore long and hard in his mind. He might have continued with his mental tirade if it were not for the voice buzzing like an angry wasp at the other end of his mobile phone.

"Do I make myself crystal clear, Detective Constable Earp?"

"Yes, ma'am."

"Good. Now be a nice boy and toddle over to the old farmhouse on Cleaton Bluff. Detective Inspector Sallow is waiting for you. Bring her straight to my office. An easy task for your first day as a detective constable. Oh, and tell your good wife not to make supper, we don't want it to spoil and her get all upset, now do we?"

Chapter Four

D ETECTIVE INSPECTOR FENELLA SALLOW knocked on
the door of the superintendent's office. It was in a long hall at
the top of the police station. Thick carpet lined the floor, and gilt-
framed photographs hung on the walls. She gave the door another
hard thump. Then whacked with more force. She was riled. She'd
been brought to the office before she visited the crime scene in Port
Saint Giles.

"The superintendent told me to drive you straight here," Detective
Constable Earp had said. "My first day on the job, ma'am. We don't
want to tick off the big boss, do we?"

Fenella gripped the handle and thrust the door open. It creaked as
she stepped inside the office. The room smelled of polish and leather
and ancient oak. A small window let in dull light.

Jeffery sat at her enormous desk with reading glasses balanced at
the tip of her nose. She was the same age as Fenella but had risen
higher in the ranks. Her lush chair had golden trim as though it were
a throne. She read a thick report. Fenella stood by the door and
waited. Jeffery didn't look up, but her lips moved as though she were
sounding out the words.

Didn't Jeffery hear the knock?

"Did I say you may enter?" The waspish voice of Jeffery filled the
room like a loudspeaker. But her head remained tilted down, eyes

scanning the report. "What do you want?"

"Ma'am, you said to report first thing."

"Oh it's you, Sallow." Jeffery didn't look up. "Come in."

Fenella walked into the room and sat at the desk.

Jeffery continued to read the report. Her lips moved very fast, although no words came out. Fenella was patient, could wait out a camel at a watering hole. But it looked like a very long report and she couldn't wait for her boss to be done.

"Ma'am, the death on the beach."

Jeffery flipped a page but did not look up.

Fenella wouldn't be ignored.

"Ma'am, is there something I should know before I visit the scene of the crime in Port Saint Giles?"

Jeffery tossed the report to one side. "Police work comes with so many things to read and sign and scan and file. When am I supposed to get quality time with my staff?"

"The death in Port Saint Giles, ma'am. You asked that I report to your office."

"This morning I've had to deal with the fallout over search warrants. Now we have got to count how many are signed by a judge." Jeffery shook her head. "The Home Office, the Law Commission, and local politicians are all over us on this. It might make sense in London, but this is Port Saint Giles."

Fenella felt tension in her neck and tilted her head from side to side. She should be in the crime scene tent, not stuck in a chair in an office. The patch of sky through the window darkened. It looked like rain. She wanted to get to the beach before it began to fall.

"Ma'am, is there news about the body on the beach?"

"And then there are the complaints from the town Ambulance Service. Well, you know all about it. Treat paramedics with respect. That's the slogan I'm taking to the troops. If I hear of anyone in my station upsetting our medical friends, they will have me to deal with. I'll make them sorry."

Fenella stood. "I need to get to the crime scene."

"Sit!" Jeffery slammed her fist on the table. "All search warrants are to be approved by me. No exceptions. Thought I'd better put you in the picture, Sallow. Spread the word, will you?"

Fenella sat and said, "And the death on the beach, ma'am?"

Jeffery's skin became taut around her jaw. It took a moment for Fenella to realise she was smiling. A wolfish grin like a politician about to lie.

"You will need a strong team to look into this one." Jeffery's lips curved further and she bared her teeth. It was supposed to be friendly. "We are short-staffed, and with the spending cuts we have to make do and mend. I've assigned Detective Hugh Earp to your team."

"He drove me over, ma'am."

"And how did you find him?"

"Punctual, ma'am."

"Anything else to report?"

"No, ma'am."

"And how did you find his... mood."

"Mood?"

"You didn't sense anything... off?"

"No, ma'am."

The superintendent went quiet for a moment.

"I think I should fill you in on his background. Earp moved from the Carlisle station a few days ago. Never an easy thing, moving police stations. But at least he has a home in Port Saint Giles. Married, with a small boy. I hear he went to the high school. He was demoted from detective inspector because—"

Fenella raised her hand. "With respect, ma'am."

"Don't you want to know why he was demoted?"

Fenella watched a drop of condensation streak down the window, then said, "Is Earp a good detective?"

"There are no complaints other than—"

Fenella interrupted. "Good enough for me. All we want is a strong team to help solve our cases, right?"

"Indeed."

"And the incident in Port Saint Giles, ma'am?"

Jeffery shuffled through papers on her desk. She didn't find what she was looking for and shrugged. "Some old biddy found by the bonfire. Might be nothing to it, but take a look, will you?"

Not an old biddy, Fenella thought, *a person, just like Nan.*

"Do you have a name?"

Jeffery didn't answer. "And stay out of the crime scene tent until the technicians have done their job. Oh, Zack Jones is now on your team."

Fenella wondered whether he was another transfer from Carlisle.

"Is he new?"

Jeffery nodded. "I met with him this morning. He is eager and straight out of the National Detective School, with top scores."

Fenella said, "He didn't come from uniform, then?"

Jeffery looked shifty. "An eye for the arts. He said a few words about old photos and girls and lighthouses. Above my pay grade, I told him. I don't have a taste for fine arts. If it is not in a spreadsheet it's hard to assess, isn't it?"

That wasn't what Fenella expected. It didn't answer her question. "How many years has he worked as a police officer?"

"He's not a fresh-faced twenty-one-year-old, if that's what you are concerned about." Jeffery shuffled through a stack of files. "Thirty-five. Worked in business for a few years, then signed up. What he lacks in police know-how is more than made up for by his grades. Top of his class in financial forensics. Bachelor's degree in history of art from Cambridge. Studied photography at the Royal Academy. And Jones will boost our minority headcount—parents from Trinidad, okay?"

Fenella's frown was answer enough. She got on well with Robert Dexter, her Detective Sergeant. She stood with him when he'd been the only minority on the force. And he'd stood by her when she was one of the few women.

"If that will be all, ma'am."

Jeffery said, "There is the question of Detective Sergeant Dexter."

Suddenly the room felt chilly. A gust of wind rose to a howl. It rapped on the window and threw rain hard against the glass.

Fenella said, "Dexter, ma'am?"

The superintendent's small eyes shrunk to pinheads.

"He's back on the bottle again, isn't he?"

"Not that I have seen, ma'am." Fenella wanted to mention his George Cross and a hundred and one other things, but she held her tongue. Jeffery also knew those things. "Dexter gets the job done."

Jeffery crossed her arms. "Both you and I are part of the modern police force. Dexter is... well he is a relic like an episode of *Inspector Morse*. If it weren't for his background, one wonders whether he'd be in the force."

"Are you saying if he weren't black, he'd have been out, ma'am?"

"It takes a sober head and clear mind to be a success in today's police force. Drunk detectives belong in the movies." The muscles in the superintendent's face set hard. "Do I make myself clear?"

Fenella counted the police officers she knew who were a little too friendly with the bottle. Good men and women. All ranks. All ethnicities. All ages. She lost count.

"A hazard of the job, ma'am."

"You might talk to Dexter about... pasture."

"What are you saying, ma'am?"

"Do you want me to spell it out?"

"I think you'll have to."

There was a pause while the superintendent slowly shuffled papers on her desk.

"Very well. I want you to have a friendly chat with Dexter. I'll accept his early retirement, say, at the end of next week? And with Jones on board, well, it won't hurt the numbers. Dismissed."

Fenella didn't move.

"Dismissed!"

Fenella remained seated.

Jeffery placed her hands flat on the desk. "Detective Inspector Sallow, you are dismissed."

"You've got it in for Dexter since he—"

"That has nothing to do with it!"

"While seeking revenge, dig two graves. One for yourself."

Jeffery sucked in a slow breath but didn't respond.

Fenella said, "And you have cleared it with the chief constable?"

"I've free rein to do as I choose."

"But Dexter put away Hamilton Perkins, ma'am."

"Yesterday's news won't satisfy today's readers." Jeffery slowly removed her hands from the desk and leaned back in her chair. "Dexter the police hero is old news. Only the old-timers know, and they will soon fade and be gone. Old news, Sallow. Don't protect him. He is nothing but a rancid blast from the past."

"Not to the Rae family, ma'am." Fenella recalled the horrific case. Even now it turned her stomach. She'd worked on it back in the days when Jack Croll ruled the roost. They felt like heroes when they put Hamilton Perkins away, and the team's success was cheered by the press. Fenella even got to shake the hand of Chief Constable Alfred Rae. "Last I heard, Perkins claimed it was a police set-up."

"A word in your ear." Jeffery stared towards the closed office door. "I've tried to keep this under wraps, but this place leaks like a colander. I've taken a personal interest in the case." She lowered her voice and her lips peeled back into a grin. "I am taking Mr Perkins to find the burial spot of his last victim. Dexter is not the only hero in our station. When I find the girl's body, we'll have a press—"

"Her name is Colleen Rae," Fenella interrupted. She spoke as if Colleen were alive, even though she knew the chances were slim to none. She always did until they found the body. "Colleen was a fifteen-year-old schoolgirl with learning disabilities when she disappeared." And she always remembered their names, and their faces. They haunted her even when justice was seen to be done. "Sickening crime, ma'am."

"Quite so." Jeffery paused for three beats. "But Perkins now recalls where Colleen is buried. Thanks to the help of Dr Joy Hall, he feels remorse for his crimes. He says he wants peace of mind. I told Chief Constable Rae about Perkins and said I would lead the search for his niece." The superintendent removed her reading glasses. "The power of psychology, eh? And Joy Hall is a good friend, as is Chief Constable Rae."

"I'd better tell Jack," Fenella said.

"This is police business. Keep Jack Croll out of it. We don't want a media circus." Jeffery shook her head. "Croll can find out like the rest of the public—after we find the body. Not before."

"Very well, ma'am. But I'll inform Dexter since his efforts put Mr Shred out of commission. He still suffers with the scars."

"I'm well aware of that fact." Jeffery's lips twitched into a wolfish grin. "Old wounds are borne by those who bear them, everyone else forgets. Old news, Sallow. Dexter and Croll are old news."

There was a reason Fenella didn't want to climb any further up the police totem pole. Today reminded her why. She stood.

"If you want Dexter to retire, you can tell him yourself. Excuse me, I've got a crime scene to investigate."

Chapter Five

B Y THE TIME FENELLA arrived at the crime scene, the weather had shifted. A grim gloom hung over the beach and a stubborn drizzle sprayed down from the low clouds. A white crime scene tent spared Maureen Brian's corpse from the worst of the elements. But the dull and the damp weren't enough to put off the crowd. They watched with their umbrellas raised and spoke in a low mutter.

Fenella paused by the side of her car to take in the scene. A generator growled above the urgent screams of gulls. The wind howled from the sea. Portable arc lamps lit the area around the bonfire. There were black embers and charred logs, and the sand was smeared with ash.

"Nice day for it," Earp said, as he stood by Fenella's side. "Not that there is ever a good day for death."

"No," Fenella replied. "I don't suppose there is."

Then she saw Dexter. He prowled around the outside of the tent, hood down, then off with big cat strides following the blue and white tape that marked the perimeter of the crime scene. She didn't expect to see him, thought he'd be curled up on his sofa in a drunken stupor. Drink didn't dim his radar for crime. *The man is a good detective,* she thought, and not for the first time. *A bloody good detective.*

They walked to the blue and white police tape. A police constable stood guard. He nodded at Fenella and raised a quizzical eyebrow at Earp.

"He's new, Constable Crowther," Fenella said. "From Carlisle, so treat him nice as he's not used to the ways of civilised folks."

"Will do," Constable Crowther replied. He glanced over his shoulder and dropped his voice to a whisper. "And, ma'am, a word in private would be much appreciated."

Fenella got on well with the uniforms, having come from their ranks. She knew what it was like to stand guard over a crime scene in the sun and rain and heat and cold.

"Of course," she replied. "I've always got time for you."

Anyway, they'd have to wait until the crime scene officers finished their forensic search. Then they would enter the tent and take a good look at the corpse. Not a nice task, but it helped get a feel for the thing. Fenella hoped Lisa Levon led the unit today, but couldn't make her out in the sea of white suits.

Fenella and Constable Crowther walked away from the police tape. They stopped a short distance from where the crowd had gathered. Earp stayed at the blue and white tape to keep guard.

"I know it is not the time, ma'am, but I wanted to thank you for the pot roast," Constable Crowther said. "From Elsa too."

Fenella had formed a group who cooked meals for police officers whose spouse fell ill. It was her way to give back to the other half. To men like her husband Eduardo, and women like Elsa. To show her support when they were sick. It was in its tenth year and still going strong.

"And how is your wife coming along?"

"Slow but improving. I'm working the overnight shift most days, so I can be with her in the daytime. And overtime when I can get it. Today it's a double shift for me." A herring gull landed on an arc lamp and screamed. Constable Crowther paused a moment to watch, then lowered his voice to a confidential murmur. "I wasn't the responding officer, but I recognise the victim. Can't recall from where, something to do with politics and I hear the press have got a whiff. Tread with care, ma'am. I don't like the smell of this."

Fenella's grey cells went on high alert. It would be a bad mess if politics got mixed in. Politicians had faster hands than a gunslinger for pointing the finger of blame.

Fenella said, "Are we talking town hall politics or national?"

"Not national, but don't quote me on that. But I'm sure I've seen the victim at town hall meetings. And I remember her face was in the newspaper a few years back. I think she is an artist, famous. I can't recall the name though." Constable Crowther reached into his tunic pocket. "For the animal shelter. I know you are on the board. Elsa loves dogs and insists. Our bit to help dogs and cats that don't have a home, as a thank-you." He stuffed a banknote into Fenella's hand, then hurried back to his post.

When Fenella returned to Earp, she ignored his raised eyebrow and said, "Go and speak with the responding officer. Find out what they know about the deceased. Let's build a clear picture of what happened as soon as we can. The more we know about this woman, the sooner we'll sort this out."

"Will do, ma'am," Earp replied, already on his way.

Fenella felt a surge of adrenalin. Who was this woman? Was she famous? Forensics would pick through the details. And her team would comb through the woman's past to reveal all her secrets. It would not be long before she found out all there was to know.

A white van arrived. People got out and suited up. More crime scene techs. Fenella looked at the crowd, and then the crime scene tent, and finally at the black embers of the bonfire. She chose the bonfire, the path taken by Dexter. She wanted his first impressions, but not before forming her own. Slowly she walked the perimeter with such an intense concentration that the chatter of voices and generator and screech of gulls vanished, leaving only the soft squelch of sand underfoot. Embers and ashes mostly. Blackened beach and a couple of crisp packets trapped by a charred log. A silver hot dog wrapper held in place by a crushed soda can. Nothing out of the ordinary. Still, she filed it all away in her mind.

"Ma'am."

Dexter was at her side.

"First impressions?" she asked, knowing he'd already been inside the crime scene tent. Dexter wasn't a man who followed protocol.

"Nasty."

Fenella's heart sank. But she waited, knowing there was more.

"An assault with deadly intent from what I saw before being hustled out by the white suits. Vicious." He stared out towards the crime scene tent, face set in a deep scowl. "She is so small, I thought at first it was a child. And whoever did it, tossed the poor lady onto the bonfire. Like I said, vicious."

In the distance, a darker line of clouds crept in from the sea, and with it, a solid wall of rain which Fenella watched with concern.

"Have the crime scene officers worked the area around the bonfire yet?"

Dexter scowled. "They haven't started. The lazy buggers like to be where it is warm and dry." But he knew, with the cutbacks, the team were down in numbers and everything took twice as long. Rain washed away evidence, and with the drizzle it would be tough enough. "Do you think the wind might pick up to hold back a downpour?"

Fenella glanced towards the slowly advancing wall of rain and shook her head. "Anything catch your eye?"

Dexter shrugged and pointed at the crime scene tent. "Let's hope they find what we need in there."

They stood in silence and watched the scene unfold. White suits came and went. Red and blue lights flashed from the parked police vehicles. Officers moved hurriedly against the backdrop of a drizzle-filled sky. But there was no sign of the press, and for that, Fenella let out a thankful sigh.

More police vehicles came. They stopped next to an ambulance where two paramedics talked by the open rear doors. One pointed at a hot dog truck which had just pulled up to the curb. A chance to make quick cash for the truck owner. Fenella doubted the uniforms would shoo the truck away. Police officers loved hot dogs and cups of sweet tea.

Detective Constable Earp stood by the crime scene tape. He talked to a constable, his back to the tape, front facing the crowds. Fenella liked that. Multitasking. She knew what Earp was doing. Listening to the officer and scanning the faces of the crowd. *He'll do*, she thought, as she considered the challenge ahead.

Now Fenella watched the crowd. Twice she scanned the curious faces. On the first scan, she noticed a woman in an orange jacket with her hair bunched into two pigtails. She wore a short skirt and Doc Martens boots. *Must be a teenager*, Fenella told herself. Then she scanned the crowd again. On the far side, partially hidden by the anoraks and umbrellas, she noticed a tall man. Not only tall, but huge. He wore a mud-brown trench coat several sizes too large. As she stared, trying to take in details, his oversized head slowly turned in her direction. A pair of feral eyes that jutted out of narrow slits returned her gaze. They did not blink.

"Fenella, we meet again," came a familiar voice. And there was Lisa Levon in a shapeless white suit, but nonetheless glamorous with her auburn hair, raven eyes, and twenty-year-old face even though she was closer to forty. "Dexter said you'd be around. I tossed him out of the crime scene tent earlier. How many times does he have to be told?" She didn't wait for an answer. "We're opening up in a moment, and we've got another one of your team inside."

That surprised Fenella. But eager to hear what they'd found, she let it slip. "And what can you tell me?"

Lisa flashed two neat rows of polished white teeth which gleamed even under the dull November sky. *A Hollywood smile*, Fenella thought, *just like the crime scene techs on the television*. Not that

Lisa Levon would be out of place amongst film stars. Not with her looks.

Lisa said, "Ever so smart."

"Eh?"

"Your new man Zack Jones. He's inside the crime scene tent. He is a fast worker, I must say." Again came the megawatt smile. "I attended to him personally."

Fenella stared at Lisa. What on earth did she mean? And how was Zack Jones able to stay in the crime scene tent when Dexter got tossed out?

Fenella said, "Any details on the victim's name?"

"Miss Maureen Brian, seventy-six. Killed by a blow to the back of the head with a blunt instrument. Then was pushed or fell onto the bonfire where she was scorched by the embers."

Fenella's neck became tense. She tilted it from side to side. It did not ease the stiffness. "Miss Brian was burnt to death?"

Lisa shook her head. "The force of the blow would have killed her before the smoke and flames. We'll know more once the pathologist looks. But by the state of the body, I reckon she died late last night or very early this morning, say between midnight and 2 a.m. More than that, I can't speculate about."

"DNA and fingerprints?"

Lisa said, "It might take days, even a week or two."

Fenella didn't have that kind of time. It let things go cold. "Put a rush job on, can you?"

"The labs are backed up." Lisa raised her hands, palms out. "I can't promise anything."

Fenella said, "Did you find her handbag?"

"Phone and purse. Seventy-five pounds and some small change."

"Not a mugging gone wrong, then?"

Lisa flashed a sad smile. "You're the detective; my job is to trawl through the bloody mess for clues." Theorising the reason for a crime was like maths to a pigeon for Lisa Levon. It made absolutely no sense. "If I live to one hundred, I'll never understand the criminal mind."

Not to Fenella though. In the end it all came down to motive. Even the crazies had a reason. She folded her arms, speaking her thoughts out loud. "What was this seventy-six-year-old woman doing on the beach in the early hours of the morning? Why would anyone in this tiny seaside town take a blunt instrument with deadly force to her head?" And, she wondered, what secrets lay hidden behind the thin walls of the crime scene tent?

Lisa shifted uneasily as if questions of who did it and why belonged to another domain. Not her world.

"Dr Mackay is on his way. He's working locum in Carlisle." She glanced towards the main road. "Should be here soon."

Fenella approved of Mackay. He was an old-school pathologist who spoke his mind and liked to visit the scene of a crime. He said it gave him a feel for the place. And Fenella liked that.

Lisa said, "Suit up, Fenella, and come inside."

Chapter Six

TEN MINUTES LATER, Fenella stood in the crime scene tent. A sickening smell of burnt flesh and wood roiled her stomach. A thin mist hovered between the thin walls like an old-time London fog. It curled in a yellow haze and got into her eyes and up her nose. Even with a mask that filtered out the worst, Fenella had to cough. *A terrible place for the living,* she thought. *A horrible place to die.*

She looked for the body, but couldn't see it through the haze and the sea of white-suited people.

"This way," Lisa said.

She followed Lisa through the tech-suited throng until she raised a gloved hand and Fenella got her first glimpse of Miss Maureen Brian. Her head turned away in revulsion. Her stomach churned in disgust. Yet, she forced her eyes to take another look.

Dear God! What a stomach-retching sight.

Fenella could watch a post mortem without missing a heartbeat. But crime scenes were more personal. They were the place where an actual human died. The harsh white light of the arc lamps exposed every detail. With sad eyes she took it all in.

Her eyes made a slow pass over the stiff black corpse. Then she took in the image once more. Like an artist with only paint and a brush, each pass brought to life new facts. Until, at last, a bright image burnt deep in the grey cells of her mind. A new name and face added to her mind's memory banks of the innocent dead.

When she'd seen enough, she turned her back and prayed they'd have an early breakthrough. Would they catch the killer through DNA evidence? A fingerprint or footprint or drop of the killer's blood would do the trick. Amazing what you can work out from a soft footprint in the sand or a splash of dried blood.

Fenella did a slow sweep to take in the full scene. Lisa Levon stood next to a white-suited figure. A man. She could tell by his stance, and he looked fit too. She strolled over to see what was going on and was surprised when he said," I'm Detective Constable Jones, ma'am."

His handsome face stared at her through swollen eyelids. He looked green around the gills. Before Fenella responded, Lisa Levon placed an arm around his shoulder and said, "I gave him the okay to come in the crime scene tent. Can be quite a shock, the first time. How are you feeling now, luv?"

He gave a weak smile.

"First time, then?" asked Fenella. She wondered what Superintendent Jeffery would make of it all. *Kittens. She'd have kittens.* Her lips curved into a minuscule smile. "Better go lie down in my car, lad. The blue Morris Minor, you'll find it."

"No, no. I can't," Jones replied, struggling to speak. "It's more the shock of it, knocked me for six. I still can't believe it!"

The first time at a gruesome murder site affected police officers in different ways. Some threw up. Some went quiet; others burst out in nervous laughter. But Fenella had never seen a babbling response quite like this. She thought about her husband Ed. He was an artist just like Jones and fainted at the sight of a dead sparrow. Was Jones like that too?

Fenella waited. Thunder roared in the distance. A scar of lightning streaked across the roof of the crime scene tent. Again came the booms and blasts and flashes of light so bright they drowned out the arc lamps. Raindrops smashed against the tent with the force of a demented heavy-metal drummer.

Jones went to rake a hand over his chin, then recalled he wore gloves and stopped.

"Ma'am. What I'm trying to say is that... I-I-I know Miss Brian. We were both in love."

Chapter Seven

W HAT THE HELL DID she have on her hands here? Fenella tried to hide her shock but felt a vein pulse in the side of her neck. She twisted her head from side to side to ease the tension. How could Jones know Miss Maureen Brian? What was all this about love? The woman was forty years his senior, old enough to be his grandmother.

"How on earth did you know Miss Brian?" Lisa Levon got in the question ahead of Fenella. Her voice crackled like sparks with hints of envy and rage. "I know you are a fast worker, but, my God, you've just got here from London. I mean, did you meet her on the train?"

Jones said, "I know this sounds strange, even a bit woo-woo, but Maureen filled my life with a fresh joy." He stopped, took a gulp and went on. "She taught my art class at the Royal Academy, and is... was... one of a few folks who still use the old-style wet-plate collodion process to make photos. Art schools from all over the country sought her out to teach her method to their students. People even came from America to see what she did. And China too. It's a bit like the Welsh language. Not many people speak it, but those who do are enthusiastic."

Fenella thought he sounded like Eduardo when he talked about his comic strips. There was a depth to Jones words her own unartistic mind couldn't quite grasp. A deep passion that lay beyond her sight.

And there was something else, hidden between the words. She sensed it, but again couldn't quite grasp it, so she said, "Tell me about you and Miss Maureen Brian."

Jones hesitated for a moment. He looked about as if he had just realised he was speaking to his boss. And in the heart of a crime scene tent with people in white suits flitting about like ghostly shadows. The pause drew out one, two, three beats. And continued through four and five.

Fenella sensed his nerves, thought he might dry up for good. She felt she should say a few words to urge him on, but knew to keep her mouth shut and wait. She was good at the wait.

Jones let out a breath and said, "Ma'am. It began with a project. Photos. I was in the last year of my master's degree when I met her. And she agreed to review my research project. It was love at first sight for Maureen, and she made that very clear. I felt the same way." He stopped as if he had run out of words.

Lisa Levon's voice rose to a half shout. "But she's seventy-six... How is that even—"

"Go on," Fenella said, raising a hand for Lisa to keep quiet. "Go on."

Jones shook his head. "We both fell in love"—his voice trailed off but there was no hiding his passion—"with pictures captured by film. Not any film. Old-style collodion positive images. They are like black-and-white photos with a hint of brown. They were the love of Maureen Brian's life, and mine too."

Fenella said, "So, Maureen Brian was an artist who took black-and-white photographs?"

Jones shook his head. "More than that. She taught her process, yes. But she was also active in historical groups. Building preservation. We are... were about to write a paper on the history of the young girls who helped work lighthouses. Maureen was to travel northern England and the Scottish borders to take photos of those that still exist or the places where they once stood."

"So, she was famous, then?" Fenella asked.

"In the circle of those who use the wet-plate collodion process, she was a legend." Jones looked back to where Maureen Brian's corpse lay and shook his head. "One of life's genuine good people. Unique and graceful. Ma'am, killing Maureen Brian, well it's like stamping out the sun. Who in their right mind would want to do that?"

Fenella took it all in without comment as the rain splashed against the roof of the crime scene tent. A picture of Maureen Brian began to take shape. It was still dim around the edges but bright in the centre. And she too wondered who would want to put out this light.

Chapter Eight

T HE FRIGID AIR MADE Fenella gasp. She had just left the crime scene tent with Jones at her side. Rain fell in icy drops, hard as shards of ice. Yes, it was only day one, and she'd been at the crime scene for only a short while, but she could not shake the image of the battered body from her mind, and it drove her crazy that the rain might wash away any evidence.

There were so many questions and a long list of known contacts to work through. They would start with close friends and widen the circle from there. A clear image would grow with time. But that was the thing. It would take time. She let out a second gasp, this time from frustration, and went over her mental checklist.

Officers rushed to set up a tent, but the gusts of wind slowed their efforts. A line formed by the hot dog van. The man who served the food moved as though time would soon run out. Even though he worked fast, the wall of odd-sized umbrellas moved as slow as a sludge-filled stream. Then Fenella saw Earp and Dexter. They huddled under a large golf umbrella and spoke in quiet tones. When she walked over, Dexter shifted his umbrella over her head.

"There you go, Guv. Keep you dry."

Fenella caught a whiff of sour whisky on his breath. They'd have words later, of course, but for now she said, "Earp, go and have a word with the gawkers."

Despite the rain, the crowd had swelled. Fenella scanned the faces and wondered at the speed at which bad news travels. A man in a clown's wig held two wood batons under his arm. An upturned top hat rested by his feet. Ready to perform and ready for donations once the rain eased. *He'll do a nice trade*, Fenella thought. Then she saw the girl in the orange jacket, face so pale she looked like death or a Goth but for the short skirt and Doc Martens. And the large man with the huge face and feral eyes remained where she'd last seen him, now with his hood up.

Fenella continued to speak. "I want the names of those who were on the sands this morning. And find out what time they closed the beach last night."

Earp was off before Fenella finished her sentence. *Keen*, she thought, *and experienced*. "Dexter, go with him. Jones, with me."

Dexter didn't move. In part because he still held the umbrella over her head. Tiny bullets of frigid rain splashed against his face. But still he did not move, jaw set firm, as though the weather were a mirage.

"Guv. A Mr Noel O'Sullivan found the body at seven forty-five this morning. He made the call from his mobile phone and said there was no rush because he knew she was dead."

"Responding officer?" Fenella asked.

"Constable Phoebe arrived six minutes after Noel O'Sullivan's call. He looked around the crime scene and then called for backup." Dexter let out a slow breath. "He's as pale as a ghost, ma'am. He knew Miss Brian."

Fenella said, "How did Constable Phoebe know Miss Brian?"

"Through his wife," Dexter replied.

"They were friends?"

"Maureen is the godmother for one of his boys." Dexter rubbed his chin. "And I'm godfather for his daughter. I guess we must have met at some do or other, but I don't recall."

Fenella saw the sharp glint in Dexter's eyes. Maureen Brian's death was personal. *He'll be like a dog at a bone now. Good!* She glanced at the sky with its thick sheets of clouds and hoped the rain would leave them a bite to chew on. A forensic clue to place their investigation on a solid path.

She stared at the crime scene tent and wondered what they would find. She knew forensics was hard, and processing crime scenes was hard. They would be meticulous and make pages of notes. But crawling in the damp ash-laden sand in a tent filled with the stench of death was not glamorous. Not like television where the techs' suits were always white and clean. It was hot and sweaty and uncomfortable, and most of all, a team effort.

She hoped they would find something they could use, but knew she couldn't rely on it. Without a forensic clue, it was down to good old-fashioned policing—identify and eliminate. Not a quick process. Fenella glanced back at the sky and thought the rain might get worse. *Better do a bit of old-style face-to-face*, she thought. And she'd start with the person who found the body.

She turned to Dexter and said, "Jones and I will have a quiet word with Mr O'Sullivan. See if we can get his statement while it is all fresh in his mind."

"He is in Constable Phoebe's patrol car," Dexter replied. "Keep the umbrella, Guv." Dexter turned to leave but stopped and pointed at the main road. Then he swore.

A truck engine growled. A blur of red and green eased through the sheets of rain. It came to a stop close to the hot dog van. Port Saint Giles locals knew those colours well. The logo of the town square television news station. A mauve and black minivan followed—the Port Saint Giles news radio station van. And behind it, a dark-green, beat-up Ford sedan.

Fenella sighed. They'd barely got a start at the crime scene and now the media were here. It was only a matter of time before the BBC showed up. But it was the battered, low-slung green Ford sedan she watched as the vehicles cut their engines.

Rodney Rawlings owned the Ford. He was a reporter for the *Westmorland News,* a local paper that sold in towns across Cumbria. Years of work on the town news beat had made his head tough and soiled his liver. He drank hard, chased stories like a fox, and foxed around women like a dog. No one dared mess with Rodney. He knew where the skeletons lay.

Thunder rolled across the dark sky. It shook loose more pellets of icy rain. Not that it dimmed the thrilled hum of the crowd. Their necks craned to watch as the crews burst from their vans. There was a brief beat of chaos as the journalists glanced around like bees on the hunt for honey. A voice yelled, "They are over there, by the crime scene tape."

The pack ran towards the detectives, their very microphones buzzing like bees.

"An update please," said a slim woman. She had bleached hair and Botoxed lips and a nose which turned up at the tip. Fenella knew her from lunchtime television news. "Can you give a word to our viewers, to help calm their nerves?"

"Stand back," Constable Crowther said. He stepped between the reporters and the detectives and waved his arms. "Do not cross the police tape. Stand well back, please."

A scruffy man in a ragged duffel coat pushed forward. "Tim Tarrant, Port Saint Giles radio host. We'll broadcast live from the scene all morning. On air in half an hour. What have you got for us, Inspector Sallow?"

Fenella would have ignored their questions but for a ratty-faced man with sharp eyes who shoved his way through the throng. He nodded at Constable Crowther, then ducked under the crime scene tape like a snake slips out of its den.

Rodney Rawlings said, "Got anything for me Fenella?" His voice rattled with the hollow ring of a smoker. "A nice bit of juice that we can slap on the front page."

Fenella said, "What I can tell you is that this was no accident. First signs suggest a vicious attack."

"Name?" The question came from the slender woman with bleached hair and Botoxed lips. "Can you give us a name?"

"Miss Maureen Brian, aged seventy-six. A local woman. We ask anyone who knew her to contact the town police station. We are trying to trace her family."

Rawlings rubbed a hand over his chin and said, "Is there a link?"

Fenella frowned. Was there another angle to the death? An angle she hadn't picked up on yet? An angle that had brought the media scurrying like an army of scavenging ants?

"Link?" she didn't like to ask.

Rawlings peeled his lips into a grin. He liked to be one step ahead of the police. "Miss Brian sat on the Lighthouse Restoration Board." He paused a beat. "Chaired by Chief Constable Rae. Any thoughts about Mr Shred? Is Maureen Brian's death linked to Hamilton Perkins?"

Chapter Nine

F ENELLA CLIMBED INTO THE back of the patrol car. The
scent of aftershave and wet dog hit her nose hard. Noel
O'Sullivan sat next to Barkie, his Irish Setter. The cramped space
didn't bother the dog, not by the volume of its gruff snores. But Noel
looked hot and tired. His leather jacket rested in his lap and she
noticed the gold crucifix on the back. Rain slapped the windows and
drummed in hard plops on the doors.

Fenella said, "Tell me what you saw on the beach."

He flashed a smile that would make a married woman weak at the
knees. "Where to start?"

Only three words, but Fenella took in his twang and guessed
Texas, tried to slow her beating heart and said, "How about you start
just before you reached the bonfire?"

"An ordinary day to begin with. I was out for my dawn stroll with
the dog." Noel's lips twitched at the corners as though about to laugh,
or cry. He did neither. "I met Mrs Collins on the beach and we
walked the sands at dawn."

"Who is Mrs Collins?"

"Elizabeth is a dear friend and dawn walker, like me. Most days I
walk the length of the beach. Not all of it, just from the dunes near
the bonfire to the pier." He pointed towards the lighthouse. But sheets
of rain hid it from view. "Today, I'd planned to walk all the way to the

pier with Elizabeth, but at the last minute recalled an early appointment. So, I doubled back on myself to the bonfire where"— his voice trailed off to an indistinct mumble—"dear God, what a terrible sight. Who in their right mind would do such an evil thing?"

Fenella waited several seconds. "And what is it you do, Mr O'Sullivan?"

"Noel, please." His lips lifted to reveal dazzling straight white teeth. "I'm a pastor at the local Free Evangelical. We meet on the beach. Mine is a small but sweet flock."

Fenella took in his easy eyes. It wouldn't be hard to whisper secrets into his soft ears. She had wanted to be a priest when she was young. Not a nun or even a monk but a priest. At the time, it wasn't possible, and she'd met Eduardo and joined the police. Now she served her flock at the high altar of crime so townsfolk could sleep easy in their beds at night.

"Noel," she said, using his first name. "Please go on."

He smiled. "I've settled into a routine. I suppose we all do in the end. So much of life is lived on automatic, and that's what happened this morning, why I forgot the meeting."

"Unusual, then, this morning meeting?"

"Well, yes, it was outside of my usual routine, if that is what you are asking." He paused and again smiled. Fenella realised it was a habit of his. A practised smile which did not match the strange stare in his eyes. "I normally take those type of appointments at the weekend."

"And what type of appointment are we talking about, Noel?"

"I really can't see the importance of it."

"It helps us build a big picture."

"With a… well… related to church."

Wouldn't a pastor expect to be called on all hours by the faithful? Fenella rolled that over in her mind and said, "Can you give me the name of the person you met?"

His jaw tightened. "Confidential, I'm afraid."

"We'll need to speak with the individual to confirm the facts. Just routine procedure, so we can check a box."

He gave an uneasy smile. "Am I a person of interest?"

Fenella ignored the question. What secrets hid behind his polished teeth?

"I'll not press you on a name right now," she said. "But I will come back to it if it is material, agreed?"

Noel waited two beats. "Agreed."

He let out a breath and relaxed. Barkie let out a contented snort. They watched the sleeping dog in silence for a minute.

Fenella said, "Can you at least confirm whether your appointment was with a man or woman?"

Noel blinked. "I can't see the—"

"Man or woman?" Fenella spoke slowly.

A pulse leaped in his neck. He stared at Barkie, then let his eyes drift to the floor.

"Detective Inspector Sallow, I—"

Fenella said, "In confidence. It will not go beyond these car doors."

"A... a... well, a woman." He sat up, but his shoulders curved as if under a great weight. "We'd arranged to meet at eight thirty."

Of course, she thought, *a meeting with a man wouldn't be so painful to admit.* "Let's get back to the beach. You discovered the body and called the police straight away?"

"Well, not exactly."

"What do you mean?"

"I called the police, but it was the screams that froze my blood. And then Barkie started whining." He pointed through the fogged-up window at the crime scene tent. "I hurried to the bonfire and found her crying."

"I'm not with you."

"Detective Inspector Sallow, I didn't discover the body, Mrs Audrey Robin did."

Chapter Ten

T HEY FOUND AUDREY ROBIN in the back of the ambulance. She sat with her head in her hands. A sharp antiseptic tang mixed with the smell of fried onions and hot dog hung in the air.

"Hello, luv," Fenella said flashing her warrant card. "I'm Detective Inspector Sallow. And that handsome young man standing outside in the rain is my sidekick, Detective Constable Jones. Are you okay to answer a few questions?"

Audrey stared with blank eyes. Her cheeks were stained with dried tears, eyes red raw. A medical blanket was draped over her shoulders. *Late thirties*, Fenella thought, *and no ring, not that a wedding band counts for much these days. Still, it is Mrs Robin, and with her large glasses and fur-like hair, she looks like a timid mouse or clever owl.* Fenella was torn between the two.

"Hey!" a voice yelled from the front. "Who let you in here? I'm responding to a medical emergency. Now get out or I'll have the union on your tail."

A paramedic glared from the front seat. Fenella realised her mistake. Should have asked for permission before she entered the vehicle. *Now the bugger's got a face like a wet Wednesday in January.*

"Just a few questions for Mrs Robin." Fenella kept her voice light. "Then we'll be out of your hair."

The paramedic said, "Why don't you give her a break?" He held a half-eaten hot dog in his hand. "The lady doesn't need a grilling. You lot poking into her business will not do her health any good. Can't you see she is in shock and confused?"

"Is that what you would like, luv?" Fenella spoke in soft tones as she settled next to Audrey. "We can come back later, but best to get it over with now."

"And close the bleedin' door on your way out," yelled the paramedic. "Look what you let happen on the beach, and on Bonfire Night too! Supposed to burn bloody Guy Fawkes, not innocent little old grannies. We don't want none of that murderin' in here."

Fenella nodded at Jones. He shrugged, then shut the doors, but remained just outside in the rain where he gave the thumbs-up. She liked that. No fuss and he waited nearby like a loyal Labrador. *He'll do too*, Fenella thought. *And it will be fun to mentor a bloke who could pass as a fitness instructor.* That triggered another thought— she'd encourage Eduardo back to the gym, have Nan cut down on his portion size, and she'd take an extra Pilates class to flatten the flab on her stomach. Maybe even encourage her daughter, Katherine, to sign Winston up for his local track and field club; he'd gotten too fond of pancakes for his own good. Jones wasn't just a pretty face. He was Mr Motivation too.

Fenella gave the paramedic a friendly smile and kept the beam on her face for Audrey. "I'm here to listen," she said. "Now, what do you say, luv, can we talk?"

Audrey looked at her hands and she looked out the small steamed-up window of the ambulance, then she looked at Fenella and nodded.

Fenella began with a simple question. "You were on the beach this morning?"

"Yes. I walk the beach most mornings at dawn, a regular, I suppose you'd call me." Audrey gave a little cough, her voice dry and hoarse. "Don't think I'll be doing that for a while. I mean... it might have been me."

"You ought to be out there catching bleedin' criminals so she can feel safe on the beach," grumbled the paramedic. "Not in here in the warm, pestering a sick woman!"

Fenella had patience, but this individual was testing her limits. "Where is your colleague?"

"Oh, so I'm now part of your investigation, am I, Mrs Sherlock?" A dry laugh. "Gone for a hot dog, not that it is any of your business."

"They serve coffee too, why don't you grab one. On me."

"Got to stay with the ambulance, I'm on duty. "

Fenella drew in a breath, turned to Audrey and said, "Not from around these parts, are you, luv?"

"Not originally, but it is home now. I live in town and work at the library."

"Want us to take you home?" said the paramedic. "My colleague will be back in a tick. You don't have to answer questions, not with you still in shock. Don't let the bleedin' police intimidate you."

Fenella tilted her head upwards as if looking for something on the ambulance roof. *Take a breath. Inhale. Exhale. Stay on task.* "Bristol? Is that where you are from, Mrs Robin?"

"How d'you know?" Audrey adjusted her glasses. "Most people guess South West England, but never the right town."

"I've visited, luv. Nice mellow twang you lot have."

Audrey grinned. "Love it here, much colder than Bristol though. This morning I walked along the beach collecting rubbish after the Guy Fawkes festivities. I've done that ever since I moved into town. The environment is so fragile and we humans leave so much mess. I worry about it and want to do my part."

Fenella leaned forward encouragingly. "Is that how you ended up by the bonfire?"

Audrey gave a nod. "This morning I was following the trail of litter. Not that there was much—a few empty crisp packets, lager cans... bits and pieces. Maybe if I'd have started at the bonfire, something could have been done?"

She let out a long wail. To Fenella's ear it sounded like the cackle of a witch around her cauldron.

"Go on, luv, have a good cry," Fenella said. "I'm here."

"Maureen's body was... charred, so very, very charred." Audrey's face crumpled and her body shook with sobs. "I should have found her sooner."

Fenella felt a pang of sorrow, couldn't help herself and gave Audrey a comforting hug. "It would have been no use, luv."

Audrey snuggled between her arms and whimpered. "If only I'd walked to the bonfire first, then I would have seen Maureen earlier and called for help. They might have been able to save her. I mean it is marvellous what medicine can do these days, isn't it?"

Fenella held her even tighter, saying nothing, sharing in her grief.

The wind picked up. It threw pellets of hard rain against the ambulance as though a mediaeval crowd tossing stones at a witch. A blast of thunder crackled. It rolled across the beach like a long jeer. The vehicle shuddered under its deep boom. *There goes what is left of the forensics*, Fenella thought with a glum sigh. She tilted her head to stare through the condensed windows. Jones turned up his collars but didn't move from the ambulance door.

"Don't blame yourself," Fenella said at last. Audrey clung to her like a newborn baby. "Not your fault, luv."

"I blame *you*!" the paramedic bawled from the front. "Can't find a cop when you need one and when you do, they interrogate you like you've just escaped from a high-security prison. Leave the woman be, for crying out loud. Can't you see she is sick?"

Fenella fought the urge to throw him from the vehicle. If she did, there'd be trouble with the union, and Superintendent Jeffery would raise hell when she found out. She sucked in a breath and let it out slow. *The cheeky bugger would be out in the rain otherwise.*

Audrey suddenly broke from Fenella's hug and wiped her eyes. "Please forgive me. I don't know what's come over me."

"Shock," said the paramedic, chewing on the last chunk of hot dog. "Go home, get some rest. We are happy to take you. Once the police start with their questions, there is no end to it. Why can't you leave her be?"

Fenella sighed. *Maybe this wasn't such a good idea.* "Mrs Robin, do you want to go on or would you rather make a statement at the station tomorrow?"

"Now, please." Audrey's hands shook. "Then it will be over?"

"It's never over," grumbled the paramedic. "Trust me. The buggers will be at you like a dog peeing on its favourite tree."

Fenella took a slow breath through her nose, then spoke in a soft sociable tone. "Another interruption and you're nicked!"

"Charming, I must say," replied the paramedic. "Whatever happened to the friendly Bobby? Wait till I speak to the union rep."

Just then, the ambulance door opened and Dexter climbed in, a savoury shroud of sour whisky and damp coming with him.

"One of my team," Fenella said in a level tone. "Detective Sergeant Dexter."

Dexter picked up the annoyance in her voice, glanced around, and asked the paramedic for permission to enter.

"Come join the party," the paramedic replied with a sneer.

Dexter rolled his eyes, then put out his hand to Audrey. "Mrs Robin?"

She reached and shook, touched her hair, dabbing it down, then adjusted her owl-like glasses and smiled. "Detective Dexter, I believe we have met."

Dexter beamed. "Are you sure?"

"*Home Brewing. A Guide for the Thrifty.*" Audrey tapped her temple with her index finger. "I remember the title. You borrowed it from the library three weeks ago. Have you had any success with your own home brews?"

"Ah," Dexter replied, avoiding Fenella's eye. "Just something to read on a rainy day."

"I'm sure Mrs Robin has no interest in what you do with your free time on rainy days," Fenella said in a pointed voice.

The ambulance door flew open and there was Jones, struggling with a ratty-faced man who wriggled from his grasp with the agility of a ferret.

"*Westmorland News*, here," yelled Rodney Rawlings. "Could I have a word, Mrs Robin?"

"Hey, you can't come in here, bloody fool!" screamed the paramedic.

"Out!" barked Dexter, stumbling to his feet and out the door to help Jones.

"People have a right to know," howled Rawlings. "Did Miss Maureen Brian say anything about Mr Shred before she copped it?"

But he was surrounded by uniforms. He struggled, more ceremony than actual fight, as they carted him away. Dexter hurried after the melee. He knew the routine with Rodney Rawlings—a stern talk and then release. Best not to press charges against members of the press. Rodney Rawlings had been around so long, he knew where Dexter's skeletons lay.

"Told you nothing good would come from talking with the police when you are sick," the paramedic said. "God knows what'll happen next."

Fenella slammed the ambulance door shut. Then she sat down. A minuscule smile kissed her lips. She leaned forward and said to the paramedic, "Where were you late Bonfire Night?"

No answer. But she saw the flare in his nostrils before he turned away to stare out of the front window.

Now Fenella got down to business.

"Mrs Robin, did you know the victim?"

"Oh yes. I knew her very well."

"You two were friends?"

Audrey adjusted her position and tugged at the blanket. Her hands still shook. She raised them to her ears for a moment, then turned to glance out of the window and let out a heavy sigh.

"Everyone knew Maureen, she is... was a marvellous person and welcomed me with open arms when I moved into Port Saint Giles. She introduced me to the community and helped me settle in and make connections. Maureen did that for everyone. But yes, we were friends, very good friends."

The rain eased to a grey blanket of drizzle, and with it, the constant *pitter-patter* turned to a soft *tap-tap*. Dexter returned and took out his notebook. *Good*, thought Fenella. *Now I can focus*. "Do you know any relatives of Miss Brian?"

"She had a sister in Cornwall. But she died before I moved to Port Saint Giles."

"Any grandchildren, nephews, nieces?"

"Not that I know of. We were close, Maureen and I; she treated me like a daughter."

Fenella changed tack. "Have you any idea who might want to hurt Miss Brian?"

"No." Audrey's face spasmed. Her hand reached out, tapped her coat pocket. "Maureen was such a lovely woman, and to find her tossed on the bonfire like a... cast-off scrap of driftwood. Who could do that to a fellow human being?"

For several seconds both women stared at one another as the soft rap of drizzle faded, leaving behind the whistle of a hollow wind and the gentle rumble of the generator.

"That will be all, for now," Fenella said. "Thank you for your time, Mrs Robin."

Audrey visibly relaxed and a broad smile crept onto her lips. "I hope I've been helpful."

"Wonderful." Fenella stood, paused, then sat back down. "Oh, just one more thing. Tell me again what happened today. Just so I can get it straight in my head."

"I just walked around the bonfire picking up rubbish when I saw something. I thought to myself, that's a bit small for a Guy Fawkes.

Then I wondered why it hadn't been burnt in last night's fire. I walked closer and there she was. I recognised Maureen and knew she was dead—the back of her head... smashed in." Audrey's hand flew to her face and she scrubbed her eyes. "Then I must have screamed, and Mr O'Sullivan was at my side."

"And he called the police?"

"Yes."

"Now think very carefully before you answer my next question." Fenella paused for three beats. "Did Maureen have any enemies?"

"No."

"An upset neighbour?"

"Detective Sallow, I can't think of anyone more agreeable than Maureen Brian. I've known her since I moved to this community and never heard her raise her voice."

"When did you last see her?"

"Yesterday evening, we met briefly before they lit the bonfire. But we lost each other at the start of the procession. That was the last time I saw her alive."

"And where were you between midnight and two this morning?"

"At home, sleeping, I suppose."

"What time did you get home?"

Audrey shrugged. "I can't say, but I left before they closed the beach and I went straight to bed."

"Anyone corroborate that—your husband?"

"I'm divorced. My husband was rather difficult. Controlling. That is why I came to Port Saint Giles, to get away from the memories. I live alone."

"And you've no inkling who would want to harm Miss Maureen Brian?"

Audrey Robin slowly shook her head. "I've absolutely no idea who might have killed her, but I hope you catch them soon."

Chapter Eleven

N O ONE SAW CATHY Wallace's tears.
It was the day after they discovered the body on the beach. She bent down over the sink in the fake pinewood bathroom and breathed in and out in short bursts. A nightmare she could no longer remember had jerked her from sleep, but it was the tune running through her head that kept her awake. *What was it called?* She didn't know. But it made her cry and she couldn't make the tears go away.

A hot shower might ease the sick feeling she felt in the pit of her gut. But she groaned when she opened the cracked plastic door where mould curled around the edges. There was grime and stink everywhere. Her dad hadn't cleaned up after himself. He never did when he came home drunk. Taking care of him was a lot of work, but she had promised her mum to look after him. Though Mum had done little of it herself while alive.

She closed the narrow shower door. She couldn't face that, would clean it till it sparkled like new after school. But not now. Too early in the morning. She shoved the door shut and opened the small square window that rattled and shook when the wind picked up. It shifted an inch on its rusted hinge. Cold air flowed in. Then Cathy looked in the cracked mirror of the medicine cabinet. More spots. She'd been up since dawn, and swore there were one or two more.

Cathy closed the lid on the toilet and sat down to think about last night. She'd met Belinda Yates. They sat on a bench on the pier by the lighthouse. Under the florid orange glow of a rusted streetlamp, they drank cans of cheap long-life lager. Six cans of the brew, bought by Belinda from the newsagent opposite the launderette. The owner knew she was underage, sold booze to all the school kids, and made a nice profit in the bargain.

They gossiped and laughed and shared the first can. Like blood sisters, they took sips in turn. Then each cracked open a second which they sipped like fine wine. Cathy wore red lipstick and painted her fingernails to feel more grown up.

After a short while the ale kicked in. Cathy let out a wild laugh. Belinda joined in. They giggled and chuckled without words being spoken. It was as if their minds had become one. Better than blood sisters. Very best friends who life would not split apart.

A frigid blast from the Solway Firth whistled across the pier. The wind howled as if to warn that rain would soon come to drench anyone outside. They drew their coats tight and raised their hoods, but did not move from the bench.

They huddled against the wind with their cheap brew and Cathy spun one of her fantastic tales. This time about a house in a country with a pond and a duck that laid eggs which hatched into children with wings. The children looked like angels but were devils inside. One child became Cathy. She lowered her voice to a whisper and glanced about to make sure no one was there. Then she told a gruesome tale of what one of the angel children did to the owner of Logan's Bakery. Mr Eye, Cathy called him in her tale, for his eyes roamed over the counter girls, peeling away their clothes as his tongue darted out. Belinda giggled with delight and urged her on to tell more.

When the story was over, Belinda said, "But you wouldn't really kill someone, would you?"

Footsteps shuffled along the pier. Through the dark, a broad shadow took form. A gang of schoolboys, all teens, appeared from the gloom. They slouched by and jeered and whistled and made rude gestures. But Belinda grinned. She yelled their names, and told each boy with delicious delight what she'd tell their mothers when she next served their crusty cobs from behind the counter at Logan's Bakery.

That shut them up fast. Everyone in school knew Belinda had no fear and would do what she said she would do. They pulled up their hoodies and scattered. Into the darkness they flew. The slap of their footsteps faded until all that was left was the quiet slosh of water against the barnacled pilings below.

"Stupid twits," Cathy mumbled under her breath. She knew every one of them by name, but didn't have Belinda's confidence to tell their mothers. Her friend confronted problems. Cathy hid and made tales. And once again she knew that was the thing she liked about her friend.

"Nothing but boys," Belinda replied, the grin still on her face. "Harmless; not children, but not quite men either." She rolled her eyes playfully. "You ought to come live with me for a while. Elizabeth has an army of little monsters who are always up to no good. But I've never seen her raise her voice, let alone slap any of them."

Cathy marvelled at the easy way Belinda spoke with older folk. It was Mrs Collins to her or Mrs Elizabeth when she hung out at their house, while Belinda called her Liz.

Cathy said, "Like it at Mrs Elizabeth's place, don't you?"

"Love it!"

Cathy took a long sip from her can. "I still think a quick clip round the earhole would set those lads right about how to treat women."

"Oh come on! My dad was quick with his fists, and Mum was just as bad—that's how I ended up in foster care."

"I'm sorry." Cathy wondered why her mouth always ran ahead of her brain. Not like Belinda who spoke with maturity. *Like a mother. So sensible.* And Cathy liked that.

Belinda gave Cathy a quick hug, then said, "They are only a bunch of silly boys out for some teenage fun. In a year or two you'll be batting your eyelids at them. Anyway, it's not like they go about cracking old ladies on the back of the head and shoving them onto the bonfire." She pulled a tissue from her pocket, blew hard. "I'm so sorry about what happened to Maureen."

"Miss Brian?" Cathy knew who she was talking about but asked anyway. She didn't like to think about what happened.

"Aye. I can't stop crying when I think about it." Belinda fished around in her pocket and this time pulled out a cloth handkerchief. "She was... lovely. I mean, I know what the police are saying but, it just had to be an accident, didn't it?" She gazed at Cathy with watchful eyes. "It was an accident, wasn't it, Cathy?"

Cathy didn't like the way she stared at her. It made her feel uneasy. What did she know? So, she tried to spin a tale about Miss Brian getting drunk on a thimble of beer, and how, dizzy and dazed, she stumbled on a chunk of driftwood and cracked her head as she rolled onto the glowing embers.

"See," Cathy said. "It really was just a silly trip and a fall. An accident."

But the entire town knew it was murder, and when Cathy finished her story, the laughter stopped and the conversation turned sour.

"Bonfire Night," Belinda began, drawing out the two words as if they were poisonous pus. "Where did you go?"

"Nowhere."

Belinda just stared at her and didn't say anything.

"Oh, that," Cathy said after five beats. "Well, you know how it is."

"No. Tell me."

Cathy crossed her fingers and decided to say nothing. She felt uneasy at the silence that followed until a childlike guilt urged her to speak. "I wasn't gone for long, was I?"

"Long enough to be seen under the pier with a mysterious man."

Cathy gulped a mouthful of lager, almost gagging at the bitter taste. She thought she had been careful, and anyway, she'd left overweight Belinda at the bonfire.

"Loo break. You know how it is."

Belinda sipped from her can, her eyes focused on Cathy's face like beams of white light.

"Who is he?"

"Drinking this cheap brew isn't good for me," Cathy said. "My bladder feels like it has shrunk to half its usual size. Belinda do you think that is normal?"

"You are still a child, Cathy."

"I'm sixteen and can get married."

"A child."

"Look who's talking."

"Tell me what happened."

But this time Cathy kept her lips sealed. She thought of her primary schoolteacher, Mr Stanhope, and pretended to be a palmate newt. She always became a newt when she didn't want to talk. She shifted on the bench as she wriggled deep into the dark weeds of the Port Saint Giles town square pond.

"Cathy, what are you doing?"

She didn't answer.

"You're bonkers." Belinda's eyes never left Cathy's face.

"I'm not."

Belinda lowered her voice. "He might be the killer!"

"Don't be daft."

"Ah, so you did meet a man!"

"None of your business."

"Aren't we best friends?"

Cathy shrugged and sipped from the can. "You know where I went."

"To the loo, you said, but you were seen under the pier with Mr Mysterious. Gorgeous. Name?"

"It's not what you think." Cathy put her lager can on the slatted beams beside the bench, then waved a hand vaguely. "Belinda, there is no Mr Mysterious; I went to pee."

For several minutes they sat huddled on the bench in silence as a wind picked up from the sea. It blew sharp gusts of chill which whipped up the water against the barnacled pilings so it sounded like voices roaring at a foul in a football match.

"Then I'll go to the police." Belinda toyed with her lager can. "They are asking for people to come forward with anything unusual. If I do, they'll want the pervert's name, so you might as well tell me and save yourself the trouble."

Cathy laughed. Her cackles rose until they sounded like the frantic screams of a herring gull. And then Belinda whined and charmed and cried about being best friends. Then she spat out spite. But Cathy wouldn't say.

Belinda stormed off.

Cathy sat on the bench in the cold and dark and drank until she'd drained the final three cans. Then she got up and staggered home.

Chapter Twelve

THE MORNING BRIGHTENED. A dull sky gloomed through the open bathroom window. Cathy dabbed away the last traces of lipstick. It left a bright red smear on the tissue. She stared at it and wished she'd gone easier on yesterday's beer. A tune played in her head as she swatted away tears.

From outside the door came heavy footsteps. A fist pounded the bathroom door.

"You in there, Cathy?"

"Won't be long, Dad. Getting ready for school."

"Well hurry up, I need to dump a motherload. And for God's sake, wear your uniform today."

She heard his footsteps shuffle away, and a moment later, through the thin walls of their plywood and corrugated-metal cabin, the sound of voices on the television.

"Dull with a light drizzle and a gentle breeze," said the weather reporter in an enthusiastic voice. "With a high of eight degrees Celsius; that's forty-six Fahrenheit for those who prefer old money."

Cathy ran the sink tap and splashed water over her face. It woke her up. Her thoughts drifted to Miss Maureen Brian. An accident, wasn't it? That's what she'd told Belinda. And her friend lapped it up, believed every word of her story. Hadn't she? Sure, they'd fallen out, but that was nothing new. Belinda would come creeping back for more outlandish tales just like she always did. Best not say any more about Miss Maureen Brian and what happened on Bonfire Night. Her stomach turned over. *Better to let sleeping dogs lie.*

"Got some fried chicken leftovers from last night. Want me to warm up a leg for your breakfast?" The words, from her dad, came out almost musically, all singsong and treble so that Cathy knew he'd already fuelled his body with a hit and would be good until later that day. "Hey, there are two bags of fries as well. Feast time!"

The sharp bang of plates echoed from the kitchen. Then came the creak of the rusty microwave door. Cathy's stomach lurched. Sour vomit spewed from her throat. The vile stench tore at her nostrils as she doubled over to unload another splashdown. From the television, she heard the headline news, and moments later, the singsong voice of her dad.

"Poor sod. Beaten and pushed onto the bonfire and the stupid police haven't got a clue. Those buggers couldn't catch a fly trapped in a bottle."

The microwave pinged.

Cathy retched again. She fished about in the sink for the plughole, then wiggled her finger to unblock the drain.

"Breakfast's ready. Come on Cathy, hurry, else it will get cold." Her dad went quiet for half a minute. "Hey, did you hear that? Miss Maureen Brian was an artist?" The question mingled with the creak of the microwave door and rustle of packaging. "The newsreader just said her latest snapshots went for a pretty penny. Wouldn't have to go out to beg and rob if I had a couple of those in my back pocket, would I, luv?"

Cathy's skin prickled. She wished he wasn't so brazen about his thieving. *Just like those teenage boys.* Why couldn't her dad be like a cat burglar in the movies? They worked under cover of night with a hidden daytime identity the police didn't know about. Instead, her dad, the balding beatnik druggy known by every police officer between here and Carlisle, bungled his jobs in the glare of bright daylight and CCTV cameras. Still, he didn't bail on life like her mum, and her dad put food on the table.

"Hurry up, Cathy, my arse is about to explode!" He spoke as if his mouth were filled with food. "The newsreader says there is going to be a conference at the town hall. Waste of taxpayers' money. I tell you, there's more chance of me dumping right here on the carpet than the police catching Miss Brian's killer."

"Almost done."

Cathy wiped the sink clean, taking her time to get it all. Tears came as she hummed the tune trapped in her head. *What is it called?* No answer came. But her lips pursed, turning the hum into a whistle and she wasn't sure whether that thrilled or infuriated her.

Chapter Thirteen

THAT SAME MORNING, Fenella stood at the whiteboard in Incident Room A and breathed in the aroma of coffee and aftershave. She held a cup of the hot brew in her hand and kept her face blank as she watched the team amble into the room. No rush. They'd done this a hundred times before. A stroll to the coffee pot, pour, and take a seat. Familiar sights and sounds. The scrape of a chair against the tile floor. The soft *slosh* of coffee as it poured into paper cups. The *glug* of the tea urn. And the hushed voices. Everyone keen. They knew it was a big day. The first full day of the hunt.

Good, a full house.

For several minutes, she sipped and watched. Stragglers shuffled into the room, but her core team were in place. They had arrived even before she first walked into the room. Earp leaned backwards, sipping his cup. Jones opened his laptop and fired it up, then took a gulp from his small coffee cup. Dexter prowled three walls of the windowless room and stopped at the coffee pot to pour. His third.

Sound came from the hallway. People poured into the room. The last-minute rush. They snatched up coffees and hurried to find seats. Within a few seconds, it was standing room only.

Fenella's lips quirked at the corners but she stifled the grin. Now was not the time for showboating. Still, she felt good about this one. And word had flown around the station that if they didn't crack it, the big guns from Carlisle would come in. Now everyone saw it as a chance to stick it to headquarters. Show the big shots what a small-town police force could do.

Fenella smiled when Tess Allen came into the room and pushed her way through the throng. She nabbed a seat on the front row when its owner got up for a tea. Fenella liked Tess. The press officer was a whizz in front of the camera.

The quiet murmur rose to a buzz. Fenella knew the noise. It sounded like the fast beat of bee wings. A high-pitched drone which hummed as though it were a wild beast about to attack. The best investigations started this way. Anticipation mixed with excitement and adrenaline. This is why they signed up for the job. She hoped they'd get a quick result, because the buzz didn't last. It would be gone in a day or two. After weeks of hard slogging, interest would fade. Even the best detectives got jaded at the edges. Chasing down dead ends did that to you.

As she considered her opening lines, Constable Crowther walked into the room. *Looks tired. How is his wife?*

Then she noticed Constable Phoebe. He stood next to the tea urn, arms crossed and as still as a statue. He'd found Miss Brian's body. She was a good friend of the wife. His body language told Fenella everything, and she made a mental note to make time to pay him and his wife a visit. Take them a meal and have a quiet talk with the wife. Get her view on Maureen Brian. Two birds with one stone. Useful. And she'd have a quick chat with Dexter about Phoebe's family. *Godfather to their daughter, isn't he?*

The buzz grew louder. If the beast wasn't fed, it would sting.

It was time to begin.

Fenella let out a slow breath and tilted her neck from side to side. The tension eased, her mind kicked into high gear, and she waved for Tess Allen to join her at the front. Then she pointed to the gruesome crime scene photograph of Miss Maureen Brian. It hung at a sharp slant, pinned by magnetic force to the whiteboard.

"What do we know?" Fenella's question stilled the room. The quiet tick of the clock and glug of the tea urn rang out like shouts. "Miss Maureen Brian, seventy-six, killed late Bonfire Night or early the following morning on the beach, a fatal blow to the back of the head. Nasty." She stopped, took her time to make eye contact with each person in the room. "Then the poor luv was shoved onto the embers of the town bonfire where she died." She paused. Faces looked, expecting her to continue. "I want the person who did this. And so do you."

Fenella walked two paces towards Tess and touched her arm. A signal. She'd passed the baton for the moment.

Tess placed her hands on her hips, legs planted wide and said, "I needn't remind you that Superintendent Jeffery will be all over this one."

There was a long murmur. The entire station knew Jeffery was under pressure from the bigwigs in Carlisle. And that meant pressure for Fenella. Her boss had the patience of a gnat and the focus of a lion on the kill in protecting her career. If Fenella didn't get the perp, she'd be tossed off the case. Jeffery wouldn't bat an eyelid about that.

Tess said, "There'll be a press conference at the town hall at eleven. The superintendent would like a big turnout, so if you are free, it would be great if you showed up. There'll be lots of media. This case is growing like a snowball. Our focus is on Cumbria radio and local television. We are asking for anyone who knew Miss Brian to come forward. And there'll be politicians on the stage as well."

A collective groan filled the room.

Tess raised her hands, palms out. "I'm just the messenger. But you should know Councillor Ron Malton will speak—"

Another groan. This time a voice booed.

Tess shrugged. "Mr Malton is a champion for law and order and will speak first since he sits on so many police boards. But others will get a chance. Equal time for all." She paused and placed her hands on her hips. "This is a joint effort. The Cumbria Constabulary is doing its part for town relations. Please spread the word. Any comments?"

"Will Chief Constable Rae attend?" The question came from Dexter, more growl than voice.

Tess responded with a quick shake of her head. "He wants to play this one down since the victim served with him on the Lighthouse Restoration Board."

"Any word about Mr Shred?" This from Earp.

Tess turned to Fenella as if for the okay to go on. Fenella gave a swift nod and Tess said, "There are online rumours about a link to Hamilton Perkins. They are baseless. Our line to the media is, there is no link. You all know that, don't you? So, no gossip on our side, please."

Fenella waited for Tess to return to her seat, then said, "Ideas?"

Jones sidled sideways without getting up. Then he raised a quick hand, still holding his cup. "Mugging gone wrong, ma'am."

"Go on," Fenella said. "What have you got?"

"I'd guess a local yob in need of cash to fuel the next hit. The person botched up the attack." Jones lowered his arm and squeezed his eyes tight for a moment. Eduardo did that too, when he got a hairbrained idea. "Yes! The thug wanted cash. And Miss Brian wasn't much taller than a nine-year-old child but she wasn't the type to be pushed around. She put up a fight, and the yob knocked her on the head with a log. Might not have meant to kill her."

"Seventy-five pounds and change in her purse though," Fenella said. "Why didn't the yob take the cash?"

"Someone frightened the person off and they legged it," replied Jones.

"We are talking about an attack that took place between midnight and two in the morning. Even on Bonfire Night, the beach wouldn't have a lot of folk about." Fenella thought it over. Did he have a point?

She said, "Why hasn't the person or people who scared off the yob come forward?"

Jones shrugged. "They might not have heard the news yet. I'll check with the tip line to see if anything comes in."

"And see what you can find out about the whereabouts of town louts. Make a list and follow up."

"Will do, ma'am."

"Family?" Fenella continued before anyone responded. "Miss Brian had a sister who passed a few years back. Jones get on it, see if the sister had any children, a husband, or cousins. Find anyone related to Maureen." Fenella liked to use the victim's first name, felt it made the investigation more personal.

Jones began typing into his laptop.

Fenella moved to the next item. "Earp, what did you find out from the gawkers at the crime scene yesterday?"

"Got a decent list of names, ma'am." He pulled out a spiral-bound notebook. "Twenty people were on the beach between five a.m. and the time Mrs Audrey Robin discovered the body. I'm working through them."

"Eliminate as quick as you can. Until forensics get their act together, it's old-school and shoe leather. And get onto Dr Mackay. Hurry him along. We know it was a blow to a head, but what else has our pipe-smoking pathologist got for us?" A thought wriggled into Fenella's mind. She took a sip of coffee, waiting for it to take shape. "Yesterday, in the crowd, did anyone notice a tall man, large... big head?"

"Name is Martin Findlay," responded Earp. "Local man, lives in town."

"Check his alibi for the night of the murder." There was something else. Fenella closed her eyes and saw it immediately. "And a young woman in an orange jacket, tall with pigtails?"

"I saw her," Dexter said still prowling the walls. "Teenager."

"I noticed her too," Jones added. "I'd say fifteen at most but dressed older."

"Anyone get a name?" Fenella asked.

No one responded.

"Earp?"

"Sorry, ma'am, she was gone by the time I made my way over."

"Why wasn't she in school?" Fenella folded her arms, but the question faded into the next as she continued. "Dexter, what do we know about Maureen's friends?"

"Bugger all, Guv."

"Well find out, will you?" Fenella moved to the next item on her mental list. "Mrs Audrey Robin found the body, like a daughter she said, so there's another one for you, Dexter."

"Aye, will do."

"Tell you what," Fenella raised a hand. "Why don't we both pay her a visit, get a list of contacts from the horse's mouth as it were." And this time there'd be no annoying paramedic to hamper her questions. "Mrs Audrey Robin lives in Seafields Lane, if my memory serves me well?" It did. She'd memorised the addresses. She filed it along with all the other facts of the case in her brain cells. Every detail. Down to the blue headscarf wrapped tight around Maureen Brian's head.

"Constable Crowther," Fenella said. "Can you visit with Mr Noel O'Sullivan, get a formal statement. Call ahead, Pastors are busy, and a flock of crusty Cumbrian folk aren't easy to tend. And will someone find out what time they closed the beach on Bonfire Night. Earp, that ball's in your court."

Fenella gazed at the enlarged photograph of Miss Maureen Brian's corpse.

"And Dexter…"

"Guv?"

"After the press conference, let's you and me have a butcher's around Miss Brian's home. See if we can't get a more flattering photo of her to pin on our board."

Chapter Fourteen

F ENELLA KNEW IT WOULD be a rugby match, but did Jeffery have to steal all the air time?

The public and press squeezed between the oak walls of the town hall's great room. Jeffery shoved her face into the spotlight, grinning with her wolfish smile. She knocked about the media's questions like a tennis pro. Even Tess Allen, the press officer, could barely get a word in. Fenella had planned to make an appeal for witnesses. She had prepared a brief speech, if asked. But no one asked. And the questions from the press led to squabbles across the political divide. Jeffery stayed clear of that melee, but dropped her sound bites when a chance opened.

"A tragic event."

"A one-off."

"No. no. Not a serial killer."

"The public can sleep easy in their comfortable beds. This is a quiet town and my officers will catch the killer."

Fenella left before the press conference finished, with Dexter in tow. They drove to Miss Maureen Brian's house on Seafields Lane. Only there wasn't a row, just a narrow dirt lane with bare hedges on either side, and trees with branches so low they almost touched the ground.

"Be careful," Fenella said to Dexter, who drove. "Don't scratch my car. I know it's a banger, but I have some pride."

"Damn branches are like witches' hands out to block our path," Dexter replied.

The lane snaked up a sharp slope. At the end, on a patch of gravel and tufts of brown grass, stood a run-down, three-storey Victorian red-brick house. It had wide windows and thick net curtains. A faded sign proclaimed—Seafields Bed and Breakfast. Luxury Accommodation at Great Rates.

They climbed out of the car to dull clouds and a brisk breeze which softened the splash of the sea. The beach was near; they could smell it in the air. Fenella glanced around, and through the broken fence saw a broad sweep of sand dunes and the white surf of distant waves.

The detectives took quick steps through a rusted iron gate. They hurried along a gravelled path which snaked in a slow arc to stone steps. Twenty at least. They stopped and peered up at the faded front door.

"Stairway to hell," Dexter said as he took the first step. "Wonder if we have the right address. I can't see a seventy-six-year-old skipping down these first thing in the morning to do her shopping. And she'd have to climb back up with her bread and milk."

"Come and join my Pilates class," Fenella replied as she skipped two steps at a time. There was nothing like being outside of the office and working a case. She felt as energetic as a beagle on the scent of a fox. "We've got three octogenarians. The other women are in their thirties and forties. You never know, one of them might like a bit of stale gristle. Then you'll thank me for introducing you to the new love of your life."

"Guv," Dexter huffed. "I've no plans to perform the double leg stretch or kneeling side plank, even with a gaggle of fit sweating ladies."

It was tough going. Fenella paused midway and dabbed a handkerchief at her brow. She pretended to wait but couldn't hide her long drawn-out gasps. Dexter laughed, but knew better than to rub her nose in it. Instead, they sucked in cold air and gazed at the wide sweep of beach and the dark sea farther out. A squawking flock of black-headed gulls walked the sands.

Now they took their time. There was no rush and the slow pace gave Fenella time to run things over in her mind. Who else lived in the place? Where were they on the night Miss Brian was killed? They shuffled close together like rock climbers easing along the ridge of a Himalayan mountain range. As they shambled and huffed onto the top step, the front door opened.

"I was expecting you," said a grinning man with black button eyes and a beard that tapered off into a devil's wisp. "You guys must be keen, most folk use the side ramp. Few tackle those steps."

Fenella didn't have the breath for speech, noted the gold loop in his nose, and pulled out her warrant card. He waved it away with an easy smile.

"I'm Ben Griffin. I run the place with my wife, Safiya. We wondered when you would show up. Come on in, I've just brewed a fresh pot of coffee."

Fenella and Dexter panted like beagles back from a fox hunt. They followed Ben along a dark hall with soft carpet. It smelled of boiled vegetables and pine and bleach. There was no sound other than their soft footfalls. He stopped at a frosted glass-panelled door.

"This is the dining room. We can talk in here if you don't mind."

"Perfect," Fenella replied.

The door squeaked open.

"Ladies first." Ben flashed a dazzling smile and made a low bow.

Charmer. Fenella had a soft spot for compliments. Eduardo had charmed her into dating. He was a poor starving artist with nothing but a pencil, sketch pad, and a head full of beautiful dreams when they met. And she on the first rung of her police career. He still had his dreams and pencil and sketch pad. Fenella loved that about her husband. Then she thought of how Jones had dazzled Lisa Levon in the crime scene tent. Now she wondered whether Ben had dazzled her too. Nice skill to have with the ladies.

They sat at a long table with a red-and-white tablecloth by a window that gave them a view of the flat sands and sea. The faint trace of fried food and coffee and boiled dinners of long ago mingled in the still air. Ben poured three mugs and joined them.

"A Bonfire Night I'll never forget," he said. "Safiya and I got back home after the fireworks, around ten. Maureen wasn't home yet. But there was nothing strange in that. She often stayed out late, and given the festivities, we thought nothing of it." He paused. "I'm sorry, you have questions?"

Dexter gulped his coffee down in two sharp swigs and said, "Which room can we find—"

Fenella touched his arm. "No point rushing. Especially as Mr Griffin has gone to the trouble of making coffee. We might as well take our time. Let's do our bit for community relations, shall we?"

Dexter frowned. "Guv?"

But Fenella just sipped and watched Ben as he returned to refill the coffee pot. She wanted to get her breath, clear her mind and think about the next steps. This was not what she expected. She'd expected a cottage, not a dilapidated bed and breakfast. She wondered who would want to stay here. Not tourists with money. Even in the dim light, she could see the threadbare swirls on the worn red carpet. The dark furniture from two decades ago was stained and chipped. And the patterned wallpaper with giant green peacocks didn't sit well with her image of Miss Maureen Brian the artist. The place looked like an orphan from a slum street the town council knocked down in the nineteen seventies.

"Busy?" Fenella asked.

"One or two guests," Ben replied. "We are lucky to get even that at this time of year, and with the wet weather this summer, it's been tough."

Fenella's phone buzzed. "Excuse me," she said, and picked it out of her handbag. She knew it was a message from Superintendent Jeffery before she glanced at the screen:

Civic meeting went well for everyone. Community relations on a solid footing now. Missed you at the end. Is everything on track?

The superintendent had outpoliticked the politicians at the press conference. She came up smelling of roses. Fenella had never been great at politics. Not even the office kind. All those weasel words and doublespeak made her stomach queasy. She'd joined the force to be a detective, not to tangle in the political debates of the day. But the higher you went in today's force, the deeper the political mire. Not for her. Best left to Jeffery. Still, the superintendent's political adroitness sent a cold tingle along her spine.

She continued to read:

Please speak with Dexter and then send him in to see me for a nice little chat.

Fenella stared gloomily through the window at the beach and flat sea. The black-headed gulls took to the air, a shimmering blanket of cackles and screams.

At the sound of the dining-room door creaking open, she turned away from the window. A short goose-faced woman with long greasy black hair waddled into the dining room. She wore a sky-blue sari and white pumps which bulged at the edges with her fat feet.

Fenella watched her splay-footed gait, felt a motherly glow, and said, "When's the baby due, luv?"

"Oh, this is Safiya, my wife." Ben got to his feet and helped his wife to the table. "You should be in bed having a nice nap, luv."

"Not too long now till the bairn arrives," Safiya said, ignoring her husband's words. She had a deep voice which honked from her throat. "I'm seven months."

Seven months! Fenella put down her mug. Oh my God, she looked like she was going to burst. Poor lass. Fenella recalled a slim coach in her gym. Her husband worked at the fish-tinning factory in Maryport, a small coastal town. The coach was forty-two when she went through infertility treatment. The quadruplets grew large and fast, but the birth was hindered by high blood pressure, rupture of membranes, and caesarean section. After, the coach blew up from stress. Her weight had grown even more with the late nights and feeds at dawn. Babies aren't easy, and four fresh from the womb would test the nerves of a saint. She got diabetes and lost the use of her legs. Now she scuttled around in a wheelchair.

"Are you expecting twins?" Fenella asked.

"Only one boy," Safiya replied.

"Must be a biggun," Dexter said.

"Takes after his dad. Fifteen pounds, weren't you, darling?" Safiya smiled. "Our first; makes us a proper family at last."

"We can relax now, honey," Ben spoke in soothing tones, like the presenter on a late-night radio jazz show. But there was also the hint of an alert in his voice. "These nice people are from the police. They are here at last."

"About bloody time," Safiya said, in almost a shout.

The loud honk startled Fenella, but she kept her voice level. "We are sorry to have kept you waiting."

"I thought you were travellers come to stay as guests." Safiya gave her husband a quick look. "I suppose Ben told you we saw the press conference on the local news. At the end they asked for anyone who knew Miss Maureen Brian to come forward, and since no one has been here yet, Ben called the station. We didn't expect you so soon."

"We aim to serve, madam," Fenella replied. She detected a sense of disappointment that they weren't paying guests. And something else. But she couldn't put her finger on it. "My name is Detective Fenella Sallow, and this eager-to-serve gentleman is Detective Robert Dexter."

"Detectives!" Ben stared as his face turned a greasy grey. "I thought you were community support officers. I... I... well, I don't know if what we can tell you will be of any help."

Dexter opened his notebook.

Fenella said, "Normally, we'd send a constable around to inform the relatives. We appear to have messed up on that one. We hope our delay wasn't too disturbing for you." She paused for a moment, watchful. "You say you called the station?"

"Yesterday morning when we realised Maureen didn't come home," Ben replied. "We were told she was an adult and not to bother the police until she'd been missing at least forty-eight hours. Even then, since we aren't relatives, the officer said there wasn't much they could do. Later in the morning we heard about what happened on the news. We called again yesterday around noon and again in the evening, and just now after the press conference at the town hall. But each time, we got a different person and they said they'd pass the message along."

Fenella fumed. *Damn cutbacks have turned the service into a shambles.* But she leaned forward like a close friend eager to hear good news. "Please go on."

"And I would have gone to the police station myself," Ben continued, "but as you can see with my wife..."

Safiya spoke. "We are not one to make a fuss, but when there is trouble you hope the police will be there for you. That is why I made Ben call our local councillor last night. Do you know Mr Malton? He said he'd take up the matter with your superiors."

Everyone in town knew Councillor Malton. He was a man of the people who'd lost his legs in the army. He rolled about town in a wheelchair and snarled like a rottweiler. And he bit, too. Frequent and hard. Fenella imagined him in the superintendent's office, and for an instant felt sorry for Veronica Jeffery.

"We are here now, luv." Fenella sounded apologetic. "Let's make a fresh start, shall we?"

Safiya said, "From what I've seen of the police, half the town will be dead before you catch the bugger." She jerked to her feet. "Find the person who killed Maureen before they strike again."

Ben hurried forward, wrapped an arm around Safiya and tried to ease her back into the chair. "Don't get excited, honey."

"Get off me!"

"Please sit down," Ben said, the smooth tone still in his voice. "The police are trained to find deviant fiends. They'll get the killer. Now think of the baby and sit and rest."

Safiya slumped back into the chair. "I'm sorry. The baby makes me moody."

Fenella sensed a deeper tension between the couple. It simmered just beneath the surface. Maureen or the baby or something else? She wished she were a fly on the wall so she didn't have to speculate. Perhaps with a gentle prod it would all come out.

"Let's talk. We want the person who hurt Maureen caught, don't we?"

"I'd like to strangle the bugger who did that to her." Safiya tugged at a strand of hair. "Ben, fetch me a coffee."

"But the doctor said—"

"Coffee!"

Ben rose and strode to the coffee pot. He poured and walked back slowly holding a diminutive china cup and saucer with both hands.

"Here you go, honey."

"A bloody doll's thimble! I want a mug. Strong and black."

"How about I get you a glass of lemon water? It will help with your digestion, good for the baby too."

"Stop trying to control me! You are always trying to box me in. I'm not a robot. I'm a woman who wants a bloody mug of coffee, okay?"

"We don't want a caffeine-addicted baby, do we, honey?"

"You are freaking me out." She was almost screaming now, her voice hissing like an angry goose. "And with Maureen dead, our world has turned upside down."

"Things will work out, honey." Ben kissed Safiya's cheek. "I promise."

"I've so many questions running around my head, Ben." She stared at her husband with pleading eyes. "You heard what they said on the news? A blunt instrument to the—"

"Hush now," Ben said and gave her another kiss.

"Why was it so brutal? I mean, I want to die in my bed."

"Okay, okay. I hear you. We'll talk later, but please drink the coffee slow."

Musical chimes rang out—the opening bars of Mendelssohn's Wedding March.

"Doorbell," said Safiya. "Quick, it might be a guest,"

Fenella wanted to hear more. If only she could continue to listen like a fly on the wall. But the solid chimes brought an end to the couple's argument. The detectives were back in the room.

"Detectives, will you please excuse me." Ben flashed his charming smile, smooth radio voice back. "I'll only be a moment. No more questions until I return, okay?"

Chapter Fifteen

A FTER THE DOOR CLOSED, the dining room was still. The coffee pot gurgled in a low hiss. Safiya stared through the window at the sands and the flat sea beyond.

Fenella's lips curved into a minuscule smile. "I'll top your coffee up when you are ready, luv."

"Ben fusses," Safiya replied. She made a face and gave an eye roll. "Since I've become pregnant... well things have changed. Now with Maureen gone, I suppose they'll change again."

"Happen you are right about that, luv. Best not to sugar-coat these things, eh?" Fenella made a sympathetic murmur. "Tell me about your relationship with Miss Brian?"

"Ben said not to—"

"It's okay, pet. We are here to help."

Safiya gazed at her china cup and she gazed at Dexter who hunched over his empty mug, and she gazed at Fenella with a sad frown. "Maureen lived here before we took over the place, five-going-on-six years now. A very nice lady, quiet, respectful, and she got on very well with our guests."

"She rents a room?" asked Fenella.

"Oh no, we didn't charge her rent. We couldn't. She came with the place... a fixture, I suppose."

"I'm not with you, luv." Fenella took another sip of coffee.

"Maureen is... was our landlady. She owns the building. We sublet and run a bed and breakfast." Safiya closed her eyes. "Ben and I run our dream business and Maureen got to stay in the home she loved. We considered her a member of the family. Our own fairy godmother."

Fenella took in Safiya's long gooselike face. Unusual and lopsided with those fat lips, wide eyes, and patches of ashen skin surrounded by dark. And trusting. For an instant she wondered how she and Ben had met: Safiya short and plump and Ben tall and handsome. *Opposites,* she thought with a sly glance at Dexter, *attract.* Her mind began to click through eligible opposites for her sergeant, but she forced it to stop and said, "And Maureen lived here?"

Safiya's eyes opened. "In the dormer. Would you like me to take you to her room?"

"There is no rush," Fenella replied. Her mind went back to the steps at the front door and she wondered how many to the dormer. "There are one or two more questions we'd like to clear up first, just routine you understand. It won't take long and once we are done, my colleague and I will take a little look around Miss Brian's room. I hope that is okay?"

Safiya fiddled with the china cup. "Sometimes I forget my limitations. I couldn't climb the steps to the dormer if I wanted too." Her left hand fluttered over her mouth as if dusting crumbs. "I'll have Ben take you. Now, what do you want to know?"

Fenella said, "Let's start with a list of people who recently visited Maureen. What can you tell us?"

Safiya shook her head. "Maureen didn't invite guests here. She met her friends at the Grain Bowl Café in town or on the pier by the lighthouse. She allowed no one into her quarters."

Fenella considered that and said, "But you've been inside her room recently, right?"

"It's been a long time. A year ago, Maureen came down with the flu. I took soup every day and left it on the dormer landing."

"You haven't entered her room since she was reported missing?"

"Like I said, I can't make the stairs, and Ben's not visited yet either. But now she is gone, we've a good excuse for poking around but we don't want to be the first to breach Maureen's privacy. That is for the police; we think too highly of her to nosy around her private belongings."

Fenella gave her an inquisitive look. Did she really mean that?

Safiya turned to stare through the window.

"We are trying to trace Maureen's movements up until the moment she died," Fenella said. "Let's go back to Bonfire Night; did you see her that evening?"

"No. But Ben did. He bumped into her near the lighthouse. Maureen was with Audrey; that is Mrs Audrey Robin. They chatted for a couple of minutes, then he came back to the car to sit with me."

"And you watched the fireworks from the car?"

"Quite honestly I don't like flashing lights and the noise. I go for Ben."

"And what time did you get home?"

"Oh, I don't know, a little after ten."

"I see." Fenella paused, knowing it would prompt Safiya to continue.

"I had a shower. Ben gave me my sleeping pills and I went to bed."

"And Ben?"

"He sat with me for a while, as he always does these days. He is a wonderful husband, wonderful. My Ben idolises me and the baby. You passed our rooms on the way in here. No stairs, Ben insisted, and he always gets my medicine from the chemist."

"You are a lucky lass," Fenella said.

Safiya ran a hand over her protruding stomach. "We are all Ben lives for. It scares me sometimes, how much he loves me and the baby. On Bonfire Night, he held my hand as I drifted off to sleep. He always does that because he loves me."

"I know," Fenella said. "And what time was that, approximately?"

"I don't know, but he spoke to me as I drifted off. Told me how much he loved me. But I didn't look at the clock."

"That's all right; not to worry," Fenella placed her hands flat on the red-and-white tablecloth. "What else do you remember?"

"Not much, really. I woke up around one, bad dream. Can't remember what it was about, but I heard the front door click shut."

That would be Maureen. Fenella reworked her theory. If Maureen Brian came home and went back out, that placed her death closer to 2:00 a.m. She watched Safiya with keen eyes. "So, Maureen came back home after the fireworks?"

"It was only my Ben," Safiya said. "He went out for drinks with his friends. He's been restless since we discovered we are having a baby, and he works so hard with so little reward." She paused and looked around the tired outdated room. Her eyes glistened. "This place is too far off the tourist path. Money has been difficult and I don't want to be an old nag and spoil his one night of fun. I'm so lucky to have a man as gorgeous as my Ben to love me. I know which side my bread is buttered on."

Fenella took Safiya's hand. Warm, hard. A woman used to manual work. "It has been tough for you, hasn't it, luv?"

Safiya winced, and for a moment Fenella thought the baby had kicked. On her own third child, it had been terrible. Would they have to help her back to her room or call for an ambulance?

"Are you okay, luv?"

Safiya winced again, and Fenella realised the sound conveyed an unburdening: more psychological than physical.

"It has been a tough year," Safiya began. "A wet summer, few visitors, and now Maureen. The only bright spot is the baby."

"Go on, luv, I'm listening."

Safiya's hand reached out for the cup, hovered, then withdrew and fell to pick at imaginary lint on the tablecloth. "This place is losing money. It was Ben's dream, really. It's sucked up all my inheritance and now needs more. But Ben, well, he is not great with business."

She looked up with a sad smile. "We are scraping the cash together to buy a doughnut cart. Ben borrowed a cookbook from the library and sold me on the idea. We'll sell them on the shore front during the summer season. The extra cash will make a big difference."

Fenella didn't have the heart to tell her they'd need a licence to sell food. The council charged double for vendors selling on the beachfront and they'd have to get in a long line. The wait was a year at best. She switched the conversation back to the reason for her visit. "Tell me about Maureen's friends."

Safiya sniffed back a tear. "It's awful. Our landlady is killed on the beach on Bonfire Night. I can't stop thinking about it." She burst into tears. "I don't know why it happened or who would do such a terrible thing."

"That's what we are here to find out," Fenella said and gave her a tissue. She waited until Safiya blew her nose and gave a weak smile. "I'd like you to tell me about her friends."

"Maureen mixed with all ages. I think she had a special gift with teenagers, but everyone loved her. Not a mother figure, more a wise companion." She squeezed Fenella's hand. "Her death has torn a hole in my heart, but it is going to hit Elizabeth and Audrey the hardest."

Dexter's pen moved swiftly over his notebook. The faint scrape filled the temporary quiet. He glanced at Fenella and nodded.

Fenella said, "And who is Elizabeth?"

"Elizabeth Collins."

Fenella recalled the name. "Are they close friends, then?"

"Aye. We called Maureen, Elizabeth, and Audrey the Port Saint Giles Trinity. You never saw one without the other." She dabbed at a tear. "Those three women hung together like chain-link rope."

Chapter Sixteen

B EN GRIFFIN DIDN'T RETURN to the dining room, so Safiya waved them up the stairs to Maureen's room with a long iron key.

"Right at the top, as far as you can go. If you need me, I'll be resting in my room."

Fenella waited in the eerie dull of the landing while Dexter searched for a light switch. The smell of boiled cabbage hung in the motionless air. It stirred memories of school dinners. Sloppy brown gravy over tough leathered beef with bland pink blancmange for dessert. It was hotter up here. The heat of the climb brought warmth to Fenella's cheeks and beads of sweat to her forehead.

"Found it," Dexter said.

Moments later came a sharp *click*. A weak orange glow shone from a single light bulb to reveal a red-bricked wall with an arched oak door. It was secured with great iron hinges and had a huge keyhole, the type you'd find in a castle. Ornate panels ran in vertical slats with diagonal iron strips overlaid for support. A dungeon door. The detectives stared in silence. Was it there to keep folk out, or protect what lay within?

"Solid," Dexter said, rapping the wood with his knuckles. "A sodding vault door like that bloody crypt in the village of Irton."

Fenella remembered the grim case. They'd worked it years back. She stared at the locked door and wondered what lay beyond.

Dexter said, "Shall I call it in, Guv?"

His words hung like particles of dust in the stale cabbage air.

Fenella sniffed. "We believe Miss Brian lived alone?"

"As far as we know."

"No visitors either?"

"Aye, Guv, that's what Safiya Griffin said."

The Irton case called from the edge of Fenella's mind. It turned her blood stone cold. What would they find behind Maureen Brian's solid oak door? A hint, perhaps, about her secret life. Maybe a diary on a bedside cabinet with a clue about the murderer. What were the odds they'd find a pile of partially decomposed bones like Irton?

Fenella said, "We'll call in the crime scene techs after we've had a good look. Superintendent Jeffery's been going on about costs. We don't want to upset her with a large bill."

"Aye," Dexter said. "Right you are, Guv."

Fenella heard the hesitation in his voice. For a fleeting instant she considered changing her mind. But she was curious. Her job was to find the killer of Maureen Brian, not to worry about events from the past. No matter how much they haunted the quiet corners of her mind.

Dexter's phone buzzed. He glanced at the screen, let out a soft groan, and shoved it into his jacket.

"The library about your overdue books?" Fenella asked, prying. "Or have you upset the new love of your life?"

She didn't like to interfere in his private life. Neither could she help doing so. She wondered whether her obsession was an addiction or just part of her genes. Whatever the reason, she'd played matchmaker since Dexter's last divorce. Alas, Cupid's arrow had always fallen short. Not an easy man to pair. Still, if there was a new love in his life, she wanted to know. That way, her brain could switch off its matchmaking circuit.

Fenella said, "I'm betting it's from a lovely lass who enjoys walks on the beach and jars of home-brewed beer."

Dexter cracked his fingers. "Nope."

"Well then?" Fenella knew her question wasn't subtle or discrete or professional, but she had to know now. After all, he brought up the subject, didn't he?

Dexter pulled out his mobile phone, gazed at the screen and said, "Superintendent Jeffery wants to see me." He turned to look Fenella directly in the eyes. "Any idea what about?"

Fenella didn't respond. *How would Jeffery start the retirement conversation? Like a politician,* she thought. *A disarming compliment and mention of Dexter's heroic past. Then she'll stick the knife in and twist. Jeffery will get what she wants. She always gets what she wants.* And she wanted Dexter out.

Dexter was talking. "It smells fishy and you know Jeffery has it in for me. If you hear anything, you'll let me know, won't you?"

The noise of a soft shuffle caught Fenella's attention before she answered. It sounded like footsteps creeping along the stairs below. She raised her hand and listened, then turned to look down the stairs but saw only shadows. Dexter strode by her and sped down a handful of steps.

"Everything all right up there?" Safiya asked. She sounded out of breath.

"Fine," replied Dexter.

"Give me a shout if you need anything." Safiya's footsteps retreated. This time firm and solid.

Dexter returned and said, "And Jeffery?"

"Whatever she wants, say no." *I'll put up a bloody good fight before I let my detective sergeant go.* "Or ignore it."

"Guv, I'll keep my head down for now, hope she forgets and moves on to her next victim." Dexter laughed without mirth.

They put on shoe protectors and gloves in silence.

Dexter took a step towards Maureen Brian's sturdy oak door. A hollow pang buzzed in Fenella's gut. It hovered like the slow beat of a kestrel's wings—the thrill of anticipation intermingled with deep sadness. Always the same feelings as she prepared to cross the threshold into the living quarters of the recent dead.

"Ready, Guv?"

As Fenella nodded, she recalled an article about Egyptian archaeologists. They had discovered a trove of treasures in an ancient city buried deep in the sand. *We are tomb raiders*, she thought. *On the search for clues rather than gold.* And once again she wondered what awaited them beyond Maureen Brian's sturdy arched oak door.

Chapter Seventeen

A UDREY ROBIN DID NOT know what persuaded her to do it. After all the publicity, she should have known better. But she climbed into her car and drove to Miss Maureen Brian's house on Seafields Lane that morning. If she were caught or seen, how would she explain herself?

They'd even filmed her for the television news. She tried to cover her face and hide, but they took pictures anyway. She should have stayed at home.

But another force pulled at her, an unseen power she could not resist. If she had to guess, one word would suffice—routine. Routine made her feel alive, gave her strength. It got her up at the crack of dawn to walk the beach. It brought her back home for a quick read over a milky coffee. And earlier, routine had pushed her, hurried and flustered, out the door and into her car for the drive to work. When the engine turned over, she remembered with a nauseating jolt her time off.

The morning before, at the library, they'd been ever so understanding. Audrey smiled when she thought about the sympathetic voices. She played them over in her head. It seemed everyone knew Maureen Brian. They knew she was friends with Audrey.

"A terrible shock."

"Must be distressing for you, luv."

"Who'd do such a wicked thing to such a wonderful person?"

The gaggle of chittering co-workers around Audrey's desk brought the head Liberian scurrying.

"I've seen the television pictures. It was your friend who was beaten to death, wasn't it? Oh my God! What are you doing here? Grab your handbag, leave now. Go. Go now. I insist."

They ushered Audrey out the main doors with strict orders not to return until she felt better. So, this morning instead of her routine drive to work, she made a snap decision to visit Maureen's home. She'd never been invited inside but went anyway.

She pulled into a potholed car park. It was used by dog walkers and runners to access the beach. A sparse place off the tourist path with only a dozen parking spaces and a single whitewashed bench which faced the sea. Audrey felt a tinge of joy when she saw the small wicker-framed trash bin. There'd be rubbish on the beach, for sure. The voices would keep quiet if they saw any mess.

For a moment, she waited. Her mind worked slow these days. All that medicine. Still, it gave her time to think about the plan. Only a single sheet of paper written neatly in her own hand. How could it wield so much power? She patted her coat pocket. The envelope was secure.

She switched on the car radio. It played the press conference from the town hall. Audrey listened. The superintendent of police was speaking. She reassured the public that everything would be done to catch the killer. The politicians all agreed, and the audience clapped and cheered their applause.

Audrey stared out of the windscreen at a large woman in a blue duffel coat with a ratty terrier trotting at her side. The dog turned its head, opened its mouth, and Patrick's voice, soft as mice, came scurrying out.

"Turn yourself in. The police will find you."

Audrey blinked, took off her glasses, then rubbed her eyes. Of course the dog didn't speak. And it wasn't her ex-husband's voice. Just her mind playing tricks again. Now, though, she had the feeling that she was being watched. Her eyes tracked the blue duffel coat and terrier until they dipped out of view. With an anxious flick of the switch, the voices in the radio died. *Keep to the routine so you can think clear enough to stick to the plan.*

For a long while she sat very still. Her head did not move as she stared at the bland beach with the dark sea shimmering below dreary clouds. Her eyelids fluttered down, and she was back in the ambulance. The smell of hot dogs, onions, and antiseptic filled her nostrils. Rain drummed a soft rhythm against the roof. The slender woman detective with the grey hair was talking, watching, and listening to her answers with a concentration that reminded her of Patrick.

Her husband's focus had been as intense as corked wine in the months before he demanded the divorce. She tasted the taut bitterness as his work dragged him home later each night. Looking back, she suspected those late evenings at work were when he slept with his new wife. They'd wed days after the decree absolute. The twin babies were born inside the year.

Audrey tensed, mind back in the ambulance. The grey-haired detective was speaking as the doors swung open. The grizzled black detective who smelled of sour rum climbed in. *What had she told him?*

Apprehension clutched like a tight hand against her throat. She took a deep breath, holding it in until she remembered—*home-brewing on the cheap.* "Detectives! Nothing but a nosy old maid and a bloody drunkard. Catch the killer? The only thing they'll catch is a cold. Politicians are bloody liars!"

Audrey laughed, relaxing at the sound of her voice. For a long while she savoured her secret revelation.

Outside in the car park, other dog walkers were starting out towards the beach. An elderly man in tight green shorts and a mop of bleached white hair jogged to the bench, did push-ups, and sped away. Retired with no work to go to. Just the freedom to exercise when he wished. No crumbling cottage. No repairs that sucked money from your purse before payday either. On an assistant librarian's salary, Audrey did not know if she'd be able to retire. Finances were meagre enough. How would she live on a state pension?

Maureen Brian retired to a good life. Even her bloody black-and-white photographs sold for high prices at auction. She didn't have to count the pennies, did she?

A watery sun peeked from behind the low clouds. It blazed streaks of feathery yellow across the sand. The sea glistened as if covered in frost. Audrey's hand, steady, reached for a black bin bag. She kept a stack on the passenger seat.

May as well pick up rubbish along the way. Do another good deed to clean up the environment. And it will keep those voices at bay.

Audrey stepped from the car, and again she had the distinct sensation that she was being watched. Clusters of clouds swamped the sun's feeble yellow rays, and November's gloom returned. She put up her hood and walked a half mile along the flat sand. A stiff breeze slowed her progress and the black bin bag remained empty. No human debris on this stretch of the beach. Then she saw the large dune that led to a rickety garden fence. She climbed through a dense strand of marram grass, taking care to avoid the grey-green tufts of spiky leaves. At the top she peered through the slats of the fence. The Seafields Bed and Breakfast stood like a run-down Roman fort.

As she watched the dark building, a memory stirred. There was Maureen. The retired artist threw her head back and laughed. Then she twirled and jumped between a gaggle of excited children. She was showing them something. How to make play swords with marram grass. Then she vanished like a ghost. Where did she go?

Again came the laugh as the children found her kneeling low between the tufts. The kids giggled like a flock of common gulls. Elizabeth's flock, she recalled. Audrey joined in too, but it was Maureen and Elizabeth Collins who doted on children.

Elizabeth had magical powers with youngsters. The woman loved to take care of children who came from difficult homes. They'd arrive at her house as tight as clamshells. Like a good witch in a fairy tale, she'd get them to open up through spells cast by her cooking, easygoing style, and the constant chant, "You are somebody. Who do you choose?"

Maureen's power was more mysterious to Audrey. She didn't have words to explain. A kind of charismatic empathy for human need. Or a deep connectedness with the soul. Yes, that was it: empathy and connectedness. Audrey felt she had neither.

Lost in remembrance, she didn't hear the engine or the slam of the car door. It was the urgent scream of a herring gull which jerked her into the present. She saw them then. The grey-haired detective in the lead, making her way up the steps with her sidekick several paces behind.

Instinct kicked in. She crouched low in the marram grass, watching. The woman detective skipped up the steps, then paused halfway up to glance around. Like holidaymakers from London, they didn't move for ages. It seemed they were sucking in the cold salt air, boggled by the vastness of the flat quiet sea.

What were their names?

She couldn't recall. The past few days had seemed like a dream, everything soaked in a green fog so dense it tasted like bitter parsley. The detectives' names remained just out of reach, waiting like lost children on the other side of the fog.

Audrey squeezed her eyes shut. Now she was back at the burnt-out bonfire, her throat raw, with Noel O'Sullivan at her side. A policeman appeared out of the green fog. He spoke with an excited buzz into his radio. Then more police came in a great blue swarm. She'd tried to play her *know thy neighbour* game, but their faces were so many that it all became a jumble.

The detectives' names? She'd memorised their faces, but their names remained hidden in the bitter green fog.

A rhythmic grunt caused Audrey to freeze. She had heard no footsteps. Nothing to show that she, too, might be watched. That ratty terrier dog flashed into her mind with its open mouth and words from Patrick. Mind tricks. The grunt came again, closer, human, real.

The blustery breeze continued its low whine. That perpetual whisper where land meets sea. A constant comfort to coastal dwellers, like the soft coo of a mother to child. But the whine set Audrey's nerves on edge.

She was sure no one knew she'd come here. Unless... her ex-husband bugged her car, attached a tracking device like she'd read in a spy novel. Anxiety rose. Had she stepped into Patrick's trap?

Again came the grunt as if calling her name.

She muttered her secret mantra and spun around.

The elderly man in tight green shorts scrambled along a sand dune. His thick legs, with veins like knotted oak tree roots, propelled him forward against the resistance of the blustery wind. She crouched lower. Did he see her?

He didn't look back.

When he was out of sight, Audrey reached for the envelope secured in her coat pocket. Her hand hovered for a moment and withdrew. *Nothing's changed.* She placed her elbows on her knees and buried her face in her hands.

After thirty seconds she wiped her eyes. Her gaze returned to the steps of Seafields Bed and Breakfast. The detectives were still admiring the view. When they turned to continue the climb, Audrey eased to her feet. Now she didn't think, wouldn't think, let instinct be her guide. Walking carefully on the uneven ground, she found a break in the fence and slipped through.

Much better view from here.

The detectives were on the top step. The front door opened. Audrey hoped she'd glimpse Ben. He'd let her in, show her around Maureen's room. She'd like that. But she couldn't tell if Safiya or Ben answered. Her jaw clenched. She scurried closer, keeping low to the ground. But the detectives were inside and the door shut as she reached their parked vehicle—a dark blue Morris Minor.

Crouching at the side of the detective's car, a thought struck.

It struck hard like a burnt log propelled with great force.

It caused Audrey to shudder.

It was the realisation that the paramedic was right. The detectives would be back, and if she didn't get her story straight, she'd be their favourite tree to pee on.

Her hand trembled as it reached into her coat, pulling out a small, dark glass bottle. She sniffed the bitter mint fragrance—hyssop. The bracing scent rolled up her nostrils and turned her mind over like a combustion engine. On each revolution, she got her story more organised. She muttered answers like an actor in dress rehearsal. At last she was ready. *I'll bake a cake, a sweet-scented Victoria sponge. My own personal illicit pleasure.* She felt a sudden surge of renewal.

The soft purr of the motorcycle crept slowly into Audrey's consciousness. It came to an easy stop at the steps. Even in jet-black leathers and polished helmet, Audrey recognised Noel O'Sullivan. He swaggered up the steps two at a time, pressed hard on the doorbell, then stepped back.

The door opened.

Audrey strained to hear the conversation. With a sense of elation, her ears picked up Noel's Texas twang. She edged closer. But the wind picked up and carried away the words so their meaning was incomprehensible.

Another sound caused her to turn around, look back along the driveway. The elderly man was there. He lumbered across the sand, following the line of the fence. He didn't appear to notice Audrey as he skipped across the pitted driveway. A sudden fog of green envy enveloped her. She resented the old man's easy life. Nothing to think about except his breathing. Nothing for her but bills.

She turned back in time to see Ben step out of the entrance. An impulse to rush forward, ask what the detectives had uncovered, surged. But how would she explain herself, crouched low behind the car?

No. Better to stay here out of sight. She crouched lower and watched.

The two men strolled down the steps. At the motorcycle, they stopped and talked in low whispered tones—the priest and the confessant.

Audrey wasn't entirely sure which was which.

Chapter Eighteen

D EXTER CLANKED THE KEY in the lock of Miss Maureen Brian's door. It turned with a sharp click. He pushed the door open and stepped aside for his boss to enter.

Before the slow tick of the clock on a shelf. Before the scent of vanilla potpourri hit Fenella's nostrils. And before her eyes took in the neat order of the well-furnished room. She knew Miss Brian and Nan would have gotten along well, and a sharp pang of regret stabbed at her gut.

She stood in the entrance and blinked. It took a moment for her eyes to adjust. The main room was divided in two. The small kitchen fitted into an alcove where the roof slanted down. It had a sink, electric cooker, and microwave.

The living room was larger. A quilted camelback sofa with thick mahogany legs sat next to a maple-veneered cabinet. There were four dials on the front of the cabinet and a hinged door. A Persian rug with red and gold flecks covered part of the polished oak floor.

A pile of magazines lay at one end of a cherrywood coffee table. At the other end, a crochet hook and two balls of yarn: one pink the other blue. A built-in bookcase ran the entire length of one wall. Four shelves in total: three filled with books, ordered by size, spines facing out. The fourth held trinkets: seashells, pebbles, a rusted cowbell, Kodak Brownie camera, wooden mantel clock, and a fat china

Buddha. They all jostled for space with a large spider plant with long dangling leaves. And it was quiet up here in the dormer. Only the distant *slush* of the waves and the soft *whoosh* of the wind.

Fenella took photographs with her phone.

Dexter padded across the rug to the cabinet. "Haven't seen one of those since my granddad was alive." He stared with wonder at the ancient device. "Looks like an Ace radio. Valves rather than electronic transistors. Takes an age to warm up, but Granddad swore by it."

With a gloved hand, he tugged the cabinet door. It swung forward and down to reveal a record player. He peered inside. "Hasn't been used in a while; bet it spins though. Can't beat valve technology, works like a dream, reliable." He closed the door and fiddled with the knobs. A backlight glimmered behind the dial. The cabinet let out a low hum.

Fenella sat down on the couch and looked around. After a few moments she wondered at the neatness of the space. Clean and tidy. Nothing out of place. *Like an image in a magazine, almost as if someone has been in here to tidy up the room.*

She watched Dexter at the radio. With a jolt, she realised it was the same model her own granddad once owned. Childhood memories swarmed her mind. The family around the scrubbed pine table in her grandparents farmhouse. A woodstove crackled in the corner. Blasts of warm heat wafted savoury scents from the oven through the air. Roast beef with Yorkshire pudding and homemade gravy with potatoes roasted in drippings. Even now, in Maureen Brian's room, the memory made her stomach rumble. It felt so real.

"My granddad had one of those and shelves of record albums," Fenella said. "We'd visit for Sunday dinner and, after, listen to classical music or watch a show called *Songs of Praise* on the television. I liked the radio most. Me and Granddad would dance and he'd make up words to go with the music."

Dexter rocked back on his heels. "On Sundays my granddad cooked dinner, played reggae, and drank rum. Later his friends would visit. They played dominos in the front room while Grandma and we kids sat in church pews."

"Explains a lot," Fenella said.

But Dexter didn't hear; he was fiddling with the Ace radio knobs.

From her seated position, Fenella realised the room wasn't quite rectangular. It tapered in from the front door to the bedroom. She stood and wandered through the kitchenette. A copper kettle sat on the far ring of the cooker. Several pots and pans dangled from overhead hooks. Nothing in the sink. Bottle of milk in the fridge.

Fenella had not expected such order in an artist's home. Eduardo's studio contained drawings scattered about, and inkpots and pens too. There was even an old laptop with floppy discs so large they looked like table mats. No, this place was nothing like Eduardo's work studio, and that made her stop and think.

Fenella looked around again, then walked into the tiny bedroom. There was a built-in wardrobe, and a small square curtainless window let in what there was of the November daylight. She peered through the windowpane, with a view of the front of the house, steps, and the ramp they'd missed earlier. An elderly man in tight green shorts jogged along the line of the fence. He turned his head in her direction, staring at the dormer window as if sensing she was there. She gave a little wave, but he continued as if not seeing.

Farther out, she could see the sweep of monotonous sand. The people were like dots. Dog walkers, more joggers, and couples out for a stroll. She was about to turn away when the motorcycle parked near the bottom step caught her eye. It wasn't there when they arrived, she was certain of that. She watched for a while, hoping to get a glimpse of the rider. After two minutes she lost patience with the wait—only a courier of some sort.

Turning back to the bedroom, she took it all in. The bed hadn't been slept in. She touched the lavender bedspread, then looked under the pillow to find a lemon nightdress and a pink hot water bottle. The nightdress was neatly folded, the hot water bottle empty. No diary.

A swing-arm brass lamp sat on the bedside cabinet. A magazine lay open at an article about prehistoric cave paintings in the Ardèche region of France. No clue to point to the killer here, then. Fenella sighed, stooped, and looked under the bed.

Nothing.

For a long while she stared at the photographic landscape which hung on the wall. Was it Port Saint Giles? The image was strangely coloured and distorted as if viewed from beneath rippling water. Fenella thought she could make out the pier with the lighthouse at the end. There was nothing else on the walls except a wooden crucifix above the bed. Not a lot of photos about the place for a photographer. When she and Eduardo first got married, he'd hung his drawings all over the place. All those comic sketches drove Fenella crazy. That's why they'd built the studio. The images now hung in odd-sized frames on the studio walls, but not in the kitchen or the bedroom or anywhere else.

Fenella pushed the wardrobe door. It slid into the wall on well-oiled rails. Not very deep though. Only a handful of feet. Skirts, dresses, blouses, even headscarves all hung from racks in neat lines. Shoes at the bottom, some in boxes. all arranged in orderly rows. Everything spotless. Everything in its place. No boxes of photographs.

Fenella slid the door closed and left the bedroom. It felt as if an hour had passed, but Dexter was still fiddling with the Ace radio.

"First impressions," Fenella said as she sat back on the couch.

For a long moment Dexter was quiet. Fenella was about to repeat the question when he said, "It reminds me of the beach, Guv." He twisted a knob.

Fenella said, "How do you mean?"

"Nothing was taken from Maureen's purse." He straightened, running a hand across the top of the cabinet as if stroking a thoroughbred horse. "Nothing taken from her apartment either." He stooped back down to fiddle with the dials.

"And?"

"Whoever killed Maureen Brian didn't come back here to turn the place over. Unless they knew what they were looking for and didn't need to."

Trumpets blasted.

Dexter leapt away from the cabinet like a mashup between Frankenstein and a demented ballerina.

Fenella laughed. It was only the opening bars of Purcell's Sonata in D Major for Trumpet. She clapped her hands as a classical music aficionado might for a wonderful performance by a great maestro. Then she thought of her granddad and how they used to dance on Sunday evenings, and felt sad.

Dexter regained his composure, returned to the Ace, and jabbed at a knob. The dial light faded first, followed a few moments later by Purcell's trumpets.

"Sorry, Guv. My granddad's radio used to do that all the time. Thank God for electric transistors. Bleedin' valves are a bugger to work with."

"Anything else?" asked Fenella, still grinning.

"Nowt that I can think of." Dexter rubbed a hand over his chin and stared at the radio as if he wanted to kick it. Then he shook his head and grinned. "Guv, I'll let the crime scene techs know, then?"

Fenella stood, did a slow 360-degree turn. "No sign of a break in. No sign of anyone looking for something." She didn't want Superintendent Jeffery on her back over costs. "Let's wait to see what Dr Mackay has for us or if anything comes out of the forensics from the bonfire."

"Aye, my thoughts too." Dexter walked slowly into the kitchen. He opened the microwave door. "Wish there was more to chew on here."

"There is one thing," Fenella said. She gazed at the bookcase. "Maureen was renowned for her colloidal photographic images.

That's old-style photo-taking to you and me. None of your digital malarkey. If I understood young Jones, those old black-and-white photos require chemicals and glass plates."

"She didn't have none of that here, Guv."

"Exactly. Where did Maureen Brian store her art?" Fenella placed her hands on her hips. "Where is her art studio?"

Chapter Nineteen

A S DETECTIVE CONSTABLE EARP stood in the car park of the Quarterdrigg Activity Centre, he felt annoyed. It was a whitewashed one-storey concrete structure surrounded by brown-bricked walls as high as a bus. He'd parked next to a row of black council wheelie bins which overflowed with bloated bin bags. One of said bags had snagged under the driver's-side front wheel. Its contents spilled like a split gut around his car: crisp packets, coffee cups, a dozen or more apple cores, banana skins, empty bottles, chicken bones, fast food containers, and soda cans.

He gasped in the rancid plume, spluttered a cough, and cursed as he kicked away rubbish. So far, he'd only spoken with seven from his list of people on the beach, and endured seven irate lectures on how the police were failing in their duty to keep the public safe. Sue hadn't packed his lunch either. Only his flask of coffee which he'd long drained.

Everything dragged under the dreary dull sky. The sound of traffic on the main road rumbled in the distance. Two pigeons landed on the brick wall. A gust caught a crisp packet sending it upwards in a demented spiral. Earp kicked away more rubbish, stamped hard on a rolling ketchup bottle. Its congealed sauce splattered on his shoes. He stamped again. It spluttered like an old dog with flatulence.

Next on his list was Martin Findlay. He'd tracked him down to the Quarterdrigg Activity Centre thanks to a chatty neighbour—Mrs Claire Sutherland. She watched her narrow street like a hawk.

"He's across the street in the flats: big bloke, doesn't talk much, but friendly enough. Goes to the Quarterdrigg during the week. Well, he's not fully there, in his head, like."

"Cheers," he had said, but she took his arm.

"Now what you lot doing about that murder on the beach? Ought to be chasing down the killer, not pestering nice Mr Findlay. A right ruddy disgrace. Call yourself a detective! The kids playing cops on the street do a better job. It's not safe anymore, is it?"

Earp wanted desperately to visit Maureen Brian's address with Sallow and Dexter. Instead he'd spent his morning taking verbal beatings from irate members of the public. And now he had to chase after the mentally impaired. He gritted his teeth and sighed. He took orders now, took a back seat in the investigation, did as he was told. His mind flashed back to when he ran the show. Detective Inspector Earp got results, banged up criminals by the dozen.

I should be centre stage. Show the buggers how it is done.

By now he'd have had an army of officers turn Maureen Brian's place over for clues. Tear the place apart. Then a hard chat with the witness Audrey Robin—squeeze her like a lemon for information. Frighten the silly cow if necessary. Make her pee her pants. There'd be something between her sobs, complaints, and wet knickers that would help him catch the killer. That's what the job was about, wasn't it? Putting perps away. Getting a result. *I'm the last stand for the old school*, he thought. He knew he did his job well, however much the higher-ups cautioned him to curb his unconventional ways. They'd brought it up in the tortuous demotion hearing which lasted for innumerable hours. It seemed like ages ago.

Sod the lot of them. Only a bloody detective constable. Grunt work with no food.

He swore.

His stomach rumbled.

Why hadn't Sue packed his lunch?

In the damp dullness, he recalled with weary acceptance she hadn't been awake when he left. He'd slipped out of bed before daylight, leaving Sue with her dreams. As water boiled for coffee, he'd gazed through the growing dawn at the frozen branches of the Egremont Russet apple tree. Nick had stirred as he crept along the hallway. If it weren't for the creak of the boy's bedroom door, he'd have been out into the morning chill, picking his way across the white hoar frost towards his ice-covered car.

Nick called out as he reached the front door.

"Can't sleep, Daddy," said his boy, already in his wheelchair and out in the hall. "Can I come with you?"

"It's early, son. Go back to bed, else you'll never wake up for school."

"Don't want to go."

Thomas, their cat, trotted along the corridor. Earp stooped, picked him up. "You need to go to school if you want to grow up to be a policeman."

"I've got no friends." Nick let out a soft sob. "The kids in Mrs Ledwidge's class don't like me. They call me names."

Earp's skin prickled. "What sort of names, son?"

"I don't want to go, Daddy."

Earp wasn't sure whether to wake Sue. He set the cat down slowly. Then he remembered Walter, another wheelchair-bound child in his son's school. "What happened to Sandra, Tim, and Walter?"

"They are not my friends anymore."

"But you are in the same class, aren't you?"

"Yeah, but Mrs Ledwidge won't let me play with them."

Bloody teachers! I ought to go to that school and crack a few heads, starting with Ledwidge.

Earp placed an arm around his boy's shoulder. "Why won't your friends play with you, son?"

"They say I'm a fibber because I told them my dad was a detective and would speak to the class."

Earp pinched the bridge of his nose, closing his eyes. "Next time, son, I promise."

"Can I go with you, Daddy, and be a policeman today?"

"One day son. One day. But you need to go to school this morning, okay?"

"Promise?"

"Promise, son."

"When."

Again he rubbed the bridge of his nose. "Soon son. Soon."

A coffee cup rolled towards Earp, bringing him back to the present. He kicked it with a vicious swing. It spun and bobbled sideways, coming to a stop with the cardboard bottom facing him like the rear end of an exhibitionist flasher. He cursed again and stared with irritated eyes at the brash welcome sign:

Quarterdrigg: Fun activities for people with a disability. Everyone welcome.

Earp pulled a paper tissue from his pocket, wiped his shoe clean of ketchup, and threw it down. Then his lips curved into a hard smile.

"Martin Findlay, disabled or not, here I come."

Chapter Twenty

T WO THINGS SURPRISED EARP as he entered the wide doors of the Quarterdrigg. First, the polished flagstone floors and the wide windows. They let in more light than he'd expected from the dreary November sky. The lavender walls reminded him of an upmarket art gallery in Carlisle. Images hung in simple rosewood frames—of men working the pits and women weaving on great looms. A fragrant tub of potpourri sat on the reception desk. On either side stood large porcelain vases filled with roses the colour of plums. Soft classical music, vaguely familiar, played low from hidden speakers.

The second thing that surprised Earp was the welcoming face of Gloria Embleton. She was all smiles, her eyes shining expectantly as if he were an old friend.

"Welcome to the Quarterdrigg. How may we best serve you today?"

The buoyant greeting threw Earp. For a moment he stood staring at the short plump woman. She had huge looped gold earrings, afro speckled with grey, and a Glaswegian accent.

"I'm Detective Constable Hugh Earp. Can I speak with whoever is in charge?"

"My God, we were just talking about you."

"Me?"

"Well, the police. The name's Gloria Embleton," she said extending her hand. "I called the police station earlier, after the appeal for information." She stopped, as if realising she was getting ahead of herself. "This place is run by volunteers, and for my sins, I'm in charge today. Why don't we go through to the office? That way we'll have a bit of privacy."

Without waiting for his response, she yelled something he couldn't understand. Scottish dialect, he thought. A thirty-something woman wheeled through a set of automatic doors. Then he realised she'd called a name—Abertha.

Abertha wore a dark jacket, white blouse with matching skirt. Very professional. Very office. She moved quickly, manoeuvring her wheelchair behind the reception desk. She had no legs.

"What's up, Gloria?"

"Mind holding the fort for me, darling." Gloria lowered her voice. "This gentleman is a detective and we need a bit of privacy."

Abertha stared at Earp as if he were an exotic exhibit in the zoo. She smiled, showing two rows of irregular teeth. "Right you are, Gloria. Just holler for help if he brings out his handcuffs."

Earp followed Gloria through electronic doors and into a wide rectangular room. It had floor-to-ceiling windows along one wall. A contented murmur filled the space, somehow in harmony with the classical music. Several armchairs faced the windows, with men reading newspapers or sleeping. Others cluttered around a rectangular table playing a game of cards. There were women too, although less in number. He noticed three in wheelchairs. They clustered in a semicircle at the far end, middle-aged, knitting as they nattered. No one looked at him, but they all stared. He felt it. A police officer's sixth sense.

Gloria paused at a noticeboard filled with flyers, posters, and announcements.

"The centre is for all ages. During the day, it's mostly adults. Weekday evenings is a mixture of children with their mothers, and our teens." She straightened a flyer. "Weekends it's every man for himself—chaos!"

Earp wanted to hurry the woman on and get away from the prying eyes. Once in the enclosed space of her office, he would ask about Martin Findlay. Then a quick round of standard questions with the disabled man, and he'd be on his way to the next witness. He'd wasted enough time today and felt tired and hungry.

Gloria pointed at the picture of a boy, nine or ten, in a wheelchair. Then another of the same child in a canoe. "Gold medallist in the Aira Beck White Water Challenge. Only been at it for a year. Follow the path of your infinite potential, that's what we tell these boys and girls. Sometimes I can't believe what they achieve."

"Aye," Earp replied. As he stood with his arms folded tight across his chest, a thought hit him. Nick. Maybe he'd mention the centre to Sue. He wasn't sure his son would take to water, but maybe there was something else here he'd enjoy.

A few moments later, Gloria and Earp were in a cubical office: glass walls, no desk, two wing-backed armchairs placed shoulder to shoulder, humid air.

Gloria eased into a chair. "No one can hear us in here." She stood up, turned around several times like a cat, then settled deep in the cushions, letting out an inaudible sigh. "A bit of privacy, Detective Constable Earp, so we can have a nice natter."

An elderly man in a flat cap hobbled over to one of the glass walls. He leaned on his stick and peered into the office. Abertha arrived soon after, had a few words with the man, and opened a packet of crisps. She was soon followed by the three women in wheelchairs Earp had seen earlier. They parked, continued to knit, natter, and stare. Earp felt like a guppy in a tropical aquarium. The humidity was getting to him, so he took off his jacket and sunk deep into the soft velvety cushion. Despite the stares of the gathered crowd, the earlier tension began to drain away. He half wondered if Gloria had worked some Scottish magic like the witch in the bedtime story he'd read to Nick.

Gloria leaned sideways, tapped the glass, and pointed at Abertha. "Reception desk," she mouthed without making a sound, and again she pointed.

Abertha pulled a face, swivelled, and wheeled away.

"Ignore the eyeballs," Gloria said. "They are just curious. And this fish tank is better than talking outside in the car park."

Earp squeezed his eyes shut for a second and tried to focus. He felt sleepy. "You'll have heard about the death of Miss Maureen Brian," he began, feeling his way into the subject. "I'm trying to trace everyone who might have been on the beach the morning the body was discovered."

"Oh, then you'll want to speak with me and Peter. We knew Maureen well and walk the beach most mornings."

More friends of Maureen. *Did she know the whole bloody town?* More names to add to the list. A wave of tiredness washed over him. He scribbled down the names and shifted in his seat trying to remain focused.

Gloria was still speaking. "Peter Jarman is my fiancé. He runs Jarman Automotive Repair in town. Maureen got us together, so you can imagine our distress at what's happened. We have been friends for years, her and I. Almost like sisters. Well maybe not sisters. I always fought with mine. Still do, all these years later, imagine that? But we were close, and to think…"

The early morning start, humidity and lack of breakfast finally got to Earp. He felt his eyelids flutter shut. He wasn't sure how long they remained in that state, but jerked his head up at the sound of Gloria's voice.

"And Bonfire Night, Peter and I walked the beach planning our wedding; met Audrey Robin too. She was looking for Maureen, quite frantic she was. Anyway, are you any closer to catching the person who did this? Well, I suppose it is early days in the investigation, so…"

He sat up straight, snatched out his notebook and pen, then tried to scratch a few words onto the page. What did she say? He couldn't remember. Sod it! Anyway, he'd taken pages of notes, carefully scribbled, but considered them a waste of good ink. He'd been at it too long to care about the death of an old boiling fowl. Old people didn't have much to live for anyway. Still, if Sallow asked, he'd have evidence that at least he'd tried. Not how he'd run the investigation though. He stopped himself, knowing if he let his thoughts run in that direction, he'd become agitated. So he tried to think of Nick and Sue. He was doing this job for them. That's all that mattered. They'd soon have the money to go to America, and when he came back, his boy would walk.

"Then when Maureen found out it was true love between me and Peter, well, I can't tell you how happy she was for us both. Not just me, but us both…"

As Gloria continued to speak, Earp's mind grew foggier. He saw not even the vaguest clue in the conversations he'd documented. No leads. No names. No pattern. Nothing.

"There isn't much else I can say, really." Gloria stared at him with expectant eyes. "I hope what I have told you is useful. Seems like inane chatter to me, but I'm not a detective skilled in the art of piecing things together, am I?"

His mind fought to escape the swamp of creeping sleep. *Keep your eyes open.* He stared back, gave a professional smile. He glanced at his notes and scrambled for something to say. "I'll have to have a chat with Mr Jarman. Can you give me the details?"

She did, with quick words as if she'd been waiting for the moment.

"Oh, and there is one thing, Miss Embleton." He'd almost forgotten the reason for his visit. "Can you point me towards Martin Findlay? I'd like a quick word."

"Ah! I'm so sorry to disappoint you, Detective Earp. Martin isn't here today. His group are on a day trip to Derwentwater. They won't be back until after ten this evening."

Chapter Twenty-One

A UDREY KNEW THEY WOULD come.

She'd had a bath, soaked in the bubbles, and put on her work clothes—a striped lemon cotton blouse with khaki cargo pants. Not standard librarian dress. She preferred jacket and skirt, but felt it better to appear less formal. Anyway she needed roomy pockets. She'd taken the envelope from her coat and placed it in the large side pocket of her pants. Better to keep it close.

In the kitchen, the kettle simmered on the stove, the low hiss filling the room with soft steam. A moist Victoria sponge baked in the oven. The fragrant vanilla set the sweet tone she wanted to portray. Better than the stink of hot dogs and onions on her first meeting with the detectives.

Now she watched from the window and waited. She could see the Solway Firth and, on a clear day, for miles until the sky joined sea in a horizontal blue line.

"That's why they call it Clearview Row," Maureen had said when she introduced Audrey to the idea of buying the little stone cottage. "Unobstructed views to the horizon. A perfect place for you. Help keep you focused on the future. On a clear day you can sit at the window and read a book or paint or daydream. A clear view across the water."

Not today though. There'd been no let-up in the clouds. They hung their spidery tendrils in restless swirls over the flat water. But on that day with Maureen, it was clear, and the cottage cast a spell on Audrey. Through rose-tinted glasses, she'd made the offer and purchased the cottage.

They were an odd-shaped assortment of houses on Clearview Row. Orange, browns, blues, even pink hues, and Audrey's two-bedroom whitewash faded to grey. Like a family, she often thought, connected by the lane as straight as a vein. Her cottage was in the middle. A pink bungalow on one side. On the other, a three-storey Edwardian town the colour of honey converted into flats. Most people parked on the lane as the front gardens were small, built before the popularity of cars. Today, she had parked farther along the lane. That left space outside her window so she could see when the detectives arrived.

The rhythmic hum of a car engine slowing to a crawl first alerted Audrey of their appearance. In slow motion it eased along the lane around a parked van and came to a stop where she expected—in front of the cottage. She smiled. So, they owned the dark blue Morris Minor she had hid behind at Seafields Bed and Breakfast, did they?

The detectives sat in the car for a long time. Audrey peered through the net curtains and strained her ears. The steady sputter of the Morris Minor and the distant murmur of the sea echoed along the lane.

Then the grey-haired woman detective, crisp and alert, climbed out. The engine roared and the car sped away. Audrey did not notice who was driving, had her eye on the woman detective.

The woman opened the garden gate, glanced around, then started towards the front door. The light *clop-clop* of her footsteps echoed like goat hooves of a recurrent dream. It came to Audrey on days like these. The voices first. Then an unremembered nightmare which crept into her unconscious as the pills pushed her into the free fall of deep sleep.

Audrey took a step away from the window when she saw a two-legged devil with horns and a pitchfork walking up the garden path. She snatched off her glasses, wiped them with a tissue, and continued her gaze.

A woman. Not a devil.

Now she turned her attention to the car, but it was out of sight although she could hear its low rumble. The driver must have been the other detective, the grizzled-looking black one. What was his name?

It came to her along with a rush of adrenaline. Dexter, Detective Sergeant. And the grey-haired woman—Detective Inspector Fenella Sallow. A wave of relief. Her *know thy neighbour* skills were back in full flow. That she'd remembered their names sent a thrill through her body. She tapped her pant pocket two times, stopped on the third; she didn't need luck. She had her plan.

Audrey continued to watch. The woman detective couldn't see her through the net curtains and the clouded glass. It felt like a show on the television. She sat in the audience and saw it all, while the actors knew only their next lines. Except... She held her breath for a moment. Why was the woman detective on her own?

The knock on the door pushed a wave of adrenaline through her body. It surged so hard, her next memory was of the grey-haired detective seated at the kitchen table with a notebook and pen in hand.

"Just a routine inquiry," said the woman detective as she gazed around the kitchen. "Smells good. Baking?"

"Victoria sponge. It is about done. Would you like a slice with a cup of tea?"

Audrey thought neither of them ate much cake, too fattening. Now she worried the detective might get suspicious, decline her culinary creation. Would it be a bribe to offer fresh-baked goods with a cup of tea? They were firm about gifts in the library. No tips or packages. Patrons who wanted to leave cash were sent to the charity collection box. It was at the checkout desk, out in the open. That made things difficult, but when no one was looking, Audrey emptied the box into her purse. How else was she expected to pay the bills on what they paid her?

It was more difficult at Christmas. Satisfied readers brought in chocolates, cakes, cards with cash, even bottles of wine. The head librarian put them in a box in her office. Audrey would sneak in and grab a few things. One at a time. It was surprising how they mounted up. At the end of her shift, she'd smuggle them out. There were so many last year, she'd even rewrapped one and gave it as a gift to the head librarian. She thanked Audrey with wide eyes and smiles. So sweet.

Now Audrey worried she'd made a big misstep. Weren't the police very strict about gifts? She imagined they had an army of folk tapping out policy and procedures on keyboards. She wanted no more trouble. Things were bad enough in her job at the library. These days the head librarian watched her like a hawk. The woman was always trying to catch her out. Always nagging about some violation or other of library regulations. She tried her best, but it was never good enough for the damn witch.

"This isn't the lunch I'd planned in my diet journal." Audrey smiled. "Today was supposed to be a turkey-lettuce wrap with a dollop of cottage cheese. But I've baked it now and don't want to eat it all myself. How about a slice each and I'll give the rest away to my neighbours?"

"Aye, that'd be lovely," said the woman detective.

Audrey felt very clever. She went to the oven, placed the cake on a cooling rack and poured a pot of tea. Things were off to the perfect start.

They didn't speak again until after everything was on the table. She used her blue-and-white china teapot with matching teacups. It came from the Christmas box in the head librarian's office. The pot for the milk didn't match. Nor did the tub for the sugar. But she used the little silver teaspoons with the fancy handles. And the cake, moist and warm, she placed on a china stand. Very posh. Like a teahouse in Carlisle.

"I'll not take up much of your time," the detective said after she had taken two bites, said it was delicious, and sipped her tea. "Just a few questions. We had rather a tough time having a conversation in the ambulance, didn't we?"

"It was a shock finding Maureen like that by the bonfire." Audrey added milk to her cup, took a sip, tasted bitterness. " I suppose my mind was a little messed up. Anything I can do to help?"

The detective didn't answer. Her gaze fell on the sideboard where Audrey stored her trinkets. A framed photograph, pebbles, seashells, little mementos of her trips to the beach. And there was a spider plant too, with long dangling leaves.

"Is that Maureen?" The woman detective pointed to the rectangular frame. The photograph contained three women, a large man, and a brood of grinning kids.

"That's her," Audrey said. She got to her feet to fetch the photograph. "Taken last summer. That's me, Maureen, Elizabeth with her foster kids. And those two are Gloria and Martin."

"Findlay," added the detective looking at the man. "Martin Findlay?"

Audrey didn't reply for a moment. She stared at the woman detective and took another sip of tea. "Maureen had a soft spot for"— she stopped, considered her words with care—"people who are different."

"Disabled?"

"Oh, I don't think there is anything wrong with Martin physically, more in the mind. Maureen took a shine to him when he was a kid, kept an eye out. His mum had her problems, lived alone, spent her days at the pub making friends with married men. It helped pay the rent, I suppose." Audrey thought it would be helpful to paint a picture. Broad outlines only, let the detective fill in the rest. "Not that I was around. As I understand it, Maureen introduced Martin to

Gloria, years ago. Gloria got him a spot at the Quarterdrigg Activity Centre. He goes there most days."

"Friendly lad, is he?"

"Oh yes, very friendly. Sometimes."

The detective looked at her like a CCTV camera so that she felt like a shadowy image caught in the act of a crime. She took a bite of cake, thinking.

Outside in the lane, a van lumbered by the cottage. Its exhaust pipe rattled above the persistent hum of wind and sea. The clap of the letterbox echoed a tuneless melody as the postman pushed through mail. Audrey felt the urge to get up, run to the door, see if there was anything other than bills. Maybe if she hurried to the hallway, to return a few moments later, more slowly, walking softly, holding the mail with both hands, the grey-haired detective would be gone. Just like the ratty-faced terrier who spoke Patrick's words. Just like Maureen. She felt a sorrowful weight.

The detective was speaking. "Tell me about Mr Findlay."

"Martin comes to the library several days a week, a regular." Audrey took a quick breath, quick to see the possibilities. "He is the sweetest person when he is himself."

The detective blinked, tapped a pen on her notebook. "And when he is not?"

"Well, it's not for me to say." Audrey sipped her tea. "Oh look at me, I'm rattling on again."

"Not at all. We are trying to build a picture of Maureen Brian. That includes her friends and acquaintances."

"Then you may as well put the entire town down, including the staff of the library." They'd never catch the killer if they did that. Audrey imagined *Wanted* flyers plastered to lampposts all over town asking for help. She felt giddy, electrified. "Are you close to catching the killer?"

The detective said, "We are in the very early stages of the investigation. Most of what we are doing now is about gathering the right information. Later we'll shift our focus and sift through it to see what we've got."

A robot response, Audrey thought. *Like the woman officer who spoke at the press conference. A string of important-sounding words, which when taken apart told you nothing.* She wanted to hum, but not aloud, quietly in her mind so that ratty terrier wouldn't come—*tat-de-da-da-de-de-dah.*

The detective watched with the laser-focused eyes of a mystic. Could she read minds?

Audrey stopped mid-hum and said, "I'm sure the person knows they'll get caught." She took a big bite of cake. "In the end."

The detective picked up her teacup and leaned forward. "Tell me about Mr Findlay?"

"Like I say, he is the sweetest person you'll ever meet. A big bloke. A bit simple. Harmless." Audrey gazed at the detective with interest. "Once a week, Maureen visited the Quarterdrigg Activity Centre. She read from Dickens, Shakespeare, or a bestseller in crime or science fiction. Her readings were very popular with the attendees. Martin never missed it."

"Really?" The detective's eyes seem to glow, or that's how it appeared to Audrey. "And Mr Findlay never missed a reading? Interesting."

Audrey felt alive. She sat up straight like a child in a classroom eager to answer the teacher's next question. Ready responses about Martin Findlay hovered on the tip of her tongue. She'd tell her about how he was locked away. Not his fault. Not right. But he'd spent time in a cell. *Tat-de-da-da-de-de-dah.*

The questions didn't come.

"Why don't you tell me about Maureen?" The woman detective leaned back. "Nothing is off limits. Talk and I'll listen."

Audrey stared at the detective. "As I said earlier, Maureen helped me settle into the community. Not just her, but Elizabeth Collins and Gloria Embleton. Even Martin Findlay did his part to make me feel welcome. Nothing was too much trouble for Maureen. She even helped me buy this cottage. It's a work in progress, but I'd never have afforded it without her help."

"How so?"

Audrey felt like she'd made a mistake. "Oh not with money or anything like that. It was her advice that was so valuable. Worth its weight in gold."

"I see. So no loans, then?"

"Maureen was the type to offer, but I'd never accept. She found workmen to fix things up in the house on the cheap. The electric, plumbing and so on. You know how it is in these old stone cottages."

"Aye, luv. I know. Nothing but repairs and bills and more repairs, eh?"

Audrey laughed. they could become friends, couldn't they? She relaxed. "And I'm only an assistant librarian; they pay us peanuts." Then she added, "But I'm a good saver thanks to Maureen. She always said spend less than you make to make a stress-free life."

There was a pause while the detective wrote into her notebook. Then she turned and pushed a strand of hair from her face. After another sip of tea, she tilted her head to the left, then to the right in some kind of neck-stretching exercise.

"Why don't you tell me about Maureen's photographic art."

"Oh, I don't know much about that. It was all hush-hush. I know she was working on another project with a bloke from London." Audrey closed her eyes. "Jones. Zack Jones. Never met him, but she always had her notebook with her to write down ideas. I also hear her photos are selling at high prices these days, but like I say, that's not a secret. Everyone knows."

The detective took careful notes.

All that writing made Audrey uncomfortable. What had she told her that merited such careful precision?

In a rush, she said, "I thought I saw Detective Sargent Dexter in the car." Suddenly she realised she'd admitted snooping. "Thought he might come in for a cup of tea as well."

There was an extended silence. The detective took a sip of tea and appeared to decide.

"He'll probably come in for follow-up questions." She placed the cup in the saucer. "There are always one or two I forget to ask."

"I'll be here. I'm not going anywhere."

The detective stared at her for so long, Audrey thought the hawk-eyed woman could see into her khaki pocket. Her hand dropped to pat the envelope. Could they order her to turn out her pockets?

That thought terrified her. She should have thrown the bloody plan on the bonfire. She didn't want anyone reading her handwritten instructions, let alone a policewoman. And for an instant, she saw that ratty terrier dog in her mind's eye. That frightened her even more. It would speak in Patrick's voice and tell the police where to look.

The detective was speaking. "Earlier we visited Maureen's apartment. Everything was in order as far as we could tell. Did you ever visit?"

"No. She never invited guests back to the boarding house."

"Do you know why?"

"Not really, although she said she didn't want to impose on Ben and Safiya Griffin. They run the bed and breakfast, lease it actually from Maureen." Audrey's mind drifted. She wondered where the other detective went. "I suppose Detective Dexter has gone back to the station for his lunch?"

The grey-haired woman detective laughed. "No luv, we get little in the way of lunch breaks. He is on his way to visit the community college and then the local art galleries. We asked Mr and Mrs Griffin about Maureen's art. They couldn't tell us much. So now we've got to do a little research on our own."

"Oh, that's not surprising." The words came out without Audrey thinking ahead of time. "Ben and Safiya are in a different bucket."

"Come again." The detective leaned so far forward, it felt to Audrey as if she wanted to reach into her mind. "Why do you say that?"

Audrey detected a touch of formality in the voice. She didn't like the tone. It reminded her of a stern nurse in the hospital or a guard as they closed the cell door. So she recalculated their chance of friendship. Was the grey hair and smiles all surface?

Yes, everything was an act. Still, she narrowed her eyes as if sharing a great secret with an intimate acquaintance.

"Maureen organised her life in neat buckets. Friends, home life, photographic art, and teaching. They rarely crossed. No, I'm not surprised Ben and Safiya knew nothing about her photography. Why would they? I only know a little myself. As I've said, Maureen kept her art close to her chest. Elizabeth Collins might tell you more I suppose. But I know nothing about it."

"We'll have a chat with her." The detective wrote into her notebook. "Anything else?"

"If it is her art that interests you, then I suppose you should visit the studio on the *Pig's Snout*. That's a boat in the harbour."

Chapter Twenty-Two

E ARP TOOK THE PHONE call while still parked in the Quarterdrigg Activity Centre. He considered himself fortunate to have sounded alert at all when the mobile rang. He'd taken a few minutes shut-eye which had extended, as he looked at his watch, to a full thirty minutes.

"Hello ma'am... yes I'm making steady progress... at the Quarterdrigg... no, nothing to report... Find anything at her home, ma'am? Another name... yes... uh-huh... uh-huh... her studio... the harbour... Pig Snout... got it... I will... I know... I'll go straight there."

Earp gave the phone two fingers along with a volley of sour words. Another wild goose chase. He started the car and reversed. The front wheels ran over another black bin bag. It burst with a pop. He didn't stop, swung the car around, and headed for the exit.

As he signalled to turn into the street, he glanced into his rear-view mirror. Gloria Embleton, Albertha, and the old man in the cap stood in the Quarterdrigg entrance. The old man raised his walking stick. He pointed at the litter as it swirled around in the wind.

Earp knew he should turn back, clean up his mess. His son had shown an interest in the environment. Nick had read about the plight of the red squirrel in the woodlands of the Lake District. Sue's voice swelled with pride when she told him Nick had written a report in his spare time. The lad got an A and a gold star from the teacher. Now his son insisted they use the council recycling bin. Earp agreed, although he thought they jumbled it all together anyway.

His stomach rumbled.

"Sod it!"

Earp continued, taking a slight diversion to stop at Mustard's Chippy. He bought a large battered haddock with steaming-hot chips, a pickled onion, curry sauce, and a large can of pineapple soda. He ate the crisp fish and fried chips in his car with the heat turned up high. As it began to drizzle, he scooped up the last of the sauce with a slab of batter. Then he reclined the driver's seat, and again closed his eyes. Just a quick kip.

Earp awoke, refreshed, to a light rain drumming on the window and the lingering smell of chip shop curry. Could do with a battered sausage and another can of soda. He stared for a while at the steamed windows of Mustard's Chippy. It was packed with lunchtime patrons. He couldn't be bothered to wait in the queue. His mind turned to the earlier phone call. Sallow and Dexter hadn't found anything interesting at Maureen Brian's home. Why didn't they call in a crew to tear the place apart?

"Soddin' idiots."

Earp put the car into gear, but didn't let it move. Today had been one dreary slog. Where was the excitement he used to feel at the start of an investigation? He hadn't felt that in years. Still, he needed brownie points to get his career back on track. With a fast result, he'd be on the road again to inspector. That came with a higher salary and more savings to pay for his son's treatment in America. But he needed a quick win.

The drizzle stopped.

A vague idea formed.

He smiled.

Yes, he'd find the *Pig Snout* in the harbour, take a nosy around the outside of the boat. Better yet, he'd check the doors. Not a problem if locked. He'd jam the latch so it opened and take a quick look inside. Maybe he'd find enough to persuade Sallow to send in uniformed officers. They'd find something, he felt sure of it, and he'd take the credit, all of it. He wondered what they'd make of his instant success back in Carlisle. Solving this murder would get their attention.

His smile swelled to a grin.

Miss Maureen Brian is my passport out of this hell hole.

He clung to this thought as his car jerked into the traffic.

Chapter Twenty-Three

E ARP RESTED HIS ELBOWS on the harbour railing and idly watched a fishing smack navigate its way through the entrance channel. The drizzle had stopped, but the threat of heavy rain loomed so that the air smelled of brine with a faint trace of sulphur. Low waves lapped against the harbour wall; a soft rhythmic murmur broken by the screams of herring gulls as they hovered above the deep water. Port Saint Giles kept a working fishing fleet. Commercial boats bobbed by the wet dock. There were private boats too, a few shiny and new. Most were well-worn and used for more than the occasional weekend sail around the Solway Firth.

From this distance it wasn't obvious which boat was the *Pig Snout*. He walked along the harbour wall towards the stone gatehouse with its pitched slate roof and ornamental turrets. It reminded him of Carlisle castle.

On the boardwalk, a man kicked a ball about with his son. A sudden surge of jealousy caused Earp to stop and watch. Another few years, and he and Sue would have the money to take Nick to America. After the operation, they'd play kickball on the boardwalk and snap photos by the gatehouse. He and Nick would pretend it was a citadel and defend it from imaginary Viking hoards. Provided all went well with the operation. It would be a success; he could feel it in his bones. The Americans had put a man on the moon. They could fix his boy's legs. He felt a tightness in his chest and returned his attention to the gatehouse.

The uniformed security guard dozed behind a small glass hatch. The newspaper at his side was turned to the sports pages with a bookie-office pen pointing at the 16:23 greyhound race at Owelerton Stadium. Earp watched for a while, noted the circle around Carney Jill, and wondered whether it was worth a flutter. He knocked on the window.

Nothing.

He tried the door.

Locked.

He thumped again, several times, continuing to drum his fist against the glass in rapid bursts.

"Open up."

The shout roused the man from his slumber. He rocked in his chair. It tilted over, spilling him sideways onto the floor. He lay there in bewilderment as if he'd awoken in a strange bed and didn't know how he got there. He rubbed sleep away with the backs of his hands, sat up, looking about wildly. With a jerk he scrambled to his feet and opened the hatch.

"What the bleedin' hell do you want?"

"So sorry, sir." Earp tried to keep himself from laughing out loud. "Are you all right?"

"You ought to be locked up for creeping up on folk like that. Could have given me a bleedin' heart attack."

"You appeared to be sleeping, sir."

"Nowt wrong with taking a nap on me lunch break."

"You are the security guard, aren't you?"

"Watchman, that's what I am, not some bleedin' ninja warrior."

Earp did not speak for a while. He stared at the man and listened to the relentless slap of waves against the harbour wall, the susurrous *whoosh* against stone that separated water from land. Was there another security guard who'd be more amenable?

Earp said, "Has your workmate popped out for a smoke?"

"They don't pay enough for two watchmen. I'm all there is."

"So, you are on duty?"

"Ever worked a double shift, mate?"

"I'm with the police. A detective." Earp kept his voice polite although the man's tone was beginning to irritate. He waved his warrant card, glanced at the man's name tag and smiled. "Can I have a quick word? Finnegan Woodstock, isn't it?"

"Aye." Finnegan looked him up and down. His eyes rolled over the crumpled suit, curry-stained tie, and scuffed shoes. It appeared to fit his perception of a Cumbria Constabulary detective. "Now what's all this about?"

"I'm investigating the murder of Maureen Brian. I understand she rented a boat, the *Pig Snout*. I'd like to have a quick butcher's."

Finnegan didn't reply, simply stared at Earp through the little glass hatch. An outboard motor rumbled in the distance. Giggles and laughter came from behind. Earp turned. A group of schoolgirls in uniform hurried along the boardwalk towards the lighthouse. They had their umbrellas raised, although there was no rain. There was something about the girl in the orange jacket. The Doc Martens boots? He wondered why they weren't in school, then realised it was still lunchtime. It felt much later. The haddock and chips had sucked his energy or maybe it was the curry sauce. Good stuff. Worth it. He might return later for a battered sausage and another can of pineapple soda. It'd cost, and he and Sue needed to save every penny, but that's what happened when his lunch went unpacked. He contemplated another snooze. *After I've finished poking around the boat.*

Finnegan was speaking. "Maureen Brian was a wonderful woman. A real-life angel whose time on this earth was too short."

"You knew her, then?" Earp took out his notebook.

"She helped me and my wife, Tammy, with babysitting when our Danny was small. Years ago now, but I still remember the great advice she gave us when he wouldn't sleep at night. Worked like a charm." He fell silent and stared past Earp towards the boardwalk.

Earp turned to follow his gaze. The father and son kicked the football back and forth. Neither spoke, but it was clear they were having fun, creating memories that would last a lifetime. The clouds seemed lower. There'd be more rain soon.

Finnegan said, "When I was a kid, Maureen would take a bunch of us to the beach to kick ball and play stick cricket. Miss Maureen, we called her. Always Miss Maureen. We got up to mischief and had lots of fun. On the way home she'd buy us each a glass bottle of cola with little straws and a bag of chips with scraps." He stopped speaking, gazed at Earp, but his eyes were seeing the marvellous past. His face radiated.

Earp struggled to put a word on the glow—*sadness*. But there was happiness too. He pondered what to make of it, drew a blank and decided he would stop by Mustard's Chippy as soon as he wrapped things up here.

Finnegan was speaking. "Bonfire Night. That was the last time I saw Maureen. My boy, Danny, got lost in the crowds. Maureen found him. She was with her friend, Audrey Robin." He leaned forward so his face almost touched the glass hatch. "You'll find who killed Miss Maureen, won't you?"

Earp hesitated, taken aback by the intensity of Finnegan's question. "I have a few questions of my own; routine, if you don't mind."

"Looks like it's going to chuck it down. Come inside; not a lot of space, but it's dry and warm. I'll put the kettle on."

"No thank you."

"Suit yourself. What do you want to know?"

"Where were you between midnight and two in the morning, Bonfire Night?"

"At home with my wife and boy."

Earp made a note. He'd check with the wife later. "Is Miss Brian's boat, the *Pig Snout*, berthed here?"

"Aye. Maureen used to visit once or twice a week. She came with a big canvas shopping bag most times. A huge thing, like she were hauling coal. Sometimes I'd walk with her to the boat, just to stretch my legs and talk, but she wouldn't let me help carry. She'd give a little wave and disappear inside."

"She was a hobby boater, then?"

"Never took it out on the water. Well, not least so I saw. Most times she would stay a couple of hours, then go home."

"Any idea what Miss Brian used the boat for?"

"She liked to sit and watch the water, I suppose."

"Ever been aboard?"

"I'm a watchman, not a crew mate."

"Weren't you curious?"

"I get caught snooping around a yacht and I'm out of a job. The last guy held late-night parties on the boats, got fired." Finnegan paused, thinking. "Wayne Wingfield, that was his name. I believe you lot put him away for drug dealing."

Earp made a note. "So, you've never been inside the *Pig Snout*?"

"I've got a family to feed."

A squally shower splattered down. It splashed against the window. Water dribbled from the roof. Earp cursed under his breath, turned up his collar and said, "Why don't you show me where the *Pig Snout* is berthed so I can have a quick look around."

Finnegan considered for a moment. "You got some sort of paperwork, a search warrant?"

"We are trying to find out who beat and murdered Miss Maureen Brian."

A cold gust swept heavier drops across the boardwalk. It slanted down, drenching Earp's trousers. He almost let loose a tirade of foul words but held himself in check. It'd be worth it if he got on that damn boat. He'd tear the place apart himself now, wouldn't stop until he found something. And if anyone complained, he'd have a good excuse—Finnegan Woodstock let him board. He didn't move, and set a pleasant expression on his face.

"Just a quick look, Mr Woodstock; won't take more than ten minutes."

"I dunno about that."

"It will help our investigation." He heard the irritation in his voice but hoped Finnegan missed it. "Just point me in the right direction, I'll have a wander about, simple."

Finnegan frowned. "Not easy finding work about these parts."

"Then we'll keep your afternoon kip between ourselves, shall we?"

Finnegan looked at him, his eyes clear and focused. "Sorry mate, it is more than my job's worth." He scribbled on a slip of newspaper with the bookie-office pen. "Why don't you give Ron Malton a bell? Councillor Malton owns the *Pig Snout*. Get his say-so and I'll do anything you ask."

Earp stood in the cold and the rain, cursing under his breath. Drops, icy cold, slapped his face as he slowly turned away from the hatch. He cursed again and stamped his soaked trouser legs. He stomped back along the boardwalk and didn't notice the man and his son, umbrellas raised, dancing.

Chapter Twenty-Four

CATHY SAT IN WANDER'S Wash Laundrette feeling like a great big lump of coal. A November wind gusted against the plate-glass windows. It turned the drizzle into smears of grime and glitter. Inside, the tumble dryers and washing machines spun with an urgent hum. They spat out damp and heat so that it was warm. She shrugged off her orange jacket and waited for the wash to be done.

Thursday was wash night.

She'd pushed the soiled clothes in a shopping cart her dad had nicked from Tesco years ago. If she didn't do the wash, it wouldn't get done. So, once a week she scrounged money from her dad and came to sit, watch, and catch up on her homework. Not that school mattered much anymore. Dreams of a farm in the countryside pulled her away from her books these days.

Chickens and goats and a vegetable patch. In the rich soil, she'd grow organic carrots and cabbages and potatoes. Some she'd cook and eat, the rest she'd sell in the local farmers' market.

But daydreams of rural life weren't enough to sustain her this evening. She felt weary and frightened and sad, and needed to speak with him again. With Maureen Brian dead, doubt crept in. She'd saved some money for flowers. Not enough yet, though, for the bunch of orange roses and yellow sunflowers. They were pricey but Miss Brian deserved it. And now she was dead, it was the best she could do. So she picked them out from a display in Laurie's Florist and counted the pennies until she could afford them. Her way of saying sorry.

At one minute past six, she fiddled with her phone. She scanned for a message from Belinda. They hadn't spoken or texted since they'd argued on the bench under the lighthouse on the pier. So she watched an inane video of cats dancing to nineteen-seventies' disco music. At six twenty, her mind drifted to him. At six thirty, she pulled out her geography homework, then put it back.

Too boring.

Should she send Belinda a text message?

But then there'd be questions, and she wasn't ready for that yet.

At six thirty-five, she went to the laundrette door. She peered into the amber lamplight of the drizzle-swept street. Most of the shopfronts were dark, except the convenience store and the newsagents next to it. They closed late to cater for the evening rush. The occasional person hurried along, coat drawn tight against the blustery wind. At the end of the street, as it curved on a slow bend, stood the Three Tuns pub. A handwritten sign was taped to the frosted glass of the saloon window—Pub Grub Sold Here. Her dad would be in there now, drinking the evening away. He'd beg a box of food at closing time, bring it home for breakfast or a late lunch. Nothing unusual. Nothing to see.

As she turned to go back inside the laundrette, a boxy car belched to a stop in front of the newsagent. A man flitted like a graveyard shadow from the driver's side into the shop.

Cathy spun around.

It was him.

She drew in a breath. Her stomach churned as if riding the Tilt-A-Whirl at the town theme park.

A sign.

She started out after him, almost calling his name. At the edge of the pavement she waited for a break in the traffic. Cars trundled along. Commuters on their way home to a warm house and evening meal. When a gap came, she darted across the road as if a hare pursued by a fox.

Cathy stopped under the awning of the newsagent. It wasn't until then that she realised she was holding her breath. The wind gusted its chill and her hands flew to pull tight the hood on her jacket. Only then did she exhale.

There were people moving about the store; she could see them through the window, but not him. Easy to see. Dark into light. Not so easy on the inside to see out. Light into dark.

Better wait outside. He won't be long.

Like a loyal puppy dog waiting for the return of its master, that was she. Or a palmate newt awaiting the warmth of spring. Both animals. Both constrained by their biological urges. She thought again of Belinda. The girl had her craven need for stories, bright and gossipy and extravagant. *But I'm here too,* she thought. And standing outside the newsagent in the damp and cold and dark when I should be in the laundrette where it is bright and cosy and talking to Belinda on my phone while folding crisp warm clothes.

Cathy peered through the plate-glass window. She had to speak with him tonight, tell him everything. He was so pure and honest and true. He made her feel safe. But she knew he'd ask lots of questions.

Over and over in her mind she practised what she would say. There was Maureen and the baby and her violent death on the beach in the dead of night. It jumbled around her head and she couldn't get it straight. And she needed to get it straight when she spoke with him. She didn't want him to get angry, or have him say she didn't trust him. And her mind was already a mess. It was hard to keep things straight and clear.

Cathy stepped back and glimpsed herself reflected in the window. A useless lump of coal. And she reached for her phone to text Belinda but caught sight of him before it came out of her pocket. He had his back to her and stood still and rigid by the magazine rack. His head tilted upwards at the shelf—porno magazines with big-breasted women and computer-enhanced butts. Every face beaming with welcoming smiles. He pulled down a glossy publication, head drooped as he flicked through the pages. It went under his arm and his head once again craned upwards.

A momentary wave of dizziness rose in Cathy. She'd heard about men who liked that, but... not him. Please, God, not him. Perverts, Belinda called them. She'd have used stronger language herself. Her mind raced. She tried to slow her pulse and think about what to do next. Drizzle fell in a fine mist, pooling in puddles on the uneven pavement.

Cathy couldn't think. Drops of icy water dripped from the shop awning. They splashed against her face as she felt something inside break that could not be put right again.

Once more his head tilted up. But this time his hand hesitated. It was like watching a grocery shopper choose between two ripe plums. Then his big forceful hand darted out as fast as a lizard's tongue. His forked fingers grasped a glossy magazine as if it were a juicy blue-bottle fly.

The drizzle stopped. The drip from the awning beat in time with the rhythmic trundle of cars along the street.

Cathy decided then.

She'd go back to the laundrette, fold the washing, pretend it hadn't happened, be a palmate newt. Forget about him. Forget about the baby. Forget about the police. But before she turned away, he spun around.

It was the greyness of his face that caused her to scream. Skin drawn taught and leathery across sharp features like some hideous cadaver woken up from the tomb.

It wasn't him.

It was some old bloke.

Cathy ran.

Chapter Twenty-Five

"All right, ladies and gentlemen, your attention please." Fenella stood at the whiteboard in Incident Room A. She held a thick, bound folder under her arm. Her eyes watched the faces. Not too bad for an 8:00 p.m. briefing. She knew her core team would show—Dexter, Earp, and Jones. But there were other faces too. She nodded at the press officer, Tess Allen, and Constables Crowther and Phoebe.

She kept evening briefings short, but she'd not get home in time to enjoy supper with Eduardo and Nan. They'd already be sat around the scrubbed pine kitchen table. Part of her wished she was there too.

Not possible tonight though. Important to keep up the momentum.

The room went quiet.

"I've read through the crime scene report," Fenella began as she flicked through the volume. "Lisa and her team have done an outstanding job, as always."

Lisa Levon's reports were always typed with the precision of an engineered instrument. The pages were bound into a thick tome. It detailed every aspect imaginable: from a fibre collected from near the bonfire to estimates of time of death. It even detailed dog paws and herring gull tracks from three different birds. There was no immediate sign of animal damage to the corpse. And there were six distinct sets of footprints. One set were jogging shoes, size seven.

The others were for boots or shoes which ranged from size nine to size fourteen. The size-fourteen footprints matched Constable Phoebe. One pair matched Audrey Robin, the other Noel O'Sullivan. The dog paws were believed to be those of Barkie, Mr O'Sullivan's dog. But that awaited confirmation. The owners of the other footprints were not yet known. But one, by the size of the boot and uneven impression, was likely a male, over six foot with a limp.

The crime scene team had photographed the body from every imaginable angle. Plus the charred wood, scorched sand, and single metallic ring pulled from the top of a cola can. As for Miss Brian's corpse, there was no evidence of drug abuse. Samples of sand awaited analysis in the labs. Analysis of DNA swab samples from areas of likely contact were also pending. And so it went on.

Fenella closed the report and for an instant thought about Eduardo and Nan. At home she was a wife, mother, and daughter. Never a cop with her head full of dark crimes. She'd mastered the switch and could slide from murder to domestic bliss and back again. The drive home from work helped. That's where she made the change. The Cumbria countryside with its neat hedgerows and winding lanes helped her to unwind. But even she couldn't switch off that pang she felt when she missed an evening meal with her family.

Those gathered in incident room A watched their leader and waited. Fenella flipped the switch, brought herself back to the present. She said, "Anyone else looked at the report?"

Every hand went up.

Fenella studied the gathered faces. They were eager. The first furlong of the investigation was now well underway. Her own hopes were high. Doubts as soft as forgotten dreams. No need for her to pick through the report and read the relevant sections aloud. Everyone in the room was on the same page. She moved on. "Earp, where are you with the statements from the list of beach walkers?"

"About halfway."

"Anything interesting?"

"I've heard nothing but Miss Maureen Brian's good deeds and no end about her brilliant advice. It's insane, no one's got a bad word. Seems like the old broiler clucked with everyone in town, can't figure who'd want to wring her neck." Earp glanced around in the hopes of a laugh.

There came none.

The room became still.

Earp shrunk low in his chair and stumbled on. "Uh... er... well... makes it tough for us police folk when you've got no enemies." He gave a self-conscious laugh, thumbing his ear. "Anyone find any dirt on the woman?"

The room went as mute as stone.

"Come on, people," said Earp, his voice as scratchy as a stand-up comedian who'd bombed. "Where's your sense of humour?"

"This is a murder investigation, not the ringside in the circus." The blank expression on Fenella's face spoke more than her quiet words. "Okay?"

Earp stared hard. "Yeah."

Fenella held Earp's stare. "I didn't hear you."

"Yes, ma'am." He looked away.

"Okay." Fenella continued to stare. "What time did they close the beach?"

Earp flipped through his notebook, avoiding eye contact. Then he glanced around. "Anyone have the details?"

"I asked you to follow up on that item, Detective Constable Earp." Fenella kept her face fixed. She had a soft heart, knew that, but she wouldn't accept slackness in her team. Nor clowns who disrespected the memory of victims. Earp needed to understand that. "When I ask, I expect your commitment. Jones, follow up on it, will you?"

"Will do, ma'am." Jones beamed.

Fenella turned away from Earp and continued, her voice level. "I visited Miss Brian's home, a dormer in Seafields Bed and Breakfast run by Mr Ben and Safiya Griffin. Not what I expected, but that's bye the bye. What is important?" She gathered her thoughts. "First, Miss Brian was sociable, but she didn't take visitors to her home. Strange, eh? Second, there were no signs of a break-in when Dexter and I examined the place." Again, she paused. Nothing unusual except the lack of photographs. Then it hit her. Could someone have taken them from the walls? *I'll send Dexter for a second look tomorrow.* She continued without missing a beat. "One line of inquiry is the location of her photographic art studio. We believe it is on a boat in the harbour, the *Pig Snout*. Any thoughts?"

Jones raised his hand, back straight, eyes alert, like the bright kid in school. He sat at the front too. Fenella liked that, and his charming smile.

"Go on, Jones."

"We spoke about the storage of her collection when she taught my class in London."

"Well, don't keep us in suspense; this isn't a horror movie."

Everyone laughed, including Earp.

"Maureen was always a bit secretive about the exact location. But I recall her mentioning several times she kept a portfolio of finished images in her studio. I think she kept them there until they were shipped to either an art gallery or a dealer. So that would mean they are stored on—"

"The *Pig Snout*," interrupted Fenella. Now she turned to Dexter. "What can you tell us about her recent sales?"

Dexter looked at his notes. "Her art was sold through a broker in Carlisle. A company by the name of Wingfield and Morton. I spoke with one partner, a Mr Wingfield."

"And?" Fenella knew there was more. Knew Dexter.

"Mr Wingfield said his art shop has sold three of Miss Brian's works. All for high prices. Two went to America and the other to an oil man in Nigeria. The bidding was fierce."

"Isn't it strange what people will buy when they have too much money," Fenella said. "Go on, we are listening."

Dexter lowered his voice as if about to share a great secret. "One of Mr Wingfield's Chinese clients was very upset at missing out at auction. The nouveau riche in China can't get enough of Mrs Brian's work. He reckons they'll do anything to get their hands on her prints. Anything."

"What else?" Fenella spoke in a low voice, thinking.

"Mr Wingfield said his gallery had the rights to sell another four items." Dexter paused as if for dramatic effect. "He was very upset because he had not taken delivery before Miss Brian was killed. So, where are those photos?"

"In China," Jones said as he jumped to his feet. "I read about smuggled art in a spy novel. Maybe the Chinese government had a hand in it?"

"I'm with the boss on this one, reckon it's on the *Pig Snout*," Earp said, trying to be more helpful. "Unless Jones thinks we need to pay a visit to the Chinese Embassy in London?"

Everyone laughed.

Fenella did her best to stifle a grin. She liked her young detective's ideas even though this one was way outside the box. "Wherever they are, we will need to find those photos fast. Jones, get on the line to the forensic finance investigator. See what you can find out about Miss Brian's financials."

This was it.

They were moving in a direction at last. Fenella sensed the atmosphere in the room change. Energy crackled along the walls. She turned to Earp and smiled. "Root out anything interesting for us on your forage around the harbour?"

Warm chuckles filled the room, although Earp kept his face straight. He'd made one misstep this evening with his boss, wouldn't make another. He kept his tone formal. "I can confirm the *Pig Snout* is in the harbour. But I could not get access to the vessel without a search warrant. The security guard, Mr Finnegan Woodstock, refused to let me on board."

Fenella wasn't surprised. Earp simmered with discontent. It oozed like pus from an old wound. He probably peeved off the security guard. She'd send in Jones and Dexter to have a word; they knew how to work the public. Might even go herself. She paused, wondered what Nan had cooked for supper, knew it'd be in the oven. It wasn't the same when she arrived home late. Nan would be in bed and Eduardo listening to the play on BBC Radio Four.

Fenella pointed at Earp. "Are you trying to tell us the magnificent skills you learned in charm school failed you?"

Once again everyone laughed.

Earp joined in, then rubbed his ear. "Ma'am, the boat belongs to Councillor Malton."

"Okay," she said. "I hear that."

Something shifted in the room.

Dexter said, "Guv, we'd best tread with care with Councillor Malton."

"We don't want any bad publicity," Tess Allen added. "And he is good friends with Chief Constable Rae, not that it is important. But it's good to know."

"I'll have a word with Superintendent Jeffery," Fenella replied. "Once we get her say-so, we'll get the magistrate to issue a search warrant. By close of play tomorrow, we'll have searched Miss Maureen Brian's boat."

Chapter Twenty-Six

E ARLY THE NEXT MORNING, Fenella stood inside the mortuary and shuddered.

Dr Mackay's kingdom was in the oldest part of the Port Saint Giles Cottage Hospital. It dated back to Roman times. The weathered tan brick of the morgue was colder than the rest of the hospital. A sharp tang of disinfectant mingled with the stench of death. It lingered in the rooms and hallways. No matter how hard the cleaners scrubbed the stainless-steel tables, it hovered in the still air. No amount of rinsing down the blackened blood off the brown-tiled floors shifted the grim scent of the long dead. The shadows of those who'd gone before haunted the ancient place, if not literally, in the recesses of Fenella's mind.

Dr Mackay bent over Miss Maureen Brian's corpse. He clucked and muttered as if unaware of Fenella's presence. If he were an actor, the stage director would have demanded he tone it down. But the good doctor was no actor, just a man fascinated with death and all it entailed. Full of stories too. Many too gruesome for even Fenella. But he knew how to draw his listeners in. He mesmerised them like a Moroccan snake charmer, his words as melodic as a pungi flute.

Fenella had first met him when she was a rookie constable. There'd been a murder and she'd been assigned to guard the body. The stench of the place churned her stomach, and she trembled, turning pale green in this very room as Dr Mackay stood over a rotted corpse.

"Human decomposition," he had declared, "is the ultimate way to give back."

Now Fenella glanced at the steel table where the childlike form of Miss Maureen Brian lay. Lifeless, pale as dawn, naked, and cold as the night. She couldn't quell the sad question that crept into her mind. What would Maureen have achieved if she'd had an extra year or two? How many more people would she have touched through her friendship and art? Sorrow opened like a crack in dry earth.

Dr Mackay hovered over the corpse like a carrion crow. He was always doing something. At times with a scalpel. Or tugging at a body part with both hands. Even chipping at the head with a skull chisel. Forensic pathology seemed to Fenella to be a depressing job. How did he do it day in day out, and with so much zeal?

At least she took criminals off the street, but to stare at rot and decay and with the stench in your nostrils every day. That, she couldn't comprehend. Still, she admired his passion, professionalism and enjoyed his little quirks.

Few like him left.

The new breed of pathologists were a dull bunch. They hedged until the labs confirmed beyond any reasonable doubt. Not Dr Mackay. He spouted theories of the cause of death as freely as he imbibed a good Scotch whisky. Frequently and often.

Quirky, but human with it.

"Bloody awful." Dr Mackay stood up and turned to face Fenella. He held an enterotome, large stainless-steel scissors like those used by a butcher chef. It dripped with some vile bodily fluid. "Filthy business, this."

"Aye."

There was no denying it.

"A bloody awful business." Dr Mackay had a way about him that reminded Fenella of a scalpel. He peeled away the disinfectant, chemical deodorisers, and bureaucracy to expose the simple truth. "Last meal, fried chicken and chips with a can of cola. I've got the lab gals working on the brand." He placed the enterotome on the table. "Thank God I arrived at the crime scene before they shifted the body. Useful to see where the deed took place, much better than photographs. Got a feel for the situation, amount of blood, splatter patterns and the like."

Dr Mackay walked to where Fenella stood by the door. He raised his gloved hand for a shake, realised the error, and withdrew his bloodied hand.

"What can I tell you, Fenella?"

He always used her first name. Never detective, never Sallow. Not even constable when they'd first met all those years ago. Fenella liked that.

She said, "We're struggling to build up a picture of Maureen's last movements. We know she was on the beach for the Bonfire Night celebrations. She spent some time with a friend, Mrs Audrey Robin, the woman who found the body. Other than that, her movements between, say, nine p.m. and time of death remain a mystery."

"One forty-seven. That's the time of death."

Fenella marvelled at the precision of modern science. "I'd ask how the lab knows that, but the explanation would go over my head."

Dr Mackay snorted. "I can't wait for some snotty-nosed graduate to look down a microscope and then swirl foul-smelling fluids in some godawful chemical solution to tell me the obvious. The time of death is my best guess. Bet you a good bottle of Glenmorangie I'm right."

Fenella declined. She'd lost that bet once too often. And Eduardo didn't like it when she gave away bottles of his favourite whisky.

She changed the subject. "What else have you got for me?"

"Let me begin by putting all my cards on the table." He raised his gloved hands in mock surrender. "I knew Maureen, saw her Bonfire Night, maybe an hour after the procession." He paused for a moment and raised his gloved hand so it partially covered his face. "She was surrounded by a crowd of people as always. No one I knew though."

Dr Mackay turned to look at the body. For a brief moment he had his back turned to Fenella. She heard a noise. A sob or a laugh?

She couldn't say, but his stoop was more pronounced than last time, she thought. How long had he been working here? Before her time certainly, before Detective Inspector Jack Croll too. Thirty years, forty?

"I'll send Detective Constable Jones over to take a formal statement."

"New?"

"Just out of the National Detective Programme."

"I'll give him a tour as we chat, show him all the details, hands-on, just like I did when you were a rookie." Dr Mackay grinned, then turned his attention back to the matter at hand. "Like I say, a bloody awful business. Blunt-force homicide. Well you know that; not a knife. A fist, boot, a baseball bat, hammer... you get the picture. Blunt force." He shook his head. " Definitely not an accident. I wish it was otherwise for Maureen's sake and my peace of mind, but that's not the case according to my gut."

"Your gut?" Fenella respected his opinion. Gut was as important as fact. But she couldn't put how he felt about things in a report. "Your professional gut, I take it?"

"Of course." Dr Mackay lifted his arms, gloved hands hovering just above his ears. "My professional gut is informed by the hat brim line rule."

"Go on."

"Friday night in Carlisle. Young men. Pubs closing. You with me?" He waited until Fenella nodded. "One punch. Down the young man goes, smashing his head against a wall. Now, imagine the victim wearing a trilby. Not much call for those these days, not even in your line of business, but picture it nonetheless."

"Croll's boss used to wear one," Fenella said, a smile touching the corners of her lips. "I've seen the pictures in an ancient photo album." "Todd Stamford, wasn't it? I remember him. Died ten years back. Bad ticker." Dr Mackay tilted his nostrils, so they pointed towards the door. He sucked in the antiseptic-laced air as if a tourist cleansing his lungs on a beach. "Anyway, here is the kicker—fall-related injuries generally happen below the hat brim line. Not above it. Case in point, I recall a woman who was pushed in a New Year's Day sale in Barrow-in-Furness. Cracked her head on the haberdashery counter —dead before the ambulance arrived. Nasty. Blood all over the place. The key thing, though—her injuries were below the hat brim line. Accidental death."

"And Miss Brian?" Fenella asked, knew the answer.

"Above the hat brim line. Not accidental. Too many splits to the skin, long and linear. Intentional blows. Maureen Brian died of blunt force trauma." He half folded his arms across his chest. "A crude crime of passion I suspect. Have you considered a lover?"

The mortuary door opened wide. A young woman spoke from the entrance.

"Dr Mackay, I've a call from the medical director."

"Five minutes."

"He is rather insistent."

"Let Dr Oz wait; won't hurt the bugger."

"But sir."

"Tell him I'm with the police and helping our Fenella with her inquiries."

The door closed.

"Any ideas on the murder weapon?" Fenella hoped he would give her a clear picture of what was used.

"Blunt instrument, heavy. Bludgeoned." He sucked in a long breath. "Everything crushed in like that, reminds me of a case over in Workington. Husband hanging a curtain rail. The wife complained about the slant. He reached in his toolbox for the hammer. Only swung it once. That was that for the wife." Dr Mackay stopped speaking. He turned to stare at the remains on the table. When he turned back, he'd aged ten years. "The person who killed Maureen had multiple goes at it. The bugger bludgeoned her skull to a pulp. Not a hammer though, wrong skull fracture pattern. Mercifully, Maureen was well dead before the embers seared her face."

Fenella closed her eyes, remembering the crime scene. The charred remains, burnt embers, blackened sand. It all turned over in her mind. A ragtag collection of images with no form, no shape, no purpose, as if random. Yet a quiet voice nagged. It itched in some lost corner of her mind. Her stomach churned over like a faulty starter motor. There was something else. She was sure of it. What had she missed?

She opened her eyes and Dr Mackay said, "Has Lisa Levon found much of interest in her forensic search?"

"Still with the labs."

"Pity. If you found the murder weapon... well, you'd have half a chance. The gals in the labs have made quite remarkable progress in evidence recovery."

Fenella gave a sad smile. "And I thought you were an old-school luddite."

"Only to my boss. All that blasted form-filling drives me crazy."

"Got anything else for me?"

"Whoever did this to Miss Brian didn't know their own strength. They must have carried a giant club." Dr Mackay stretched his arms wide to illustrate. "A great big bloody-mindless Neanderthal, swinging a great big bloody club."

Chapter Twenty-Seven

F ENELLA STOOD BY HER car and thought about her next step. She had just left the morgue and now had a clear picture of how Maureen Brian died. The murder weapon might be a log from the bonfire or a chunk of driftwood. Either way, it was a club-like weapon an apeman might swing. She climbed into her Morris Minor and sat in silence. Her eyes watched the low clouds, mind elsewhere.

It was the phone that broke her quiet focus. Stunned by its intense din, Fenella stared at it in a dreamlike state. For several moments it rang. The superintendent's tone. What did the boss want? Then she thought about the *Pig Snout* and the search warrant and scooped the phone into her hand and pressed it tight to her ear.

"This business about Councillor Malton," Jeffery began, "comes at a tough time."

There was a long pause as if she were waiting for agreement. But the sight in the morgue had chilled Fenella to her core. She wasn't in the mood for games.

"I've never known murder to come at any other time, ma'am. We need to get on that boat and look around."

"It's a hot mess, Sallow. I'm under pressure from all sides. Headquarters in Carlisle want a daily update on the case. Progress, stats, status."

"Okay," Fenella said. She thumbed the phone to turn down the volume. "I will keep you informed. And the search warrant, ma'am?"

Jeffery said, "If we don't get a quick result, this will look bad. Might dent our careers beyond repair. I'm not sure it is worth the risk."

The line went quiet.

This was it. This was what the phone call was about: ambition, numbers, and her boss's climb up the ladder. The hush was total. Fenella thumbed her phone to turn up the volume.

"Are you there, ma'am?"

No response.

But she heard a soft breath. It was as if Jeffery had begun some massive calculation. Fenella waited. She was good at the wait.

At last, Jeffery said, "Are you one hundred percent certain the missing art photos are on Councillor Malton's boat?" Jeffery's waspish voice creaked with a strange hiss. "One hundred percent, Sallow?"

There was no way Fenella could answer that question and Jeffery knew that. Fenella said, "We believe Miss Brian used the *Pig Snout* as her art studio. There is reason to believe she also stored her finished works on the vessel."

"Reason to believe, Sallow? We'll need a good sight more than that if I'm going to poke the hornets' nest."

Fenella felt tension in her shoulders. She tilted her neck from side to side. It didn't help.

"Ma'am, the missing items are of considerable value and may prove the motive for Miss Brian's death. We need to search the boat to find them."

"Is Councillor Malton a suspect?"

"We can't rule anyone out at this stage. Once we look around the boat, we will have a clearer idea."

"Rather a sticky wicket here." The superintendent's voice grew in volume, until by the end, she was shouting. "Sallow, you've bowled me a bloody googly."

Fenella enjoyed ladies' cricket, preferably from the clubhouse with a glass of red wine and a slice of cheese with a dash of brown pickle on the side. She'd cheer with the crowd at a six or a four or a well-taken wicket. But it was the batswoman's duty to deal with the ball as bowled. It was Jeffery's duty to get the search warrant.

"Sorry, ma'am. But you understand we need to access the boat."

"Well, of course." The line went quiet for so long Fenella thought the superintendent had hung up. But Jeffery's voice came back, soft, like buzzing bees. "I'll need time to work through this. I can't give you an answer today. Oh, and send Dexter in to see me, will you?"

The phone went dead.

Fenella started the engine and weighed her options. It was useless to dwell on the search warrant. The weather forecast said there'd be clear skies, a warmer day. Already a watery sun had begun to show through the sullen clouds. She might stop by the Grain Bowl Café, grab a cortado and butter croissant, and sit outside to think things over.

Then she thought about Maureen Brian's apartment and her heart did that little flipping thing. She'd forgotten to ask Dexter to take a second look. She could do that herself. And anyway, her team were at full stretch. It wouldn't hurt to get a bit more fresh air.

Chapter Twenty-Eight

T HE WEATHER FORECAST WAS wrong. Rain fell in great grey sheets which smashed hard against the Morris Minor's windows. Cumbria weather, ever changeable. The urgent beat from the heavens was like a hard fist pounding a door at night to warn of danger ahead. It poured down for the entire drive to Seafields Bed and Breakfast.

Safiya Griffin greeted Fenella at the door.

"Help yourself, Detective Sallow," she said. "I'll be in my room. Give me a shout if you need anything."

"And Mr Griffin?"

"Ben's out shopping, so you are on your own, I'm afraid." She waved Fenella up to the dormer with a weary nod of the head.

Fenella entered Maureen's room and looked around. A faint smell of vanilla-scented potpourri hung in the still air. Same rectangular space partitioned into two rooms. A living room with a small kitchen in the alcove where the roof slanted down. She did a slow 360-degree turn looking for change, but nothing. She walked to the Ace radio and again looked around. No markings on the walls.

She padded across the rug, stopped, stepped off the autumnal swirls and stooped to lift the edge.

Nothing.

She went to the bookcase, pulled out books at random and flicked through the pages. Then she ran a hand over the wooden backing of the bookcase. Next, she went to the cherrywood table and stared at the loose pile of magazines. Again, she flicked through the pages. She stared at the balls of yarn, pink and blue, but did not pick them up. Then looked back towards the door. She hurried over to close it and examined the wall either side. No sign of a hook or nail or faint outline where a frame once hung. No sign of the missing photos.

In the bedroom, the same unslept-in bed, same lavender bedspread, same pillow. Underneath, the same lemon nightdress next to the same empty hot water bottle. On the wall above the bed, the same crucifix. She touched the crucifix, weighed it in her hands. Same for the swing-arm brass lamp. For a while she stared at the open magazine. Then she read the article about prehistoric cave paintings. It contained nothing useful, so she searched the bedside cabinet.

Nothing.

Fenella walked to the window and stared out. Beyond the garden fence, a bleak beach with a bland sky. There was only one person on the sands; a jogger in green shorts with a mop of bleached white hair. He moved with slow precision through the sheets of slanting rain. She turned away and thought about Maureen Brian in the morgue and felt sick in her stomach. She riffled through the built-in wardrobe with an urgent sense she could not explain. Skirts, dresses, blouses, headscarves. Shoes at the bottom, some boxed. Boxes in neat rows. Just like last time. What had she missed?

She went to the photographic landscape hung near the small rectangular window. Definitely the lighthouse but viewed through a distorted lens. She eased it off the wall, half hoping to find the outline for four smaller images once hung beneath.

It was a long shot.

It missed.

In the reluctant November light that filtered through the window, she studied the small bed. She bent over, looked under the mattress.

Then knelt to stretch her arm deep under the slats, feeling about the bare floorboards. When she'd finished, she stood by the window, thinking.

After a while, she once again looked about the tiny bedroom and tried to think of something else but could not. A feeling she dreaded clawed at her gut. A numbness of dull despair that she was chasing a stick in a stream. Always one step ahead. Always just out of reach.

Chapter Twenty-Nine

E ARP FOUND HIMSELF ON yet another doorstep. The sixth
this morning. This time at the frosted glass door of a
semidetached house in a quiet cul-de-sac. The cars parked in the
driveways of these homes suggested business executive. A vague
hunger gnawed in the pit of his stomach, with the knowledge of only
a half flask of coffee in the car.

The weather had turned against the meteorologist's hopeful
predictions. Rain fell hard. With his umbrella raised, and in a foul
mood, he wondered how they could get it so wrong and still have a
job. At least it was Friday. He cursed as he rang the doorbell.

The melodic chimes faded away. A woman with the face of a
fashion model answered. She wore a cotton dress the colour of
avocado with masses of wavy brown hair. Under the dim light, Earp
took her for a teenager or young twenties at most.

"Can I speak with Mrs Collins?" He peered hard, uncertain and
flashed his warrant card. "Your mum?"

"That's me," Elizabeth replied with a broad smile.

Takes good care of herself, Earp thought and repeated her name
just to make sure.

"Come in out of the rain, Detective." Her words fizzed and
effervesced as if they were old friends. "We can't have an officer of
the law dripping wet."

He caught a better look as she turned into the hallway. Forty at least, maybe more. Pretty though.

The hallway smelled of floral scents. Two dark amber pots held golden chrysanthemums. There was cherrywood furniture and cream-coloured walls with polished waxed floorboards. A long narrow Persian rug ran the length of the hall. Elizabeth took his mackintosh coat and hung it on a coatrack next to children's hats and gloves and a pink jacket. She put the umbrella in a cherrywood umbrella stand. Affixed to the bottom, Earp noticed a brass oval drip pan polished so hard it shone like a bedroom mirror.

Elizabeth turned to Earp. "Let's talk in the kitchen, warmer in there. I'll put on the kettle for coffee, or would you prefer tea?"

No surprise at the visit, or resentment or angst, just a friendly welcome. Earp's mood improved.

"Tea would be nice."

"And a slice of cake?"

"I wouldn't say no."

In the kitchen, the floral scent from the hallway mingled with the faint trace of curry. It was a broad room with a chef sink and wide windows. They looked out onto a green lawn with a swing set and sand pit and a box filled with toys. At the end, almost hidden by the slanting rain, lay rose beds and a freshly dug vegetable patch next to a garden shed. On the fridge and the walls were pictures drawn by children. Stick people. Stick dogs. Stick trees and boxy buildings with slanted doors, all in garish colours. They reminded Earp of the oil paintings he, Sue, and Nick had seen on a trip to the Lowry museum in Salford.

The rain was slanting hard against the kitchen window. Earp watched it for a few moments. Then he gazed at the chef sink. There was a large cutting board, knife holders, drainboards, drying mats and sponge holders. His wife, Sue, was more of a packet-mash-and-frozen-veg cook. He couldn't imagine her peeling and chopping and scraping. Not when she could whip something out of the freezer and put it in the microwave. Still, it would be nice to eat something fancy every once in a while. Not curry or Chinese or frozen lamb cutlets dashed under the grill. His stomach rumbled.

"Please take a seat, Detective Earp." Elizabeth pointed to the pine kitchen table. It was broad, like the benches Earp remembered from a pub he and Sue visited in the village of Crossthwaite. "I'll get the kettle on."

After two cups of tea and a slice of Battenberg cake, Earp pulled out his notebook. He read for a moment, then gazed at the children's paintings.

"Kids in school?"

"Thank goodness, a few hours peace when the army are gone."

Earp hesitated for a moment, unsure of what she meant.

"Army?"

"Oh, I thought the police knew everything. I'm a foster parent. I've got five under twelve."

Earp glanced around the orderly kitchen and tidy yard. Nothing like the mess and chaos at his place, and he and Sue only had one.

"Five! My God, how do you keep the place so"—he struggled to find the right word, thought about the brass oval drip pan polished to a mirror-like shine—"pristine."

"I've a teenager too; she helps."

"But still."

"I'm organised, Detective Earp. It's the only way to keep the ship moving, and the kids know the rules and generally stick to them." She wagged a finger, grinning. "Tidy away your toys. Finish your meal else no pudding. No shouting. No biting. Start your homework. Turn that light out, it's bedtime. You know the drill."

"Aye." But he thought there had to be more to it than that.

"Anyway, I give the place a quick tidy while the nippers are at school—Saint Giles Elementary. They finish at three thirty; that's when the chaos begins." She laughed. "Madness, pure and simple lunacy when they return."

Earp realised she loved children, loved having them about, loved the chaos and the mess and bringing order out of everything. He adored Nick and so did Sue, but he felt resentful at this superwoman who made it all seem easy.

Elizabeth was talking. "And Belinda, my teen, is volunteering this morning at the Quarterdrigg Activity Centre."

Not just a whizz with little kids, then. She can work her magic with teenagers. He let out a low whistle. "The Quarterdrigg, eh?"

"Twice a week and she loves it, likes to help. Later she's picking up the afternoon shift at Logan's Bakery. When she gets back home, she'll help me with the kids."

Earp pondered for a moment. "I'm thinking of signing my boy, Nick, up for their after-school club."

She raised an eyebrow. "At the Quarterdrigg?"

"Aye."

"Mental health challenges?"

"No."

"Physical, then?"

"A bit."

Elizabeth stared at him over her cup. "Well, he'll love it. I volunteer one weekend a month, in the kitchen. Let me know when your son visits, I'll keep an eye on him. It helps them to settle in if they feel someone is looking out for them."

Earp realised he'd drifted off course, didn't care, and took a sip from his tea and another bite of cake. He felt sure they'd find the evidence they needed on the *Pig Snout*. How long would they have to wait for the superintendent's green light? In the meantime, he had to spin his wheels speaking with people who resented his questions. No point rushing away from here.

They fell into silence. A soft drumming rattled the kitchen window. Rain slanted down in white sheets. He wondered how long he could stay before moving on to the next name on his list.

Elizabeth got up, went to the fridge, and came back with a package wrapped in brown paper.

"You may as well take this. Turkey stuffing with cranberry sauce sandwiches, wholemeal bread. There is a homemade vanilla crème brûlée for pudding. I prepared it for Belinda, but she forgot. Late as usual."

Earp thought about the half flask of coffee in the car. It would go down a treat with that. It seemed like he'd stumbled on a pleasant witness at last. Those he'd spoken to earlier crackled and spat at being disturbed. Or were annoyed the police hadn't caught the killer.

"Just a few questions," he began, on guard for a change of Elizabeth's generous mood. He placed a protective hand on the brown package just in case. "I believe you were friends with Maureen Brian?"

"Best friends." Elizabeth's voice wavered. "Along with Audrey Robin. Gloria Embleton was close too. Maureen had so many good friends and we are at a loss to understand. Why did it happen?"

In his early years on the force, he'd pursued the same question. The quest powered the long days and longer nights. It kept him going despite dead ends and stony silences. With careful diligence, he sought to dig up and expose the root cause. Over unrelenting years, he'd moved from sympathy to empathy to nothing at all. He'd lost any interest in who did what to whom or why. His job was to ask tough questions, make people sweat, cry, pee their pants so the perp would be put away. That was how he saw his role as a detective, and he detested himself for it. But today, in the bright kitchen with his belly filling with hot tea and warm Battenburg, and the stick-figure children's drawings and the prospect of a gourmet-packed lunch, he glimpsed something he'd lost.

"Is Mr Collins about? Your husband might want to sit with you through the questions."

"George was quite a bit older than me, went suddenly—heart attack, fifteen years ago."

"Widowed, then?"

"My husband was a banker, and I worked for a staffing agency as a bookkeeper. They assigned me to his branch when his regular clerk was out on maternity leave. We fell in love." Elizabeth went silent, looking off at the drawings on the fridge. "George left me well endowed. I want to give back. I live for the children and my volunteer activities. And now he is gone, I'm on my own and will always be so."

If he hadn't already done so, Earp would have blown another low whistle. A woman with her looks could definitely attract another bloke with a fat wallet. Why would she willingly accept growing into an old grey spinster? He wanted to pry further, out of curiosity, but it wasn't germane to the investigation.

The melodic chimes of the doorbell rang.

"Please excuse me, Detective Earp."

He watched her leave the kitchen and shook his head slowly. Then grabbed another slice of cake and topped up his tea. But he couldn't restrain his inner detective and crept to the kitchen door, eased it open, and listened.

Elizabeth muttered a greeting followed by a woman's voice. It travelled along the hallway but was too mumbled for him to make out the words. He recognised the tone—worry.

Footsteps.

He closed the door and darted back to his chair, picked up the cup, and was about to take a sip when Elizabeth hustled into the kitchen. At her side stood a boy, six or seven. If she was flustered, it didn't show in her voice, only perhaps her movements which were quickened.

"They sent Timmy home from school. He's got a temperature." Elizabeth stooped down to place the back of her hand on his forehead.

Timmy said, "Feel poorly, Ma."

"I'm right here." She gave him a hug. "We'll get you up to bed with a hot drink and two paracetamols."

For several minutes Elizabeth fussed around the kitchen preparing a hot drink for the boy. She moved with swift efficiency, then disappeared with the youngster in tow. She was gone for so long, Earp considered leaving and coming back Monday, around lunchtime. But she hurried back into the room, all apologies as he took another chunk of cake. He said he fully understood and pulled out his notebook.

Earp said, "Are you a regular walker on the beach?"

"Most days. I go on my own, meet up with Noel O'Sullivan or Audrey Robin, and we wander to the pier and back to where they built the bonfire."

Earp recognised the names and made a note. "When did you last see Maureen?"

"The day before Bonfire Night. I'd hoped to see her on the beach, but this year there were just too many people. The event seems to get bigger every year. Anyway, I didn't meet up with her, but kept an eye out."

"Did you notice anyone unusual on the beach?"

"Unusual?"

"A drunk or an argument amongst a group of people, or maybe a stranger?"

"Well, I didn't know all the faces; we are a growing town."

"Anyone acting strange?"

"No."

Earp leaned back, tapped his pen on the notebook. The Battenburg had blunted his hunger and the warmth raised the damp from his trousers. Still, he was in no rush to get back to the rain and the door-knocking and the scowling faces. He put his pen down and changed the subject in the hopes of another five minutes in the pleasant kitchen.

"And what did you do Bonfire Night?"

"The usual."

"Which is?"

"Well, now let me see. Where would you like me to begin?"

"Anywhere you choose."

"Before the fireworks, I gathered the kids around the bonfire. Easier to keep an eye on them on the beach, and they can run wild. We watched the fireworks display in the same place." She picked up her cup, took a long sip as if thinking. "Audrey showed up after the fireworks display and we chatted about this and that. Then we went searching for Maureen while Belinda watched the kids."

Earp picked up his pen.

"What time would that have been?"

"Maybe thirty minutes after the fireworks ended." She closed her eyes for a moment. "Audrey worries about little things. That night she seemed concerned."

"Over what?"

"I've no idea. I suggested we track down Maureen so the three of us could have a natter about it. I suppose we'd have talked if we'd found Maureen; she had a knack for listening and giving good advice, but we didn't find her."

She stopped speaking.

Earp glanced out the window. The rain continued to pour. *Another ten minutes here, then I'll have a quick nap in the car.*

Earp said, "Anything else?"

"Not really."

"And what time did you get home?"

She shrugged. "Probably a little after eleven. The kids were in bed and the house quiet by midnight."

He wondered what else to ask, glanced at the pelting rain, and came up with a new line of questions.

"Where did you search for Maureen?"

Elizabeth rested her head in her hands. "We walked along the beach in the opposite direction from the pier. It was dark and quiet until we came across Noel O'Sullivan. He's a pastor. Around him were a group of people, teenagers mostly, and they sang. It was so"— she struggled to find the right word—"stirring."

Earp kept quiet, but nodded as if he understood.

Elizabeth's face bubbled with girlish excitement. "Audrey and I joined for a while." Her eyes closed. She swayed from side to side as if back on the beach in the dark with Noel O'Sullivan strumming his guitar to the pulsing beat of the surf and harmonious hum of the crowd. "We wandered off before the preaching began and..." She stopped suddenly, sat upright and stared at Earp, eyes wary.

"Go on, Mrs Collins. You were about to say something."

"Later we met Martin Findlay." She spoke slowly as if measuring out each word. "He is such a good man, a little simple, but kind-hearted..." Again, she stopped.

Earp wasn't sure why her voice trailed off. He thought about it for a moment. The rain continued to fall.

"Mrs Collins," he began with an air of authority, "we are having a chat to put us in the picture about Maureen, and that includes all her friends. Tell me about Martin Findlay."

She slowly nodded. "Martin on his own in the dark sat by a saltwater pool, all hunched up. When I asked him what was the matter, he didn't reply, just kept throwing rocks into the pool. Over and over."

Earp leaned back. He felt weary to the bone and wanted the weekend to begin. *So, Martin threw rocks into pools on the beach; who didn't?* He often did that himself. The ripple would spread out slowly and he'd watch until it vanished. He'd even shown Nick how to throw flat pebbles so they bounced like fleas across the surface. *Another minute or two and I'll be on my way.*

Earp said, "Martin was having a bit of fun, was he?"

Elizabeth didn't reply. The only sound came from the electric hum of the fridge and pitter of rain on the windows. At last, she looked at Earp with sad eyes.

"Martin was so very angry. He threw the rocks with such savage force that it quite frightened Audrey and I."

Chapter Thirty

A UDREY TOOK OFF HER glasses, wiped them with a tissue, and continued to stare. Detective Sergeant Robert Dexter sat at her kitchen table sipping a cup of her tea and eating a slice of her Victoria sponge cake. She hadn't heard his car come creeping along the lane. Nor the squeak of the iron gate. Or his footsteps on the path. Only the sharp clank of the door knocker which announced his sudden arrival.

"I was lost in *Little Dorrit*, Dickens," Audrey explained. She still felt as if she were in a fictional dream, imagined herself in the satins and lace and silks of Miss Havisham's bridal dress. The image faded and yellowed as she came back to the present. "Such a good read, like being with an old friend. I barely heard the door. Were you knocking long?"

"We get used to waiting." The detective gave a wide pleasant smile. "Part of the policeman's lot. Waiting."

"I'm so sorry, and with all this rain."

"Little secret, Mrs Robin." He flashed his friendly smile. "I saw your car and knew you were at home. We're full of tricks, us detectives."

Audrey wondered what else he held up his sleeve. She thought he'd keep his best concealed and, like a street magician, bring them out with sleight of hand one by one to bamboozle her. One thing she knew: there'd be more tricks. Her librarian mind liked things orderly, catalogued and shelved in the right place. How could you do that if you didn't know exactly what the police had up their sleeve?

He continued to chew. He took a long slurp from the cup, glanced about the kitchen, and returned to the crumbs on his plate, shaking them into his hand.

It pleased Audrey that the police were always ready for another slice of her Victoria sponge, washed down by a refill of tea or coffee. It was one of her secret ways of keeping an eye on the investigation, made her feel useful. She picked up the plate and went to the kitchen counter and sliced a thick wedge, returning to the table with it in both hands as if carrying precious stones. Then she heard a soft scurrying sound. Whispers. Patrick's voice, and she wasn't taken in by the detective's charm or the pleasant words or the way he smiled at her. Patrick smiled like that.

His first slap surprised her.

They were together on the sofa with soft jazz drifting from the radio. A Saturday evening. They'd made love, then argued over Patrick's late nights at the office. He flicked the back of his hand hard against the flat of her nose as if swatting a bluebottle fly. A sudden wicked smack. She placed a hand to her nose. There was a small dark drop of blood where his wedding ring cut her nostril. He struck her again. It stung less than his vile words—"Mummy was right. You tricked me into marriage. Cheated me of a child, but now the scales have fallen from my eyes. You are nothing more than a working-class shark."

He wanted a divorce.

The following day, she'd visited Patrick's mother whose broad smile betrayed sentiments other than sympathy. When Audrey went to the police, the officer smiled too.

The physical blows and verbal abuse continued until, locked in the dark of the wine cellar of their three-storey townhouse, Audrey agreed to Patrick's mother's terms for the divorce.

A small cash settlement.

Nothing else.

Audrey didn't have the emotional strength to fight. Suddenly she remembered the day of the divorce. Goose bumps prickled her skin. A blue sky with fluffy white clouds like soft faces, and the air filled with the blossoms of May. Patrick smiled at her after the court hearing; so did his wife-to-be, the ex-mother-in-law, and even the magistrate. And for a terrifying instant, Audrey saw the ratty terrier from the car park on the beach sitting at her kitchen table next to the detective, and it was smiling too. She stifled a gasp, turned it into a cough, but the detective didn't appear to notice. He was still talking.

"Very tasty bit of sponge cake. Not like the processed stuff in the supermarkets. Mouth-watering, Mrs Robin. Delicious."

Audrey waved her hand to show she didn't take the compliment seriously but decided to bake another cake in case he came back. But her thoughts lingered on Patrick and his new wife living in her townhouse in Bristol with their happy kids. At least she had gotten away with the cash. More than even Patrick realised. The fool hadn't changed his account passwords. It was payment for her time in that dark cellar with its stink of antiseptic and white walls.

She stood, walked to the sideboard and picked out a small bottle from amongst the trinkets, framed photograph, pebbles, seashells and other little mementos of her trips to the beach. She twisted the top and sniffed.

"Smelling salts. Hyssop. My mind's been so bunged up since... well, it clears my head a little."

"What a terrible experience." He slowly shook his head. Audrey thought he was building up to ask a question. "I can see you are still in shock."

"A little."

"Did the paramedics take you to your doctor?"

Audrey sensed genuine concern in his voice, but something else hovered behind his question. "They brought me straight home."

"Nothing prescribed to help you sleep, then?"

"No."

He tutted as if the National Health Service's failure to provide tranquillizers was a shameful disgrace. "I wonder if you have any booze in the house, rum, whisky? A shot or two will ease your nerves."

"Oh, I don't know."

"I'll join you if it helps."

Audrey thought police officers weren't allowed to drink on duty, but went to the kitchen cupboard and came back with two shot glasses and a bottle of supermarket brandy. The detective watched as she poured.

"Don't spare the horses, Mrs Robin."

Audrey filled his glass to the brim and shook out a shot into her own.

"You have news of Maureen?"

He shook his head. "Just a passing visit. The investigation is ongoing, but we have arrested no one in connection with her death. I'm sorry I don't have better news." He took a sip from his glass. "It's like following a trail of breadcrumbs. You do not know where they will lead."

The detective seemed to be in no hurry to pepper her with dangerous questions. A tinge of relief bubbled in Audrey's stomach. "I suppose most of the time the breadcrumbs lead you in circles."

He laughed. "We'd like to expand the circle, make it into a net so we can reel in the person who did this to your friend. That's why I'm here."

"But Detective Sallow has already asked a lot of questions. You were there in the ambulance, weren't you? I told her everything. Then she came here and was very thorough and wrote it all down." Audrey knew she spoke too quickly, so she added, "Live more and worry less, that's what Maureen always said."

"Think I'll steal that one, if you don't mind." The detective drained his glass.

"Another?"

"Oh, go on, then."

Audrey topped up his glass. Her own drink remained untouched.

He swirled the drink and took a chug. "Listen, I'm not here to fire off a bunch of questions, but to ask a favour."

Audrey squinted at the detective as if peering at an unfamiliar shape through fog. The police wanted her to do them a favour? Astonished, she leaned forward, poised.

"I'll do anything I can to help with your investigation. Another drink?"

"If you don't mind."

After she poured, the detective took a quick sip and said, "The Guvnor asked me to stop by with a request." His head turned towards the sideboard. "I wonder if we might borrow that photo of Maureen?"

"My picture?" She stared at him in confusion. "I'm sorry, I don't know."

The image captured so many memories that Audrey was reluctant to share. She wanted him to understand. To feel what she felt when she looked at the photograph in the mornings over her breakfast or late in the evening over a mug of milky tea—a kind of confidence that anything was possible.

Audrey said, "When I remember back to that day that photo was taken, I see golden-yellow sands under a sky dotted with thumb-sized clouds. The air smelled salty, sweet, mingled with seaweed, and crisp and damp at the same time, like you get after a bitter storm." She looked the detective directly in the eyes. "We were lounging about with a gang of kids, Maureen, Elizabeth, and I. Elizabeth's foster kids. Playing stick cricket, hide-and-seek, and kicking around a ball. I still recall their names, although some have moved on to new homes." Audrey picked up the photograph. "It had been a rough few years for me, and this picture, more than anything, captures what the three of us had together. Maureen called it our armature. I called it friendship."

The words which had come so fast and furious from deep down in her gut suddenly dried up. Audrey felt a wave of embarrassment and glanced down at her hands which cradled the frame like a newborn baby.

"We won't keep it for long," he muttered. "We'll make a copy and return it as quick as we can."

The quiet reasonableness of his request made Audrey shudder. She couldn't win. No point putting up a fight. They'll get what they want in the end, just like Patrick. If she resisted further, the detective might probe, ask uncomfortable questions, uncover the plan.

"Promise you won't lose it."

"I'll bring it back personally."

"Oh, very well, Detective Dexter, but I'll hold you responsible for its safe return."

He was on his feet with the framed photograph in his hand. He stared at it for some moments. A sudden burst of thunder clapped overhead. The room darkened. After several moments, Audrey flipped on the overhead fluorescent lights. They flickered and brightened and illuminated the kitchen with stark white light. The detective didn't move, his eyes cast down on the photograph. Something about his stillness as he examined the image reminded Audrey of a tiger before it pounced. Now she felt like a goat tethered to a stake by hunters, tempting the savage beast to come close. She shook the image out of her head, replaced it with the picture of her in the satins and lace and silks of Miss Havisham's bridal dress.

"Detective Dexter, I'll see you to the door."

He didn't move.

"The door, Detective Dexter, I'm sure you have other people to see."

He put the photo into his jacket pocket and looked up with eyes blazing.

"Perhaps you would like another drink, Detective Dexter?"

"No thank you." The intensity of his gaze frightened Audrey.

"Are you sure, it is no trouble."

"Who else was on the beach when you discovered Miss Brian's body?"

"It was just a normal morning stroll. I've made it a hundred times before. I saw nothing unusual. Nothing at all." She moved towards the kitchen door.

The detective said, "Humour me, Mrs Robin."

"But I've already given the details to Detective Sallow."

"Tell me. Describe what happened. Close your eyes if you have to, but tell me who you saw."

"I didn't see anything."

"Please. Close your eyes and focus."

Audrey sighed, folded her arms, and closed her eyes. "When I started out, it was dark. It always is at this time of the year. I walked the beach with a black bin bag in my hand scanning for rubbish left over from the Bonfire Night activities. No tourists at this time of year and it was way too early for school kids or the office workers who like to stroll along the boardwalk."

"So, no school children?"

"No."

"Or clerical workers?"

"I've just said so."

She wanted to open her eyes and see him to the door, but felt it best to play his little game. It was like the game she played with Patrick after he locked her in the wine cellar.

"Now, Mrs Robin, you have told me what you didn't see. Please concentrate and tell me what you did see."

"Is this really necessary?"

"Concentrate."

She didn't want to play anymore, but said, "When it began to get light, there were only a handful of people about."

"How many?"

"I don't know."

"Think."

Audrey's hand drifted to her chin. "A mother played with a toddler at the water's edge, and a tall figure in a mud-brown trench coat"— her eyes snapped open but the words tumbled out before she could stop them"—hurried away from the bonfire."

His pen and notebook were already in his hand.

"Who?" The single word came out like a boxer's left jab. He followed it with a right hook. "Mrs Robin, did you recognise the person?"

"No," Audrey said, even though she did.

Chapter Thirty-One

F ENELLA PULLED HER CAR to a stop. She was on a pot-holed lane on the edge of town. The rain continued to fall, fast and hard. It had been two years since she had last travelled this way. She'd had her reasons then too. It was a Friday afternoon in summer and the hedgerows were heavy with foliage. Yellowhammers perched on top of hawthorn bushes. They sang their "a little bit of bread and no cheese" ballad. On a slope shaded by broadleaved sycamore, she'd watched a badger sett. Later, she'd walked to Detective Inspector Jack Croll's cabin.

Now, as the wipers worked hard, she peered along the barren lane. She was looking for the dirt track that snaked to Croll's home. After her futile search of Maureen Brian's apartment, she didn't want to return to the office. She wanted to do something. Not stare at the bleak walls and wait for news from her team. Of course, there was the administration she always left for Friday, but it could wait until next week. As soon as she filled it all in, more forms arrived. It was a never-ending paper chain of forms and reports and procedures. All had to be read, memorised and implemented. And she'd promised herself a visit to her old mentor. A break from the case, she thought, with someone who understood. Later, she would look back on their meeting as the lull before the storm.

The retired detective's house was a single-storey shack with a thick iron roof rusted to russet. He came onto the porch and watched. Fenella eased her Morris Minor to a stop in the muddy front yard. He'd grown a beard, bleach white, and leaned on a chestnut staff held firm in his right hand. If he'd worn a cloak rather than blue jeans and a tee-shirt, he'd have made a passable Fagan from Dickens's novel *Oliver Twist*. But he could have dressed in high heels and a tartan kilt for all Fenella cared.

Jack Croll saved her career.

Fenella climbed out of the Morris Minor and walked to the porch wondering why she'd left it so long.

"Hello, Jack."

"I knew you'd come today," Croll said, flashing a crooked grin. "A little bird tells me there has been a spot of bother."

Chapter Thirty-Two

T HE FRONT DOOR LED straight into the living room. Fenella stomped her shoes on the welcome mat, feeling the warmth as the rain pattered on the windows. She inhaled the smell of floor wax, beer, and embers.

Nothing's changed.

An old but respectable Axminster rug patterned with faded blue-and-beige floral medallions covered much of the living room floor. Fenella slipped off her shoes and headed for the wingback armchairs which stood side by side in front of the wood-burning stove. She settled into the soft cushions. Croll looked at her as if about to speak, changed his mind, and left the room.

Fenella stared into the flickering flames, remembering. It was two years since she sat in this room and, within two minutes, she was back in the memories of the crimes they'd solved around this stove. Croll shuttered his team in his cabin when they worked a tough case. They'd eat pizza, drink craft beer while each person put forward their theory. Everyone's idea, whatever the rank, taken by Croll with professional interest. Then they argued good-naturedly until the truth emerged. They worked the Mr Shred case from this room. Tracked down Hamilton Perkins and put him away.

Fenella realised once again what a remarkably good detective Jack Croll was and wished she was back working a case with him.

It was always very quiet in Croll's cabin. She turned in her chair and folded her knees to one side to get more comfortable. The only sound was the patter of rain as it hit the windows with such a constant beat that you almost had to listen for it. She thought about what might have been if he'd found the right woman. There'd been girlfriends, too many to recall. She sunk deeper into the chair trying to remember their names. Janet with her dark eyes and brown skin stood out from the rest. Gentle, kind, caring Janet. She'd stayed the longest. Years. But like the rest, moved on when she realised there was nothing outside the police in Jack Croll's life. It took you over like that if you let it. The work so intense, so overwhelming, the desire to catch the perp so deep that it left a toughened outside but hollowed-out the core. Now Croll's era had passed, but she couldn't get used to her boss as a retired bloke.

"Putting a pizza in the oven."

Croll's voice came from beyond the door that led to the kitchen.

Fenella turned from the fire to glance around the sparse room. A fold-down table with two stools sat by the window. No television. In its place, a mahogany Davenport desk with the hinged desktop down and a laptop resting next to a pile of handwritten notes. A handcrafted bookshelf with perhaps a hundred books. She thought of Maureen Brian's apartment. Neat and tidy and organised and clean. In his cabin, too, Jack Croll kept things simple.

Croll returned with two half-pint tankards and four bottles of ale on a tray that folded out into a table.

"Loweswater Gold. From Hawkshead village."

Fenella poured half a glass of the amber liquid and sipped.

"Delicious, almost tropical in flavour."

She poured the rest into the tankard, kept it in her hand.

They didn't speak again until after Croll stoked up the fire so it cracked and spat above the patter of the rain.

Croll said, "Five years."

"Already?"

"Feels like ten. Don't retire early, it's a bloody lifetime." He took a gulp from his tankard. "And you? Tough times I hear. With the police cuts and the body on the beach."

Fenella sighed. For a long moment she gazed intently at the bare panelled walls, skimmed with a coat of dark varnish. No gilt-framed certificates or pictures of Jack Croll shaking hands with bigwigs. Just an enlarged photograph of the Port Saint Giles beach and pier and lighthouse. But he'd made more impact than a dozen gilt-framed certificates in his time. Much more than a ripple. He'd told her to master the switch, not to be on all the time like him. She'd listened and applied his suggestions. Jack Croll saved more than her career, and for that, Fenella remained forever thankful.

"The investigation into Miss Maureen Brian's death is bogged down," she said. "But we are working several lines of inquiry. Including her art studio which is moored in the harbour."

"Clear sight on a motive?"

"Not yet."

Fenella felt slightly light-headed, not from the Loweswater Gold, but from thinking about the Maureen Brian case. She couldn't get a good handle on the motive.

She said, "Theft of her photographic art seems the most likely possibility." Yet she still felt wary of that explanation. Once they got access to the *Pig Snout*, they'd have an answer. "And she didn't appear to have any enemies. As far as we can tell, she was one of those women who everyone loved."

They lapsed into silence, gazing at the stove. The flames cast miniature shadows which danced, then vanished moments after they appeared. It was Croll who broke the quiet.

"Not a mugging gone wrong, then?"

"Nothing stolen as far as we can tell. Her handbag and purse were found intact."

"Family, then?"

"None that we can trace."

"Interesting," he said slowly. "I can see why the newspapers are whipping it up as a sort of mystery. An elderly artist who everyone loves and does good deeds is slain on a quaint Cumbrian beach as the fireworks flash."

Fenella unfolded her legs to stretch. Croll continued to speak in his quiet understated voice.

"There are no mysteries in our world. Only crimes of passion or vengeance or greed." He paused. "Whatever the headline spin, integrity beyond doubt. Remember that and you'll be fine."

That was Croll's mantra back in the station when they'd worked together in the pressure cooker of internal politics, public opinion, and political demands. He never used that phrase unless something was wrong.

"Anything I should know?" Fenella asked.

Croll said, "A little bird told me this one is not going down well with police headquarters in Carlisle. Doubt you've got long before they and their political masters jump in to dish out healthy portions of blame." He stopped abruptly, ran a hand over his beard. "There's one other thing…"

"Go on."

"They'll be out for a scalp if this isn't cleared up fast. It won't be Jeffery. The woman is like Teflon. Nothing sticks. Watch the higher-ups and watch your back."

Fenella stared at Croll's face. It held so much of her loyalty that she knew it well. The ever-so-slight twitch in the corner of his right eye and the little pulse beating on the side of his jaw. Suddenly she knew that Croll was working up to something more. She shifted in her chair, eyes fixed like bright beams on his face.

"Jack?"

Croll's gaze drifted back to the flames. He cleared his throat.

"How is Dexter?"

"That's what I came to speak with you about."

"Back on the bottle, isn't he?"

"Seems so."

She didn't ask how he knew. Croll cared about his people; that's what they told her when she joined his team. Five years retired, and he still did. She suspected it was innate in him, like a mother bear protecting its cubs.

Croll said, "How is Priscilla?"

"She left him."

"Really?"

"More than a year ago."

"Shame." Croll shifted in his seat. "And you and Eduardo?"

"He is still drawing superhero cartoons and I'm still chasing down the bad guys."

"And little Winston?"

"He's nine now."

"Time flies."

For the first time since settling into the armchair, Fenella realised Croll appeared exhausted. His eyes swelled as if he lacked sleep, and he'd lost weight. Until the day he had retired, he'd been like a dynamo. Now she wondered if he was sick.

She'd seen it happen before.

Police officers who devoted themselves to their job and nothing else. When their time came to retire, bereft of relationships outside of the uniform, there remained nothing but memories and the prospect of long empty days ahead. Melancholy settled like dust. Disease and sickness soon followed. Had the void of retirement's endless days overwhelmed her mentor?

"And you, Jack?"

Croll's quiet eyes fixed on Fenella. He sipped his drink.

"Tell Dexter to stop by. He owes me a chat."

"Not if you two are going to knock back more than a few bottles of Loweswater Gold." She delivered the line like banter, but if Jack was sick, she wanted to know.

"Oh come on." He grinned, the old Jack back. "It'll give me a chance to evaluate things."

"Really?"

He nodded towards the Davenport desk. "Been doing a spot of research. The section of the mind that detects criminals is also the part that looks inward. Like a mirror. The mirror mind."

Fenella leaned forward, curious. Where was he going? But she didn't interrupt, knew it would be somewhere extraordinary.

"We can deceive the world, but not the mirror mind." Croll took a long gulp from the tankard. "We can train it too. That's what all great detectives do. Makes us curious, active, alert, instinctive, get deep into other people's heads."

"And?" Fenella couldn't help herself.

"Dexter is too good a cop to let drink destroy his mirror mind."

Fenella nodded at the bookshelf. "Read that in one of your books, did you?"

"Aye. Open University course. I'm completing my doctorate in psychology. Long days. I've been burning the midnight oil. Overdoing it, I suppose."

Fenella sipped her ale, thinking. "Not sick, then?"

"Fit as a fiddle."

"Dr Jack Croll, eh?"

"Has a ring to it."

She pointed to the empty mantelpiece and bare wall.

"Oh come off it, Jack. You don't have any of your commendations or medals on display. Why would you suddenly want an academic title?"

"Wanting a thing is reason enough."

"I'm not buying. What is the real reason?"

"To hang above the mantelpiece."

"And mice don't like cheese."

"They don't, actually."

Fenella stared at him, mouth open. He had a way of sucking her into a silly argument. She knew she shouldn't argue the point, but somehow couldn't resist.

"Oh, come on! Everyone knows mice eat cheese. *Tom and Jerry*, anyone?"

"They prefer to nibble on something sweet."

"And cheese."

"Fruits or grains, actually."

"What about cheese?"

"Or if they are half starved, a chunk of stale cheddar."

"Told you."

"Okay, okay, but I said starving."

Fenella grinned. "Now, just what are you up to with this PhD?"

"Nothing."

"And mice don't eat cheese."

He laughed. "You are quite right; I have an ulterior motive." He poured the rest of the ale into his tankard. In the distance they could hear thunder, and after a while lightning lit the sky. The rain continued to lash against the windows. "I've a favour to ask."

"Anything; you know that, Jack."

"I'm planning to come back."

Fenella stared, wide eyed. He'd reached the mandatory retirement age. There was no way back. But she kept her mouth shut and listened.

"The force are looking for retired detectives to work cold cases. The doctorate will help with my application. You'll put in a word to the admissions committee for me, won't you?"

"If they ask about mice and cheese, you are sunk." But Fenella grinned.

The ping of the oven timer sounded from the kitchen.

"A word in your ear," Croll said, getting to his feet. "Keep a close eye on Detective Earp."

"You know him?"

"Solid record but driven. Too much at times. No switch."

"Like you."

"Aye, like me. No way to live though. Kills the body. Almost killed me." Fenella remembered his heart attack. It was a close call. "Earp was demoted to a detective constable. From what I hear, it was his own fault."

Fenella thought about that. "We all make mistakes."

Croll turned, squinted with one eye. "They told you what he did?"

"I didn't ask."

"You should have been a priest, Fenella."

"I've dropped my share of clangers." She put the tankard down. "They didn't stop you taking me on board. You were very tolerant of my foibles."

"Still, it helps to know."

"If it doesn't colour my judgement. But the way Jeffery sneered, I feared it would. So I've given him a chance before I peek into his files."

"Aye, perhaps you are right." He smiled. "Now, before the pizza burns, tell Jeffery she's made a mistake."

"About what?"

"Two things."

Fenella waited.

"First, Hamilton Perkins won't lead her to the body of Colleen Rae."

Fenella picked up her tankard and stared at Croll for a long moment. How the hell did he know about that? She tried to hide the surprise in her voice and said, "You said two things."

"Second," he said with a smug smile, "she'll never get Dexter to retire early."

Chapter Thirty-Three

I T WAS PAST LUNCHTIME when Audrey arrived at Martin Findlay's flat on Fleetwood Lane. She carried a cardboard box of fried chicken and a double portion of chips. The girl in the tatty uniform and baseball cap had offered a plastic bag.

"Two if you like, it will keep it from getting soggy from all this rain. Keep it nice and dry so you can eat it in the car."

Audrey refused. The bag would live in the landfill forever. At least the cardboard box was decomposable. Now she stood with her hood up underneath the dingy porch with its rusted tin roof. But she did not knock. Instead, she waited outside Martin's front door and listened to the splash of the rain.

She felt anxious.

If she were caught, there'd be big trouble. But she had to speak with Martin before the police arrived. She had gone over and over what she would say, but each time the words came out wrong. She felt like a child on stage performing at a school play. All those eyes watching you on stage from the dark. That freaked her out. She turned to stare back into the street to see if anyone watched.

A figure moved through the rain, but she could not make it out. Just a jogger. *Silly buggers run in any weather*. She raised her hood, just to be careful in case anyone was watching. Soft whispers spoke between her ears, a murmuring of voices as though clearing the throat.

"No," she yelled. "I won't listen."

The rain continued to splash. Great sweeping squalls rattled along the rooftops and down the drainpipes. The tenacious drumming echoed on the porch as if hideous voices warning her away. She hesitated, thought about returning home. With a surge of momentary confidence, she tried once more to practise what she would say. She reworked the words so they'd come out just right. But it did not work, so she closed her eyes and thought about the last time she visited Martin's flat.

It had been a while. The last time? With Maureen. The two of them had a late-morning coffee in the Grain Bowl Café to celebrate the sale of another of Maureen's photographic creations. Maureen paid and afterwards ordered a takeaway meal for Martin.

"Something different for him." she had said in her chatty voice. "He eats nothing but fried chicken and chips. Do you mind driving me over? On Fridays, it's mornings only at the Quarterdrigg. He'll be at home by now."

"Ginger-marinated grilled tofu with red peppers is a long way from chicken and chips," Audrey had replied, doubtful whether it was something Martin would eat.

But they'd also stopped by the fried chicken shop. Maureen ordered drumsticks and a double portion of chips.

"For my supper," she had said with a sly grin.

Audrey drove to Martin's flat and waited in the car, while Maureen, talkative as ever, delivered the food. The woman had stayed for ages inside. Talking in her rapid-fire voice no doubt.

Audrey raked her memory for a time when she'd been inside Martin's flat. *Never*, she realised with a start. Every time, she'd sat outside in her car and waited. It served as her own safe space, where she'd hide when the head librarian shouted at her. A peaceful oasis away from the inane literary chatter of workmates. The perfect place for making her plans. That day, as always, it was her chariot for carrying Maureen to her do-goody tasks, and she'd stayed in her car and thought of Patrick.

The daylight steadily dimmed so that it felt almost like dusk. The air turned ice-cold. Would Martin welcome her in, or would she have to stand on the doorstep outside? Again she glanced back towards the street. It wouldn't be wise to be seen out here. But Audrey thought the rain and the cold would keep the nosy neighbours away.

Now her imagination conjured what lay inside Martin's flat. Maureen often visited, and she was so orderly: everything in its own place. Audrey wondered again why she hadn't been inside. Was it that she'd never been invited by Maureen? Yes, that had to be it, and she'd never realised that trick! Now she suspected Maureen ate the tofu while Martin dined on chicken and chips. Had she been nothing more than Maureen's personal driver? She stood very still, engrossed in that thought until damp seeped through her hood and moistened her mousy hair.

This rain made everything miserable. So it was too cold and dark for anyone to be about. Audrey's body began to relax. She and Martin could talk on the doorstep without any fear. That cheered her up a little.

She lowered her hood and let the rain splash over her head. But now she wanted to get inside, her curiosity was so great. She stared at the door and anticipated what awaited her. Neat and tidy with a shoe rack in the hall—even a floral tablecloth thrown over the dining room table—and one of Maureen's photographic pictures hung on the wall? Her heart raced faster. Would Martin know how much it was worth? She didn't think so, and that made her feel better.

When Maureen first shared her art, Audrey thought they were just blurry photos. But she'd soon found out what people paid, and it made her head hurt. Now nothing would stop her from having a nosy around Martin's flat. *Who knows what treasures I'll find? Once Martin gets a whiff of the fried chicken and chips, he'll hurry me inside*. She hummed, quietly, in syncopation with the tap of the rain —tat-de-da-da-de-de-dah.

She stopped her merry hum and was about to knock when she sensed the presence of a heartbeat before she heard the noise—a scraping shuffle above the drum of the rain. At first, she thought it was her mind playing tricks and that ratty terrier would come into view, mouth open, baring the small sharp teeth of a rabid fox. Her heart froze in fear as she braced herself for Patrick's whispered words.

"He's not back long, pet. Got his lunch I see."

Audrey spun around. A skeletal woman peered at her through sharp eyes. She wore a yellow plastic mackintosh with the hood up and held a floral umbrella opened wide above her head.

The woman said, "He's inside now. I saw them drop him off. They came in the big white van with the yellow stripe along the side and the funny poster of that American bloke eating a hot dog stuck on the back doors. You know him, don't you? Pastor at that church that gathers on the beach when the weather's good. Funny folks if you ask me. Guitars and singing are not what church is supposed to be about. In my day it was hard wooden pews with wild-eyed preachers screaming fire and brimstone. And to see him on the beach strumming and grinning with all those young women google eyed. It ain't proper. No wonder crime's gone barmy. Flogging's too good for the buggers. Anyway, they always bring Martin back at the same time on Friday. Are you from social services?"

Audrey fingered back a tuft of her mousey hair. It stood up in damp punk-rock spikes. She muttered a non-committal answer.

The woman said, "Me hearing's not what it was?"

"Social services," Audrey shouted.

That seemed to satisfy the woman. She shuffled away, inspected a row of dustbins, only turning back when she was at her porch door. She watched Audrey and gave a little wave.

A sudden squall blew in from the Solway Firth. The rain fell like a great white curtain for half a minute, then eased to a soft cold drizzle. The skeletal woman in the yellow plastic mac was still there, watching.

Eyes like a bloody hawk, Audrey thought.

The fried chicken carton's warmth leached into her hand. Suddenly the greasy aroma unsettled her stomach so that she lurched forward and thumped the door knocker.

For an instant after the door opened, Audrey stared with confusion at the woman who smiled back.

Chapter Thirty-Four

"IT'S AN ADMIRER," ELIZABETH shouted into the flat. "Come inside, luv, and get yourself dry." She glanced at the soggy fried-chicken box. "Oh, you've brought lunch for Martin? Well, I made him a curried chicken and mango salad. I suppose he can eat yours for his supper."

Audrey shuffled along a musty hall into a dim space. It was a fusty room, split in two sections by a Formica breakfast bar. The walls were papered with a foliage pattern full of browns and khaki-coloured swirls. A dingy pair of yellowed net curtains dimmed the room to dusk. Peeled paint curled on the windowsill. An oversized television was perched on an orange plastic table. It was tuned to cartoons with the volume turned down. The flickering lights illuminated the grim room like New Year's Day fireworks.

Everywhere were dirty clothes, overturned fast-food cartons, and empty crushed cans of soda. Martin Findlay lay on an old sofa. His oversized head rested on a tiny pink pillow and he stared at the television. A china plate of curried chicken salad sat untouched on the coffee table. He didn't look up when they entered the room.

"Jesus," Audrey whispered. She cleared a pile of soiled underwear from a three-legged stool and sat, still holding the sagging cardboard container. The stink of the place. "Oh Christ."

She wanted to open the windows, throw out those dingy net curtains. Even repaint the room in modern tones and take the piles of stinking clothes to the launderette. But most of all she wanted to think.

"Look who's here to see you," Elizabeth said in a primary-schoolteacher voice. "Your good friend Audrey."

Martin didn't respond.

"And she has brought you supper." Elizabeth placed her hands on her hips. "Martin, eat your salad."

Audrey's mind whirred. What was Elizabeth doing here? What should she say now?

Elizabeth's appearance at Martin's flat had caught her off guard. She and Maureen were a couple of do-gooders. They were almost like town saints with all they did for the community. Audrey had tried to copy their well-intentioned actions, but held secret thoughts filled with hate. Her ex-husband, his new wife and their kids were top of the list. A chill settled around her heart. She resented Elizabeth's wavy brown hair, youthful looks and the way she breezed easily through life. Then she thought about Maureen with her army of friends and hobbies and art, and wanted to sob. No matter how hard Audrey tried, she'd never make a saint. Why hadn't Elizabeth let her know she'd be making lunch for Martin?

Audrey's heart pounded with anxiety. She felt left out just like when she'd lived with Patrick. He'd kept her away from his work. Worse, he'd stayed long hours in the office, all the while making secret plans with his new wife. She'd put it all together when she was locked in the wine cellar. And Maureen and Elizabeth whispered together too. Always just out of earshot. What the hell were they talking about?

That question upset Audrey.

If she'd known Elizabeth would be here, she would have come by later. It would be better to speak to Martin when they were alone. Then it occurred that she hadn't told Elizabeth about her visit either.

Still, she had to do this. She had to say the words to Martin Findlay before the police arrived. But she'd have to be careful now, so she reworked her words yet again.

"Now come along, Martin, try to eat your salad." Elizabeth's voice remained light, almost playful. "It's real food, organic. It'll make your brain grow."

Audrey went to the kitchen sink, urged on by the sudden need to wash her hands. She cleared a space between the dirty plates and placed the fried-chicken box on the Formica counter. She let the water run for a count of ten. Then she squeezed washing-up liquid onto her hands and plunged them into the cold flow.

The rain continued to fall.

Audrey returned to the stool. Elizabeth stood by the sofa. Martin didn't move. It was as if he was unaware of their presence.

"Martin." Elizabeth placed a gentle hand on his shoulder. "Organic greens are good for you."

His head turned slowly from the television. He stared at Elizabeth through feral eyes. They jutted out of narrow slits. He did not blink.

"Curried chicken and mango salad. One of my favourites." Elizabeth continued to speak as if urging a child to eat its green peas. "It's delicious. Why don't you try a little?"

Suddenly Audrey found her words. They formed as if by magic into a coherent sentence in her mind. But they still had to be spoken. She had to speak before they became a jumble and flew away.

"Martin, I have to talk with you about something important."

"He hasn't eaten his lunch," Elizabeth said. "Let him be until he's finished."

"It's about Maureen"—Audrey got to her feet and wanted to pace, but there wasn't enough space for that—"and the police." She said it so softly, she wasn't sure whether it was only a thought, so she tried again. "And the police."

Elizabeth stared at her with disbelief. Her mouth opened and closed. At last she said, "What about the police? Martin, what's going on?"

Cartoon images flickered across the television screen. An oversized cat chased a cunning mouse but got trapped when it tried to enter the rodent's den. Then the mouse picked up a pot and smashed the cat on its head. Martin turned his head to watch the screen but said nothing.

"Martin?" Elizabeth again placed her hands on her hips. "Have you been rummaging around Mrs Shari's garden shed again?"

Still nothing from Martin.

Audrey cleared her throat. Would there be an argument about what she was going to say? An argument wasn't in the plan. Nor was finding Elizabeth in Martin's flat or telling the detective about Martin at the bonfire. She looked at him, feeling sad. But it had been done now, and she supposed it was for the best.

Audrey said, "They may come to speak with you, Martin. Not folk in uniforms. But police officers in regular clothes. Suits. With pens and notebooks to write everything down. A man in a suit, or a woman with grey hair, or they could send someone else. They are called detectives and ask a lot of nosy questions. They will ask you a lot of nosy questions."

"Let him be." Elizabeth appeared annoyed. "What we all want is for Maureen's killer to be caught and put behind bars."

Audrey almost lost control and stifled a shout. "When the police get a whiff, there is no stopping them."

There was an awkward silence. Elizabeth's face turned purple. She stared through wide eyes and said, "Audrey, we all want the truth. We all want justice for Maureen."

Audrey realised her mistake and lowered her voice. But she still wanted to shout. "Elizabeth, I'm thinking of Martin. He is a friend; we have to protect our friends."

"But that's ridiculous, Audrey. What are you trying to say? Surely you can't think..." Elizabeth's youthful face clouded with doubt and she fell silent.

Now the words came easy and Audrey spoke with cold precision. "Those detectives are like bloodhounds. They are nothing but half-starved dogs on a scent. The only thing on their minds is the kill. You understand that, don't you Elizabeth?"

Audrey stared hard at Elizabeth. The moment had come. The words were in order and ready. She turned her attention to Martin. "It is very important when the detectives come to speak with you, that you—"

"I talked with Detective Earp this morning."

Elizabeth spoke so softly that Audrey almost missed her words. But her subconscious mind flagged their meaning before she took her next breath. She stopped, mute as a stone.

"I told him all I know." Elizabeth held Maureen's gaze. "Everything."

A dull thud pulsed at the back of Audrey's mind. "But if they ask Martin questions—"

"He must tell them the truth." Elizabeth turned to Martin, replaced her hand on his shoulder. He looked at her, but did not blink. "If the nice detective comes to visit you here or at the Quarterdrigg, you must tell them everything, and no fibs."

Martin turned his head back to the television.

The words drained from Audrey's mind, their order blotted out by the dull thud of anger. When she finally spoke, all that came out was a bitter shout.

"Martin Findlay, if the police come, don't say a word. Tell them nothing."

Chapter Thirty-Five

F ENELLA DID NOT KNOW what possessed her to leave Croll's house while the thunderstorm raged. She supposed it had to do with the two beers she'd drunk and the guilt. She should be at the police station filing and signing reports and poised to respond to new information on the Maureen Brian case. Not stuffed to the brim with pizza and rather fine ale. And there was another message from Jeffery. It blinked on her mobile's message icon like Cyclops's eye. If she left now, she'd be back in the office by 3:00 p.m.

She set off in the rain, along the muddy lane with its growing pools of standing water and sharp bends which caught you by surprise on the clearest of days. The first warning toll rang out as she pulled out of Croll's yard. The Morris Minor splashed through a deep puddle and stalled. It restarted after she let out the choke. Her spirits remained high as the car crawled forward, its wipers at full pelt.

"Croll's coming back."

She let out a laugh. They'd talked theories about the Maureen Brian case, with each line of thought countered with another. The *Pig Snout*, they agreed, held the vital clue. That quelled her internal doubts and pushed her spirits even higher. Better yet, Croll knew Ron Malton. If Jeffery failed to come through with a search warrant, Croll would have a word with the councillor. Fenella sensed a break in the case was just over the horizon.

Thunder tumbled across the heavens like the clap of a shaken-out bed sheet. The rain fell so hard the wipers couldn't keep up. They screeched back and forth in an agitated yowl. A wall of white mist cut the view to a handful of feet. Just enough to see the grassy bank shaded by a stand of broadleaved oak by the gated entrance to a pasture field. There'd be no farmers on their slow-moving tractors in this weather. The lane only led to Croll's shack, so there'd be no other drivers coming this way either. Fenella pulled off the lane. She parked on a grassy bank, doused the lights, but kept the engine ticking over with the heat turned up high. Then she pulled out her mobile phone to play the message from Jeffery. Before she pressed the icon, the mobile rang.

"Hi, Earp... an update... yes... go ahead... Martin Findlay... Bonfire Night... rocks in a pool... the connection? Yes... and what does he have to say for himself? I see... on your way to his flat now... we'll need to find an appropriate adult... well, let me think about that. Wait outside until I call back."

She hung up. A chink of light at last.

"Martin Findlay, eh?"

Fenella remembered Martin in the crowd by the crime scene tent. Tall, odd-looking head with that dirty mud-brown trench coat. You couldn't miss him if you tried. She thought him a ghoul, interested in seeing the grisly activity around the murder sight. Or a concerned member of the public who wanted to help with their inquiries. But he hadn't come forward after the television appeal. Had he seen someone watching Maureen on the beach late Bonfire Night? Or had he met her, argued, lost his temper and struck out?

Martin Findlay's probably a long shot, she thought as she stared out of the windscreen. Then she recalled Dr Mackay's words about a club and a Neanderthal. And the photograph on Audrey Robin's sideboard, he was in that too. Now she wasn't quite so sure.

The mobile pinged. A text message from Dexter:

Eyewitness saw figure in mud-brown trench coat hurrying away from the bonfire. From description, believe it is a Mr Martin Findlay. No record of him calling the police station to report the find. Awaiting your instructions or call.

Fenella sat bolt straight. They'd have to bring him in for questioning. But at this time on a Friday, finding an appropriate adult would be a challenge. And she wasn't aware of the extent of his disability—mental or physical?

She considered that for a long while and felt a little depressed. Only one thing for it. She would get on to social services, have someone who knew Martin attend the station. Get an assessment of the man. Did he have a history of violence? It would require the calling in of favours. Maybe some shouting, but she'd get an appropriate adult in place before they hauled him in. That was a trick she'd learned from Croll. They get agitated if you keep them waiting. A waste of time if they clam up.

Fenella began to type her reply when she glimpsed headlights. They advanced slowly like an old man treading on ice. She wondered who would drive this way in all this rain. Not a farmer. Had someone taken a wrong turn from the main road? Or were a couple looking for a quiet spot to be alone?

After several moments staring through the clouded windscreen, she lowered the window. She peered through the rain but could see nothing except the bright headlights reflected through the raindrops. So she waited with the driver's-side window half down. The wind blew drops of rain into her face. The low growl drowned out the slush of the rain.

From out of the white rain, a Ford came into view. Its single occupant crouched over the wheel. Fenella recognised the battered, misshapen green vehicle—Rodney Rawlings, the *Westmorland News* reporter. And she knew he had only one destination on his mind— Croll's house. *Like a hungry fox after a rabbit,* she thought. An instant later came a disturbing revelation: the press were only one step back. The politicians wouldn't be far behind.

She hadn't expected to see the reporter. *Like a rat sniffing out cheese*, she thought dryly. He needed a big story to boost sales. She could see the headlines blasted across the social media sites:

"PC Plod Arrests Beloved Disabled Man. Another Cumbria Police Cock-Up?"

Fenella thought it over. Then she quickly typed into her mobile phone. The message was for Dexter and Earp:

Leave Martin Findlay. We'll speak with him on Monday.

If the press caught a whiff they'd hauled in a disabled man, it would be all over the weekend media sites. Fenella didn't want that.

Chapter Thirty-Six

C ATHY WENT TO MEET him because it was the only thing she could think to do. It was only 4:00 p.m. in the afternoon but as cold and dark as midnight. The rain had stopped. Heavy clouds covered the moon in a cloak of angry black swirls. They pressed down with the threat of more rain to come. It held off for the moment, air calm and still. The lull before the storm.

She stood outside in the shadows with the orange hood of her coat pulled tight, pigtails sticking out like two devil horns. By the dustbins she waited and watched, knowing he'd soon be out to empty the bins.

A dustbin truck rumbled and came to a stop, filling the air with stink. Two men in donkey jackets clambered out and lumbered in her direction. She shrank back further, out of sight, watching as they dragged bin bags to the truck, tossing them in without a word.

Only after the engine's rumble disappeared into the night, did she return to her previous place and watch. A weak moon peeped suddenly through the clouds, and it became very cold. Cathy wished she'd worn long pants rather than her miniskirt, but they hid what Belinda called her runway-model legs.

Belinda hadn't texted or called, so Cathy assumed they still weren't talking. *People say if you want to make a friend you should be a friend,* so she thought Belinda should reach out first and apologize for poking her nose in where it was none of her concern. Then they could get back to the good old days where she'd tell outlandish tales with Belinda egging her on.

But she couldn't wait for Belinda to see sense. She needed to speak to someone now and knew standing outside his house made things complicated. Like his home telephone, the house was a forbidden zone. He'd said never to visit or call. When she needed him, he would know. *Like a wishing well,* she thought. Although sometimes she wished and he' never turned up. Other times, he would show when she had never wished at all. Or, perhaps wishes were like palmate newt pheromones, produced when she needed him most.

And there he was.

He shuffled through the doorway with a black bin bag in his hand.

Cathy hesitated, but only for a heartbeat. Then, panicky and breathless, she called his name.

He dropped the bin bag and looked around.

"Cathy, is that you?"

His voice echoed through the still air like a frightened choirboy. Its high-pitched screech startled Cathy too.

When she stepped out into the dim light from the doorway, she was surprised by the hostile glare in his eyes. Yes, he had told her never to visit or call, but she expected to see his soft smile. Now she wondered why he kept her away. Weren't they going to run away to the countryside where he'd buy her dream cottage and they'd live happily ever after?

"What the hell are you doing here?" He looked like he couldn't believe his eyes, face scrunched up, lips twisted, everything sour. "What the hell!"

Cathy felt her heart break. He said he would show up whenever she wished. Well, she wished, and here he was. So what if she'd given the wishing well a little kick by showing up on his doorstep? *Why is he so angry? Has he changed his mind?*

But then she remembered his work, and breathed. Dealing with the public was stressful. Belinda had told her there were days after a shift at Logan's Bakery when she came home and cried. And he dealt with the public, day in, day out. Stressful.

Over the Solway Firth, thunder growled. It shook the frigid air and whipped up dead leaves in spinning swirls. They tumbled in sullen clusters, making a patter sound like drops of rain. He glanced at the heavens, then at the half-open door, grabbed her arm and tugged her deep into the shadows. Cathy wanted to believe he did it to protect her but wasn't so sure. When she left school, they would run away together. She was sure about that. He had told her many times.

"Someone might see you," he said in a hiss. "I told you never to come here."

Cathy struggled for words, her mind going blank. If anyone found out about them and their plans, she would be in big trouble. Why did she kick the wishing well?

"Cathy, look at me. You are never to come here again, understand?" He placed a hand on her cheek. "The police are snooping around and asking questions about Maureen Brian. If anyone asks, and I hope to God they don't, I was with you on Bonfire Night, right?"

Cathy shook off his hand and stepped farther back into the shadows, afraid to look him in the face.

"But you weren't with me!"

"Listen, I'm saving your bacon here, like I always do." His voice softened to honey. "It's not like you are telling a lie or anything. We met under the pier. No one will ask, but if they do, you'll tell them I was with you all night."

Another clap of thunder pressed clouds closer to the ground. Black with ice and wet, like bloated balloons ready to burst. Cathy felt completely paralyzed. A palmate newt in deep hibernation. They didn't wake until things warmed up, and in his mood, it would be a long hard winter.

A streak of lightning snaked across the sky. Suddenly, Cathy's mouth opened and her feelings tumbled out.

"You want me to get rid of our baby and now you want me to lie for you."

"Cathy!"

"You weren't with me."

Rain fell from the heavens. He tried to place his arms around her, but she broke free and ran. A palmate newt wriggling from the weeds of the Port Saint Giles town pond.

Chapter Thirty-Seven

THE RADIO WOKE AUDREY up.

Perspiration seeped through her mousy hair, icy-damp like hoar frost. The early-morning news bulletin crackled from the radio. She struggled to her feet and turned up the volume with one hand. The other gripped a duster. She'd lost track of how long she'd dozed in the armchair or even where she was.

It was Sunday morning, wasn't it?

Yes, she'd fallen asleep after midnight while reading *The Layman's Guide to Police Practice and Procedure.* And now it was 3:00 a.m. The fire was out, with cold seeping into every corner of the room. The announcer rattled off the top headline: "No Progress in the Maureen Brian Investigation." Soft swipes muted the other stories, as with care she dusted the radio.

Martin Findlay is sound asleep, she thought, *but it won't be long before the detectives show up.* She thought they'd take him in over the weekend. But they didn't. It drove her crazy not knowing what they would ask.

"Say nothing," she said to the empty room.

"An unseasonably warm day with clear skies," whispered the radio.

She padded across the carpet, intending to use the kitchen sink to wash her hands. But she hesitated, thinking about the filth and mess of Martin's dim little flat. So, she dusted the windows and the walls and the rail from which the curtains hung, and the rod attached to the wall with the tiny silver screws. The pictures on the wall were dusted and behind the pictures too, and she took out the vacuum cleaner to suck up grime from the floor. Next, the mop and bucket over the hard kitchen tile, then down on her knees to scrub and polish.

Audrey cleaned every spot, double checked, then cleaned again.

Yes, living room.

Yes, kitchen.

Yes, doorknob and front door.

She'd not leave a trace. The habit, picked up long ago when Uncle Don, stuffed full of greasy haddock and chips, threw up after his ninth can of long-life lager. It splattered over the scrubbed pine kitchen table. He sat silent and staring as she, only eight and small for it, cleaned up the pungent mess. By then she knew it wouldn't be gone in the morning.

Audrey recoiled from the memory as if the stale patch of vomit in her mind's eye reeked afresh in stinking sour blasts up her nostrils. Uncle Don replaced Uncle Sid who replaced her father, Markus. There were others after Uncle Don, but Audrey didn't bother to learn their names. Now, after all these years, their faces were an indistinct blur. All dirty old men in her child's eyes.

Hot and exhausted, she gave the curtains a final dust. She stared out into the dark still street and remembered the old jogger in tight green shorts who'd seen her crouching at the fence of the Seafields Bed and Breakfast, and again beside the detective's car. *Another dirty old man,* she thought, *but what if he went to the police?*

Audrey moved abruptly from the window.

She was almost sure the old jogger hadn't seen her that day on the beach, Almost. Tension simmered as she considered her next move. *How are you supposed to stay hidden from the authorities these days when there are people watching on a windswept beach, and CCTV cameras everywhere?*

She was taught to mind her own business.

"Keep your nose out of my affairs," her mother had yelled when, at nine years old, she had asked why she had so many uncles.

A thought struck. If the jogger had seen her, he would have stopped to ask if she was all right, given sympathy, and offered soothing words. Or maybe he'd have asked her what she was up to. Isn't that what normal people do? And he hadn't done that.

Relief came in a tidal wave.

Tat-de-da-da—de-de-dah.

Then she remembered the skeletal woman in the yellow plastic mackintosh outside Martin Findlay's flat. A sudden thud of her heart caused her to gasp. She didn't expect anyone would be out in all that rain, thought she'd never get caught. But she'd told the nosy parker she was from social services. Her gut pulled as tight as a drawstring bag. She knew the old biddy would check.

And that put everything in a different light.

Chapter Thirty-Eight

MONDAY MORNING, EARP SAT in his kitchen staring out the window at the Egremont Russet apple tree. He watched the shadows cast by the bare branches morph by the minute as the pre-dawn light gave way to the dull shine of another November day. His hand clutched tight around a coffee mug, mobile phone on the table. He could barely admit it to himself—he was nervous.

He'd woken a disgraced detective constable, but anticipated with delicious delight going to bed as a local hero. Anytime now, Sallow would call to give him the all clear. *Martin bloody Findlay*, who'd have thought? He sipped the bitter coffee and wished Sue had bought a larger bag of the Grain Bowl Café brew. They'd run out of that treat. When word got around he'd fingered the perp, they'd be able to buy more than good coffee. He gulped a mouthful of the supermarket discount acrid grind with a smile that soon swelled into a grin.

There were no sounds in the house this early in the morning. Just the slow tick of the kitchen clock and hum of the fridge. Before Earp could stop himself, he picked up the mobile phone, weighing it in his hand as if assessing the quality of the workmanship. Once his eyes caught sight of the still message icon, he placed it carefully back on the table and tried to throw himself into his plans to re-fence the garden. But he couldn't get excited at that prospect and instead watched with anxious breaths as the shadows crept into day.

It had started quite innocently as the sun lightened his garden view. That anticipatory sense of imminent success like a coil wound tight or a child's excitement on Christmas eve. He could hardly believe his good luck and couldn't quell the triumphant feeling. *A little dram to celebrate*, he told himself, as he riffled through the kitchen cupboards for a bottle of supermarket discount brandy. It wasn't like he was a problem drinker. He knew it was too early for hard liquor; only drank socially, but he deserved it after the crap he'd been through.

When he hauled in Martin Findlay and the perp confessed, the toffee-nosed buggers in Carlisle would have to admit they'd made a mistake. Admit he was a good detective. A bloody great detective. Anyway, they'd send a car to take him to the Quarterdrigg with a constable as a driver. Like the old days. He opened the bottle and splashed a generous dollop into his mug, sipped, and topped it up with a splash more.

He picked up his mobile phone again. Nothing yet. He sighed and thought about Sue snug in bed and played for a long while with the idea of joining her for a frisky tumble, when he heard a familiar soft electric whizz. Nick wheeled into the kitchen, Thomas the cat in his lap.

Earp wasn't one for woo-woo thinking, but knew at once that his son's arrival so early in the morning was a sign. The last time it happened, he'd been on his way to the Quarterdrigg to speak with Martin Findlay. Now he wondered if the stars had aligned in his favour or if they were about to deal him another blow. He sipped nervously at his coffee.

"Daddy," Nick whispered in a weepy voice. "We have a big problem."

He knew it! The stars had rolled their dice and dealt him another unfair blow. Why couldn't he get a break? He felt like he was riding a sea serpent intent on dragging him down. That's what comes from being a family man trying to do a good job. Now his six-year-old little boy was coming to him with big problems. *What the hell is the world coming to?*

He felt like he might lose it, right here in the kitchen in front of his son. Perhaps if he hadn't become so anxious waiting for Sallow's call, he wouldn't have felt so angry. He could feel his heart racing, hard. Felt the thuds at the base of his throat. Almost shaking with a combination of rage and anxiety, he forced comfort into his voice. A devoted father speaking softly for the sake of his beloved son.

"What is it, Nick?"

"Thomas is thirsty. Can he have some milk?"

"That's the big problem?"

Nick nodded and swallowed as if his own throat were bone dry.

"Very thirsty, Daddy, and he needs a saucer of milk."

The tension drained from Earp's right shoulder, but he couldn't slow the fast beat of his heart. "You know he must wait till feeding time." The vet had warned them that the cat had grown too fat. There was one meal a day for Thomas. Saucers of milk were definitely out. Earp moved towards the toaster with the mug in his hand. "How about I make us some toast?"

Nick cocked his head to one side. "Just a teeny bit of milk."

"No."

"Aargh... Thomas is so thirsty." His face crumpled into a grumpy old man with his tousled hair up like a brush.

"Then he can have some water."

"It don't taste good."

"Water or nothing."

"But—"

"But, nothing, young man."

"He isn't that thirsty."

Earp couldn't help but smile. His boy had spunk. A chip off the old block. He took a gulp of his boozy coffee and gestured towards the cat. "Your mum will feed Thomas later. Strawberry or raspberry jam?"

"Strawberry, with lots of butter."

Earp looked in the fridge and found what he needed. Butter, jar of strawberry jam. From the breadbin he took a crusty loaf which he sliced into thick wedges. The aroma of toast filled the kitchen. It popped up, golden brown. He slathered on butter, then jam, and returned with two plates to the table.

"Now, young man, once you have eaten, straight back to bed."

Nick took a greedy bite, swallowed and said, "Can't sleep, Daddy."

Mrs bloody Ledwidge again! Earp felt his face flush. That damn teacher made his blood boil. Why wouldn't she let his son play with his friends in the classroom? I'm going to tear a strip off the lazy cow. He placed a hand on his son's shoulder, looking down at him while counting slowly to ten. At nine he remembered what Dr Joy Hall had said about teachable moments and felt there was a lesson in this for Nick.

"I've made some mistakes, son. Sometimes I wish it were possible to turn back the clock." He sighed. "But time only moves forward. One thing I've learned is, a friend is a gift you give yourself."

Nick looked at his dad with sad eyes. "Do daddies have friends?"

"Yes, son. Your dad has plenty of friends."

"I've never seen them." Nick spoke in a halting voice as if he didn't quite believe him. "Where are they?"

Earp's only acquaintances were fellow police officers. *The buggers are always trying to stab me in the back,* he thought with a sigh. Still, this was supposed to be a teachable moment for his son, not retrospection into his own miserable life.

Earp said, "When I was your age, I'd go into my classroom with a smile and make new friends every day. If your old school friends won't play, make new ones."

"But School's all right now, Daddy. Me and Sandra and Tim and Walter are friends again. Mrs Ledwidge lets us play together. She's an ace teacher."

"Oh." Earp stared at his boy. Did he break and make friends so readily as a child? He'd long ago lost touch with his school friends and couldn't recall. "Bad dream, then, Son?"

"I'm practising." Nick rocked his wheelchair backwards and forwards, his version of jumping up and down. "For next Saturday."

Earp stared at his son with confusion.

"Next Saturday?"

"When I get to go back to the Quarterdrigg." Nick squealed with delight. "I've to get up early, cos me and my new friends have a day trip to Derwentwater. If I'm late, they'll leave without me, so I need to practise getting up early. And Mum is taking me out of school to go shopping for clothes this afternoon."

Earp had heard nothing but excited chatter from his son since Sue took him on a whim to visit the centre on Saturday morning. They'd stayed all day, returning home after dark. "He's found a new social circle," she had said. "It'll do him good to make more friends like him. It'll do us all good. A bunch of them have travelled to Europe. Nick could go when he is older too, imagine that. They'll give him support."

Earp felt uncertain about that. After the operation in America, his boy would walk. There'd be no need for the Quarterdrigg. Tension crept into his shoulder. Tightness clutched at his chest. He got up and walked to the kitchen counter, topped up his coffee, and added a dram of brandy. It sloshed into his mug. More than a dram. Why didn't brandy bottles come with a measuring device so you didn't pour out too much into your cup? They'd managed it with those little malt vinegar bottles he doused over his fish and chips. Yet the boffins couldn't do the same with a bottle of booze? The greedy buggers want you to drink too much. Well, he'd down it anyway. No point throwing away good money. He took a gulp of the bitter coffee, gagging at the strength of the brandy.

"Practice is over when you've finished that toast. Then straight off to bed and get up when your mum calls you, else we'll both be in for it."

"Can I come with you to work and play at being a detective?"

"No, son."

"Awww!"

"Tell you what, how about we play wheelchair cricket in the garden when I get home?"

"Promise."

Earp placed a hand over his heart. "I promise, son."

"But it will be dark."

Earp looked at his boy. Yes, it would be dark. He wanted to celebrate with his colleagues. It wasn't every day the spotlight of success shone on him. But his son came first; he'd not stay long in the pub. Only a pint or two, then straight home.

"I'll bring a Chinese curry for dinner and string up some lights so we can play night cricket. Like they do on the television."

"That will be fun." Nick paused. "Promise, Daddy?"

"I already did."

"I love you, Daddy."

Earp gave his son a hug. "One day you'll be a detective like me."

And he'd walk and run and jump and dance and climb high in the branches of that damn apple tree. But Earp mentioned none of those things.

Nick said, "That's what I want most when I grow up, Daddy."

"You'll be better than Sherlock Holmes, son."

"As good as you, Daddy?"

"Better."

"No. Just as good."

"Aye son, happen you're right."

It wasn't until Nick had caught the bus to school, Sue had gone shopping, and Earp had drunk another three mugs of boozy coffee, that his mobile rang. His anxiety spiked as he listened to the call. Detective Inspector Sallow wanted him to go to the Quarterdrigg to pick up Martin Findlay and bring him in for questioning.

There'd be no constable to pick Earp up and drive him to the activity centre. They were too short-staffed. This wasn't like the old days. He wasn't a detective inspector any more. He'd have to drive his own car and meet Constable Phoebe in the Quarterdrigg car park. An appropriate adult from social services would join them at the police station for the interview.

"Don't go in heavy-handed," Sallow had said. "The press are all over this one. We don't want any trouble."

Chapter Thirty-Nine

I T WAS A LITTLE after ten in the morning when Fenella and Dexter arrived at the harbour. They were met by Finnegan Woodstock, the watchman. He led them to an oval room that looked like a captain's cabin. The detectives sat on one side of a glass-topped oval table with yellowed nautical charts beneath.

On the other side sat Ron Malton. Jack Croll had set up the meeting. Fenella hoped to get access to the *Pig Snout* without a warrant. It wasn't a done deal. She felt like a student about to take a test, her hands clammy with nerves. She rummaged in her handbag, pulled out a handkerchief to wipe her palms. There had been a rumour that Malton had cancelled an important catering contract because the head chef's sweaty palms didn't reflect a suitable standard of hygiene. Fenella did not know whether it was true. She dabbed her palms again, not willing to take any chances.

Ron Malton looked like a doddery physics professor in a rickety wheelchair, but he wasn't.

"You're Fenella, are you?" He spoke in a thin gasp like air deflating from a tyre. "And you must be Dexter."

"Aye," Fenella said, speaking for them both. She hadn't seen the councillor this close up before. His sagging expression reminded her of week-old bread turned green at the edges. Odd-sized eyes, stained the colour of a smoker's fingers, sized her up.

"So, tell me what this is all about," Malton said. "As your humble public servant, I'm here to listen."

"Thank you for sparing the time," Fenella replied. "We are here regarding the death of Maureen Brian."

"A dear friend and co-conspirator in my work as a councillor." Malton had one of those faces that gave nothing away. Even when he spoke in plain English, you were never quite certain he meant what he said.

"You knew her well?" The question came from Dexter.

"As a member of the harbour society and a friend."

"We are interested in any friends of Maureen Brian." This was Fenella. "Routine, you understand. How long have you known her?"

Malton gave a superior smile. "Would it surprise you to learn Maureen funded my re-election campaign?"

Fenella tried not to show her shock. But her brows crumpled. Could Maureen's death have been political? They hadn't considered that. She'd read the forensic finance investigator's report. Nothing out of the ordinary in those dry pages. Now she made a mental note to check again. This time she'd look for political donations.

Malton said, "Maureen donated to my last election campaign. I believe the money came from the sale of her art."

Fenella said. "Do you know if Miss Brian had any enemies?"

Malton shrugged. "Maureen was the least partisan person in Port Saint Giles. She must have supported all sides of our political divide in her time. She simply chose the best candidate, irrespective of party. A dogmatic woman and very generous with it."

Fenella glanced at Dexter, then back at Malton. She wouldn't be doing her duty if she didn't question the man further. But if he became angry, he might refuse access to the *Pig Snout*. They'd be back to square one if that happened.

Fenella said, "How long were you and Maureen friends?"

"Years. Fifteen… no, twenty at least."

Dexter took out his notebook and began to write. Malton watched him with sharp eyes.

Fenella said, "Were you aware of any problems in Maureen's life?"

"She listened, didn't judge, and brought you solutions."

"She didn't mention anything out of the ordinary to you?"

"No."

"And her harbour rent was on time?"

He shifted uneasily. "Not exactly."

Fenella tilted her head, considering how best to proceed. She had to be very careful. If she pushed him too far, the interview would be over. So would her chance to search the *Pig Snout* without a warrant.

"I'm not quite with you, Councillor Malton."

The councillor's face flushed, and for a moment Fenella thought it was all over. But he leaned so far over the table his breath caught in her nostrils—the rancid stench of a stale packet of cheese and onion crisps. "I want you to catch her killer. Maureen's death is very untimely and intensely personal. Now let's continue off the record, shall we?"

Fenella nodded at Dexter. He put down his pen and folded his arms.

"Please go on, Councillor Malton," Fenella said.

"Maureen and I had an agreement... for tax purposes, but no actual money changed hands. Her use of the boat was free. A gift from me, if you like. Mutually beneficial for both sides."

"Can you explain?"

"Let's not go there," He said, voice snapping like a trapdoor. For a moment the room became still. Then his wheelchair creaked as he leaned back and looked from Fenella to Dexter. "My private affairs are not relevant to your investigation. Need I remind you that I can end this meeting at any time."

Fenella wasn't sure how much more she could get away with. Was the famous Malton temper about to break? There was one more question she had to ask. She rolled the dice and hoped Ron Malton would not explode.

"Do you know if Miss Brian was involved in a romantic relationship?"

A slight flush came to his face. He jabbed a finger. "Like I said, I can end this meeting at any time."

"You haven't answered my question, Councillor Malton."

He lifted his head and held Fenella's gaze. A slight quirk touched the corners of his lips. "I do not know about the romantic relations of that woman."

Fenella detected the politician's blarney in his tone, but sensed it would be a waste of time to push, so she changed direction.

"How did you first meet Maureen?"

"Oh, a pure fluke." The quirk twitched into a grin. "I'd been invited to a fundraiser for the coastal lighthouses organised by my Uncle, Malcolm Buckham. His wife was friends with Maureen and they were both interested in the restoration of historic buildings. Malcolm is a civil engineer, retired now. Maureen and I got along very well, although she was quite a bit older than myself. But then again, she seemed to get along with everyone."

"And you are certain Maureen didn't have any"—Fenella searched for the appropriate phase—"male acquaintances?"

"I cannot comment on her romantic relationships, Detective Sallow."

Fenella got the message and moved on.

"What about financial problems?"

Malton shook his head. "Not with the prices her artwork is selling at. Maureen lived a very modest lifestyle. She had a healthy pension and income from her art and teaching. She gave away more than most." He folded his arms across his chest. "Do you have any idea who might have murdered my friend?"

"Not yet," Fenella replied. "We are working a number of leads."

Malton sat straight in his wheelchair. He stared at Fenella for a long time.

"I hear through the grapevine you have a person in your sights." He watched Fenella closely as if searching for a reaction. "A man with mental health problems. Isn't that so?"

Fenella kept her face blank. "I can't comment on that."

Malton said, "I want you to move quickly on this case. The more days slip by, the colder the trail. I think you should know that Superintendent Jeffery is keeping me informed." He gave a self-satisfied chortle. "Anything else?"

Fenella cleared her throat. "Can you verify your whereabouts on Bonfire Night?"

Malton raised an eyebrow, suddenly tense and alert. "Am I to take it that I am under suspicion of murder?"

"Just routine, sir." Fenella smiled. "It is our job to check alibis and eliminate. The faster we do that, the quicker our progress. I'm sure you understand."

There was a moment's hesitation. Then he spoke in an irate tone.

"This year I was invited to open the parade. After the fireworks I joined the after-party at the Giles Breeze Hotel. It finished rather late, around two thirty a.m."

"And I suppose someone can confirm that?" Fenella would check either way.

His voice crackled like a distant thunder storm. "I'm sure Superintendent Jeffery will vouch for me. She spent much of her time chewing my ear about the very issue which brings you here."

"The *Pig Snout*," Fenella said.

Malton nodded. "I've complained no end about the police's flagrant abuse of search warrants. Given the political tension over the issue, you'll not get a magistrate to sign one anytime soon." His voice trailed away. He picked up a device which looked like a remote control.

A short while later, Finnegan Woodstock strode into the room.

"You buzzed, Mr Malton?"

"My conversation with these two detectives is over. Please take them to the *Pig Snout.* Give them full access and anything else they require."

Chapter Forty

J UST AFTER TEN O'CLOCK that same morning, Earp pulled his
car into the Quarterdrigg. The piles of overflowing rubbish bags
by the trash cans had swelled to double his previous visit. There were
only three other parked cars, all dark inside. They gave the place an
eerie abandoned atmosphere. For an instant he was reminded of a
haunted house where you know something terrible will happen. The
sooner this is over, the better, he thought. Where the hell is Phoebe?
Tension tightened in his shoulder.

Earp parked on the opposite side, as far away as possible from the
bloated bin bags. He poured a coffee from his flask and felt the
warmth seep into his hands. As he sipped and inhaled the nutty
aroma, he listened for the growl of Constable Phoebe's patrol car. He
hoped the coffee would sober him up. The brandy was still taking its
effect. Combined with only a splotch of jam on buttered toast, his
stomach felt queasy.

He was anxious. His right shoulder ached and there was a tightness
in his chest. He clenched both his fists and let them relax. Then he
rolled his shoulders, forwards and backwards. The rotary movement
more than anything gave him a sense of ease. As soon as Phoebe
arrived, the tension would go.

He thought about how the rest of the day would turn out, felt
certain there'd be a confession in the interview room. The sooner that

came, the sooner he'd be hailed a hero. In the old days, before CCTV and recorded interviews, he would have been able to jolly things along. Squeeze a confession with a sly blow to the groin. The do-gooder higher-ups were none the wiser. *No rush,* he told himself, although he wished the evening celebrations would come. But he forced himself to take his time, sipping, watching, wondering where all the people were.

The car park was deserted with the front entrance of the Quarterdrigg shrouded in dark and quiet. Fantastic! Couldn't be better. They'd slip in and out with no fuss at all. Bringing in Martin Findlay for questioning would be a doddle. Nothing could go wrong.

After he'd finished the coffee, he popped a mint into his mouth. Would it get rid of his boozy breath?

He'd have another before he showed up at the police station. Maybe even the whole bloody pack. He smiled at that and got out of the car to stretch. Golden rays shone from a clear blue sky. A crisp November day with no rain, although the weather forecaster said there'd be a hard frost overnight. *At least this time the sun's out,* he thought. Still, he'd expected more activity at the centre this morning. Sue said the place was jumping on Saturday with no place to park but out on the street. And on his last visit, there'd been at least triple the parked vehicles. Like a ghost town. Where the hell is everyone?

Now he had a bad feeling.

He did a slow 360-degree turn. Nothing but the three parked cars. He stood perfectly still, listening to the rumble of traffic from the road. The rattle of a motorbike. The distant toot of a horn. An energetic young radio voice introducing a tune. A harsh techno-beat mix of "Kung Fu Fighting" pounded the frigid November air, then faded away.

Too damn quiet.

For a while he gazed at the street entrance, half hoping to see someone walking to the centre on foot. But there was no one else about. So he turned his attention to the building and stared, apprehensive, as he considered his options.

Bloody Sallow.

If she'd called him earlier, they would have nabbed Martin Findlay at his flat. Much easier. Now he'd have to haul the bloke in surrounded by a gang of disabled folk. That was it. That's what bothered him about all of this. Being a dad whose son wants to make friends with the kids who attend the centre. *Just as well it's Monday and the little buggers are all in school.* That thought eased his nerves a little. *Once Phoebe arrives, we'll be in and out like a whippet.*

Earp returned to his car, clicked on the police radio, and listened. A crash on High Road. Nothing new in that. He let out a savage curse as the dispatcher diverted Constable Phoebe's patrol car to deal with the event. *How long will Phoebe take now?*

He called in to request another car to assist him. His heart skipped a beat, and he held his breath to count to ten. Then the dispatcher responded.

"None available for interview transportation."

Earp's right shoulder throbbed. Should he wait for Constable Phoebe? Or haul in Martin Findlay on his own?

He chewed his lower lip. He'd rather have uniform backup even though the buggers usually got in the way. Annoyed and uneasy, he poured another coffee.

As he sipped, he sized up the situation. The cuts and lack of uniforms meant all hands on deck all the time. Transporting an individual to the station for questioning was not the dispatcher's highest priority. What if Constable Phoebe got called to another incident? Maybe it would be better to talk with Martin Findlay on his own. Assess the man, call for help if needed. There was the question of a responsible adult for Martin. It was a requirement the bloody rule-makers had introduced years back. And police officers were supposed to work in pairs. Just in case of trouble.

Earp drained the cup, tossed it into the back seat, and strode purposefully to the entrance. Sod the bloody rules. He'd identified the perp. He'd bring the bugger in.

Chapter Forty-One

A CRISP BREEZE BLEW across the harbour as the detectives and the watchman scurried along the jetty, loud as soldiers in their combat boots. It was still a shock to Fenella that Malton had given them access, and she gave a silent prayer of thanks to Jack Croll. They picked their way through the clustered boats and along the motionless pontoon to the silent berth where the *Pig Snout* stood waiting.

"There she is." Finnegan Woodstock pointed to a sleek fifty-foot sloop which glowed with teak and polished brass. It bobbed gently at the end of a wide pontoon, hidden in shadows, out of sight of prying eyes. He adjusted his watchman's cap. "A beauty."

Dexter let out a low whistle.

"Twin auxiliary engines for when there's no wind," added Finnegan with a hint of pride. "Cuts through the swell like a knife through butter. Mercedes. Smooth."

"Mercedes, eh?" Dexter rubbed his chin. He drove a rusted Volvo with a dodgy passenger door. "Mercedes makes boat engines too? Fancy that."

Fenella had imagined a small dingy of a boat held together by rusted nails and rope, or a refurbished fishing smack with scuffed floorboards splashed with faded paint. Nothing was farther from her mind than gleaming brass and polished teak. Definitely not the hovel of a starving artist, more like a floating upscale art gallery. How could Councillor Malton afford such a vessel? Why did he lease it to Maureen Brian for free?

As if mirroring her thoughts, Dexter muttered, "Pricey. We'd better take a closer look at Miss Brian's financials. See if we can't find a bit of something to chew on."

Fenella stood quietly and watched the boat. It looked like it would have a polished bar inside. And a bearded barista to serve the drinks. Dainty cups of espresso, latte, or shots of single-malt Scotch whisky for eager buyers of Maureen Brian's art. So this was her studio. Her perception of Miss Brian shifted again. She was a savvy sales woman *and* a creative artist.

Dexter was speaking. "Take the rich nobs out on the water, wine and dine them, then return to shore with a sale and a fat cheque. That's what I call classy."

Fenella turned to Finnegan. "Did Miss Brian use the *Pig Snout* to showcase her photographic art?"

Finnegan shook his head. "Not since I've been here. As far as I'm aware, the last person who took the boat out to sail around the Firth was Wayne Wingfield, the former watchman."

"And where can we find Mr Wingfield?" This was Dexter.

Finnegan shrugged. "I believe he spends his days and nights in one of Cumbria's finest institutions. At the taxpayers' expense, if you get my drift. Four years, if my memory is correct."

"Drug pusher to teenage girls, I recall," Fenella said. "Now tell me about Maureen and this boat."

Finnegan said, "She visited most days, stayed a while, then left. Always on her own."

Fenella stared back unable to hide her disbelief.

"No visitors?"

"Check the guest book."

"Anyone been on the boat since Miss Brian's death?"

"Nope."

"Are you sure?"

"I walk the jetty and pontoons several times a day." He turned and pointed at a tall silver lamppost. "And we have CCTV cameras."

"What about Mr Malton?"

Finnegan placed his hands in his pockets. "I just work here and do as I'm told. It pays well and I have a family to support."

High above them, silhouetted against the bright sky, a herring gull flew in a slow arc, landed atop the CCTV camera, and screamed.

"This must be very difficult for you," Fenella said. "I hope you understand our job is to find out what happened to Miss Maureen Brian. Anything you say to help will be kept in confidence."

Finnegan cleared his throat. "I'm sorry for what happened to Maureen. I'd like her killer caught." From his jacket pocket he took a folded piece of paper but didn't immediately hand it to Fenella. "Mr Malton is wheelchair bound. Since I've worked here, I have never seen him on the jetty or by these pontoons. Yes, he owns the place, but apart from swanning around his office like the captain of the bleedin' Titanic, he spends most of his time at the town hall and doesn't have much to do with the hands-on day to day."

"So who manages the place?"

"A bloke called Malc. He is a retired engineer."

Fenella thought for a moment. "Would that be a Mr Malcolm Buckham?"

"Aye, that's him. Everyone calls him Malc. He is Mr Malton's uncle. Ten years before he retired, Malc bought this place. Over the years he built it up. But during the last recession he ran into financial problems, and his nephew bailed him out by becoming the largest shareholder. They say the stress killed Malc's wife."

"Malc about today?" Dexter already had his notebook out and was writing. "Since we are here."

"He's not been about much since Bonfire Night. Used to stop by on a regular basis. Very regular if you know what I mean."

Fenella said, "Perhaps you can enlighten us."

The herring gull screamed.

Finnegan tilted his head to gaze at the gull. It sat on the CCTV camera and screamed and screamed. When he looked back, his cheeks were flushed.

"Like I say, I've got a family to care for." He handed the folded paper to Fenella and nodded at the *Pig Snout*. "That is the combination lock number. Go ahead. I've still got to finish my rounds. If you need anything, you'll find me in the gatehouse."

He adjusted his cap, swung around and hurried away, swerving around a pile of rope so he had to balance along the edge of the pontoon.

Chapter Forty-Two

E ARP FELT HIS PULSE thumping so hard he didn't take in the polished flagstone floors or wide windows or hear the gentle classical music playing from unseen speakers. An adrenaline jolt from the chase or the kill? He didn't know. He had Martin Findlay in his sights now and needed to convince him to come quietly to the station. No fuss. That'd be easy with the dunce. He felt like a kung fu master about to take out an untrained pleb.

A well-dressed thirty-something woman sat in a wheelchair behind the reception counter. She watched him warily as he approached.

Earp remembered her name—Albertha, the lass with no legs. He popped another mint into his mouth, feeling confident it shrouded his boozy aura. His heart continued to beat fast, and he knew now it was the excitement of the kill.

"Morning, darling," He said with a polished lilt. "I'm back again. Remember me?" He gave an easy smile. It wasn't every day a detective showed up at the Quarterdrigg. The curious stare gave him a thrill of importance, like a minor soap opera actor recognised on the street. "You keeping the riff-raff out today, are you, luv?"

"You got in, didn't you?"

Her tone simmered with something he couldn't read. He'd have to watch it with her. He knew her type. Demanding her rights and complaining at the slightest indiscretion. One word out of place, and she'd be on to the police complaints committee like a dog at a bone.

Earp said, "They tell me I've got a memorable face?"

"Unforgettable. I agree." She laughed, but her eyes watched him as if he were a cockroach crawling along her arm.

Earp didn't care if she didn't like the police. He had a job to do. "Is the centre open?" He glanced about. Definitely less hustle and bustle than his last visit. "Seems quiet today."

Albertha said, "A group of our daytime regulars are in Normandy on an exchange visit with our partner organisation in France. But we are still open seven days a week for as long as the funding lasts. There is so much need in the community I wish we could open twenty-four seven. Not enough funding for that though." A yellow-and-white plastic collection box appeared in her right hand. She shook it with vigour. "Anything you can spare will help."

Earp kept his face friendly as he deposited two pound coins.

"Always happy to give a hand, luv."

He wasn't a bleedin' cash machine. His chest tightened and his stomach turned sour, but it was Albertha's hard-staring eyes that made him more uneasy.

She kept her arm outstretched, snorting slightly. "Some of our members cannot find employment through no fault of their own." Again she shook the collection tub.

Earp deposited another coin, cursing under his breath. He didn't like the way she watched him—like a shop assistant all eagle eyed as if he were about to nick something. Then it came to him all at once. The woman hated the able bodied. He saw it in her eyes, a dull simmering resentment. He'd read about the militant disabled marching in London. They'd wheeled along Whitehall demanding everything from more pay to paved tracks through the National Parks. Now the buggers were in Port Saint Giles! Not that the liberal politicians would do anything about that. He sensed trouble ahead. He could smell it. She was already getting on his nerves.

Albertha was speaking. "The centre is always on the lookout for able-bodied volunteers to pick up any litter, carry stuff, empty the bins, and scrub the toilets. Your face fits the bill."

Earp knew her game now. Poke the hard-working police officer and, when they strike, go running to the complaints board with allegations of abuse and discrimination. He breathed in long and hard to quell the desire to punch the cheeky lass. But he considered himself a professional, like a kung fu master, and wouldn't let her get under his skin. So he kept the playful tone; didn't want her to go all militant on him.

"Then sign me up, will you."

"For dustbin duty or the toilets?"

"I was thinking about reception."

"Sorry, I can't." Albertha sniffed. "There is a waiting list. Perhaps instead I can add you to our regular donations sign-up sheet? A pledge of twenty pounds a month. Not much for a man of your means, but it makes the world of difference to those of us who are less fortunate."

The way she spoke unsettled him. He swallowed down his annoyance. He was here for Martin Findlay, and he intended to take the man in without fuss.

"I'm a public servant, luv. We don't get paid enough to share."

She put the collection box under the counter. "I suppose you want something?"

He'd had enough of the snooty cow and said, "Mrs Gloria Embleton about?"

"You on duty?"

"No I'm on my bleedin' holiday!" He flashed his warrant card to ram home the point. That always got their attention. He'd not be intimidated by political correctness or a crowd of misshapen militant buggers. It wasn't his fault the cow had no legs.

Albertha sniffed again. "Gloria is a volunteer. She doesn't work Mondays."

"Who's in charge?"

"Me."

Now he'd have to deal with her. He put on his professional smile. "Can I have a quiet word?"

"You caught Miss Brian's killer yet?"

The entire town wanted the answer to that question. Earp thought Martin Findlay was the most likely candidate but racked his brain for a more caustic answer. It couldn't come up with anything fast. *That bloody brandy's slowing me down.* So he stood staring at the woman like a deranged kung fu master trying to decide upon the right killer blow.

But Albertha spoke first. "What exactly are you after?"

"A quiet chat with Martin Findlay." He still wanted to take a verbal jab at the woman, but his mind wouldn't play ball. "Is he around?"

"He is a nice man."

"Is he here, then?"

"A personal friend. Everyone loves him."

"Can you just answer my question."

Albertha snorted. "You'll not find a murderer here. Not within these walls. The members of Quarterdrigg are law-abiding people. You are wasting your time." She sniffed, watching him with sly eyes. "Anyway, Martin leaves early on Fridays. Have you tried his flat?"

"Today is Monday."

"Is it?" Albertha lifted her head, eyes wide in mock shock. She flashed an uneven smile. "Well, he won't speak with you, so you'd better turn around and leave because you're making the place stink."

Militant and a hater of the police, Earp thought. He glanced around furtively to make sure he could not be overheard, then he leaned so close he could count her eyelashes and see her pupils suddenly contract.

"You militant little bugger. I bet you were one of those dossers wheeling down Whitehall demanding something for bloody nothing." His voice started out quiet but rose to a shout. "Now, Miss No-Legs

Nancy, you are going to point me towards Martin bloody Findlay or you're nicked."

A high-pitched scream sent Earp's hands to his ears. He staggered backwards, confused. Albertha was in front of the reception desk racing her wheelchair backwards and forwards like a Friday night drunk nerving themselves to throw a punch.

"Do you want to know how I got like this?" she screamed, face a deadly shade of purple. "An accident when I was fifteen. A car crushed them so badly they had to be chopped off. Fifteen and studying for my 'A' Levels."

"Calm down, luv." Earp heard his words although they seemed to come from a great distance. "Please calm down."

Albertha was still shouting. "They called it an accident but it wasn't. I've killed myself a thousand times in my dreams rather than live like this. Nasty deaths, painful. And I cry with bitter sobs every night. Not because I hate the man who did this to me but because I trusted him to know better. We all did." Her mouth was open so wide Earp could see her tonsils. "He was a police officer. Drunk on duty. And you come in here stinking of drink! I'm going to call the police station and have them breathalyse you. You'll not do to others what that drunken fool did to me."

Earp had no memory of how he ended up at the door. He recalled his hand feeling for the handle, the stab of cold air in the car park, and the yelling screams of Albertha as he scurried back to his car.

Chapter Forty-Three

T HEY HADN'T YET CLIMBED aboard the *Pig Snout* when Dexter cursed.

"It's busted," he growled as he stared at the cabin door. He put on blue N-DEx gloves and leaned in close. "The combination lock's been jimmied."

Fenella was at his side, hands already covered by gloves. "Okay," she said standing in the sun and chill wind. Everything looked so picturesque: the wooden deck with a lacquer shine and gleaming brass rails, and a glossy black cabin door with the oversized golden letters PS etched in a stylish font. But the brass-plated combination lock hung at a sharp angle. Its cover snapped back and forth in the cool breeze. "We'll get the techs out once we've taken a look."

They walked inside. The still air smelled of polish and leather and the faded floral scent of rosehip potpourri. It looked like something owned by a banker, so plush and lavish. A deep-piled rug covered the floor like a shorn sheep's new coat. They stepped with care on the soft fibres, not wanting to blemish its impeccable design. They picked their way through the huddle of low leather seating. Then along the polished railing that led to the wet bar. An empty bottle of Johnnie Walker stood next to a shot tumbler.

Dexter picked up the bottle in his gloved hands, shook it as if to confirm its emptiness. "Drained dry, eh?" He examined the shot tumbler, placed it under his nose and sniffed. "Maureen Brian didn't strike me as a hard drinker. But then again, my old gran could knock it back. Granddad too."

Fenella walked behind the bar and saw a low glass display-case table. It was of a similar design to the one they'd seen in Councillor Malton's office. She stared at where the photographic artworks should have rested. There was nothing but an open glossy magazine on top of the green velvet lining. Fenella flipped up the glass lid. She peered at the open magazine pages. A cave painting of stick people. They were engaged in a hunt with one warrior breezily spearing a ferocious beast, apparently unconcerned that the creature held him between its sharp claws.

There was no sign of Maureen Brian's artwork. Only a faint outline showing where they might once have rested. Fenella counted four markings, but couldn't be sure they represented anything more than shadows and the imagining of her mind. She was tempted to drag the display table on deck so they could examine it in natural daylight. But the techs wouldn't like that.

"They knew what they were looking for," Dexter said, glancing at the empty case. "Maureen Brian's photographs."

"Aye, happen you're right," Fenella replied, hands on her hips. That was exactly how it appeared. A headache throbbed. Things had suddenly become more complicated.

Dexter was speaking. "Hear me out, Guv. Suppose it was the same person who killed Miss Brian."

"Go on."

"Well, they are short of cash, and seek out Maureen after the Bonfire Night festivities. They know about her artwork, know it sells for record prices and decide they want a piece of the action." Dexter paused, glanced at the empty case, and shook his head. "Miss Brian was a tough cookie and refuses to play along. It got rough, too rough. The death on the beach might have been an accident."

Fenella warmed to the idea, nodded for him to go on.

"And after she died, they thought about where she'd likely stash her finished works, broke into the *Pig Snout*, and pinched the four missing photographs."

"So, we are talking about someone who knew Maureen well," Fenella said. "A friend or a close associate."

Dexter nodded. "Rules out Martin Findlay. Although he is a friend, I can't see him being that calculating. Not unless someone else is pulling the strings."

Fenella agreed but said, "Only one problem with all of this. We've no evidence anything has been stolen. Once we've interviewed Mr Findlay, we'll see where we stand." She chewed her lip. "I think I'll join Earp for the interview; you'd better come along too. And I suppose we should have another chat with Councillor Malton. This time down the station." Fenella knew that would go down as well as a circus clown at a coulrophobia convention with Superintendent Jeffery.

A phone rang.

"The super," Fenella whispered.

Dexter signalled he'd call in the techs and left the cabin.

Fenella spoke in a brisk tone. "How can I help you, ma'am?"

"Didn't you see my text messages?" Jeffery's voice sounded stressed. "You'd better come into the station so we can talk."

Fenella couldn't leave the *Pig Snout* now. She wanted to speak with the techs and be the first to know if they found anything.

"With respect, ma'am, I'm in the middle of an investigation."

"Listen Sallow, this is bloody important. I want you—" the line went quiet. Fenella heard the waspish voice of Jeffery but it was too indistinct to make out the words. They sounded cautious and filled with trepidation. "I've got to go. Chief Constable Rae is on the other line. My office in forty-five minutes. No excuses."

Fenella paced. Fifteen more minutes here and she'd have to return to the station. Now she'd miss the action and hear what the techs found, second-hand. She turned off her mobile phone.

She needed to focus and began again to pace with her head down and a growing brew of annoyance in her gut. If she had been paying attention, it would never have happened—but she wasn't, and bumped into the starboard bulkhead. To the casual eye, there was nothing to show an opening. Only a slight irregularity to the wooden skirting. Fenella bent down and tugged at the strip that hung loose from the base. It came away to reveal a long shallow cavity.

She scrambled to her knees and shined the light from her mobile phone into the crevice. Nothing visible. But when she placed her hand into the gap and felt around, something moved. Carefully, she grasped it between her fingers and pulled the slim object into the dim light of the cabin. She held it up with a sense of growing delight.

It was a photographic image of a flat beach and white sky. The sort of thing they frame and put on museum walls. She felt around for more, but it was the only one.

"Dexter. Come quick."

He was by her side before she finished the sentence.

"Well, well, well," he said turning over the image in his gloved hands. "Now where—"

The cabin door flew open. Detective Constable Jones hurried inside.

"Ma'am," he gasped. "A body has been found on Fleetwood Lane. It was beaten about the head and thrown onto a fire. Dr Mackay sent me to get you."

Chapter Forty-Four

F ENELLA'S MORRIS MINOR SCREECHED to a halt in Fleetwood Lane.

She clambered out of the car, leaving the keys in the ignition. The engine growled as if in protest. Jones scurried behind.

They picked their way along Fleetwood Lane, littered with dustbin cans. Collection day. Later, the refuse trucks would clear it all away. A violent knot tugged in the pit of Fenella's stomach as she sucked in the hazy air. Damp and rot and embers. It twisted again at the sight which lay ahead.

Crime scene techs scuttled about in their white suits. They moved as quiet as clouds in an uncertain sky. A thin crowd of anxious onlookers gathered by the blue and white tape. It slithered in the slight breeze. In front stood a police constable as stiff as a Roman centurion. He scowled at the eager gawkers who came up close to snap photos with their phones.

"Stay back," he boomed, planting his legs wide, arms outstretched.

Behind him stood a low wrought-iron gate. It led to a narrow path that stopped at the crime scene tent. Beyond the marquee stood a porch attached to a three-storey red brick house.

Fenella slowed to a stop and glanced at the gathered crowd. Is the killer watching? She scanned the faces at the front, eyes darting from person to person for any she might recall from the Maureen Brian crime scene. Then those at the back. No one stood out, so she glanced at the messages on her mobile phone. After a moment, she turned to Jones.

"Have a word with the crowd. See if anyone saw anything. Get names and details, then get on with the door-to-door."

"Will do, ma'am."

"And turn my car engine off when you get a chance."

Jones hurried away as more people came from the houses. They peered over garden hedges or from the windows. Others wandered into the street, their feet wrapped in soft slippers. Small children pointed at the police cordon.

Fenella flashed her warrant card, stepped over the tape and stared to where the crime scene tent stood waiting. *Like a portal into another world,* she thought.

A familiar thrill of excitement tingled along her spine. This was why she had signed up for the police force all those years ago. To see behind the crime scene tent and to protect the good from the bad. She felt like a guest at a magic show who got to go backstage to see how the tricks worked. Her heart beat a little faster. There was no knowing what she might find.

She tramped along the narrow garden path as a diesel engine growled to life. The rattle grew louder until it reached a solid rhythmic *thud, whir, thud.* A tech peered upwards at tall portable lamps. They blinked on and cast a bright arc of white light over the hastily built crime scene marquee. The tech returned to the diesel engine and pulled a lever. A gruff rattle, then the motor quieted to a soft purr.

The crime scene tent door flapped open. A halo shrouded the stooped figure who stood for a moment in the bright gap.

"There you are, Fenella," said Dr Mackay, stepping out of the arc of white light. He wore a tartan jacket and red bow tie with brown corduroy trousers. Blue N-DEx gloves encased his delicate hands. Midnight-black wellington boots covered his enormous feet. "I'm done for the present. Once the techs give the all-clear, I'll make a start on the body in the morgue."

Fenella said, "Is Lisa Levon inside?"

She wanted to have a word with the forensics head about what the crime scene techs had found. She hoped for fingerprints or genetic evidence—anything to give them a clue to the killer.

The doctor shook his head. "Only the twelve-year-olds are on duty today, I am afraid. Lisa is in training in Carlisle, and with the cutbacks, there's no one else to head the team. But they are well-organised for a bunch of newbies. I hear Lisa has dialled in to check things are on track."

Fenella pulled on shoe covers and gloves, then glanced at the tent with unease. "What have we got?"

"I'll brief you on it if you like, but best come see for yourself." His face seemed thin, hollowed out, eyes rimmed with dark. "Nasty one. Come on, this way."

The brightness of the lights inside the tent surprised Fenella. For several seconds she stood blinking.

"This way," Dr Mackay said. He spoke in soft tones like a priest to a confessant.

She followed him to a row of dustbins, their mouldy stench filling the still air.

The doctor pointed. "There she is."

A wizened figure in a yellow mackintosh lay atop a crude bonfire of refuse sacks. The plastic hood was still up, arms splayed in a ragged arc.

"Dear God," Fenella muttered, taking in the gruesome sight.

She stepped closer to peer at the victim's face, but felt the gentle hand of Dr Mackay.

"Not a pretty picture. Please let me."

He stooped forward and, with a gloved hand, lowered the hood. Fenella turned away in disgust.

Outside the crime scene tent, the whir of the diesel engine continued its harsh rumble. Anxious voices carried from the street, and a childlike voice let out a frightened yell.

"Not much of the face left," Dr Mackay said at last. His hollow voice hinted at more, but he paused, his eyes watching Fenella.

She braced herself.

"Go on," she said. "Go on."

"The first blow didn't kill the victim. It injured her. Then the bugger shoved her onto the fire and gouged her eyes." The doctor spoke in quick stabbing breaths. "Look, there are signs of a struggle. And you've seen what's left of the head. No need for the hat brim line rule here. A savage Neanderthal did this."

Fenella spoke, but it was more to herself. "No accident or a suicide, then?"

"I'm afraid not." He shook his head. "The labs will no doubt agree with what I have diagnosed. I'm telling you now in the hopes it will save you some time. You'll need to get your skates on to catch the monster. No point hanging around for weeks for the boffins in the labs to confirm. Nothing beats a seasoned eye."

Fenella's gaze remained glued on the victim. Her mind churned and her stomach roiled. She didn't have a name or background, but knew no one deserved to die like this. A slow anger began to brew. She turned her head from side to side to ease the tension. But she could not take her eyes from the charred corpse. The pictures filled her memory bank. Like a camera *click-clicking*, she took it all in.

At last, her thoughts drifted to the killer. What on earth are we dealing with here? It had all the hallmarks of a manic attack. Crazy, deranged. They would have to redouble their efforts, go over things with an even finer comb. Slowly, she considered the next step.

Her mobile phone buzzed—a voicemail from the superintendent. *Jeffery's meeting!*

She glanced at her wristwatch. There was still time to get back to the office. Just. But before she hurried back to her car, an idea struck

—an idea she did not like. Resources were tight, and the police stretched thin. Only those on the inside knew that. Did the killer have inside knowledge?

For a fleeting instant, a laugh carried from the street, high-pitched and mocking. The weight of the investigation suddenly pressed down on Fenella like the twist of a vice. She closed her eyes and saw the body of Maureen Brian and placed her head in her hands.

"Are you all right?" Dr Mackay looked at Fenella with concern.

"Fine," she said, but her voice sounded dull and wooden. She sucked in deep breaths. At last, her inner detective kicked in. "Do we have a name?"

She didn't expect an answer from the doctor.

"Mrs Claire Sutherland. She retired ten years back. Her husband worked on the bin vans. He died three years ago."

"You knew her?"

Dr Mackay let out a ragged breath. "Aye. A midwife in her day, a bloody good one. She was a bit of a nosy parker too. You couldn't get anything past Claire. For her to end like this..."

Fenella wanted to reassure Dr Mackay. A sudden urge to say they'd catch the killer swelled in her chest, but she couldn't give that promise. Her team would wear out their shoe leather and persist, but success would also require a healthy dose of good luck.

"I've got Detective Constable Jones on the door-to-door." Fenella spoke in as bright a tone as she could muster. "There's a good chance he'll turn up a lead."

Dr Mackay didn't look convinced. His women friends were dropping like flies and not through old age. The man's face seemed to sag under a weight Fenella couldn't imagine. He leaned in close and spoke in a hushed tone.

"I do not want to start rumours or cause a panic." He glanced over his shoulder. "But the death of Maureen Brian and Claire Sutherland... are we talking about a serial killer here?"

"There is an outside chance, I suppose," Fenella replied.

He snorted. "Two deaths where the victim is beaten about the head and thrown onto a fire. Too eerie for my tastes. Anyway, this isn't Claire Sutherland's garden. She lived across the street. This path leads to flats: two vacant, the other let to Mr Martin Findlay. I took the liberty of looking around his place before you arrived. Constable Woods let me in. You won't believe what it was like. Not what I expected from a man who doesn't work. Quite strange."

Fenella opened her mouth to ask a question, but Dr Mackay waved it away and got in his request first.

"Is it true Mr Findlay is a person of interest in the death of Maureen Brian?"

Dr Mackay stared at Fenella with the intensity of a surgeon's knife. She shifted uneasily.

"Detective Constable Earp has orders to bring in Mr Findlay," she said.

Given the turn of events, they would hold Martin in custody. It niggled in her gut. There was no record of violence in his past, not even a parking ticket. But Earp said he was seen angrily throwing rocks into a pool. It made little sense. She hoped forensics would turn up a clue.

She said, "I'll speak with Mr Findlay later today at the station."

"Good," Dr Mackay said, breaking into a smile. "Very good."

He shuffled towards the body and squatted. His hands hovered over Claire Sutherland's battered face like a mystic's palms gliding over a crystal ball. Then, with an audible sigh, he leaned forward. The gloved fingers extended as if the proboscis of some hideous tartan fly. They moved with practised dexterity as he re-examined the fractured skull.

Two minutes later, Fenella left the crime scene tent. When she glanced back, she was surprised to see Dr Mackay at the tent flap door, watching.

The generator hummed. A growing crowd filled the air with nervous voices. Fenella's mind raced over the next move. Better call

Earp. She pulled out her mobile phone. It pinged before she'd even glanced at the screen—a text message from Superintendent Jeffery:

Remind me to discuss Detective Sergeant Dexter. We need to move on this item. Are you on your way?

The generator beat out its rhythmic thud. There was nothing more she could do here. The crime scene techs were on top of things. And Jones would report back on his door-to-door. If she hung around any longer, she'd be late for the meeting with the superintendent. Yes, better go back to the station. It is time for a frank talk with Jeffery.

A herring gull landed on the gutter of the red brick house and screamed. Fenella gazed beyond the crime scene tent to where it squawked. What did Dr Mackay say about Martin Findlay's flat? "Quite strange."

She turned to the street. Her Morris Minor waited like a police attack dog, key in the ignition but engine quiet. Fenella pivoted and hurried to the dingy porch with its rusted tin roof and screaming gull.

Chapter Forty-Five

F ENELLA MOVED ONTO THE porch, looking around.

"Good day, ma'am," said a short fat constable. He shuffled from the shadows like a hog from its watering hole. "Terrible what's happened, isn't it? These quiet streets are the worst. You never know what's going on behind the closed curtains."

Fenella recognised him: Constable Woods. What was he doing lurking about in the shadows? She glared at the officer.

"Shouldn't you be helping on the street?"

"Doing my duty right here, ma'am." He gave a salute. "As much as a uniform can."

But Fenella smelled the acrid stench of cigarette. If there was a chance to skive, Constable Woods would find it. He was lazy, besides being addicted to nicotine. A bad blend.

"You been smoking on duty, Constable Woods?"

"A quick tea break, ma'am. With us being so short-staffed, you have to take it when you can. Just five minutes to clear the head."

Fenella wished she could take a five-minute break. With two deaths on her plate, she couldn't take her eye off the ball. If Dr Mackay's hunch about a serial killer was right, there'd be more deaths until they caught the perp. How could she take a break? How could any police officer?

Constable Woods gazed at Fenella with innocent eyes. "If you need an extra body on your team, I'm game for a bit of overtime. As long as it is the paperwork variety. I'm good at sorting through files."

"Get back to work," Fenella snapped. "And don't let me see your sorry face again today else I'll have you up for disciplinary. Do I make myself clear?"

He hurried away, his thick legs moving with surprising speed.

Fenella strode in the opposite direction, curious to get inside Martin Findlay's flat. She hurried along a musty hall, heavy with the stale odours of fried food and sweat. At the end she turned into a bright room, split in two sections by a Formica breakfast bar. The still air smelled of pine and polish with faint traces of mint. A contrast so stark from the dull and stink of the hall, it caused her to stop and stare.

There were no net curtains in the window. Drapes, soft and velvety and forest green, hung from the curtain rail. An oversized television rested on a matching teak stand. The sofa and armchairs looked new, carpet cleaned. In the kitchen, the hard tile gleamed. Every surface clean, everything put in its place. It looked like a picture from a glossy magazine.

Fenella folded her arms. Was this Martin Findlay's flat? She had read his social services report. It said he spoke little, dined on chicken and chips daily and got along with everyone at the Quarterdrigg. "A kind-hearted man if a little muddled at times."

She walked to the kitchen, opened the cupboards. Yes, everything in its place. At the fridge, she opened the door. Milk, cheese, eggs, ham and butter, with bottles of ketchup and brown pickle. Nothing unusual. She turned to the sink, empty, and lifted the lid of the bin— empty. Now she thought of her cottage on Cleaton Bluff. Of Nan in the kitchen surrounded by mess. Of Eduardo in his study with drawings on the floor.

This place wasn't right.

A sudden revelation gripped Fenella. It spilled from her mind and into her gut in sour waves of dread. She recalled a teenage girl who tidied her room before disappearing into the night. A young mother who placed her baby in pretty clothes, then left the sleeping child on a church pew. And the executive who settled all his accounts before killing his wife and fleeing to Peru. Her heart sped up.

Has Martin Findlay gone to ground?

She had the chance to bring him in on Friday and passed. She gazed around the room. The faint trace of polish and pine and mint was suddenly sweet and sickly. Had she made a mistake? A mistake which led to the death of Claire Sutherland?

Again, her stomach roiled and her chest tightened so she could barely breathe. To this point, she was certain of her course. That the answers lay in the *Pig Snout* and tracing Maureen Brian's missing photographs. But the wheel of fate had turned, shattering her theories into a thousand puzzle pieces. For now, nothing seemed clear. Nothing.

Fenella steadied herself against the Formica countertop. She breathed in and out in shallow breaths. With a trembling hand, she grappled with the contents of her handbag. She wanted to know the instant Martin Findlay arrived at the police station. She speed-dialled Earp.

His phone rang for several moments, then clicked to voicemail.

She left a message, her voice dry and hoarse. Next, she called the station.

"Earp in?" she asked, her voice uneasy.

"Not yet," came the reply from the clerk.

Fenella ordered a patrol car to check at the Quarterdrigg. She hung up and gazed around the room in growing agitation. She walked around the kitchen and into the living room. Her eyes scanned the walls, and she noticed tiny brass hooks where pictures once hung. She examined the patch of dark wallpaper. Even with modern forensic science it would be impossible to say what hung there and for how long. Still, Fenella speculated. A Gift from Maureen Brian or a family portrait?

She moved to the velvet drapes, stared out the window, but saw nothing. The mowed lawn did not enter her conscious mind. Nor the crazy paving path which led to a shabby shed with cracked clouded windows. Not even the crime scene tent along the path which led to the front door. Sightless, she stood there for a long while, listening to the slow tick of the clock. Dimly aware of the police officer hurrying towards the house. Only a single image swelled in her head. The broken face of Claire Sutherland.

Fenella passed a hand through her hair and turned back to the room. She paced to the Formica counter and sat on a stool. She spotted it then. Face down on the carpet underneath the table where the television sat. A small slip of paper almost hidden by the carpet. As she approached, she realised it was a business card. She put on blue N-DEx gloves, then picked it up and read:

Jack Croll
Retired detective and Crime Consultant
Port Saint Giles 619-0703

Nothing prepared her for what happened next. Not the corpse of Claire Sutherland, nor Martin Findlay's neat room. Footsteps sounded from the hall. Constable Woods appeared, his eyes dark and troubled.

"Ma'am, I've been sent to get you. They've taken Detective Constable Earp to the hospital."

Chapter Forty-Six

I T WAS NOON WHEN Fenella and PC Woods arrived at the Port Saint Giles hospital. They ran through the main entrance. A man on a gurney sat up and watched. He coughed with hacking breaths as they dashed to the reception desk. A uniformed greeter with peroxide-blonde hair waved them into a wide passage where halls snaked in every direction. It took several seconds to get their bearings. Constable Woods, breathing heavily, doubled over for air.

"This way," Fenella said. She rushed along a ramp. It turned at a sharp angle to a staircase. Constable Woods fell several paces back. He wheezed and groaned like an old-time accordion. An awful *slap–slap* of his boots echoed off the hard concrete floor. The fierce white glow of overhead lights lit their path through door after door. Their pace slowed to a steady trot then to nothing, now outside an entrance marked Cardiac Care Unit.

A nurse stepped through the door.

"Detective Constable Earp is in here," she said. "This way please."

"Wait here," Fenella said to Constable Woods, as she followed the nurse.

A disinfectant odour shrouded the still air as dense as a London fog. They walked by a trolley filled with medical devices. They moved too fast for questions. A red light flashed. Hidden speakers let out a high-pitched shriek.

The nurse turned to Fenella and spoke in an urgent tone. "That's the patient alert. We are short-staffed today. The reception room is on the left. Make a cup of tea. Someone will stop by in a moment to answer your questions. I must go."

Fenella watched as the nurse ran along the hall and turned into a room.

"Cup of coffee?" The question came from a familiar voice.

Fenella turned.

Dexter stood in the doorway, his face grim. He held out a paper cup. She took it but did not sip.

"What happened?"

Dexter rubbed his chin and said, "Heart attack. Outside the Quarterdrigg."

"Oh my God," Fenella said. "Oh my God."

A woman wearing a white coat ran by the open door. Her long brown hair flapped like the mane of a frightened horse.

Dexter was talking. "Miss Albertha Crow found him slumped in his car. She works reception in the Quarterdrigg and is trained in first aid. She went outside for a smoke and saw him with his head against the steering wheel. Although she tugged the door open, she couldn't pull him out because of her wheelchair. So, she grabbed his arm, took his pulse from the wrist. She felt something."

"Thank God."

"But she couldn't see him breathe. She raced back inside the Quarterdrigg to call for an ambulance. It arrived in seven minutes, Constable Phoebe in eight. I heard it over the police radio and got here just after he arrived."

Fenella almost bit her tongue, but she had to ask. "He's alive?"

Dexter nodded. "Thanks to the swift actions of Albertha."

"Good," she said. "Very good."

The red light stopped flashing. A moment later the screaming speakers quieted. Fenella inhaled deeply and let out her breath in short bursts, a relaxation technique she'd learned in her fusion yoga class. She reached for her phone.

"I better call Sue."

She did not want to frighten the woman. But what wife wouldn't freak out when their husband is rushed to hospital?

"I phoned earlier, Guv. She is on her way."

Fenella nodded and closed her eyes. She could depend on Dexter, and Earp was in excellent hands. She twisted her neck from side to side and tried to relax. There was nothing more to say or do, so they sat in silence and sipped weak hospital coffee.

It was a long, grim, wait.

Just after twelve thirty in the afternoon, a woman in a white coat entered the reception room. Fenella recognised her. The person she'd seen running along the hall earlier. She stood, aware of Dexter at her side.

"I'm the duty cardiologist. Are you Mrs Earp?"

Fenella shook her head. "Inspector Sallow, and my fellow Detective Sergeant Dexter. We are work associates."

The heart doctor's expression became solemn. "Mr Earp suffered a second heart-related event. We did everything we could, but he never regained consciousness and slipped away from us. I am sorry."

Fenella remained very still. Only this morning she'd spoken to Earp on the phone. He hadn't complained of feeling unwell; the opposite, he was jovial.

"I am so sorry for your loss," the heart doctor said again.

The red light flashed as the ceiling speakers screamed.

"Another crisis, I'm afraid," the doctor said as she hurried from the room.

Fenella sat, stunned. Dexter did the same and put his face in his hands. The truth had barely sunk in when a soft electric hum carried from the hall. A small boy appeared in a wheelchair with a woman at his side.

Fenella stood straight up. She recognised Sue and her son Nick.

Sue stared at the detectives and her face drained. As though warding off the unspoken words, she raised hands to her ears. "No. Don't say it. It won't be true if you don't say it." Her eyes were wild with fear. "No. Please, God, no."

"I'm sorry, luv," whispered Fenella wrapping her arms around Sue. "I'm so terribly sorry."

"Don't worry, Mummy," Nick said in his small voice. "This is a hospital. That's where they fix things that are broken. Mrs Ledwidge, my teacher, said so. How long before Daddy is mended?"

Sue began to sob. Her limp body trembled in Fenella's grip.

"That's all right, luv," Fenella said. "Just let it out and cry." She held Sue tight, saying nothing, sharing her pain and tears.

"Where's Daddy?" Nick began to cry. "Daddy said we would play night cricket and eat Chinese curry. Where's Daddy? I want to see my daddy."

Dexter kneeled and whispered into the boy's ear. "Hey, Nick. Your daddy is very proud of you, he told me so himself. Told me you're going to be a detective like him. Told me you would look after your mummy if he wasn't around to help. He even told me about his plans to build a tree house in your Egremont Russet apple tree."

Nick yelled, "Where is Daddy? I want my daddy."

Chapter Forty-Seven

F ENELLA COULD SEE THE full sweep of the hospital cafeteria despite the dim light in the booth where she sat sipping lukewarm tea. Her wristwatch said it was 2:15 p.m., but there was a healthy flow of late lunchtime patrons. Sue's sister and mother had arrived. She left the family to grieve and make the necessary arrangements. Then she told Dexter to take the rest of the day off. He refused and returned to the *Pig Snout* to keep an eye on the crime scene techs. Finally, she made the call to inform Superintendent Jeffery.

Now she sat alone in the cafeteria surrounded by people as grief seeped into her bones. There was nothing she could do for Earp or Maureen Brian, or Claire Sutherland. Death had thrown its cloak around the day and squeezed so hard she felt her heart ripping apart.

Maybe it was time to speak with the living.

She reached into her handbag and toyed with her phone. She never called home when she was on duty. Ever.

But today had been no ordinary day.

Perhaps she should call Eduardo or Nan?

Perhaps...

She dialled home.

Eduardo picked up on the first ring.

"Come home," he said before she spoke. "Come home, honey, and get some rest."

Fenella knew he didn't listen to the news during his working hours. His focus was so complete that Nan often had to call him for lunch.

"You've heard?"

"About the murder of Claire Sutherland? Yes. Nan told me, and it is all over the social media sites." He paused, and Fenella heard Nan's voice in the background. "And about Detective Constable Earp too. It was just on the two o'clock radio news. Come home, luv. Nan is making cabbage and bacon soup."

Nan only cooked cabbage and bacon soup when there was trouble.

"On my way," Fenella replied.

She felt a tinge of disappointment in herself. Going home to rest wasn't exactly a role model for action. There was desk work to be done, which would take up most of the afternoon. And there were lawyers' briefs to read. She was due to appear in the magistrates' court the following morning and had asked Dexter to go home, but he refused. Shouldn't she stay on the job too?

"And Fenella, I love you," Eduardo said.

"Oh, you daft sod."

But she blew back a kiss before she hung up.

Now she'd heard Eduardo's voice, she felt settled. She drained the remains of her lukewarm tea. Slowly, reluctantly, she stood and was about to leave when she noticed a man waiting in line at the food counter. It was the guitar slung across his shoulder that first caught her eye. And the black leather biker's jacket with the oversized crucifix on the back.

Noel O'Sullivan, the American pastor.

Was he at the hospital to visit a patient?

Her detective instinct pinged. She eased back into her chair, toyed with the empty cup, and watched. Even from this distance, she could tell he was happy. From the tilt of his head, he might even be laughing. A young girl appeared with a tray on which balanced a large bowl of ice cream. Noel's arm snaked around her waist.

There was something about her orange jacket. Fenella took in the short skirt and Doc Martens boots and leaned forward on the table as an alarm bell rang at the back of her mind. Had she met the girl on a school visit? Or at a youth club when she gave one of her talks to encourage young girls to consider the police force as a career?

They walked to the checkout, where Noel pulled out a fat wallet and paid. Again, he gave the impression of laughing. This time the girl joined in.

Fenella remembered her then.

The teenage girl was in the crowd the day Audrey Robin found Maureen Brian's body on the beach. Fenella closed her eyes to remember. Yes, she stood amongst the crowd near the crime scene tent. They hadn't traced her.

Fenella picked up her handbag and jerked to her feet. She wanted a word with that girl. Her name and her address would be a good start. Other questions would follow. Now she had the teenager in her sights, she would not let go.

A hand tugged Fenella's arm. She wheeled around.

"It's only me," Rodney Rawlings said, palms out. "Thought you'd like to help me out with a comment about the body on the dustbin bonfire."

"Her name is Claire Sutherland," Fenella said. "And no, I've no comment other than that."

"Come on Fenella, I got a job to do." His rodent face twisted into what Fenella supposed were doleful eyes. It just made him look shifty. "Can you help me out, please?"

She considered for a moment. The news media played an essential role in criminal investigations, not least in the appeal for witnesses. And she and Rodney Rawlings went back a long way. He knew where her skeletons lay.

"I've given you her name," she said. "Why don't you get cracking on that?"

"Facts don't make good copy." There was something about the way his nose twitched that Fenella found distasteful. Like a rat sniffing out the cheese. "We can't sell newspapers with facts. It's all about the sizzle."

"And the steak?"

"I'm vegetarian." He sneezed, wiping his nose with the back of his hand. A line of snot streaked across his upper lip. "Come on Fenella, just a nugget for old times' sake."

"Why don't you speak with the press liaison officer?" Fenella stared at the line of snot as it meandered along his upper lip. If it were a poisonous snake, she'd take a shovel to it. Instead, she handed him a tissue. "She will answer your questions better than I can. I've got nothing for you."

Rodney Rawlings stuffed the tissue in his pocket without wiping his nose and pulled out a digital recorder which he thrust under Fenella's chin. "When will the Port Saint Giles Slayer strike again?"

"No comment."

"Is it true you have a person of interest, a Mr Martin Findlay, who you let slip through your hands?"

They were still trying to track down Martin Findlay. He had disappeared.

"No comment."

"Can you explain why you didn't bring him in on Friday evening?"

Fenella stared hard at Rodney Rawlings. Where the hell did he get his information?

"I cannot comment on the details," she said. "It is an ongoing police investigation."

Her tone made it clear the conversation was over.

Only, it wasn't over.

"Give me some sizzle, luv," Rodney Rawlings snarled. "Is it true your dead detective was pissed out of his skull?"

Fenella glared. "Get out of my sight, else I will have you arrested."

She shoved by him, somehow clipping his jaw with her handbag. An accident, she would claim, if the rodent complained. She hurried towards the food counter, but the girl in the orange jacket was gone.

Chapter Forty-Eight

TWO HOURS AFTER NAN and Eduardo were sound asleep, Fenella lay on her back staring at the ceiling. The magical cabbage and bacon soup hadn't quelled her stomach or calmed her mind—too much death for the broth to prevail. Silence closed in. The dreary moonlight cast a blood-orange glow. She thought of all that had happened since sunrise and feared what was to come.

The taste of hot bile bubbled in her throat and her ears rung with the wail of the dead. Long after the funeral of Detective Constable Earp, she would remember Nick's tears. Long after they buried his father in the ground, she would hear the boy's lonely cries. She sucked in several breaths, holding them for seven slow ticks of the bedroom wall clock.

It didn't help.

An impulse caused her to leap from the bed and dash into the bathroom. In the moonlit dark and the cold and the still, she threw up Nan's cabbage and bacon soup. Next came the tea and the coffee and everything else—until her stomach was empty, throat raw. She washed out her mouth with blue antiseptic and crawled back to her bed and cried.

Chapter Forty-Nine

F ENELLA SPENT THE FOLLOWING morning on the hard benches of the magistrates' court. With each case, she felt a sense of growing chagrin.

Two acquittals.

One case dismissed.

The blame game began before the prosecution team stepped out of the courtroom. The lawyers, social workers, and Fenella clashed. Each pointed the finger at the other. Their quiet arguments grew to angry shouts until the judge threatened to throw them behind bars. They escaped with a stern warning and their mutual hostility intact. Fenella hoped the day wouldn't get any worse.

It had begun to rain when she got into her car. Pools of dark water glistened in the dim light. Fenella called Lisa Levon.

"Anything from the Maureen Brian crime scene?" she asked.

"I'm so sorry to hear about Detective Constable Earp," Lisa said. Then she clicked into professional mode. "Too early for DNA. No fingerprints."

"No news on Claire Sutherland either?"

"It is in line. The labs will get to it."

"And the *Pig Snout*?"

"Let me see," Lisa said, followed by the clacking of a keyboard. "We've finished with it. There are several fingerprints which we are still going over, and a shoe print near the bar, male—not Dexter. Other than that, nothing yet."

It all sounded vague to Fenella. "Help me out, Lisa."

"We are doing our best. It takes time, and with the cutbacks..."

"Understood." Fenella sighed. "You know where I am."

When Fenella arrived back at the office, Jeffery's assistant waited.

"The superintendent would like a word. Please follow me."

At the solid oak door, the assistant knocked as timid as a mouse. Fenella didn't wait for a reply. Today she wouldn't take any crap: last night was rough, the magistrates court not much better, and the conversation with Lisa Levon soured her mood to an acidic swill. She strode into the carpeted office and took a seat at the desk.

"You wanted to see me, ma'am?"

"Nasty business," Jeffery said, looking up from a stack of papers. "I've sent my sympathies to Mrs Earp. Chief Constable Rae and I will attend the funeral service. What do you think of the Cumbria Police Band playing the Funeral March? A solemn send off for a much-loved officer."

"I'm sure his family will value that, ma'am." Fenella waited. There was more.

Jeffery tapped a manila folder, then pushed it across the desk.

It was Earp's Medical Report. Fenella took her time as she read the clinical words. A blockage of the left major artery caused the heart attack. She read and reread the section on the level of alcohol in his blood. She knew about Dexter's battle with drink, but Earp? At last, she flipped the folder closed and shook her head.

Jeffery was speaking. "No reason to mention his blood alcohol in our public account. Let's keep it to ourselves. Agreed?"

Fenella wasn't sure that was possible. Not since Rodney Rawlings mentioned it at the hospital. Was it just a guess, or did he get the details from someone inside?

"I'll do my best."

"Your best, eh?" Jeffery's eyes narrowed. "Remember he was a detective on your team. Were you aware of his drinking problem?"

Fenella sensed more behind the question. She knew a set-up when she saw one and didn't answer.

Jeffery said, "A minor annoyance which I hope to keep out of the public eye. At least until after the funeral. The press will have other rabbits to chase by then. Earp is not why I invited you here."

"Ma'am?"

"These past few days have been tough. Pressure."

"Part of the job, ma'am."

"It is imperative we do everything in our power to catch the killer."

"That's our job, ma'am."

Jeffery smiled, but Fenella saw through the wolfish grin. "You need a break."

"What are you saying, ma'am?"

"The public are asking questions. They want results."

"An inquiry unfolds at its own pace."

"The public and our political masters want more. I want more."

"There are no magic formulas." Fenella wanted to shout as she had at the lawyers and social workers in the courtroom. Her voice rose. "No shortcuts. Only careful police work, and that takes time, ma'am."

"We need answers, Detective Sallow."

Jeffery's impatience annoyed Fenella. True, it had been slow going. They had only begun to dig when the second body showed up. Anyway, the fiasco at the magistrates' court reminded her they needed to take their time. Get all their ducks in a row. And that was a detective's first rule of thumb.

Fenella said, "We need time to follow up."

Jeffery jerked to her feet. "We don't have time. What we need is progress."

"We are working our leads. The techs have crawled over the *Pig Snout*. Same for the crime scene of Claire Sutherland. The pathologist's report will be on my desk soon, along with lab results. As for Maureen Brian—"

"Yes, yes, I know all that." Jeffery waved her hand and sat. "But we need—"

"We have found one of Maureen Brian's missing photographs." Fenella was on a roll, wouldn't give up without a fight. "It might give the motive for her death."

"And the other three?"

"No news on their location."

Jeffery picked up a pen and tapped the manila folder. "Why don't you take a break. Go on a long vacation."

"In the middle of an inquiry?"

"We don't want another Earp." Jeffery smiled, but it was all wolf.

It was all clear now. Jeffery wanted a quick win. To get that, she'd push her aside. Assign another detective. Fenella would not go without a fight. Her temper hovered on the edge of an uncontrolled blast, and her breath felt hot in her nostrils.

"Are you asking me to step aside?"

"There is no one else in my team who could take on the case. You, Dexter, and Jones are all we've got." Jeffery couldn't hide the venom in her last sentence.

"Then what," Fenella asked, "have you invited me here to tell me?"

Jeffery steepled her hands. "Carlisle Police will take over the Maureen Brian and Claire Sutherland cases under my direct command. Detective Inspector Frye will be in charge from Friday."

Chapter Fifty

AUDREY SAT AT THE kitchen table drinking tea when she heard the knock. She hastily placed her cup on the table and wondered if it was the detectives coming back to ask more questions. For an instant she saw the face of that ratty terrier with its fox-sharp teeth and thought the knock at the door was all in her head. But the knock came again and she jerked to her feet, her mind running over what she would say.

When she opened the door, Elizabeth Collins stood on her welcome mat with her hood up against the chill. For a moment Audrey doubted whether she was there at all. Maybe it was the detectives in disguise? Or her mind playing tricks again? Then she took in the bloodshot eyes and ashen cheeks—Elizabeth had aged.

"Are you going to leave me standing in the damp and cold?" Elizabeth spoke in a jovial tone, but something about her wary expression put Audrey on her guard.

"Come in. I've just put the kettle on for a fresh brew." Audrey stepped from the doorway. "A surprise visit. How nice."

The door closed with a quiet click.

Elizabeth lowered her hood and shrugged off her coat, placing it on the hook on the wall. "Don't want to tread the mess and muck all over your nicely cleaned floor." She stomped on the doormat, slipped off her shoes and sniffed. "Lavender and mint; been doing a bit of spring cleaning?"

Audrey had taken great pains to tidy the place. She had mopped and swept and washed the windows so they sparkled as if they were new. The kitchen, she'd spritzed with fresh air spray to dull the scent of fried food. She had even begun sewing new curtains, though she doubted they'd look as good as bought. None of this did she dare mention to Elizabeth.

Audrey said, "Just a quick clean to spruce up the place. Don't want it going to the dogs." She watched Elizabeth closely as she spoke. Her curly brown hair was a mess. No makeup. No lipstick. "Elizabeth, is something wrong?"

Elizabeth gave a weak smile. "Let's get that brew going, shall we? I'm parched."

Audrey busied herself with a fresh pot of tea while Elizabeth sat at the scrubbed pine table. As she poured milk into a delicate china jug, she felt Elizabeth's eyes on her back. When she spooned out sugar into the small bowl, she was once again seized with the uncomfortable sense of being watched. She placed the tea things on a flat tray and spun around, almost toppling them over.

Elizabeth's chin rested on her hands, her eyes wide and wary.

"Careful Audrey, we don't want a mess. Come and sit down so we can talk."

Audrey sat and said, "Are you all right?"

"This is really awkward." Elizabeth stopped abruptly as if not wishing to go on.

"What is it?"

"I'm concerned about Martin. He's gone missing."

Audrey felt herself relax. Not Maureen Brian. Not Claire Sutherland. She didn't know what she would say if Elizabeth brought up the topics of the murders. She knew how upsetting it all was.

Elizabeth was speaking. "He is on a lot of medication. God knows what will happen if he fails to take his dose."

Audrey spooned sugar into her cup and stirred. "I'm sure he will be fine. How far could he have gone?"

Elizabeth shrugged. "I remember when he forgot to take his pills and ended up in the Port Saint Giles Hospital. He almost died."

"He'll be fine," Audrey said. "We will all be fine."

Elizabeth stared at her in silence for a moment.

"But he has disappeared, Audrey!" Her voice rose to almost a wail. "And with the murder of Claire Sutherland, it won't take long before the police start asking questions. I'm really concerned."

Audrey felt her anxiety rising and grasped her teacup with both hands. She wanted to scream and throw Elizabeth outside. Her nosing around interfered with the plan. With sharp gasps, she sucked in air. In. Out. In.

"Are you okay?" Elizabeth gazed at her with concern.

"Fine." Audrey tried to smile. It came out wrong. "It is difficult for us all. When did you see him last?"

"Friday, when we were in his flat." Elizabeth ran a hand through her untidy hair. "You saw the mood he was in. He didn't touch my food, not a bite. He's been like that since Maureen's death."

Audrey said, "Don't worry, Elizabeth, everyone's taking it hard."

Elizabeth shook her head. "Maureen would have seen this coming." She began to sob. "I feel like I have let her down."

Audrey placed an arm around her friend, kissing her on her forehead. "It will be all right. Nothing's going to happen to Martin. The police will find him."

"What will happen to him when the police catch him?"

"I don't know." Audrey thought they would charge him with murder, lock him in a cell and throw away the key. "I just don't know. Maybe it is for the best if he stays away for a while. Let this blow over."

"How can it blow over?" Elizabeth said, her voice filled with alarm. "We are talking about murder. Audrey, it won't blow over."

"I know. I know."

"This has to stop." Elizabeth shrugged from Audrey's grip. "You told Martin to say nothing, but he needs to tell the police the truth." She was shouting, her bloodshot eyes wide and wild. "Martin has to tell the truth. Maureen and Claire deserve that."

Chapter Fifty-One

FENELLA STOOD BY THE whiteboard in Incident Room A. She clutched a cup of lukewarm coffee and glared at the empty rows of chairs. It was 7:00 p.m. Evening briefings were not popular, even when bigwigs attended. Tonight, there were no bigwigs present, nor did Fenella expect any to show. Bad news spread around the police station quicker than norovirus on a cruise ship. So yes, she was off the Maureen Brian and Claire Sutherland case. But the handover didn't happen until Friday.

She had hoped for more people. Dexter and Jones sat in the last row.

"I'm sure a few faces will show," Dexter said.

But Fenella counted the empty chairs—twenty-two—and let out a gloomy sigh. She had invited Tess Allen, the press officer. No show. No Constable Crowther. No Constable Phoebe. Even the cleaner passed the room without a sideways glance. They had scattered like rats fleeing a stricken ship. Why bother to attend an evening briefing for a captain whose vessel is sunk?

"Another five minutes, Guv?" Dexter said, shuffling to the door and looking along the empty hall. "For any stragglers."

They waited for ten.

Dexter returned to the back row, sat, and said, "It is not looking good."

"Aye," Fenella replied. "Everyone has given up and gone home." She was unable to mask the bitterness in her tone. "Everyone."

Jones glanced towards the door and spoke for the first time. "They'll wait for the new inspector. A fresh set of eyes. New orders. I suppose we ought to go now as well, ma'am."

It was the kindest way for him to say it. It was over. Finished. He'd given up like the others.

Fenella put down her lukewarm coffee and stomped to the door. As she looked along the vacant hall, she reminded herself not to get frustrated and blame her team. She was the leader and had to take the balls as bowled. She twisted her neck from side to side, then sucked in a breath and held it for a count of ten. On Friday, Detective Inspector Frye took over the case. His responsibility. His call. Maybe she should close the file and wait?

But frustration seeped into her bones and she came to a slow boil. She became a detective to solve complex cases, find justice for the victim and their family. To see things through.

That's who she was.

That's all she knew.

She'd keep pushing until they told her to stop. But what could she do in forty-eight hours?

Something.

An idea formed.

She turned to Jones. "Got plans for the evening?"

"Nothing special. A shower, quick meal, and a television show. Then tomorrow, I'll do it over again."

"Tell you what," Fenella said. "Let's head to the pub. I'm buying."

Jones looked dubious but didn't get to reply. Dexter got there first.

"Right you are, Guv," he said with a grin.

Jones said, "Thought you were laying off the booze?"

"Team building," Dexter replied. "Are you in?"

"Okay," Jones replied. But he looked as excited as a child on Christmas morning tearing open their present to find a lump of coal.

"If you are sure about it. Okay."

"Let's go," Fenella said in an upbeat lilt, although her stomach bubbled with nerves. Was it a mistake to invite Dexter to a pub? Could her day turn much worse?

Chapter Fifty-Two

DEXTER KNOCKED BACK HIS drink like a man who'd stumbled into an oasis, and Fenella laughed. It was a nervous cackle, filled with relief.

She sat with Dexter and Jones around a wooden bench in the Sailors Arms. It was a dingy pub with hardwood floors and a barman with the face of a bulldog. A shroud of booze and ancient tobacco and savoury pies clung to the scuffed dark wood. The red leather furnishings were well worn. The thick frosted glass of the windows encased the saloon like a time capsule from the nineteen seventies. Nothing had changed in decades. It was a favourite watering hole for old-timers of the Cumbria Police fraternity. Young officers drank elsewhere.

Two elderly men sat at the bar. Under the dim light, they looked like etchings drawn with thick strokes of an artist's brush. Fenella remembered when they were a group of ten. Their number had dwindled over the years, pulled from this Earth to meet their maker. She recalled the names and faces of every one who had departed.

"Another?" Fenella asked with a grin.

"Oh, go on, then," Dexter replied.

"Not for me," Jones said, his hand clutching his pint. "Still working on this."

"Aye," Fenella said giving Dexter a wink. "It doesn't pay to rush the Sailors Arms' ale, else it will come back to bite you in the morning."

Fenella laughed again, this time through relief. Dexter drank orange juice rather than ale. His choice.

He hadn't given up on the case.

Neither had she.

She sipped her pineapple juice and felt pleased.

"So, what's the plan, Guv?" Dexter asked.

Fenella reached into her handbag and pulled out a spiral-bound notebook. From the docket she pulled a folded sheet of paper and spread it on the table: a copy of the photograph of Maureen from Audrey Robin's sideboard. There was a long moment of silence as Dexter and Jones stared at the smiling faces. Fenella liked that. She had their attention.

"Let's start with Maureen Brian." Fenella returned her notebook to her handbag and reached for her mobile phone. She glanced at the screen and switched it off. *Do not disturb, detectives at work.* "A popular woman who created art from her photography using a process known as—"

"Colloidal photographic images," interrupted Jones. "It involves glass plates and—"

"Yes, yes," Fenella said. "None of your digital malarkey, we get that. And her snapshots sell for a decent chunk of change. Problem is, four went missing." She paused and glanced around to make sure they were still with her. They were. "We found one on the *Pig Snout*. Where are the other three?"

"We searched her apartment," Dexter said.

"Only a quick scan," Fenella corrected, thinking about the hidden compartment in the skirting board on the *Pig Snout*.

"Ma'am," Jones said, his voice high pitched. "Should we be discussing the case in a pub?"

"Probably not," Fenella replied. "But we shall do so anyway, if that is all right with you?"

Jones shrugged and said, "Is it too late to bring in the crime scene techs to do a fingertip search of Miss Brian's room?"

"Aye," replied Fenella. But she made a mental note to return to Maureen Brian's room to check. "I couldn't get the resources earlier; perhaps Inspector Frye will do better."

The barman appeared. He carried a large tray with three plates of steak pie, green peas, Beefeater chips and a ladle of thick brown gravy. Fenella hadn't eaten since breakfast: Nan's scrambled egg and two slices of toast. Hunger hit hard as the savoury aroma wafted up her nostrils.

"On the house," the barman said in a voice which carried to the bar. Then he let his voice drop to a whisper. "It ain't right what Jeffery did to you and Dexter."

"Thank you," Fenella said, her stomach squeezing in a tight knot.

The barman turned to Jones. "And who might you be? One of us, I hope."

"Aye, he is that," Dexter said. "Fresh out of the National Detective Programme, but he'll soon learn the ways of us seasoned folks."

"Nice to meet you, son." The barman placed the tray on the table. "People around here call me Sarge. I retired ten years back from the police station you call home. I know Inspector Frye. Hard-nosed bugger. He won't go down well around these parts." He turned and ambled back to the bar.

They ate their meal in silence.

The barman stacked crates behind the counter, his loud puffs mixing with the rhythmic jingle of bottles. With quiet voices, the two old men at the bar continued to talk and sip their ale and cast curious glances at the detectives.

"Ben and Safiya Griffin," Fenella said tapping a finger on the photograph. "What do we know?" She didn't wait for a reply. "This business with Seafields Bed and Breakfast. Maureen Brian leases her home to the happy couple, and they run it as a hotel. By all accounts a dream come true for Ben and Safiya. But with all that rain we had this summer, and no visitors, it's turned into a nightmare."

"Question, Guv," Dexter said as he wiped the last of the gravy with the crust of his steak pie. "How are they staying afloat?"

"I ran a background check on their financials," Jones said. He had not been asked to do so by Fenella or Dexter and looked as if he regretted opening his mouth. "Thought it might help."

"You did, eh?" Fenella said. "And who else did you run financials on?"

Jones looked shifty. "Pastor Noel O'Sullivan."

Fenella read his face and knew there was more. She waited.

Jones said. "And also Audrey Robin and Miss Maureen Brian's friends—Gloria Embleton and Elizabeth Collins, as well as Ben and Safiya Griffin."

"Initiative, eh?" Fenella said. "That's what I like. Well, let's keep this bit of creativity to ourselves, shall we? Drop your report off on my desk in the morning, luv. But don't keep us in suspense; what did you find about the Griffin's business?"

"They've been losing money for quite some time and are up to their eyeballs in debt."

Dexter put down his fork. "So, Ben and Safiya are struggling financially. What do they gain by bumping Maureen Brian off?"

They fell silent for a moment. The quiet tinkle of bottles being stacked drifted from the bar.

"They might have a motive if they owed rent." Fenella had been over Maureen's numbers herself. Several times earlier. And again today to check for political contributions. Nothing stood out. She turned to Jones. "Did you see anything odd in Maureen's financials?"

Jones shook his head. "I asked the forensic financial investigator to give me a breakdown of her regular payments and income. I got the numbers going back five years. Just the usual stuff, pension coming in and utility bills going out. There were several large payments into her account which were traced back to Wingfield and Morton, an art dealership in Carlisle. Again, nothing suspicious."

"And what about the Griffins?" The question came from Dexter.

"They owe money to Tom, Dick, and Harry. But nothing to Maureen as far as I can tell. And their rent payments are up to date."

Fenella pursed her lips, then she said, "So neither Ben nor Safiya had a financial motive, so I guess we better move on." As she spoke, she had another thought. She raised her hand for silence and closed her eyes. When they opened, she was smiling. "Where did Ben Griffin go on Bonfire Night?"

"Come again?" Dexter said.

Fenella reached into her handbag, pulled out her notebook, and flipped to the page where she'd interviewed the Griffins. "Yes, here it is. Ben came home with his wife. She is heavily pregnant, and he gave her sleeping pills and put her to bed. But he went back out again, according to his wife, and came back home around 2 a.m. Did anyone follow up on that?"

Dexter cracked his knuckles. A sign she was onto something.

"Nope," he said. "Wonder if he knew Claire Sutherland?"

There was a pause, only a beat, but long enough to hear the expectant hum of the detectives like the chirp of insects after a storm. Fenella felt a sudden surge of adrenaline. They'd been so focused on gathering witness statements they had not had time to analyse them. And then came the murder of Claire Sutherland and the disappearance of Martin Findlay. On top of it all, preparation for the magistrates' court and one hundred and one other administrative tasks, all urgent. All required now. She put her frustration on hold and focused on Ben Griffin.

"Let's have a word with him first thing in the morning." She could not hide the excitement in her tone. But she wasn't about to put all her eggs in one basket. "Now what to do about Ron Malton?"

"We can't bring Malton in," Jones spoke in a reverential whisper. "Not without good cause, and I doubt he'll show up voluntarily."

"I'll find something," replied Dexter. "What about this business of leasing the boat to Maureen at no cost? It smells fishy. If we are creative…"

"Superintendent Jeffery would have our hides!" The outburst came from Jones. He grasped his ale and took a quick gulp. "We'll get fired."

Dragging Malton into the station would definitely give Jeffery ammunition. If it backfired, Fenella knew she and Dexter would be put out to grass. Still, if the councillor was involved, it would be worth the roll of the dice. She thought about that, wasn't ready to swing for the fences just yet, and said, "Okay Jones, you have a better idea?"

"I don't know… this business with the *Pig Snout* is… odd."

"How do you mean?"

"Her studio." Jones rubbed a hand across the back of his neck. "Where is Maureen Brian's studio?"

"On the *Pig Snout*," Dexter replied.

Jones shook his head, then pushed his half-finished pint of ale aside. "Where are the glass plates and the chemicals?" Again he shook his head. "Her studio is somewhere else. The boat was where she went to relax."

"But we found one of her photographic images hidden on the boat," protested Dexter.

"There is no way it was her studio. If it were, we would have found the—"

"We've got it," Fenella said. She agreed. "So where is her studio?"

Dexter shrugged, stood, and headed for the men's restroom.

Fenella said. "When you checked Maureen's financials, did you see any rent or other regular payments that might suggest the address of her studio?"

Jones pulled out a spiral-bound notebook and flipped through it. "Only gas and electric and her telephone bill. Of course there were groceries, but no regular payments of any kind. Wherever her studio is, she didn't pay rent for it."

Fenella folded her arms. Were the missing photographs in Maureen Brian's mysterious studio or somewhere else? And why was the photograph she found hidden in a compartment on the *Pig Snout*? One thing was clear. Wherever the location of the studio, Maureen didn't pay rent. She thought about Seafields Bed and Breakfast. All those rooms. Another reason to visit first thing. Her gut told her she was onto something, but her mind remained troubled.

"Any news on Martin Findlay?"

"Not a word," Jones replied. "He's disappeared like a ghost."

"Not easy for a big man." Her gut told her he was innocent; so did her head. But they had both been wrong before and she wanted to speak with him. "He'll not have gone far."

Dexter returned, but he didn't sit down.

"Guv, Lisa Levon's been trying to contact you."

Fenella fumbled for her phone. "What's she got?"

"A match on the Johnnie Walker bottle fingerprints. They belong to a Mr Ian Wallace."

"Name rings a bell," Fenella said. "Petty drug addict who lives in the East Side Caravan Park. Think we'd better pay him a visit."

Chapter Fifty-Three

D EXTER DROVE TO THE East Side Caravan Park, easing the Morris Minor to a stop outside a row of dilapidated cabins. The detectives sat for a moment in quiet contemplation. Bloodhounds taking in a scent. There were no streetlights, just the flicker of orange from the windows. A gust of wind picked up a fast-food box. It tumbled along the pavement, coming to a stop at a broken picket fence.

"These used to be holiday lets," Fenella said, glancing around. "Back in the day people would come from all over Cumbria to spend time by the sea. Me and Eduardo stayed here once when our children were little. It was like Disney World back then, with workers wearing red jackets and kids all over the place. The evenings were when the adults got to play. Now everyone goes to Benidorm in Spain."

"Not much sign of the glory days left," Jones said from the back of the car. "If it weren't for the houselights, I'd mark this place down as deserted. More like a ghost town from one of those Halloween horror movies. Which one belongs to Ian Wallace?"

"No numbers," Dexter replied.

"See what I mean?" Jones played a slow drum beat on the window. "Spooky."

Fenella laughed and said, "Guess you'll have to go house to house, Detective Constable Jones. We'll wait in the car."

"Me?"

Dexter laughed. "The Guvnor's on a wind-up, lad. We'll all go."

The first door they approached opened two inches before they knocked.

"What do you want?" asked a disembodied voice.

"I'm looking for Mr Ian Wallace," Fenella said.

"You the police?" The door closed an inch.

"Aye, that we are, luv."

"About bleedin' time." The door opened to reveal an elderly woman with bleached white hair and false teeth which gave her the look of a donkey. "I knew it. No one knocks on the doors around here at night, not even the Bible bashers."

"Can you point us towards Ian Wallace's place?" Fenella paused. "Mrs—"

"The name's Mrs Young. I used to teach elementary school in town before I retired. Moved here when it was a holiday resort with my late husband. Now it is a pigsty thanks to the likes of Ian Wallace. He uses my yard as a cut-through like some feral teenager, but he's got to be in his forties. Never grown up and too damn lazy to use his own front door. I've complained no end about it, but nothing's been done."

Fenella took out her notebook. "I'll see what I can do, luv." She wrote for a few moments and handed the woman her business card. "Which one is Ian's?"

Mrs Young came out onto the doorstep. She appeared much shorter outside, just shy of five feet. But she had the presence of authority. *Must be the teacher in her*, Fenella thought.

Mrs Young said, "Is he in big trouble?"

"Aye," Fenella replied. "As big as it gets."

"Fantastic. Bloody fantastic." Mrs Young clapped her hands, then pointed to the house on the right, next door. "He is in. I saw him staggering home earlier. Tell the judge to throw away the key."

"We don't sentence them, luv," Fenella replied. "Only reel them in."

"If you need a witness to shut him away for good, I'm game. I keep a diary. Ian and his druggy friends' activities make up half of the entries. It's his daughter I feel for. Imagine having a dad like that."

Fenella considered for a moment, then said, "Can one of my officers wait in your backyard?"

"I'll need to see your identification." Mrs Young flashed a donkey-toothed grin. "Anyone can print a business card these days."

Fenella obliged, then turned to Jones and said, "Make your way around the back in case he decides to go rabbit on us."

"And be careful not to stomp on my flower beds," Mrs Young added. "Ian's always stomping on my roses."

Fenella and Dexter walked along the narrow path which led to Ian Wallace's front door. A wind chime clattered with a rusty squeal. The place needed repair. Paint peeled from the rotted windowsills, and the cabin sagged to one side as if about to keel over. They paused on the doorstep. The stench of stale tobacco and beer and marijuana hung like a cloak above the rotted door.

Dexter sniffed. "Hasn't changed his ways, by the scent. Old dog, new tricks, and all of that."

"Let's see what he has to say," Fenella replied. " Up to now he has been more of a nuisance than anything else. Do you think he is involved in the death of Maureen Brian and Claire Sutherland?"

"Sometimes they graduate," Dexter replied, apparently thinking along the same lines as Fenella. "Never ends well when they step up to the major league."

Fenella tried the door handle.

"Locked. Guess we'll have to knock and wait."

A sharp noise interrupted their conversation. It came from the back of the cabin. The slam of a door, followed by hurried footsteps.

"Looks like Ian's gone rabbit on us," Fenella said. "Watch the front door."

She rushed around the side. A pile of wooden pallets slowed her progress. A figure flitted through the shadows in the direction where

Jones waited.

Jones gave a shout, and she heard footsteps as he gave chase. She followed the sounds of the chase, because in the dark it was difficult to see what was happening. And there was clutter and junk and mud and muck. It seemed their only purpose was to catch your foot. Twice she stumbled, but righted herself. After the third stumble, she slowed to a careful walk.

There was nothing but dark ahead and the glimmer of the cabin lights behind. She knew Ian Wallace couldn't outrun Jones who was twenty years his junior and built like an Olympic athlete. Fenella stopped and listened.

A solid *thud*, followed by a curse.

"Jones," she called. "Are you all right?"

In the light of a watery moon dimmed by black swirling clouds, Fenella held her breath. The air seemed to hang cold and still with the dark wrapping tight like a scarf. With no sound but the distant grumble of the sea, she called again.

"Jones, what's happening?"

A moment later Jones appeared, shaking his head and wiping a handkerchief across his mud-stained trousers.

"Got away from me, ma'am. Knows this place like the back of his hand. And as fast as greased lightning."

"Aye," replied Fenella, thinking. "You sure it was Ian Wallace? Average height, long hair, bald on top."

"I didn't get close enough to tell."

"Man or woman?"

Jones shrugged. "Moved as quick as a zebra. I'd have got him in daylight, but in the dark, well, it wasn't a fair game."

Fenella wondered whether the ale he drank at the Sailors Arms slowed him down. She sighed. The suspects seemed to be slipping through her fingers. First Martin Findlay and now Ian Wallace.

"Call the duty sergeant," she said. "Give a description as best you can and get a patrol car out here. If we are lucky, they'll pick up the person. Wait by the Morris Minor until they arrive."

When Fenella returned to the front of the cabin, Dexter said, "No joy with the rabbit, then?"

Fenella shook her head. "Even Jones couldn't keep up with the bugger."

"Whatever Ian Wallace is taking, I want some," Dexter laughed. "Anyway, Guv, bit of good news. Front door is open."

Fenella knew by the broad grin, Dexter had worked his unofficial magic.

"Let's have a look around," she said. "We wouldn't want anything to happen to Mr Ian Wallace's private property. Call it neighbourhood policing."

The detectives' footsteps clattered off the hardwood floors, a shuffling noise that echoed through the two-bedroom cabin and disturbed the rank air. Enough to wake the dead, but it didn't wake Ian Wallace.

Under the dull glow of a floor lamp, he lay slumped on a low sofa, mouth ajar, eyes closed, half-empty bottle of Johnnie Walker at his side. A contented snore alerted them to life. But it took several shakes from Dexter and a mug of frigid water to bring him around.

"Not cool, man," Ian said blinking awake. He flicked at his shoulder-length hair and rubbed a hand over his bald spot. "Not cool, dude. Not chill."

Dexter said, "What you been up to, then?"

"Hey, what is this?" He was fully awake now. His head turned from Dexter to Fenella. He gave a resigned sigh. The police were a constant annoyance in his day-to-day life. They'd shoo him away when panhandling or arrest him for selling stolen goods. "What now?"

"Mind if I look around?" Dexter didn't wait for a reply and left the room.

Fenella said, "Ever heard of the *Pig Snout*?"

"No."

Only a two-letter word, but came out like a lie.

"You sure you never heard of it?"

"I didn't do nothing." The words oozed out greasy. Damp glistened on his forehead.

Fenella glanced at the Johnnie Walker bottle. "I see you enjoy a dram of whisky."

"It's legit, I swear."

"Tell me about today."

"Never left the house. I'm a man of routine. I always stay in on Tuesdays."

"And the *Pig Snout*?"

"It wasn't me."

"Fine, let's do this down the station, shall we?"

"Listen, I don't like water. I don't like boats, never been on the *Pig Snout*. I don't go near the harbour."

"Who said anything about boats or the harbour?"

Ian blinked.

"I... er... like I say, I don't know nothing."

Fenella nodded as if she understood. "I'm with you on that, Ian. I realise you don't like boats, hate water, and have not been to the harbour recently."

"That's right. You got it, man." Ian let out a breath. "Now if you don't mind, I'd like to return to my dreams. You can find your way out, can't you?"

"Of course," Fenella said. "There is one minor detail we wish to clear up first. It has to do with your fingerprints. They were all over the *Pig Snout*. Are you sure you don't recall going aboard?"

"Listen, I... wait, what is all this about?"

"I'm investigating the murders of Maureen Brian and Claire Sutherland."

"Hey, man, you can't pin that on me. I'm innocent."

"Your fingerprints were found on the *Pig Snout*. Three valuable photographs were stolen from that boat; ring any bells?"

"I don't know anything about no stupid photos."

Dexter stepped into the room.

"Guv, look what I found hidden under the bed." He held out three square photographs. "Nice, aren't they? Look expensive. Not your regular holiday snaps."

"Collodion positive images," Fenella said, her heart sinking. Ian Wallace had graduated, stepped up to the major leagues. "And yes, they are worth a penny or two. So valuable, in fact, they'd be worth murdering for, right, Ian?"

"Hey, you got it all wrong, man."

"Why did you do it?" The answer often made no sense, but Fenella had to ask. "Why did you kill Maureen Brian and Claire Sutherland?"

"No. No. No." He tugged at his hair. "I don't know anything about Maureen's death. I liked the woman. She was good to me. And who the hell is Claire Sutherland?"

"You killed Maureen Brian and stole her photographs to fuel your drug habit."

"I don't do drugs no more."

But the evidence was damning. The room stunk of cannabis and tobacco and beer and sweat. And there was an ashtray at the side of the sofa filled with spliff butts. They'd find other drugs, too, if they searched. And they would.

"What's that, then?" Fenella pointed at the ashtray.

Ian Wallace stared hard, folded his arms but didn't answer.

Chapter Fifty-Four

F ENELLA PUT IN A call to the duty sergeant. She explained the situation and asked they post an officer on the front door. The crime scene techs would go over the cabin inch by inch tonight. In the morning there'd be a fingertip search of the front and back garden. If Ian Wallace was the killer, she'd nail him good and proper.

"Nice job, well done," the duty sergeant said. "I'll have every available officer on hand. Might pull in one or two on overtime too. The crime scene team will be there within the hour. The mother lode for you, Inspector Sallow. No expense spared." He paused a moment, and the line went quiet. When he came back, his voice dropped to a whisper. "I'm not saying anything you don't already know, but the way Jeffery treated you over this one... well, I'm not cutting corners here. Like the superintendent says, it is imperative we do everything in our power to catch the killer." He let out a devious laugh. "The expense will get right up her nose."

When Fenella hung up, she felt a sense of pride and accomplishment. They had found the missing photos under Ian Wallace's bed. His fingerprints were all over the empty bottle of Johnnie Walker on the *Pig Snout*. And here in the cabin, another Johnnie Walker bottle, half-empty. Coincidence?

Still, Fenella felt a pang of sadness for Ian Wallace. He sat in miserable silence on the sofa. She saw a wizened, middle-aged drug addict whose life had gone wrong. A loser, yes. But a vicious killer? She sighed. That decision wasn't her call. It was down to the Crown Prosecution Service to press charges and a judge and jury to convict. Her job was to follow the evidence to wherever it led. To get justice for Maureen Brian and Claire Sutherland.

"All right, young man," Dexter said, easing Ian Wallace to his feet. "Your transportation has arrived. Guess we'll speak again in the morning."

A uniformed officer handcuffed Ian Wallace and led him away.

Fenella checked her watch. It was roughly the time Nan went to bed. Eduardo would be drinking a cup of cocoa at the scrubbed pine table in the kitchen. She usually joined him, and they spoke about the day's events or plans for the future. Not tonight though. An evening with her family missed, but she felt it was worth it.

Her mobile phone rang. It was Jeffery.

"Sallow, what the hell's going on?" Jeffery cut out the usual introductions. Fenella knew to wait. The superintendent usually answered her own questions. "Let me remind you we are under extreme budgetary constraints. And now I hear you ordered uniformed officers and crime scene techs to the North Side Caravan Park. This better be good."

"I'm investigating the Maureen Brian and Claire Sutherland murders, ma'am."

"What?" Jeffery spat out the question before Fenella could continue. "I made it perfectly clear you are off that case. Inspector Frye takes over on Friday."

"Today is Tuesday, ma'am. And we have had a development."

"At the North Side Caravan Park?"

"We've found Maureen Brian's missing photographs. It seems a Mr Ian Wallace stole them."

The line fell silent for several heartbeats. When Jeffery came back, Fenella could hear the wolfish smile in her voice.

"Very good, Detective Inspector Sallow. I shall arrange a press conference at once. I told the public we would do everything in our power to catch the killer. And we have. It is imperative our result goes out tonight. Imperative. Now, the details."

Too early for a press conference, Fenella thought. But she knew better than to get in the path of Jeffery when she'd got up a head of steam. An announcement would go down well with the politicians. Rocket fuel for the superintendent's career. She gave the details. When she finished, she said, "Ma'am, we can link Ian Wallace to the stolen photographs. There is no evidence to link him to the death of Maureen Brian or Claire Sutherland, yet."

"Forensics?"

"Ongoing."

"Then we'll have to jolly them along." The superintendent placed her on hold. Fenella waited and wondered what was going on. At last the line clicked and Jeffery was back. "I've sent word to the labs to focus on your case. Follow up in the morning with the reference numbers. Now, when are you interviewing Ian Wallace?"

"In the morning, ma'am."

Jeffery snorted. "If he confesses, let's hope it is in time for the lunchtime news. No leaks on this, Sallow. I want to know the moment any news breaks."

Fenella hung up and began to make notes. The first priority was to interview Ian Wallace, get his story on what had occurred. He looked frightened when the uniformed officers took him away. Good. A night in the cells would loosen his tongue.

She would speak with Ben Griffin first thing in the morning as planned. She wondered if Ben and Ian knew each other—friends? Or did Ian sell them goods on the cheap? She made a note to check for a relationship. But if Ben had an alibi, she would drop him from the active investigation. That meant it would be mid-morning before she got around to Ian Wallace. But he wasn't going anywhere. The longer he sweated, the better.

As Fenella continued to think, the low murmur in the room tapped at the edge of her consciousness. She wasn't really listening to the hubbub of activity at first. She still wanted to look around Maureen Brian's room. Did she have enough evidence to call in the crime scene techs to search the apartment? But then she caught sight of Jones with Dexter at his side. The way Dexter's jaw suddenly dropped, whipped up her curiosity and sent her heart thudding.

"What is it?" She made her way across the room.

Jones held the four photographs in his gloved hands.

"It's these pictures, ma'am. They are not the originals. Just cheap photocopied prints."

Chapter Fifty-Five

THE FOLLOWING MORNING, Fenella and Dexter stood on the doorstep of the Seafields Bed and Breakfast. It was, even on this bright November day, cold and damp with another storm threatening to brew over the Solway Firth. They'd taken the side ramp this time, rather than the steps.

"A few questions for your husband," Fenella said when Safiya opened the door. She'd grown bigger since the last time they spoke. *No way she is only seven months,* Fenella thought. *That baby boy is due any moment now.*

"News?" Safiya gave an uncertain smile and remained motionless in the doorway, her short pregnant body like a blockage in a tube. "About Maureen Brian?"

"Let's get inside where we can chat," Fenella said. "Damn cold out here."

Without a word, Safiya turned and led them to the dining room where they'd previously spoken. The same smells of boiled vegetables and furniture polish hung in the air. There were no signs of preparation for paying guests. The place was empty. They sat at the table by the window with views of the desolate beach.

"Coffee or tea?" The question couldn't hide Safiya's curiosity.

"You sit yourself down, luv," Fenella replied. "I'll get it. Where's Mr Griffin?"

As if on cue, Ben stepped into the room.

"I heard the front door," he said, in a pleasant tone. The words hung in the air as he caught sight of the detectives. It was clear he'd expected paying guests. The friendly gleam quickly turned sour. "What the hell do you want?"

"To ask you questions about Maureen Brian," Safiya said, and in a tone that left no doubt she was annoyed with her husband.

"In that case, Safiya, let me help you back to our room." Ben looked at the detectives. "The doctor said she has to avoid stress." He gave his wife a weak smile. "You need rest and I don't want you getting agitated with their damn questions."

"No." Safiya's voice filled the room. "I'm staying right where I am."

Ben looked at the detectives as if appealing for help.

"Best leave her be," Fenella said. "An argument might cause her stress."

Ben's lips curved into a professional smile, but his eyes simmered like a master whose dog disobeyed. He gave a little cough, then spoke in a honey-sweet tone.

"Coffee or tea?"

"I'd love a coffee," Fenella said. She sensed a difficult discussion ahead. The caffeine would keep her alert.

"Same here," Dexter said, "black no sugar."

Fenella knew he had the same idea and waited until the coffee was made and Ben settled himself at the table before she spoke.

"Thank you for taking the time to see us this morning. I have a few questions which I'm sure you can clear up. Won't take long. One moment, please." Fenella rummaged around in her handbag and made a performance about taking out her notebook. She knew what she was going to ask, but wanted to make him wait. Rattle his nerves. Get under his skin. "Ah, here we are. I'd forget my own name if it wasn't so short."

"We are rather busy, Detective Sallow." Ben poured himself a coffee, black. "What is all this about?"

"Oh." Fenella glanced around. "Paying guests today?"

"No... well... er... there is so much to do."

"Claire Sutherland." Fenella spat out the name short and fast. She wanted to knock him off balance. "Did you know her?"

"No."

"Are you sure?"

"Absolutely."

"What about Ian Wallace?"

"Everyone knows Ian."

"Do business with him, then?"

"Here and there." Ben rubbed a hand over his mouth. "He sells me stuff for the bed and breakfast."

"Like what?"

"Cleaning products, foodstuffs. Curtains. You name it."

"Drugs?" Fenella knew Ian Wallace was a user. Was he also a dealer?

"I'm no fool," Ben snapped. "I never touch the stuff. Not my gig."

"Where were you Sunday night?" Fenella directed the question to Ben, but watched Safiya.

"At home with my wife, of course."

Safiya shifted in her seat and looked at her hands.

Fenella said, "All night?"

"Yes."

"Oh, so you didn't go out like you did on Bonfire Night?"

"Pardon?"

"Your wife told us you went back out on Bonfire Night. After you had given her sleeping pills and tucked her into bed."

Ben glared at Safiya. She didn't return his gaze.

"Oh, Bonfire Night?" Ben spoke slowly as if in deep thought. "Yes... yes. It seems so long ago, I almost forgot. I did go back out for a short while to enjoy the end of the celebrations."

His acting didn't convince Fenella. For the first time, she picked up her pen. "Where did you go?"

"Here and there, nowhere in particular."

Fenella tapped her pen on the notebook. "Can you be a little more precise?"

"The boardwalk to the lighthouse and along the beach. There were a lot of people around and I enjoy the crowds."

"Did you meet anyone?"

He shook his head.

"Oh, come on, Ben," Fenella said. "A handsome young man like you out on Bonfire Night and you didn't run into anyone you know. If this was London, I'd believe it. But this is Port Saint Giles. You can't walk down the street without bumping into a neighbour."

The room became very still, air heavy like when a thunderstorm is about to break. Fenella sensed it and waited.

"Darling, you told me that you met with Mike Swain." Safiya's quiet voice rolled across the empty dining room like the distant rumble of thunder. The room felt suddenly chill. "The two of you went for a drink, you said. Didn't you end up in the Sailors Arms, because it is always quiet in there?"

Ben did not speak for several moments. His head turned down so his eyes rested on the mug until at last his hand slowly reached out and toyed with the handle. Then he looked up.

"Yes, honey. That's quite right." He turned to Fenella. "I didn't want to mention Mike. Thought it best to keep him out of this. Silly, I suppose. So, there you are. Any more questions?"

Safiya began to sob. "Oh God! Oh God!"

"What is it, luv?" Fenella kept her voice soft and waited. "I'm here for you. I'm listening."

Safiya said, "I spoke with Mike's wife, Flo." She breathed in quick gasps. "Mike spent Bonfire Night with Flo at her mother's house in Carlisle."

"That's enough, Safiya." Ben got to his feet. "You are tired and confused."

But she kept talking. "And I didn't take the sleeping pills you gave me Sunday night. Where did you go? Ben what have you done?"

Ben's face became bread-dough pale. His hand grasped the mug and tried to bring it to his mouth. It sloshed over the brim, splattering the tablecloth like drops of blackened blood.

Fenella turned to Dexter. "Get a family liaison officer over here. Then call for a patrol car." She returned her gaze to Ben. "Mr Griffin, I think we better sort this out at the station."

Chapter Fifty-Six

I T WAS ALMOST 10:00 a.m. when Fenella and Dexter got back to the station. She called Jones from his cubicle. The three detectives huddled in her office to prepare for the interviews with Ben Griffin and Ian Wallace.

"Let's put the puzzle pieces together," Fenella said as they sat around her desk. "We have Ian Wallace's fingerprints on a bottle of scotch found on the *Pig Snout*. A boat he claims to have never been aboard."

"Pretty damning proof," Dexter said.

"What about the CCTV camera?" asked Jones. "If he shows up on the images, we've got him bang to rights."

"Aye," Fenella said. "Make a note to call the harbour. See how far the recordings go back. Now, let's get back to Ian Wallace. Suppose he is telling the truth."

"That he wasn't on the boat?" asked Jones.

"Aye." Fenella hesitated for a moment, thinking. "Maybe it is like he says."

"You don't believe that do you, Guv?" Dexter asked.

Fenella folded her arms. "I'm ready for anything. Every stone we've upturned in this case has led to a surprise. It's a stretch, but someone could have placed the bottle on the boat to implicate him. Only problem is, who?"

Jones said, "Someone who had access to the harbour. Finnegan Woodstock the watchmen? Or Councillor Ron Malton?"

They fell into a nervous silence. Fenella turned over the possibility in her mind. Councillor Malton rented the boat to Maureen. He'd know her photographs were valuable. Same for Finnegan Woodstock. They'd speak with Finnegan, again. But what to do about Councillor Malton? She felt like she was stepping into a snake's nest, blindfold. And everyone knew Malton liked to bite.

"Okay, let's move on," she said, as her subconscious mind continued to work through the possibilities. "Ben Griffin. No alibi for Bonfire Night or the time of Claire Sutherland's murder. And we know he had a business relationship with Ian Wallace." She paused, thinking. "Let's focus on Seafields Bed and Breakfast. Jones, anything new?"

Jones pulled out his spiral notebook and flipped through the pages. "I spoke to their bank manager this morning, off the record. He reckons the Seafields Bed and Breakfast will shut within a month or two. The bank has refused to extend more credit."

"There is your motive in plain sight," Dexter said.

"Aye, happen you're right about that," Fenella replied. "Jones, off you go to track down the harbour CCTV videos. Dexter, let's you and I see what Mr Griffin has to say."

But Ron Malton's involvement niggled in the back of her mind. She had to speak with him again; the question was how?

Chapter Fifty-Seven

B EN GRIFFIN SAT SLUMPED in a chair in the interview room. A plastic cup of tea rested on the table. His face hadn't lost the baker's-dough shade of pale. If anything, he had gone a shade paler, and his black button eyes glistened as if at any moment they might spurt.

While Dexter fiddled with the recording system, Fenella sat down opposite Ben and looked at him for a moment.

"You're in a lot of trouble," she said.

Ben sat up straight as if struck by lightning. He touched the gold loop in his nose and ran a hand over his devils wisp beard. But he didn't speak.

"Ben Griffin, I'm investigating the murder of Maureen Brian and Claire Sutherland."

Still no reaction.

Now Fenella didn't mince her words. "You are here under suspicion of involvement in their deaths. Where were you on Bonfire Night?"

Ben placed his hands face down on the table, spreading his fingers wide. "I... I... Listen, you've got it all wrong."

Fenella pressed him with another question. "Where were you the evening of Sunday the eleventh of November? The night of Claire Sutherland's murder."

Ben raised his eyes. Terror glistened. For a long while he stared and blinked. At last, he spoke, his voice a high-pitched tremble.

"I want a lawyer. I'm not speaking to you without a lawyer."

Fenella said. "Do you have a solicitor you can contact?"

Ben shook his head.

Fenella stood. "Okay, Mr Griffin, we'll continue this interview once we've arranged legal representation."

Chapter Fifty-Eight

OUTSIDE THE INTERVIEW ROOM, Fenella and Dexter watched Ben Griffin through a one-way mirror panel. He slumped over the table, head in his hands, body shaking with bitter sobs.

"Thoughts?" Fenella asked, her own mind clicking the puzzle pieces into place.

"Ben knew Maureen Brian, lives in her house, runs a business that is losing money and has no alibi." Dexter stared through the mirrored panel as he spoke. "Didn't his wife say they were going to buy a doughnut cart? Where'd he hope to get the money?"

"Not from the bank," Fenella said, remembering the earlier comments from Jones. "Their bank manager expects them to fold."

Dexter said, "He might have worked with Ian Wallace. We know they are business associates."

"But Ian stole fake photos."

"Ben might have got greedy and switched them."

"Aye. No knowing what a man will do under the pressure of debt." Fenella smiled. "You might be onto something."

Dexter said, "Any news from forensics?"

"Lisa Levon's not come through for us this time." Fenella had called the labs first thing, but knew it took time. "Let's go have a word with Mr Ian Wallace. I expect he'll be ready to talk after a night in the cells."

Her mobile phone rang—Jeffery.

"News?" Once again Jeffery skipped the formalities.

"Nothing yet, ma'am."

There was a long pause. When Jeffery spoke, her voice buzzed with waspish frustration. "Mr Wallace hasn't confessed?"

"On my way to speak to him now, ma'am."

"Get a move on, Sallow, else we will miss the lunchtime news. Report back the moment you step from the interview room. It is imperative I have the details. If Ian Wallace confesses, I want to be the first to know. Is that clear?"

Fenella didn't get to reply. A hand pressed her shoulder. She spun around.

"Ma'am, I've been all over the station." The duty sergeant looked flustered. "Councillor Malton wants to speak with you."

"What about?" Fenella's stomach fluttered with unease.

"Maureen Brian, ma'am."

"What was that?" The question came from the mobile phone— Jeffery.

"Sorry, ma'am, I've got to go." Fenella hung up before Jeffery fired off another question.

The duty sergeant said, "Mr Malton expects you at the Port Saint Giles harbour. At your earliest convenience, ma'am."

Which meant now.

"Come on, Dexter," Fenella said. "Let's see what this is about."

"What about Ian Wallace?"

"The lad's not milk. He'll not go off."

Chapter Fifty-Nine

F ENELLA DIDN'T LIKE IT.

Ron Malton sat in his wheelchair in the oval room at the Port Saint Giles harbour. His elbows rested on the glass-topped table with yellowed nautical charts beneath. There was no readable emotion on his poker face. On his left sat a plump man in a pinstripe suit with a wisp of a moustache covering his upper lip. On Malton's right sat a wiry man in his seventies, who wore a pink Hawaiian shirt with giant pineapples. They clashed with his mop of bleached white hair. The room smelled of potpourri and furniture polish with a faint trace of mint.

"Detectives, take a seat," Malton said, waving them to the opposite side of the table. "I appreciate you taking the time to visit with me today."

"This meeting is off the record," the plump man in the pinstripe suit said. "Detectives, we'll need your agreement on that before we begin."

Fenella was about to protest but Malton raised his hand. "Let's not get ahead of ourselves. Introductions first." He placed a hand on the shoulder of the man in the Hawaiian shirt. "This is my uncle, Malcolm Buckham. I mentioned him in our last conversation."

Fenella recalled he was a retired engineer who bought the Port Saint Giles harbour. The business ran into financial difficulties during the last recession. His wife passed away due to the stress. All this she remembered in the blink of an eye.

"Please call me Malc. Everyone calls me Malc," the man in the Hawaiian shirt said.

He spoke in a deep soothing tone, not what Fenella expected from an engineer. She had the idea from his Hawaiian shirt that his voice would be high-pitched; scratchy like the hinge of an unoiled door. Now she remembered that Malcolm Buckham and Ron Malton were business partners. But it wasn't clear why Ron Malton invited her and Dexter to the oval room, so she remained quiet and waited.

Ron Malton was speaking. "And this gentleman on my left is Mr Ward, my solicitor."

Mr Ward nodded. His sharp eyes flitted between Fenella and Dexter, sizing them up. He said, "This meeting is off the record, agreed?"

"Give me something to chew on," Fenella said. "Right now, all I got is gum with no flavour."

"Are we off the record?"

"No."

Mr Ward stood up. "Then we will have to conclude this conversation."

"Sit." The command came from Malton.

Mr Ward sniffed as if he disapproved. But he sat down and leaned back in his chair.

"Let's not be too hasty, Mr Ward," Malton said. "The detectives have been good enough to come when we called."

"Nothing less than one would expect of the police," Mr Ward replied. "Nevertheless, I shall stay if that is your wish." He let out a contented sigh, arms folded across his chest. The longer he remained, the higher his legal fee. "And I shall continue to advise should your conversation become imprudent."

Malton wheeled to the window so they could only see his back.

"I hear you sent a detective to inquire about our CCTV surveillance videos."

Fenella waited a moment before she replied. She wanted to see Malton's face, read between the lines. But with his back to them, all she had to go on were his words. *Why the interest in the CCTV surveillance?*

Fenella said, "We need to review the video for the Maureen Brian case."

"May I ask what you are looking for?"

"I cannot share information about an ongoing investigation."

"Need I remind you I chair the Police and Crime Panel." Malton didn't miss a beat and name-dropped to drive home his point. "I count Chief Constable Rae amongst my personal friends."

"That doesn't change the rules."

"Detective Sallow, I can assure you our videos will prove useless."

"Let me be the judge of that," Fenella said. "The public often think their information is of no importance. But I've known many a case turn on 'unimportant' details."

Malton spun around and wheeled back to the table. His poker face unreadable. "Tell you what, Detective Inspector Sallow, how about we make a deal?"

"I'm listening." Fenella was curious. She wanted to know what he wanted to trade. "Go on."

"Off the record?" The question came from Mr Ward.

Dexter shifted uneasily. Fenella smiled. Dexter had no qualms about using unofficial means to gain entry to Ian Wallace's cabin. But speaking off the record to counsellor Ron Malton made him anxious. It did the same for her. The man was a snake who liked to bite. She tilted her head from side to side to ease the tension.

"Off the record," she confirmed.

Malton gave a thin-lipped smile. "Let's begin with a brief history lesson, shall we?"

Fenella wanted him to get to the point, wondered how far back he would go, but said, "Okay, as long as it is relevant."

"You have met Finnegan Woodstock?" Malton paused, waiting for confirmation.

"On several occasions," Fenella replied.

"A good man, hard worker, and gentleman. I am honoured to say we have become quite close since he joined us at the Port Saint Giles harbour. I now count him as a friend, and I'm sure he feels the same about me. Now, how can I put this... let me see..."

Again, Malton halted, this time for several long seconds. There was a stillness to the room, as if the scented air waited in eager expectation. Mr Ward leaned forward, elbows on the table, watching the detectives with sharp eyes. Malc had his hands on his chin, staring at Fenella. Something was shifting in the atmosphere.

Malton placed his hands on the table, palms down. "Mr Wayne Wingfield was the previous watchmen. His name might ring a bell. He is doing time in one of your fine institutions. A rather distasteful fellow, I'm sure we all agree."

"Aye, happen you're right about that." Fenella remembered Wayne Wingfield. She slept more easily at night with him off the streets.

Malton said, "Mr Wingfield also ran a CCTV installation service. A small business, only one other worker. His prices were good. I employed him to install our CCTV cameras. The Board approved the expenditure at my request."

The picture began to emerge. Fenella was already one step ahead, knew where this was going.

"Go on," she said. "Go on."

"Would it surprise you to know the other person in Mr Wingfield's CCTV business was a Mr Ian Wallace? He is residing in one of your cells as we speak."

Fenella didn't ask how he knew. She didn't ask him anything, just waited.

"Now here's my problem," Malton said. "Your detective has asked for our CCTV surveillance videos going back as far as possible."

"That is correct," Fenella confirmed.

"There are no videos. Mr Wingfield and Mr Wallace installed a dud. The CCTV cameras only record five minutes in a continuous loop."

"And you've only just found that out?" Fenella asked.

"Port Saint Giles is a quiet town. We've never had cause to review the video from the CCTV cameras. When we did... well you know what we found." Malton sighed. "If this comes out, it will be embarrassing."

Fenella saw it in crystal clarity now. Ron Malton had supervised the purchase of the CCTV cameras. The champion of law and order had employed criminals to install the system. They'd swindled him with cameras that didn't work. The board would have his hide, the press his tail, and his fellow politicians would tear him apart.

Fenella turned to glance at Dexter. He couldn't suppress his grin. Neither could she.

Mr Ward said, "As you can see, your demand for video surveillance has put my client in a difficult spot. If you could withdraw the request..."

Fenella said, "And the trade?"

Mr Ward's eyes sharpened, and he ran a finger over the wisp of his moustache.

"Information about the death of Maureen Brian."

Chapter Sixty

I T WAS MAUREEN BRIAN'S lover."

The words came from the man in the Hawaiian shirt. Malcolm Buckham, known by everyone as Malc. He flashed a sad smile. There was a moment of stunned silence as his words floated in the oval room. Fenella's ears took in his deep resonant voice. But it took several seconds for the implications to percolate into her brain. Did Malcolm Buckham kill Maureen Brian? What about Claire Sutherland?

The answer came as fast as the questions formed in Fenella's mind.

Mr Ward said, "My client has an alibi for Bonfire Night and last Sunday when Claire Sutherland died." He reached under the table and pulled out a briefcase. He took his time shuffling through papers. At last, he lifted out a single typed sheet which he slid across the table to Fenella. "A signed statement confirming my client's whereabouts on both evenings. I've informed those mentioned to expect a discrete call from you to verify."

Fenella read the statement, her mind still working the implications. When she finished, she handed the note to Dexter. His astonished grunts echoed like the dull thud of a closed tomb door. When he looked up, Mr Ward continued.

"Superintendent Jeffery will confirm my client attended the after-Bonfire Night party. It took place at the Giles Breeze Hotel. Mr

Buckham didn't leave until well after 2 a.m. As you have read, counsellor Malton drove his uncle and Police Constable Woods to their respective homes. He dropped off my client a little after two thirty a.m., and Police Constable Woods at his place a short while later."

"Aye, I heard about that," Fenella said. "From the horse's mouth, so to speak."

Mr Ward ran a fat finger across the wisp of the moustache on his upper lip. "Councillor Malton and my client attended a dinner party on Sunday evening. It took place at Chief Constable Rae's house. Mr Rae will confirm that. The event was a fund raiser for the Port Saint Giles lighthouse. I also attended and confirm my client's presence at the event."

Fenella said, "What time did the dinner party finish?"

"The activities concluded around 11 p.m. Both men retired to their respective guestrooms and remained until daylight. They shared a rather pleasant breakfast of smoked salmon and scrambled eggs. Chief Constable Rae was present. They discussed budgetary issues, which I will not go into here. I also attended the business breakfast, as did many of the town's business leaders."

"Cast-iron alibi," Dexter muttered.

"Aye, seems so," Fenella replied. She thought again about Ian Wallace and Ben Griffin. She didn't see Ian Wallace as a cold-blooded murderer. That left Ben Griffin. Was he the mastermind who pulled the strings and wielded the blunt instrument twice?

A rich soothing tone percolated into Fenella's thoughts. Malc was speaking. "Maureen and I met five years ago. We became an instant item. I asked her to marry me on several occasions, but she enjoyed her independence. She is... was a very private person. We never met in town, only on the *Pig Snout*. That was where we relaxed together and she showed me her photographic creations."

It was clear he was an honest man, sincere, deeply in love.

Fenella said, "Do you have any idea who would want to kill Maureen?"

He ran a hand through his mop of thick white hair. "Not exactly."

"How do you mean?"

"I jog every day, keeps me healthy."

The words triggered a memory in Fenella. She stood in Maureen Brian's apartment looking out of the window. He was the man in the tight green shorts with the mop of bleached white hair. She had waved, but he didn't see her. The jogger was Malcolm Buckham!

Fenella's heart thudded against her chest. "Go on, luv. Tell it all."

"I jog by Seafields Bed and Breakfast most days. When Maureen was alive, I'd stop and wave. Sometimes she'd see me and wave back." He gave a sad smile. "It was last week, the day after they discovered Maureen's body. Old habits die hard, I suppose. I missed Maureen. So I jogged my usual path by the bed and breakfast several times. I don't know, I suppose I hoped to see Maureen. Silly, really."

His voice broke, and he pulled a handkerchief from his shirt pocket.

"Go on, luv," Fenella said. "We are listening."

"I was feeling sorry for myself, when I saw a woman crouched in the sand."

Fenella rested her elbows on the table. "How do you mean?"

"At first I thought she was ill, but I'd seen her earlier walking along the beach with a black bin bag in her hand. She was definitely crouching, hiding, by the side of a blue Morris Minor."

Fenella sat up straight. That was her car. She'd check her logbook later. For now she was certain it was the day she and Dexter visited Ben and Safiya Griffin for the first time.

"Did you call for an ambulance?"

"I thought she was ill at first, but she wasn't. I could tell by the way she crouched low that she didn't want to be seen."

"What was she doing?"

"Watching the bed and breakfast front door."

"Nothing illegal in that." But a tingle ran along Fenella's spine. "Did you pass this information to the police tip line?"

"No."

"But you thought her activity was suspicious?"

"Not at the time. But I saw her again, last Friday. Do you remember the rain?"

"Aye," Fenella replied. That was the day she got caught in a thunderstorm in the lane near Jack Croll's place.

"I love jogging in the rain, keeps an old goat alive." Malc chuckled. "The rain was heavy when I saw the woman again on Fleetwood Lane. I'm not a fast runner so I had time to observe her. She was standing under the porch of Martin Findlay's flat. I didn't see her knock, and it seemed to me she was… thinking. Then a woman in a yellow mackintosh came from one of the houses. The two women had words."

"An argument?" The question came from Dexter.

Malc nodded. "I don't know. But I heard on the morning news they found Mrs Sutherland in a yellow mackintosh. It didn't take long for my old brain cells to put two and two together. That is when I called Mr Ward and my nephew. I suppose it could be a coincidence?"

Fenella didn't like coincidences. She said, "Can you describe this woman?"

"Slender, average height. She wore glasses. They were very large, owl-like. Oh, and she had mousy brown hair."

Fenella rummaged in her handbag. She took out her spiral-bound notebook and unfolded a sheet of paper which she slid across the table. It was a copy of the photograph on Audrey Robin's sideboard.

"That's her," Malc said tapping a finger on Audrey Robin's face. "That's the woman I saw crouching beside the blue Morris Minor."

Chapter Sixty-One

A UDREY STOOD AT THE bottom of the stairs which led to the
attic. She rarely visited that part of her tiny stone cottage. It
was full of junk when she moved in and she never had the energy to
sort through it. She dreamt of turning it into a dormer with huge
windows that looked out onto the lane. But there were so many
repairs and so little money, she wondered whether it would always be
a dream.

Now she waited.

Listening.

The scraping noises were back; so was Patrick's voice and that
ratty terrier. It looked at her with its shiny black eyes, pointed teeth,
and ears pricked forward. Then it spoke in Patrick's voice.

"Turn yourself in. The police will find you."

Audrey knew the words were only in her mind because she could
hear the *slush* of waves on the distant beach. She had taken her
medicine today, although sometimes she forgot. That's when the
voices were worse. They'd tell her what to do and she had to obey. So
she walked the beaches with a plastic bin bag in her hand. If she
picked up the trash, the voices would stay away. Even if the medicine
didn't work.

But now they were back.

From her cargo pants she pulled out the envelope which contained the sheet of paper with her plan. While she waited for instructions from the voices in her mind, she reread it. It seemed so clear when she'd written the words down in red ink with a neat hand. Now all she saw was a jumble, and she knew something bad was going to happen.

From the attic, there was a movement, a noise. Audrey became still and glanced up the gloomy stairwell. A shaft of weak daylight did little to penetrate the dark. Again came the noise. Shuffling, scraping, as though boxes were being moved and rearranged.

Audrey held up her phone and flicked on the flashlight as she carefully climbed the stairs, making certain to hold the rail. An intense odour of dust and mould and rot hit her nostrils. It mingled with the savoury aroma of café fried food. At the top, she groped around for the string that turned on the light bulb. A dull orange glow chased away the shadows.

"It's only me," she said. "I've come to take away your trash."

Martin Findlay stared at her through feral eyes. They jutted out of narrow slits. He did not blink.

"Are you finished?" Audrey didn't wait for an answer. She began picking up the empty fried-chicken carton and the discarded plastic cup. "Where's the straw? Martin, what did you do with the straw?"

He didn't respond.

"You'll be safe up here. I'll bring you fish and chips for your dinner."

A hard knock echoed up the stairwell. Then a solid *thud* from the knocker on the front door. Stunned by the suddenness of it, Audrey remained still for a few moments in a state of total bewilderment. It clattered again, and again, and Audrey knew they had come.

She'd always known the police would come.

Chapter Sixty-Two

I F ONLY CATHY HAD known that it would turn out like this, she would never have agreed. She held on to Noel O'Sullivan's arm as they walked through the car park.

"Are you sure?" Cathy allowed her eyes to travel across his handsome face.

"It will be all right, honey," replied the pastor. "This is the right thing for us to do. You understand, don't you?"

She had been afraid he would say that. Fearful he would ask if she understood. She did; she'd always understood. That's what made it all so difficult. Not simple like when she was a child where life was shrouded in magic and mystery. Not like the town pond with its ebb and flow of seasons, or a palmate newt driven by simple biological urges. She had a brain. The ability to think, to decide. To make her own choices.

"I understand," Cathy said. "I want to do this."

"Good." Again, he flashed his Texan smile. And Cathy felt the magic and mystery creep back in. He placed a hand on her cheek. "Let's have an ice cream when we are done. With sprinkles."

"Yes, that would be nice," Cathy said. "I love ice cream. You know I can't resist it. When I was young, my dad would take me to the parlour on the town square. It always seemed sunny back then."

But under a sky pregnant with clouds, the rows of cars with their darkened interiors reminded Cathy of soldiers protecting a grave. She had seen the picture in a geography book about China. "A terracotta army buried underground," the teacher had said, "guarding the tomb of the dead." Now she felt a heavy weight as though soil pressed down the burdens of an uncertain future. Suddenly, she wasn't sure she wanted to do it. Her legs froze as if controlled by some demonic force. She stopped walking.

"I can't."

"Nothing to fear, honey." Noel O'Sullivan glanced about. There was a sudden edge to his voice, an adult urgency which Cathy recognised with dread. "This is for the best."

Cathy didn't move.

"The way you feel is quite natural." Noel spoke in a soft tone, honey-sweet, as again he flashed that million-dollar Texan smile. "You are exactly the way the Lord made you to be."

"But—"

"But nothing, honey. Trust me."

A gust of chill wind picked up a crisp packet and swirled it around like a giant butterfly with crumpled wings. Noel pushed up the collars on his leather jacket and placed an arm around Cathy's waist. It felt warm. She felt suddenly secure.

"Come on," he whispered. "Come on."

They resumed their walk, picking their way between the cars and up the steps of a faceless building.

Inside, the smell of bleach and sweat and stale coffee clung to the bare walls as though part of the structure. Sprawled on a wooden bench, a vagrant slept. A deep snore rattled from his throat like a lawn mower. Cathy turned away; she knew the slumbering man: one of her dad's gaggle of drunken friends. The vagrant's rhythmic snore didn't miss a beat.

"Hello there." The greeting came from a flat-faced man with slits for eyes. Cathy thought he looked like a grass snake. Then he bared his teeth in what Cathy thought must be a professional smile. "I'm the duty sergeant. Can I help you?"

Cathy supposed she would do all the talking. Tell him all she wanted to say. But the duty sergeant looked pale, almost translucent, like a snake that lives under artificial light. And she remembered what grass snakes ate—newts. Suddenly she became a palmate newt, her only desire, to wriggle deep into the mud of the Port Saint Giles town pond.

Noel said, "We would like to speak to the detective in charge of the Maureen Brian murder case."

The duty sergeant hesitated. Cathy noticed his sharp eyes. They took them in as though sifting wheat from chaff.

"Name please?" He picked up a pen. "So as I can let Detective Sallow and her team know you're here."

Cathy found her voice. "Cathy Wallace. My name is Cathy Wallace."

"Ian Wallace's daughter, eh?" The duty sergeant put down his pen.

"That's right," Cathy replied. "That's me."

Noel said, "She would like to see her dad." He turned to Cathy, lowering his voice. "While you're here, I think it would be a good idea."

Cathy didn't want to see her dad. She hated it when he got himself arrested. She didn't know why they had taken him in this time. When she'd seen the detectives at the front door of the cabin, she ran. They gave chase, but she escaped and spent the night at Mrs Collins's house. Belinda smuggled her into her tiny bedroom. They chatted and laughed like old times, with Cathy telling outlandish stories to Belinda's wide-eyed gaze. Mrs Collins didn't bat an eyelid when Cathy showed up at breakfast. She never did these days.

Noel was talking. "But we need to speak to Detective Sallow or one of the team first."

The duty sergeant said, "Leave your number and I'll have someone call back." He turned to Cathy. "We don't have visiting hours, not unless you happen to be a social worker or lawyer."

Noel said, "How long do you intend to keep her father?"

"I can't say. Name?"

"My name is Noel O'Sullivan and I would like to speak with a senior officer."

"I'm sorry, sir, but our detectives are busy. Leave your telephone number and I will have someone contact you."

At that moment a slender woman with grey hair entered from a door behind the duty sergeant. She moved quickly. *Smooth*, Cathy thought. *A peregrine falcon on the hunt.*

"Any news of Audrey Robin?" the woman asked.

"They are bringing her in," replied the duty sergeant. "And we have also got Martin Findlay. The lawyer has arrived for Mr Griffin."

Cathy recognised the woman. It was the detective she had seen at the crime scene tent on the beach the day after Bonfire Night. The woman who had chased her through her neighbour's backyard. And the very same police officer who, she had heard through the grapevine, took Ben Griffin into custody.

"I want to see Ben Griffin," Cathy screamed at the top of her voice. "I want to see the father of my child."

Chapter Sixty-Three

"**N**OW LET ME GET this straight." Fenella was having difficulty taking it all in. Noel O'Sullivan and Cathy Wallace sat on one side of a table in Interview Room B. She and Dexter sat on the other. "Pastor O'Sullivan, your church runs a wellness clinic for unwed mothers?"

"We prefer to call them single mothers these days."

"Aye," Fenella said, feeling her age. It was a challenge to keep up with the changing language, and she didn't want to offend. "You run a wellness centre for single mothers?"

"That's right, part of our church outreach activities. And Maureen Brian is… was an active member of our community of volunteers." Noel turned to Cathy who sat very still, her eyes cast down. "That's how she met you, isn't it, Cathy?"

Cathy nodded and said, "We met through Gloria Embleton. She is a teacher at school. I told Miss Embleton I might be pregnant, and she introduced me to Maureen."

"I see," Fenella said, beginning to grasp the full picture. "And the father is Ben Griffin?"

Again Cathy nodded. "He said we were going to run away together. We'd buy a house in a village in the country where we would raise chickens and goats and sell them in the farmers' market."

Fenella felt her heart squeeze, but waited for Cathy to continue.

"Ben is going to leave his wife." Cathy paused, as if considering the harshness of the words. "But he can't do that, just yet."

"Why not?"

Cathy shrugged. "He said he is waiting for the right time."

"How old are you?"

"Sixteen."

"Aye, that's what I thought, luv." Fenella glanced at Dexter. He shook his head. "But Ben is thirty-five, luv."

"Age doesn't count when you're in love, does it?" Cathy smiled. "Ben loves me. That's all that matters, isn't it?"

"Love is a challenge, pet," Fenella said. "It still leaves me baffled. Does your dad know he is to be a grandfather?"

Cathy's head drooped. She began to cry.

Noel placed an arm around her shoulder." It's okay, honey. It's okay." He turned to Fenella and gave a sad smile. "When I found out about Cathy's pregnancy, I spoke with Ben. I urged him to do the right thing, tell his wife."

"When was that?"

"I first met Cathy the day after Maureen Brian died. She came to speak with me about Maureen. Maureen befriended teenagers in need. A pastor knows his flock and I sensed Cathy was troubled both by Maureen's death and something else. It didn't take Sherlock Holmes to guess she was with child."

"I see," Fenella said. "And you spoke with Cathy's father?"

"No. She asked I not do that. But I did speak with Ben. I've known Safiya for some years. She comes to my services on the beach." Noel gave a sad smile. "I visited Ben at his bed and breakfast. We talked. He said he would think about it, but now he is in custody, the truth will come out. It will be hard on Safiya."

Fenella sighed. Ben Griffin had broken no laws. She felt his relationship with Cathy was inappropriate, but it wasn't her place to judge. His selfish actions would break two women's hearts. And what about the unborn babies? That stirred up her anger. Even if Cathy and

Safiya could put the pieces back together, they'd carry the scars inflicted by Ben Griffin for life.

"Can I see Ben?" Cathy stared with pleading eyes.

"No, luv," Fenella replied. "I'm sorry."

Cathy placed her head in her hands and let out a bitter sob.

Fenella felt a sudden surge of vengeance. There remained the matter of Maureen Brian's and Claire Sutherland's murders. She'd nail Ben Griffin, good and proper if his hand lay behind the death of those two women.

"Cathy," Fenella whispered. "Look at me."

Cathy raised her head and held Fenella's gaze.

"I want you to listen very carefully and think before you answer." Fenella waited a moment to ensure she had Cathy's full attention. When Cathy nodded, Fenella continued. "Did you meet Ben on Bonfire Night?"

"Yes. Under the pier, by the lighthouse."

"What time was that?"

Cathy shrugged. "I'm not sure."

"Before or after the fireworks?"

"Before."

Now Fenella took her time. She wanted a crystal-clear picture. No chance of a mistake. Then she'd cast her net and haul in the catch. "Did you see Ben after the fireworks?"

Cathy hesitated. Ben had told her to say she was with him on Bonfire Night and last Sunday. She wanted to protect him, but lie to the police? That's what her dad always did and look where it got him. She loved her dad but didn't want her and Ben's relationship to be built on a lie. When this was over, she and Ben would always tell their baby the truth.

"No." Cathy said. "We only spoke for a short while, about the baby."

"And you went home after the fireworks, on your own?"

"Not on my own. With Belinda."

"Belinda?"

"Belinda Yates. She is fifteen and lives with Mrs Elizabeth Collins. Mrs Collins is a foster parent."

"Aye," Fenella said, remembering. "I know of Mrs Collins."

Cathy was talking. "We walked home together with the other foster children. Belinda was in charge. I went into the house with her and she settled the kids down. After all was quiet, she walked me halfway home."

"And you didn't see Ben again that evening?"

"No."

"Are you sure?"

"Yes."

Fenella felt the pulse beating in the side of her neck. She tilted her head from side to side. Ben Griffin didn't have an alibi for the time of Maureen Brian's murder. What about Claire Sutherland? Safiya said her husband went out Sunday night after giving her sleeping pills which she did not take. The same trick used on Bonfire Night. Where did he go?

Fenella said, "Did you see Ben on Sunday?"

"No."

"You weren't with him Sunday night?"

"I saw him Friday night, after the rain. Only very briefly. He got angry."

"What about?"

"The baby."

"But you didn't see him Sunday night?"

"I did not."

Fenella's heart thudded against her chest. Ben Griffin had no alibi. His business was in trouble, he lied about his whereabouts, and he was a business partner of Ian Wallace who'd stolen fake photographs.

Got him.

Chapter Sixty-Four

I T WAS WITH THE excitement of the fox cornering the hare that Fenella and Dexter strode into Interview Room C. It reeked of nervous bodies, vomited dinners and cheap Cumbria police coffee. The bare walls and bolted table played their part in causing anxious interviewees to sweat.

Fenella used Interview Room C when she wanted answers.

Ben Griffin sat next to the duty solicitor, a balding forty-something man wearing a cheap suit and a disinterested scowl.

"So good of you to show up, Detective Sallow," the solicitor said in a sour tone. "I've got lunch with Judge Grey. Can we be quick?" He turned to Ben. "Now Mr, er"—he glanced down at his notebook —"Griffin. Do you want to represent yourself?" He arched both eyebrows as though encouraging Ben to agree.

"No," Ben replied. "I've nothing to hide, and I'm entitled to legal representation."

"Oh, very well," replied the solicitor. He turned to Fenella. "Now, Detective Sallow, I'm Mr Locke. What is all this about?"

"Mr Locke, I'm in charge of the Maureen Brian and Claire Sutherland murder investigation."

"Ah," replied Mr Locke, staring at Ben with curious eyes. He pulled a pen from his inside pocket and jotted in a notebook. When he finished, he looked up. "My client and I are ready."

"Mr Griffin"—Fenella waited a heartbeat; she wanted Ben to sweat—"let's begin with your whereabouts on Bonfire Night."

Ben hesitated, cleared his throat and spoke in a defiant tone. "Like I said before, I went home with my wife, gave her some pills and went out to see the end of the celebrations."

"Where did you go?"

"I've already told you."

"Can you tell me again?"

Ben let out a disgruntled sigh. "I walked along the beach and the boardwalk and didn't see anyone I know."

Fenella changed tack. "And last Sunday night, where did you go?"

"I... er..."

Fenella didn't wait for him to collect his thoughts. She had him off balance and wanted to keep it that way. She went on the attack.

"Do you know Miss Cathy Wallace?"

"No."

"Are you sure?"

Ben ran a hand over his devil's wisp beard, but didn't answer.

Fenella continued. "I suspect you know her rather well, since she is carrying your child."

"Okay. Okay. Yes, I know Cathy." He threw his hands in the air. "She was just a bit of fun that got out of hand. No harm done."

"No plans to elope to the country to raise chickens and goats, then?"

"The dumb cow will believe anything."

"She's sixteen!"

"It's not illegal, she is of age."

"The girl's a child."

"Detective Sallow," Mr Locke said in a warning tone. "Is there a point to your line of questioning?"

Fenella took a deep breath. "Bonfire Night, where were you?"

"Listen," Ben said, "I don't want this getting back to my wife, understood?"

Fenella waited.

"I was with Cathy. We spent the night together."

Fenella watched him closely. "And last Sunday?"

"Same again." Ben flashed a sexy smile. "Cathy can't keep her hands off me. But after this, I'm going to have to dump her."

"I see; well, that clears that up, doesn't it?"

"Can I go now?"

Fenella said, "Only one problem with your explanation, Mr Griffin. I just spoke with Cathy and she says she wasn't with you on Bonfire Night or last Sunday. She even signed a statement to the effect. So, you don't have an alibi, do you?"

Ben's eyes darted about like a wild animal caught in a trap.

"I didn't lay a finger on Maureen or Claire Sutherland. I didn't do it; you have to believe me."

"Where were you on Bonfire Night and last Sunday?"

"I didn't do it."

Fenella saw the panic in his eyes and waited.

"Okay, okay." He took a gasping breath. "I was with someone else."

"Who?"

"A friend."

"You'll have to do better than that."

"A girl. all right?"

"Name?"

Ben looked like he was about to throw up. He opened his mouth but no words came out.

"Mr Griffin, I need a name so I can check your alibi. Can you give me a name?"

"Belinda Yates."

Fenella sat up straight. "But she's a schoolgirl, only fifteen."

Ben began to sob. "For God's sake, don't tell Safiya. I spent both nights with Belinda. She will confirm, if you ask. Please ask her. I didn't kill anyone."

"I'd like to consult with my client," Mr Locke said. "Alone."

Fenella stood.

"What will happen to me?" cried Ben. "It's not how it seems. I'm a family man."

Fenella left the room without answer.

Chapter Sixty-Five

I N THE HALLWAY OUTSIDE Interview Room C, Fenella and Dexter spoke in hushed tones.

"What do you think?" Fenella asked.

Dexter said, "Mr Griffin has lied to us on several occasions. He lied to his wife, Safiya. He lied to Cathy. The man would do anything to save his own neck." He shook his head. "Hobson's choice. Murder or child abuse—which would you choose?"

Fenella did not like the way this case was shaking out. "We have to speak with Belinda Yates. Confirm his story. Even then, I'm not ruling him out for the murders."

Dexter said, "The puppet master behind the scenes pulling the strings?"

"Aye. With Ian Wallace as a puppet." Fenella didn't like that explanation. Her gut couldn't see Ian Wallace killing twice, not even for drug money. But her head knew her gut could be wrong. "I can't see Ian Wallace keeping quiet if he's been duped with fake photos. He'd squeal like a mouse caught in a trap."

"Want to speak to him next, Guv?"

"Aye," Fenella replied. Then she changed her mind. "What about Martin Findlay?"

"We are arranging an appropriate adult. Miss Gloria Embleton is on her way."

"The schoolteacher?"

"I believe so."

"And Audrey Robin?"

"In the custody suite, Guv."

"Let's get her into an interview room. See what she has got to say."

"And Ian Wallace?"

"Like I said earlier, he's not milk. He won't spoil."

Chapter Sixty-Six

A UDREY WATCHED AS THE detectives entered the interview room. The way they trotted reminded her of that ratty terrier dog she'd seen on the beach. And she wondered if they had fox-sharp teeth. Then the woman detective with the shoulder-length grey hair smiled, and Audrey knew she wouldn't hear Patrick's voice. So she relaxed and played her game of *know thy neighbour* and instantly remembered their names: Detective Inspector Sallow and Detective Sergeant Dexter.

"Thank you for taking the time to speak with us today," said the woman detective. "This is a voluntary police interview. It will be recorded, but you haven't been charged with anything. You can leave at any time. Do you understand?"

Audrey nodded. Not that she felt she had any choice in the matter. Didn't the police arrive at her cottage and bring her here? And they'd discovered Martin Findlay too. If it wasn't a formal interview, it sure felt like one.

"Do I need a lawyer?" Audrey asked because she'd seen it on television.

"If you wish," replied the woman detective. "There are questions we have to ask. If you would rather do that in the presence of a solicitor, we can arrange that for you."

The female detective shifted in her seat as if to stand up, but Audrey raised her hand.

"No. No lawyers. I don't like lawyers. They always twist things so you can't tell the truth from lies."

"As you wish," the woman detective said. "But you can change your mind at any time."

Audrey watched as the male detective fiddled with the recording device. He mumbled something about the date and time, and sat at the table next to the woman detective.

"Mrs Robin, my name is Detective Inspector Fenella Sallow; you've met my colleague, Detective Sergeant Dexter."

"We all met in the ambulance," Audrey said. "Outside the crime scene tent on the morning after Bonfire Night. I was the person who found Maureen Brian. Don't you remember?"

"Of course, that's right," replied Fenella with an uncertain smile. "My memory is not as sharp as it was when I was younger, luv."

Audrey smiled back. The police would never catch the killer if they couldn't remember who they'd interviewed. She didn't know why, but that thought made her relax even more. If these two detectives were the best the Cumbria Police offered, then, well, there would be more murders, wouldn't there?

"Can you remind us about your background?" The woman detective was looking in her spiral-bound notebook, flicking through pages as if lost. "Not from around these parts, are you?"

Audrey grinned. "I'm from Bristol, moved down a few years back." It was like being on the television with two dumb detectives who couldn't tell day from night. She'd heard the phrase taking candy from a baby, but didn't know what it meant until now. This was easy. "Last time we spoke, you commented on my accent."

"Aye, and you work as a library assistant. Are you still on sick leave?"

There was something about the way the detective asked the question that told Audrey she already knew the answer. And that made her nervous. Why were they poking around in her work business?

Audrey adjusted her owl-like glasses and ran a hand through her mousy hair. "They haven't asked me to come back, yet."

"I spoke with the head librarian, luv."

Audrey interrupted. "Oh, she is very nice. Told me to take as long as I need. They are very good to me."

"The head librarian said they let you go."

"I'm on sick leave. For as long as I need."

"They said your behaviour was incompatible with working in the library service."

"There must be some mistake. I'm going back when I'm well. They love me there. I'm their best worker."

Audrey noticed the quick glance the woman detective gave her male colleague. She even saw him roll his eyes. She didn't like that. It reminded her of the times she went to the police to complain about Patrick. The officer rolled his eyes too. And so did the doctor who gave her the pills. Now Audrey closed her eyes and saw that ratty terrier dog. She snapped them back open, suddenly afraid.

The woman detective said, "Do you know Seafields Bed and Breakfast?"

"Yes."

"Have you ever visited?"

"No."

"Are you sure?"

"Why would I visit a bed and breakfast? I have my own cottage."

"That's where Maureen Brian lived. You know that, don't you?"

"Yes, but I've never been inside. Maureen didn't invite guests into her home."

The woman detective leaned forward as if tossing a ball.

"A witness saw you outside the Seafields Bed and Breakfast guest house. The day after you reported Maureen Brian's body." She paused and watched Audrey with sharp eyes. "You were crouching in the sand by the side of a blue Morris Minor. What were you doing?"

"I... er... you see..."

"That's not an explanation, Mrs Robin. Can you explain why you were crouching by the side of a Morris Minor outside Miss Brian's home?"

It wasn't fair. The detective didn't give her a chance to answer before she fired off the next question. On television, the detectives gave their interviewees a chance to think and ponder. Then the interviewee would give an answer which baffled the police officer. This grey-haired Cumbrian Police detective wasn't playing by the rules.

"And a witness saw you outside Martin Findlay's flat. Last Friday, standing in the rain." The detective's eyes never left her face. They felt like laser beams. Blazing. "You had words with Claire Sutherland. What was that about?"

Audrey couldn't stand all the questions. They tumbled around her head, barking like a mad dog. She placed her hands over her ears to drown out the noise. But they barked and yapped and snarled. Then the ratty terrier appeared and opened its mouth and Patrick's words came out: *Turn yourself in. The police will find you.*

"No. No. No," she yelled and then became suddenly still. The voices whimpered and were gone. She felt certain the police had chased them away and they wouldn't come back. The thought caused her to grin.

"Mrs Robin, are you all right?" The question came from the woman detective. "I think we better end this interview."

"I'm fine. It's my medication. Sometimes it makes me anxious."

"Do you want to go on?"

Audrey thought about her plan. She tried to read it before the police arrived but could make head nor tail of her writing. It was as though a great sheet had descended on her mind, cloaking her ability to read her own hand. Now she felt compelled to go on. To explain it all, so the detectives would understand. Make it simple for them. Easy.

"I want to go on. I'm ready."

The woman detective placed a hand on her chin and looked at Audrey for a long time.

"Tell me about Martin Findlay."

"He's a friend."

"We've been looking for him."

"He needed a place to stay, and like I say, he is a friend."

"Mrs Robin, I'm investigating the murder of Maureen Brian and Claire Sutherland. We needed to speak with Martin to help with our investigations."

"He didn't do it."

"He didn't do what?"

"Kill Maureen Brian or Claire Sutherland. Martin Findlay didn't do it."

"Now, how would you know that?"

Audrey reached into the pocket of her cargo pants and retrieved the envelope. She unfolded the sheet of paper and slid it across the table.

"There you go. This explains everything."

The woman detective picked up the sheet of paper and read. When she finished, she stared at Audrey in horror as the penny dropped. Then she passed it to her male colleague. He took his time, reading and rereading. When he finished, he looked up and gazed at her long and hard for several seconds.

"I'm sorry," Audrey said. "So sorry."

Like synchronised robots, the detectives got to their feet and left the interview room.

Chapter Sixty-Seven

FENELLA AND DEXTER DIDN'T speak until they were inside Fenella's office. Then they waited for Jones, who hurried in a minute later with a tray of steaming hot coffee.

"Okay," Fenella said, her voice sounding as tired as her mind. "Okay. Not what we were expecting, eh?"

"Don't like to admit it, Guv," Dexter said, "But this one's got right under my skin. Cannot seem to shake it off. And now this."

"What happened?" Jones sat on the edge of the seat." Did Ben Griffin throw in the towel and confess?"

"No, lad," Dexter said. "Mr Griffin didn't confess. It's Audrey Robin. She gave us a note."

A firm fist knocked on the door. The duty sergeant scurried into the room.

"Ma'am, I've a gentleman on hold who would like to speak with you. He says it's urgent. His name is Patrick Robin."

Chapter Sixty-Eight

F ENELLA TOOK THE CALL in her office on speaker, with Dexter and Jones at her side.

"Detective Sallow, we've never met although I've seen you on the television news. My name is Mr Patrick Robin. I read in the newspaper that a Mrs Robin found a body, but put little thought into it until I saw her image on the news. That's when I realised it was my wife."

"Mrs Audrey Robin is your wife?" Fenella asked for clarification.

"Yes. We've been married for ten years. Unfortunately, no children, but not for want of trying. Both our parents died years ago and Audrey is all I've got. That we would never have children destabilized my wife's mind. She would wake up in the night screaming about voices in her head. She even thought I was seeing someone and planning a divorce. One time I found her arguing with my dead parents, but of course there was no one there. For a while I tried to cope alone. Then I sought help."

"What type of help?" asked Fenella.

"Her delusions were so frequent that she became violent and even attacked me. I've a scar on my nose where her wedding ring drew blood. When I took her to the hospital, she thought she was in the courtroom and I was asking for a divorce. That is how far gone she was. The medicine calmed her down for a short while, but she became like a zombie and said I was seeing another woman. She even thought I had married this phantom woman and started a family. In the end she was admitted to a psychiatric hospital. She told the doctors her room was really a wine cellar and I had locked her in until she agreed to a divorce. That was three years ago. I visited twice a day until the morning she disappeared."

Fenella said, "She disappeared from the psychiatric hospital?"

"Vanished without a trace. She had cash because she raided our building society account. Yesterday I was shocked to see her on the news and contacted Bristol Police who put me in touch with you. You can't imagine my relief." The line went dead for several seconds. "So sorry. I'm driving. I've just pulled over."

"We need to speak with you in person," Fenella said.

"I'm about an hour away from Port Saint Giles. Takes a while from Bristol." The line went quiet for several more seconds. "There is one other thing."

"Go on," Fenella said. "Go on."

"Before we married, Audrey had dreams of becoming a police officer. But her eyesight wasn't sharp enough."

Fenella said, "Policing these days isn't just about uniforms and detectives."

"That's what I said, but after we married, she decided to stay at home. I wish I had encouraged her to continue with a career, but I didn't. You've no idea how often I regret that. It might have saved a lot of bother."

His voice sounded troubled, and there came the sound of a soft sob. Fenella placed her chin on her hands and waited.

Patrick Robin said, "When Audrey became ill... well... it was difficult... She got involved with the police. Not crime, nothing like that. It's just that she would read of a murder in the newspaper and follow the people she suspected. She'd write it all down on the scrap of paper which she called her plan. Then she would make an appointment with the senior investigating detective and hand in her findings. She thought she was helping. But her notes were nothing but scribble and scrawl. Not readable at all."

"I see," Fenella said as she unfolded the sheet of paper given to her by Audrey. Red lettering spidered across the page. Neither the letters nor the words were distinguishable. It was as if a two-year-old had scribbled in a language known to only their own childish mind. "That makes everything perfectly clear."

Chapter Sixty-Nine

I T WAS AN UNPLEASANT task.

Fenella chose to do it.

She had to speak with Belinda Yates. To confirm Ben Griffin's alibi: that she spent the night with him on Bonfire Night and again last Sunday. A difficult conversation on the best of days, but with a schoolgirl it would be worse.

Dexter drove as Fenella considered her plan. She'd not long completed a refresh of the Specialist Child Abuse Investigators Development Programme, but had requested a family liaison officer meet her at the address. She was thankful Elizabeth Collins didn't make a fuss and agreed to bring Belinda Yates home from school. With no other children in the house, they would have space and room to talk.

Elizabeth Collins welcomed them at the door, her face pale and drawn.

"Belinda has told me everything," she whispered as she hurried them through the hall. "I try to do the best for the children in my care, but I can't have eyes everywhere."

They sat in the kitchen, around the scrubbed pine table, with Belinda looking down at her hands.

"Now, luv, let's get on with the introductions," Fenella said, keeping her tone brisk. "I'm Detective Sallow, but you can call me

Fenella. On my left is Detective Dexter. And the officer on my right is Detective Caroline Wright, a family liaison officer."

"I haven't done nothing," Belinda said, her head cast down.

"No one said you had, luv," Fenella replied.

Detective Wright added, "We've a few questions we'd like to ask. If that is all right with you?"

Belinda looked at Elizabeth. For a moment Elizabeth hesitated, then she nodded.

"Okay," Belinda said, but she kept her eyes on her hands. "I'm not going to prison, am I?"

"No, lass," Fenella replied flashing a friendly smile. "You're not in any trouble, okay?"

Detective Wright gave the signal to start. Fenella began with an easy question to loosen the atmosphere and get Belinda talking.

"Where did you meet Ben?"

"At Logan's Bakery. He's a regular. He used to come in every day to buy bread for his bed and breakfast." She mumbled her words and continued to look at her hands. "But with the wet summer and no visitors, he didn't show up so much."

"And you two became friends?"

"Not until the summer holidays when I worked a regular day shift. He would visit to chat with me, though he didn't buy any bread. There was no need, he said, because they had no guests. Then he invited me out for coffee at the Grain Bowl Café, and I said yes."

"Is that how it began?"

"He said he didn't have any money and asked me to pay. So I did. We met every day for a week before it got serious."

"Go on, luv, we are listening." Fenella kept her voice soft and waited.

"We talked at first. He told me he was going to leave Port Saint Giles and run away to the country. He planned to buy a farm cottage and raise chickens and goats to sell in the farmers' market. And he was going to take me with him." For the first time, Belinda looked up and held Fenella's gaze. "We are going to get married and raise a family. I'm pregnant with his baby."

"Belinda!" Elizabeth jumped to her feet. She looked like she'd sucked on a lemon and swallowed the pips. "You didn't tell me that."

"He loves me." Belinda's eyes glistened as if she were about to cry. "Don't you want me to be happy?"

Elizabeth sat back down and placed an arm around Belinda's shoulders. "Of course I do, luv. You know that. I want the best for you, that's all. And Ben Griffin... well... he is a predator... A filthy dirty raincoat man... a flasher... a bloody pervert."

Fenella clenched her fists. She did not need the temperature raised. She opened her mouth to calm things down, but it was too late. Belinda wriggled out of Elizabeth's grip and jumped to her feet.

"Ben is going to marry me and there is nothing you can do about that."

She stomped from the room. Her footsteps clattered along the polished hardwood floors and pounded up the stairs.

Fenella let out a long sigh and said, "Go after her, will you, Detective Wright. Have a quiet chat to calm her down. Then find out if she was with Ben Griffin on Bonfire Night and last Sunday when Claire Sutherland died. Me and Mrs Collins need to talk."

When Detective Wright left the room, Elizabeth got up to turn on the kettle.

"Cup of tea?"

"Aye, that would be lovely," Fenella said. Her throat was parched and her mind weary.

"With milk and two sugars," added Dexter.

Elizabeth busied herself at the kitchen counter. Fenella rested her head in her hands and closed her eyes.

Now she could focus.

Her mind drifted back to the day after Bonfire Night. The crime scene tent with the blackened body of Maureen Brian. Then forward to the interview in the ambulance with Audrey Robin. And forward again to Seafields Bed and Breakfast. Then the report on the financials by Jones. Now backwards, then forwards. She leafed through her memory, making mental notes and tallies. Like a game-show contestant, she kept score. Slowly, meticulously, Fenella sifted every piece of information, casting aside the irrelevant. Her excitement was mounting. Finally, when she heard the clank of the china teapot, she opened her eyes.

Elizabeth sat, then poured.

Fenella said, "Mrs Collins, I understand why you killed Maureen Brian. But why Claire Sutherland?"

Elizabeth stared at the detective, her eyes red and swollen. But she didn't speak. Fenella waited. She was good at the wait.

Elizabeth took a sip from her teacup and gave a sad smile. It would have appeared normal if it weren't for the tremble in her hand.

Still Fenella waited. The tick of the kitchen clock counted down the seconds. Each tick like the boom of a Bonfire Night firework.

"Maureen found out and was going to tell everyone," Elizabeth said, her voice cold and even. "I only borrowed the money from the Lighthouse Restoration Fund. I was going to pay it back, but sanctimonious Maureen wouldn't have that."

"And your Sudan children's charity, pet. Did Maureen find out about that?"

Elizabeth sobbed. "I need the money. It costs a packet to look after these kids, and the foster services don't pay enough."

Fenella said, "What about Claire Sutherland?"

"She was a nosy cow, started asking questions. If she kept her eyes on the television rather than the street, she would still be... I'm not greedy. I'm not a killer. I did it for the children."

"Aye," Fenella said, the weight of the truth squeezing her heart. "Happen you did, luv."

Chapter Seventy

T HE FOLLOWING MORNING, Fenella sat in the kitchen in the cottage on Cleaton Bluff, a steaming hot cup of coffee on the table in front of her. She watched Nan flip the bacon in the pan and refused to think about the day ahead. This was her time, family time.

"Fancy a bit of black pudding to go with your eggs and bacon, luv?" Nan turned from the stove and gave Fenella a hard look. "You are looking a bit pasty."

Fenella nodded. "Aye, and why don't you add a slice of fried bread."

"Did someone say fried bread?" Eduardo stood in the doorway with a greedy grin on his lips. "Pop two slices in the pan for me, Nan. Don't let it go anywhere near those damn blood sausages."

He closed the door, walked into the kitchen, and gave Fenella a hug. She never talked about her work at home. Eduardo never asked. But in the warmth of his arms and soft scent of his aftershave, she knew he understood.

"I love you," he whispered, so Nan wouldn't hear.

"Oh you daft bugger," Fenella said pushing him away.

"What's all this about love?" Nan asked, turning away from the stove. "I'm not deaf yet. You ought to watch him, Fenella, the crafty bugger wants something."

Eduardo let out a laugh. "I'll get the ketchup."

They sat around the scrubbed pine table and ate and chatted and drank Grain Bowl Café fresh-ground coffee. Not once did Fenella think about the day to come. She'd mastered the switch.

She helped Nan with the washing-up and took her time, drying each plate until it squeaked. The future would come too soon and she was happy to wait. So she enjoyed her time with Nan and Eduardo as she had done with her children who'd long ago flown the nest. It gave her peace from the job she was born to do, a little respite before she pushed on.

"Right, then," she said as she put the last dish away. "Let's get this over with."

She went to Eduardo's study where it would be quiet and still. It was so dark that she opened the shutters. Dull November clouds pressed down to the ground in thick swirls of white fog. She could see only as far as the stone fence; even the sound of the sea was muted.

Now she was ready.

She pulled out her mobile phone and called Dexter.

"Morning, Guv," he said, his voice brisk and bright. "We've found the photos. Three in a metal box. Buried in the vegetable patch in Elizabeth Collins's back garden. I hope she has a bloody good lawyer."

Fenella closed her eyes and sighed. They'd spent so long looking for the missing photographs, but there was no elation now. No celebration. It didn't seem appropriate.

Fenella said, "Can you do me a favour?"

"Anything, Guv."

"Go visit Jack Croll. It's been too long."

"Aye," Dexter replied. "I'll do just that."

"And one other thing."

"Guv?"

"About Detective Constable Earp." Just speaking his name out loud brought tears to Fenella's eyes. For a long moment she couldn't speak. "I'm making a pot roast for Sue and Nick, want to come?"

"I wouldn't miss it for the world, Guv."

Chapter Seventy-One

I T WAS A SLOW crawl through the countryside. Fenella put the wipers on their fast setting and headlights on high beam. Neither did much good against the thick fog. The narrow lanes with sharp turns made it a tough drive. Take your eye off the road and you'd be wrong side up in a ditch.

When she got to the edge of town, the mist pressed down in solid white bars. Even the light from the rows of shops couldn't cut through the thick haze. There was a stillness to the streets, a deadness to the air like the quiet before a massive storm.

Fenella pulled into her spot at the police station. Had she parked straight? There was so much fog it was hard to see the white lines. She turned off the wipers, lights, and ignition. She was ready for whatever the day threw her way. The switch had flipped.

A figure appeared from the fog and tapped the car window.

"Inspector Sallow, Superintendent Jeffery would like a word."

The assistant looked through the car window, face damp as though she'd been waiting for some time. The way she stared made the fine hairs on the back of Fenella's neck stand on end. With a slow twist, she let her neck tilt from side to side. She had checked her phone before leaving home. There were no messages. What could have happened during her thirty-minute drive?

"Come on," said the assistant. "The boss is furious."

Fenella got out of the Morris Minor and locked the door. When she looked up, the assistant had vanished into the swirls of white mist.

Fenella had no memory of her walk along the plush hall at the top of the police station. She entered the office with the barest of knocks. Jeffery stood by the side of her desk. Fenella knew then. Jack Croll was right.

"It's Hamilton Perkins," Jeffery said. "Mr Shred. He's escaped from Low Marsh Prison."

Author's Note

If you have enjoyed this story, please consider leaving a short review. Reviews help readers like you discover books they will enjoy and help indie authors like me improve our stories.

Details of my other novels can be found in the store where you obtained this book. If you would like to know more, you can email: NCLewisBooks@gmail.com

Until next time,

N.C. Lewis

ALSO BY N.C. LEWIS

DORIS CUDLOW MYSTERIES

The Doris Cudlow mysteries are set in an English seaside town and can be enjoyed in any order.

Deadly Chapel

Deadly Sayings

Deadly Ashes

Deadly Vestige

MAGGIE DARLING MYSTERIES

Offer a light-hearted look at life in a small English coastal town in the 1920s.

The Bagington Hall Mystery

The Wuthering Hollow Mystery

The Bankers Note Mystery

The Copper Moon Mystery

AMY KING MYSTERIES

The Amy King mysteries are set in Austin, the capital of Texas, and can be enjoyed in any order.

Murder in the Bookstore

Murder by the Clowns

Murder through the Window

Murder in the Bullock

Murder under MoPac

Murder in Hidden Harbor

OLLIE STRATFORD MYSTERIES

The Ollie Stratford Mysteries are set in the Hill Country of Texas and offer a light-hearted glimpse into small-town life.

Texas Troubles

Creek Crisis

Bitter Bones

Magic Mumbles

Teddy Tumpin

Double Dimple

Angry Arrow